DATING GAME

Also by Danielle Steel

DANIELLE STEEL

DATING GAME

Delacorte  Press

DATING GAME
A Delacorte Book / March 2003

Published by Bantam Dell
A Division of Random House, Inc.
New York, New York

Book design by Virginia Norey

LIBRARY OF CONGRESS CATALOGING-IN-PUBLICATION DATA
Steel, Danielle.
    Dating game / Danielle Steel.
        p.cm.
    ISBN 0-385-33631-4 — ISBN 0-385-33691-8 (ltd. ed.)
    1. Dating (Social customs)—Fiction. 2. Divorced women—
Fiction. I. Title.

    PS3569.T33828 D38 2003
    813'.54—dc21   2002073619

Manufactured in the United States of America
Published simultaneously in Canada

BVG   10 9 8 7 6 5 4 3 2 1

On ne voit bien qu'avec le coeur.
L'essentiel est invisible pour les yeux.

One can only see clearly with the heart.
What is essential is invisible to the eye.
—*Le Petit Prince*
Antoine de Saint-Exupéry

To those who are seeking, those who have sought, those who have found—the lucky devils!! And especially, with great fondness and respect, to those who have ground through this unnatural process, and not only survived with their minds and hearts intact, but managed to find the needle in the haystack, and win the prize!

Climbing Everest is easier, and surely less fraught with danger and despair.

And to all of my friends, who have tried ineptly or expertly to find the perfect man for me, in other words someone at least as weird as I.

To those of you who have set me up on blind dates, which will give me something to laugh at in my old age, I—almost!—forgive you.

And above all, to my wonderful children, who have watched and shared, and loved and supported me with humor, encouragement, and infinite patience. For their love and eternal support, I am profoundly grateful.

With all my love,

d.s.

What is a date? A date is when two people, who hardly know each other, go out to dinner, and push their food around their plates nervously, while trying to ask as many questions as possible in the shortest possible time. As in: Do you ski? Play tennis? Do you like dogs? Why do *you* think your marriage fell apart? Why do *you* think your ex-wife said you were controlling? Do you like chocolate? Cheesecake? Have you ever been convicted of a felony? How do you feel about drugs? How many alcoholics are there in your family? What kind of medication are you on? Did you have plastic surgery, or is that your real nose? Chin? Upper lip? Breasts? Behind? What kind of surgery have you had? Do you like kids? Have you ever dated any? What foreign languages do you speak? What's your ideal honeymoon? Two weeks in the Himalayas?? Really? Have you ever been on safari? To Paris? To Des Moines? Are you religious? When did you last see your mother? How long have you been in therapy? Why not? How many DUIs have you had? Where does your wife think you are tonight? How long have you been married? Divorced? Widowed? Out of jail? On parole? Unemployed? What's your next career move? I'm sure the circus does offer fabulous travel opportunities, but what about the high wire? Have you been bulimic all your life? How many twelve-step groups *are* you a member of? When is later? How soon do you think you'll call??

A blind date is when well-meaning friends select two people from opposite ends of the earth, with as little in common as humanly possible, and lie to each of them about just how fabulous, interesting, normal, well adjusted, intelligent, and attractive the other half of the blind date is. Reality hits as they come through the door. You then pursue the same formula as on a regular date, hopefully in less time, and you pray that they wrote down your phone number wrong. After that you go home and cry, eventually laugh, and never speak to the friends who set you up again. And after you forget just how bad it was, you let the same friends, or others, do it to you again.

With love and empathy,
d.s.

DATING
GAME

Chapter 1

It was a perfect balmy May evening, just days after spring had
hit the East Coast with irresistible appeal. The weather was perfect,
winter had vanished literally overnight, birds were singing, the
sun was warm, and everything in the Armstrongs' Connecticut
garden was in bloom. The entire week had been blessed with the
kind of weather that made everyone slow down, even in New
York. Couples strolled, lunch hours stretched. People smiled. And
in Greenwich that night, Paris Armstrong decided to serve dinner
outside on the flagstone patio they had just redone near the pool.
She and Peter were giving a dinner party on a Friday night, which
was rare for them. They did most of their entertaining on Saturday,
so Peter didn't have to rush home from work in the city on Friday
night. But the caterers had only been available on this particular
Friday. They had weddings booked for every Saturday night
through July. It was harder for Peter, but he'd been a good sport
when she told him about the Friday night plan. Peter indulged her
most of the time, he always had. He liked making life easy for her.
It was one of the myriad things she loved about him. They had just
celebrated their twenty-fourth anniversary in March. It was hard
to believe sometimes how the years had flown by and how full
they had been. Megan, their eldest, had graduated from Vassar the

year before, and at twenty-three, she had recently taken a job in L.A. She was interested in all aspects of film and had landed a job as a production assistant with a movie studio in Hollywood. She was barely more than a gofer, as she admitted openly, but she was thrilled with just being there, and wanted to be a producer one day. William, their son, had just turned eighteen, and was graduating in June. He was going to UC Berkeley in the fall. It was hard to believe that their kids were grown. It seemed only minutes before that she had been changing diapers and carpooling, taking Meg to ballet, and Wim to hockey games. And in three months he'd be gone. He was due in Berkeley the week before the Labor Day weekend.

Paris made sure that the table had been set properly. The caterers were reliable and had a good eye. They knew her kitchen well. She and Peter liked to entertain, and Paris used them frequently. They enjoyed their social life and over the years they had collected an eclectic assortment of interesting friends. She set the flowers that she had arranged herself on the table. She had cut a profusion of multicolored peonies, the tablecloth was immaculate, and the crystal and silver gleamed. Peter probably wouldn't notice, especially if he was tired when he got home, but what he sensed more than saw was the kind of home she provided him with. Paris was impeccable about details. She created an atmosphere of warmth and elegance that people flourished in. She did it not only for him and their friends but for herself as well.

Peter provided handsomely for her too. He'd been generous with her and the children. He had been very successful over the years. He was a partner in a lucrative law firm, specializing in corporate accounts, and at fifty-one, he was the managing partner. The house he'd bought for them ten years before was large and beautiful. It was a handsome stone house, in one of the more luxurious neighborhoods in Greenwich, Connecticut. They'd talked about hiring a decorator, but in the end she had decided to decorate it herself, and loved doing it. Peter was thrilled with the results. They also had one of the prettiest gardens in Greenwich. She'd done such a great job with the house that he had often teased her and told her she should become a decorator, and most people who saw the house agreed. But although artistic, her interests had always been similar to his.

She had a solid respect and understanding for the business world. They had married as soon as she graduated from college, and she had gone to business school and graduated with an MBA. She had wanted to start a small business of her own, but got pregnant in her second year of business school, and had decided to stay home with their children instead. And she'd never had any regrets. Peter supported her in her decision, there was no need for her to work. And for twenty-four years, she had felt competent and fulfilled, devoting herself full time to Peter and their children. She baked cookies, organized school fairs, ran the school auction every year, made costumes by hand at Halloween, spent countless hours at the orthodontist with them, and generally did what many other wives and mothers did. She didn't need an MBA for any of it, but her extensive understanding of the corporate world, and her lively interest in it made it a lot easier when talking to Peter late at night about the cases he was working on. If anything, it even made them closer. She was, and had been, the perfect wife for him, and he had profound respect for the way she had brought up their children. She had turned out to be everything he had expected her to be— and Paris was equally pleased with him.

They still shared laughter on Sunday mornings, as they snuggled beneath the covers for an extra half-hour on cold wintry days. And she still got up with him at the crack of dawn every weekday, and drove him to the train, and then came back to take the kids to school, until they were old enough to drive themselves, which had come far too quickly for her. And the only dilemma she had now was trying to figure out what she was going to do with herself when Wim left for Berkeley in August. She could no longer imagine a life without teenagers splashing in the pool in summer, or turning the house upside down as they overflowed the downstairs playroom on the weekends. For twenty-three of the twenty-four years of her marriage, her life had entirely and unreservedly revolved around them. And it saddened her to know that those days were almost over for good.

She knew that once Wim left for college, life as she had known it for so long would be over. He would come home for the occasional weekend, and holidays, as Meg had while she was at Vassar, only less so because he would be so far away, on the West Coast. Once Meg had graduated, she had all but disappeared. She had gone to New York for six months, moved into an apartment with three friends, and then left for California as soon as she found the job she wanted in L.A. From now on, they would see her on Thanksgiving and Christmas, if they were lucky, and God only knew what would happen once she got married, not that she had any plans. Paris knew only too well that in August, when Wim left, her life would be forever changed.

After twenty-four years out of the job market, she couldn't exactly head for New York and go to work. She'd been baking cookies and driving carpools for too long. The only thing she had thought of doing so far was volunteer work in Stamford, working with abused kids, or on a literacy program a friend of hers had started in the public schools for underprivileged high school students who had managed to get most of the way through high school and could barely read. Beyond that, she had no idea what she was going to do with herself. Peter had told her years before that once the kids left, it would be a great opportunity for them to travel together, and to do things they had never been able to do before. But his work hours had stretched so noticeably in the last year, she thought it unlikely he would be able to get away. He rarely even made it home for dinner anymore. From what Paris could see, for the moment at least, both of her children and her husband had busy, productive lives, and she didn't. And she knew she had to do something about it soon. The prospect of the vast amount of free time she was about to have on her hands was beginning to frighten her. She had talked to Peter about it on several occasions, and he had no useful suggestions to make. He told her she'd figure it out sooner or later, and she knew she would. At forty-six, she was young enough to start a career if she wanted to, the problem was that she didn't know what she wanted to do. She liked things the way they were, taking care of her children and husband, and attending to their every need on the weekends—particularly Peter's. Unlike some of her friends, whose marriages had shown signs of strain over the years, or even ruptured entirely, Paris was still in love with him. He was kinder, gentler, more considerate, in fact he was more sophisticated and seasoned, and even better looking than he had been when they got married. And he always said the same about her.

Paris was slim and lithe and athletic. Once the children were older and she had more free time, she played tennis almost every day, and was in terrific shape. She wore her straight blond hair long, and most of the time wore it pulled back in a braid. She had classic Grace Kelly good looks, and green eyes. Her figure was noteworthy, her laughter easy, and her sense of humor quick to ignite, much to the delight of her friends. She used to love playing practical jokes, which never failed to amuse her children. Peter was far quieter by nature, and always had been. By the time he came home at night after a long day and the commute on the train, more often than not, he was too tired to do much more than listen to her, and make the occasional comment. He came to life more on the weekends, but even then he was quiet and somewhat reserved. And in the last year he had been consumed with work. This was, in fact, the first dinner party they had given in three months. He had worked late every Friday night, and gone back into town some Saturdays, to clear things off his desk, or meet with clients. But Paris was always patient about it. She made few demands on him, and had a profound respect for his diligence about his work. It was what made him so good at what he did, and so highly admired in

business and legal circles. She couldn't fault him for being conscientious, although she missed spending more time with him. Particularly now, with Meg gone for the past six months, and Wim busy
with his own life and friends in the final weeks of his senior year.
Peter's heavy workload in recent months reminded her yet again
that she was going to have to find something to occupy her time in
September. She had even thought of starting a catering business, or
investing in a nursery, since she enjoyed her garden so much. But
the catering business, she knew, would interfere with her time with
Peter on the weekends, and she wanted to be available to him
whenever he was home, which was seldom enough these days.

She took a shower and dressed after checking the table and
cruising through the kitchen to check on the caterers, and everything seemed in good order. They were having five couples for dinner, all of them good friends. She was looking forward to it, and
hoped Peter would get home in time to unwind before the guests
arrived. She was thinking of him, when Wim stuck his head in her
bedroom door while she was getting dressed. He wanted to tell her
his plans, a house rule she rigidly enforced even at his age. She
wanted to know where her children were at all times, and with
whom. Paris was the consummate responsible mother and devoted wife. Everything in her life was in perfect order, and relatively good control.

"I'm going over to the Johnsons' with Matt," Wim said, glancing
at her, as she pulled up the side zipper of a white lace skirt. She
was already wearing a strapless tube top to match, and high-
heeled silver sandals.

"Are you staying there, or going somewhere else afterward?" She
smiled at him. He was a handsome boy, and looked like his father.
Wim had been six foot three by the time he reached fifteen, and had
grown another inch since. He had his father's dark brown hair and
piercing blue eyes, and he smiled as he looked at his mother. Wim
thought she always looked pretty, when she got dressed up, and he
watched as she wound her long blond hair into a bun as they talked.

He always thought his mother had a simple elegance about her, and he was as proud of her as she was of him. He was not only a good student, but had been a star athlete all through high school. "Are you going to a party tonight?" Paris asked wisely. For the past month at least, if not two, the seniors had been kicking up their heels, and Wim was always in the thick of things. Girls were crazy about him, and drawn to him like a magnet, although he had been going out with the same girl since Christmas, and Paris liked her. She was a nice girl from a wholesome family in Greenwich. Her mother was a teacher, and her father a doctor.

"Yeah, we might go to a party later." He looked momentarily sheepish. She knew him too well. He had been thinking of not telling her about it. She always asked so many questions. He and his sister both complained about it, but in another sense, they liked it. There was never any question about how much she loved them.

"Whose house?" she asked, as she finished her hair and put on just a dash of blush and lipstick.

"The Steins'," Wim said with a grin. She always asked. Always. And he knew before she said it what the next question would be.

"Will the parents be there?" Even at eighteen, she didn't want him at unsupervised parties. It was an invitation to trouble, and when they were younger, she had called to verify it herself. In the past year, she had finally relented, and was willing to take Wim's word. But there were still incidents now and then when he tried to pull the wool over her eyes. As she said, it was his job to try and put one over on her, and hers to figure it out when he did. She was pretty good about sussing things out, and most of the time he was honest, and she was comfortable about where he went.

"Yes, the parents will be there," he said, rolling his eyes.

"They'd better be." She looked meaningfully at him, and then laughed. "I'm going to flatten your tires and put your car keys in the trash compactor, William Armstrong, if you lie to me."

"Yeah, yeah, Mom. I know. They'll be there."

"Okay. What time will you be home?" Curfews were still a

standard at their house, even at eighteen. Until he left for college, Paris said, he had to follow their rules, and Peter agreed. He heartily approved of the boundaries she set for their kids, and always had. They stood united on that, as on all else. They had never disagreed about how they raised their children, or much of anything in fact. Theirs had been a relatively trouble-free marriage, with the exception of the usual minor arguments that were almost always about silly things like leaving the garage door open, forgetting to put gas in the car, or not sending a tux shirt out to be cleaned in time for a black tie event. But she rarely made those mistakes, and was organized to a fault. Peter had always relied on her.

"Three?" Wim asked cautiously about the curfew question, trying it on for size, and his mother instantly shook her head.

"No way. This isn't a graduation party, Wim. It's an ordinary Friday night." She knew that if she agreed to three now, he would be wanting to come home at four or five during the graduation celebrations, and that was way too late. She thought it was dangerous for him to be driving around at those hours. "Two. Max. And that's a gift. Don't push!" she warned, and he nodded and looked pleased. The negotiations were complete, and he started to back out of her room, as she headed toward him with a purposeful look. "Not so fast . . . I want a hug."

He smiled at her then, looking like a big goofy kid, and more a boy than the nearly grown man he was. And he obliged her with a hug, as she leaned up and kissed his cheek. "Have fun tonight, and drive carefully, please." He was a good driver, and a responsible boy, but she worried anyway. So far at least there had been no drunken incidents, and the few times he had had something to drink at parties, he had left his car and driven home with friends. He also knew that if things got out of hand, he could call his parents. They had established that agreement years before. If he ever got drunk, he could call them, and there would be an "amnesty." But under no condition, in those circumstances, did they want him to drive home.

She heard Wim go out and the front door close moments after they had exchanged the hug. And Paris was just coming down the stairs herself, as Peter walked in, with his briefcase in his hand, looking exhausted. It struck her as she looked at him how much he looked like Wim. It was like seeing the same person thirty-three years later, and noticing that made her smile warmly at him.

"Hi, sweetheart," she said as she went to Peter, and gave him a hug and a kiss, but he was so tired, he scarcely responded. She didn't mention how wiped out he looked, she didn't want to make him feel worse. But she knew he had been working on a merger for the past month, and the hours had been rough. The deal wasn't going well for his clients, at least not so far, and she knew he was trying to turn it around. "How was your day?" she asked as she took his briefcase out of his hand and set it down on the hall chair. She was sorry suddenly that she had planned the dinner party. There had been no way of knowing, when she did, how busy he would be at work at the moment. She had booked the caterer two months before, knowing how busy they would be later.

"The day was long." He smiled at her. "The week was longer. I'm beat. What time are the guests coming?" It was nearly seven as he walked in the door.

"In about an hour. Why don't you lie down for a few minutes? You've got time."

"That's okay. If I fall asleep, I might never wake up."

Without asking, she walked into the pantry and poured him a glass of white wine, and then returned to hand it to him. He looked relieved. He didn't drink much, but at times like these, knowing he had a long evening ahead of him, it sometimes helped him forget the stresses of the day. It had been a long week, and he looked it.

"Thanks," he said, taking the glass from her, and taking a sip, before he wandered into the living room and sat down. Everything around him was impeccable and in perfect order. The room was full of handsome English antiques they had bought together over the years, in London and New York. Both of them had lost their parents young, and Paris had used some of her modest inheritance to buy things for the house. And Peter had helped her with it as well. They had some lovely pieces, which their friends always admired. It was a particularly nice house to entertain in. There was a large comfortable dining room, a big living room, a small den, and a library that Peter used as an office on weekends. And upstairs there were four big spacious bedrooms. They used the fourth one as a guest room, although they had hoped for a long time to use it as a room for a third baby, but it had never happened. She had never gotten pregnant after the first two, and although they'd talked about it, neither of them wanted to go through the stress of infertility treatments, and had been content with the two children they had. Fate had tailored their family perfectly for them.

Paris sat down on the couch, and snuggled up close to him. But tonight he was too tired to respond. Usually, he put an arm around her shoulders, and she realized as she looked at him, that he was showing signs of considerable strain. He was due for a check-up sometime soon, and she was going to remind him of it once the worst of the merger was done. They had lost several friends in the past few years to sudden heart attacks. At fifty-one, and in good health, he wasn't at high risk for that, but you never knew. And she wanted to take good care of him. She had every intention of keeping him around for another forty or fifty years. The last twenty-four had been very good, for both of them.

"Is the merger giving you a tough time?" she asked sympathetically. Sitting next to him, she could feel how tense he was. He nodded, as he sipped his wine, and for once didn't volunteer any details. He was too tired to go into it with her, or so she assumed. She didn't want to ask if there was anything else bothering him, it seemed obvious to her that it was the merger. And she hoped that once in the midst of their friends at dinner, he would forget about it and relax. He always did. Although he never initiated their social life, he enjoyed the plans she made for them, and the people she invited. She no longer even consulted him about it. She had a good sense of who he liked and who he didn't, and invited accordingly. She wanted him to have a good time too, and he liked not being responsible for their plans. She did a good job of being what he called their social director.

Peter just sat peacefully on the couch for a few minutes, and she sat quietly beside him, glad to have him home. She wondered if he was going to have to work that weekend, or go back into the city to see clients, as he had for several months on the weekends, but she didn't want to ask. If he did have to go in to the office, she would find something to keep her busy. He looked better, as he stood up, smiled at her, and walked slowly upstairs, as she followed.

"Are you okay, sweetheart?" she asked as he lay down on their bed, and set the glass down on his bedside table. He was so exhausted, he had decided to lie down after all before their dinner.

"I'm fine," he said, and closed his eyes. And with that, she left him alone to rest for a minute, and went back downstairs to check how things were going in the kitchen. Everything was in order, and she went out to sit on the patio for a minute, smiling to herself. She loved her husband, her children, her house, their friends. She loved everything about all of it, and there was nothing she would have changed. It was the perfect life.

When she went back upstairs to wake him half an hour later, in case he'd fallen asleep, he was in the shower. She sat down in their bedroom and waited. The guests were going to arrive in twenty minutes. She heard the doorbell ring while he was shaving, and told him not to rush. No one was going anywhere, he had time. She wanted him to unwind and enjoy the evening. He looked at her and nodded in the mirror, with shaving foam all over his face, when she told him she was going downstairs to greet their friends.

"I'll be right down," he promised, and she told him again not to hurry. She wanted him to relax.

By the time Peter came down the stairs, two of the couples had already arrived, and a third was just walking toward the patio. The night was perfect, the sun had just set, and the warm night air felt more like Mexico or Hawaii. It was a perfect night for an outdoor dinner party, and everyone was in good spirits. Both of Paris's favorite women friends were there, with their husbands, one of whom was an attorney in Peter's firm, which was how they'd met fifteen years before. He and his wife were the parents of a boy Wim's age, who went to the same school, and was graduating with him in June. The other woman had a daughter Meg's age, and twin boys a year older. The three women had spent years going to the same school and sports events, and Natalie had alternated with Paris for ten years, driving their daughters to ballet. Her daughter had taken it more seriously than Meg, and was dancing professionally now in Cleveland. All three were at the end of their years of motherhood, and depressed about it, and were talking about it when Peter walked in. Natalie commented quietly to Paris how tired he looked, and Virginia, the mother of the boy graduating with Wim, agreed.

"He's been working on a merger, and it's been really rough on him," Paris said sympathetically, and Virginia nodded. Her husband had been working on it too, but he looked a lot more relaxed than Peter did. But he also wasn't the managing partner of the firm, which put even more of a burden on Peter. He hadn't looked this tired and stressed in years.

The rest of the guests arrived minutes after Peter did, and by the time they sat down to dinner, everyone seemed to be having a good time. The table looked beautiful, and there were candles everywhere. And in the soft glow of the candlelight, Peter looked better to Paris when he sat down at the head of the table, and chatted with the women she had placed next to him. He knew both well, and enjoyed their company, although he seemed quieter than usual throughout the dinner. He no longer seemed so much tired as subdued.

When the guests finally left at midnight, he took his blazer off and loosened his tie, and seemed relieved.

"Did you have an okay time, sweetheart?" Paris asked, looking worried. The table had been just big enough, with twelve people seated at it, that she couldn't really hear what had gone on at his end. She had enjoyed talking to the men she sat next to about business matters, as she often did. Their male friends liked that about her. She was intelligent and well informed, and enjoyed talking about more than just her kids, unlike some of the women they knew, although Virginia and Natalie were intelligent too. Natalie was an artist, and had moved on to sculpture in recent years. And Virginia had been a litigator before she gave up her career to have kids and stay home with them. She was just as nervous as Paris about what she was going to do with herself when her only son graduated in June. He was going to Princeton, so at least he'd be closer to home than Wim. But any way you looked at it, a chapter of their lives was about to end, and it left all of them feeling anxious and insecure.

"You were awfully quiet tonight," Paris commented as they walked slowly upstairs. The beauty of hiring caterers was that they took care of everything, and left the house neat as a pin. Paris had looked down the table at him regularly, and although he seemed to be enjoying his dinner partners, he seemed to listen more than talk, which was unusual, even for him.

"I'm just tired," he said, looking distracted, as they passed Wim's room. He was still out, presumably at the Steins', and wouldn't be home a minute before he had to be, at two.

"Are you feeling okay?" Paris asked, looking worried. He had had big deals before, but he didn't usually let them get to him like this. She was wondering if the deal was about to fall through.

"I'm . . ." He started to say "fine," and then looked at her and shook his head. He looked anything but fine as they walked into their room. He hadn't wanted to talk to her about it that night. He had been planning to sit down with her the following morning. He didn't want to spoil the evening for her, and he never liked talking about serious subjects before they went to bed. But he couldn't lie to her either. He didn't want to anymore. It wasn't fair to her. He loved her. And there was going to be no easy way to do this, no right time or perfect day. And the prospect of lying next to her and worrying about it all night was weighing heavily on him.

"Is something wrong?" Paris looked startled suddenly, and couldn't imagine what it was. She assumed it was something at the office, and just hoped it wasn't bad news about his health. That had happened to friends of theirs the year before. The husband of one of her friends had been diagnosed with a brain tumor and died within four months. It had been a shock to all of them. They were beginning to approach the age where things happened to friends. All she could do was pray that Peter didn't have news of that kind to share with her. But he looked serious as he sat down in one of the comfortable easy chairs in their bedroom where they liked to sit and read sometimes, and he pointed to the chair facing him, without reassuring her.

"Come sit."

"Are you okay?" she asked again, as she sat down facing him and reached for his hands, but he sat back in the chair, and closed his eyes for a minute, before he began. When he opened them, she knew she had never seen such agony in them before.

"I don't know how to say this to you . . . where to start, or how to begin. . . ." How do you drop a bomb on someone you've cared about for twenty-five years? Where do you drop it and when? He knew he was about to hit a switch that would blow their lives all to bits. Not only hers, but his. "I . . . Paris . . . I did a crazy thing last year . . . well, maybe not so crazy . . . but something I never expected to do. I didn't intend to do it. I'm not even sure how it happened, except that the opportunity was there, and I took it, and shouldn't have, but I did. . . ." He couldn't look at her as he said it, and Paris said not a word as she listened to him. She had an overwhelming sense that something terrible was about to happen to her, and to them. Sirens were going off in her head, and her heart was pounding as she waited for him to continue. This wasn't about the merger, she knew suddenly, it was about them.

"It happened while I was in Boston for three weeks on the deal I was working on then." She knew the one, and nodded silently. Peter looked at her with agony in his eyes, and he wanted to reach out to her, but didn't. He wanted to cushion the blow for her, but he had the decency to know there was no way he could. "There's no point going into the details about how or why or when. I fell in love with someone. I didn't mean to. I didn't think I would. I'm not even sure what I was thinking then, except that I was bored, and she was interesting and bright and young, and it made me feel alive being with her. And younger than I've felt in years. I guess it was like turning the clock back for a few minutes, only the hands got stuck, and once we got back, I found I didn't want to get out of it. I've thought about it, and agonized, and tried to break it off several times. But . . . I just can't . . . I don't want to. . . . I want to be with her. I love you. I always have. I never stopped loving you, even now, but I can't live like this anymore, between two lives. It's driving me insane. I don't even know how to say this to you, and I can only imagine what it must be like to be on the receiving end, and God, I'm so sorry, Paris . . . I really am. . . ." There were tears in his eyes as he said it, and she covered her mouth with her hands, like watching an accident about to happen, or a car hit a wall, about to kill everyone in it. She felt, for the first time in her life, as though she were about to die. "Paris, I don't know how to say this to you," he said, as tears rolled down his cheeks. "For both our sakes . . . for all our sakes . . . I want a divorce." He had promised Rachel he would do it that weekend, and he knew he had to, before the double life he was leading drove them both crazy. But saying it, and living it, and seeing Paris's face, were harder than he had ever dreamed. Seeing the way she looked at him made him wish there were some other way. But he knew there wasn't. Even though he had loved her for all these years, he was no longer in love with her, but with another woman, and he wanted out. Sharing a life with her made him feel like he was buried alive. And he realized now, with Rachel, all that he had been missing. With Rachel, he felt as though God had given him a second chance. And whether it came from God or not, it was what he wanted and knew he had to have. As much as he cared about Paris, and felt sorry for her, and guilty about what he was doing to her, he knew that his life, his soul, his being, his future was with Rachel now. Paris was his past.

She sat in silence for endless minutes, staring at him, unable to believe what she had just heard, yet believing it. She could see in his eyes that he meant every word he had said. "I don't understand," she said, as tears sprang to her eyes and started rolling down her cheeks. This couldn't be happening to her. It happened to other people, people with bad marriages, or who fought all the time, people who had never loved each other as she and Peter did. But it was happening. It had never even occurred to her once for a single instant in twenty-four years of marriage that he might leave her one day. The only way she had ever thought she might lose him was if he died. And now she felt as though she had. "What happened? . . . Why did you do that to us? . . . Why? . . . Why won't you give her up?" It never even occurred to her in those first instants to ask him who it was. It didn't matter. All that mattered was that he wanted a divorce.

"Paris, I tried," he said, looking devastated. He hated seeing the look of total destruction in her eyes, but the music had to be faced. And in an odd, sick way, he was glad he had done it finally. He knew that no matter what it cost them both emotionally, he had to be free. "I can't give her up. I just can't. I know it's rotten of me, but it's what I want. You've been a good wife, you're a wonderful person. You've been a great mother to our kids, and I know you always will be, but I want more than this now. . . . I feel alive when I'm with her. Life is exciting, I look forward to the future now. I've felt like an old man for years. Paris, you don't see it yet, but maybe this is a blessing for both of us. We've both been trapped." His words ran through her like knives.

"A blessing? You call this a blessing?" Her voice sounded shrill suddenly. She looked as though she were about to get hysterical, and he was afraid of that. It was an enormous shock, like learning that someone you loved had suddenly died. "This is a tragedy, not a blessing. What kind of a blessing is it to cheat on your wife, walk out on your family, and ask for a divorce? Are you crazy? What are you thinking of? Who is this girl? What kind of spell did she put on you?" It had finally occurred to her to ask, not that it mattered now. The other woman was a faceless enemy, who had won the war before Paris even knew there was a battle. Paris had lost everything without ever being warned that their life and marriage were at stake. It felt like the end of the world as she stared at him, and he shook his head and ran a hand through his hair. He didn't want to tell her who it was, he was afraid Paris would do something in some crazed jealous state, but he had more faith in her than that, and she would find out sooner or later anyway. If nothing else, once they found out, their children would tell her who she was. And he was planning to marry her, although he didn't intend to tell Paris that yet. The divorce was enough of a shock for her for now.

"She's an attorney in my office. You met her at the Christmas party, although I know she tried to stay away from you, out of respect. Her name is Rachel Norman, she was my assistant on the case in Boston. She's a decent person, she's divorced, and she has two boys." He was trying to give her respectability in Paris's eyes, which was pointless, he knew, but he felt he owed Rachel that, so she didn't sound like a whore to Paris. But he suspected she would anyway. Paris just stared at him as she cried, while tears dripped off her chin onto the skirt she wore. She looked broken and beaten to a pulp, and he knew it would take him a long time to forgive himself for what he'd done. But there was no other way. He had to do this, for all their sakes. He had promised Rachel he would. She had waited a year, and said it was long enough. Above all, he didn't want to lose her, whatever it took.

"How old is she?" Paris asked in a dead voice.

"Thirty-one," he said softly.

"Oh my God. She's twenty years younger than you are. Are you going to marry her?" She felt another wave of panic clutch her throat. As long as he didn't, there was always hope.

"I don't know. We have to get through all this first, that's traumatic enough." Just telling her made him feel a thousand years old. But thinking of Rachel made him feel young again. She was the fountain of youth and hope for him. He hadn't realized how much had been missing from his life until he fell in love with her. Everything was exciting about her, just having dinner with her made him feel like a boy again, and the time they spent in bed nearly drove him out of his mind. He had never felt that way about any woman in his life, not even Paris. Their sex life had been satisfying and respectable, and he had cherished it for all the years he shared with her, but what he shared with Rachel was a passion he had never even believed could exist, and now he knew it did. She was magic.

"She's fifteen years younger than I am," Paris said, starting to sob uncontrollably, and then she looked up at him again, wanting to know every hideous detail to torture herself with. "How old are her boys?"

"Five and seven, they're very young. She got married in law school, and managed the boys and her studies, even after her husband left. She's had a lot on her plate for a long time." He cared so much about her, wanted to help her with everything. He had even taken the boys to the park on Saturday afternoons several times, when he told Paris he was going back into town to see clients. He was absolutely driven to be with her, and share her life with her, and she was just as much in love with him. She had been distraught over whether or not to see him, or if he would leave his wife eventually. She didn't think he would, knowing how important his family was to him, and he always said what a good woman Paris was and didn't deserve to be hurt. But after the last time Rachel had broken it off with him, he had finally made up his mind, and asked Rachel to marry him. And now he had no choice but to divorce his wife. Divorcing her was the price of entry into the life he wanted. And it was all he wanted now, at any price. He had to sacrifice Paris to have Rachel, and he was willing.

"Will you go to counseling with me?" Paris asked in a small voice, and he hesitated. He didn't want to mislead her, or give her false hope. In his mind, there was none.

"I will," he said finally, "if it will make this easier for you to accept. But I want you to understand that I'm not going to change my mind. It took me a long time to make this decision, and nothing is going to sway me."

"Why didn't you tell me? Why didn't you at least give me a chance? How could I not have known?" she asked miserably, feeling stupid, and broken and small and abandoned, even before he left.

"Paris, I've hardly been home for the last nine months. I come home late every night. I go back into town every weekend. I kept thinking that you would figure it out. I'm amazed you didn't."

"I trusted you," she said, sounding angry for the first time. "I thought you were busy at the office. I never realized you'd do something like this." And after that, she just sat there and cried. He wanted to take her in his arms and comfort her, but he thought he shouldn't. So instead he got up, and stood at the window, looking down at the garden, wondering what would happen to her now. She was still young and beautiful, she would find someone. But he couldn't help worrying about her after all this time. He had been worried about her for months, but not enough to want to stay with her, or stop seeing Rachel. For the first time in his life, he wasn't thinking of her or his family, but only of himself. "What are we going to tell the children?" She looked up at him finally. It had just occurred to her. This really was like a death, and she had to think of everything now, how to survive it, how to tell people, what to say to their children. And the final irony was that she was not only about to be out of a job as mother, but she had just been fired as a wife as well. She had no idea what she was going to do with the rest of her life, and couldn't even think of it now.

"I don't know what we'll tell the children," Peter said softly. "The truth, I guess. I still love them. This doesn't change anything. They're not little kids anymore. They're both going to be out of the house when Wim leaves for Berkeley. It's not going to have that much effect on them," he said naïvely, and she shook her head at his stupidity. He had no idea how they would feel. Very likely as betrayed as she did, or very close.

"Don't be so sure it won't have an effect on them. I think they'll be devastated. This is going to be a huge shock to them. How could it not be? Their whole family just got blown to bits. What do you think?"

"It all depends on how we explain it to them. It will make a big difference how you handle it." It made her furious to realize that he was expecting her to clean it up for him, and she wasn't going to do it. Her duties to him as a wife were over. In the blink of an eye, she had been dispensed with, and her responsibilities to him no longer existed. All she had to think of now was herself, and she didn't even know how. More than half her life had been spent taking care of him, and their children. "I want you to keep the house," he said suddenly, although he'd already decided that after he asked Rachel to marry him. They were going to buy a co-op in New York, and he had already looked at several with her.

"Where are you going to live?" she asked, sounding as frantic as she felt.

"I don't know yet," he said, avoiding her eyes again. "We'll have plenty of time to figure that out. I'll move to a hotel tomorrow," he said quietly, and it suddenly occurred to her that not only was this happening, but it was happening now, not at some distant date in the future. He was going to move out in the morning. "I'll sleep in the guest room tonight," he said, moving toward the bathroom to gather up his things, and instinctively she reached out and grabbed his arm.

"I don't want you to," she said loudly. "I don't want Wim to know what's happening if he sees you in there." And there was more to it than that. She wanted him next to her, for one last night. It had never dawned on her that night when she dressed for their dinner party that this was going to be the last day and night of their marriage. She wondered if he knew he was going to tell her that night. She felt like a fool now remembering how worried she had been about him when he looked tired as he came in. This was obviously what had been eating at him, not the merger.

"Are you sure you don't mind my sleeping here?" he asked, looking worried. He wondered if she was going to do something insane, like try to kill herself or him, but he could see in her eyes that she wouldn't. She was heartbroken, but not unbalanced. "I can go back to the city now, if you prefer." To Rachel. To his new life. Away from her forever. It was the last thing she wanted, as Paris looked at him and shook her head.

"I want you to stay." *Forever. For better or worse, until death do us part, just like you promised twenty-four years ago.* She couldn't help but wonder how he could throw their life away and forget those vows. Easily, apparently. For a thirty-one-year-old woman and two little boys. It was as though the years he had shared with Paris had vanished in the blink of an eye.

He nodded and went to put his pajamas on, as she sat in the chair and stared into space. And when he came back, he got into bed, lay there stiffly, and then turned off his light. And then after a long moment, he spoke without looking at her, or reaching out. She could hardly hear his voice as she blew her nose.

"I'm sorry, Paris . . . I never thought this would happen. . . . I'll do anything I can to make this easier for you. I just didn't know what else to do." He sounded helpless and forlorn as he lay in their bed for the last time.

"You can still give her up. Will you at least think about it?" she said, loving him so much she was not afraid to beg. Getting rid of Rachel was her only hope.

There was a long silence from the bed, and finally he answered her. "No, I won't. It's too late for that. There's no turning back now."

"Is she pregnant?" Paris asked, sounding horrified. She hadn't even thought of that. But even if she was, Paris would rather suffer the indignity of an illegitimate child of his than lose him entirely. It had happened to other men before, and their marriages managed to survive. If he wanted it to, theirs could as well. But he didn't want to preserve their marriage. That much was obvious to her.

"No, she's not pregnant. I just think I'm doing the right thing for me, maybe for both of us. I love you, but I don't feel about us the way I used to. You deserve more than that. You need to find someone who loves you the way I once did."

"That's a rotten thing to say. What am I supposed to do? Put out ads? You're just tossing me out there, like a fish you're throwing back, and telling me to find someone else. How convenient for you. I've been married to you for more than half my life. I love you. I would have stayed married to you till I died. What am I supposed to do?" Just thinking about what he was doing to her filled her with terror and despair. She had never felt so frightened in her entire life. Her life as she had known it had ended, and the future seemed fraught with terror and danger and misery. The last thing she wanted was to find someone else. All she wanted was him. They were married. To her, that was sacred. And apparently less so to him.

"You're beautiful, and intelligent, and a good person. You're a wonderful woman, Paris, and a good wife. Some man is going to be lucky to have you. I'm just not the right one anymore. Something changed. . . . I don't know what it is, or why . . . but I know it did. I can't be here anymore." She sat and stared at him for a long time, and then slowly got up out of her chair, and went to stand next to him, on his side of the bed, and sobbing quietly, she sank to her knees, and bowed her head on the bed. He lay there in bed, staring up at the ceiling, afraid to look at her, as tears rolled out of the corners of his eyes and onto his pillow, and gently he stroked her hair. For all its tender agony, and all the ancient feelings it evoked in both of them, they both knew that it was the last moment of its kind they would ever share.

Chapter 2

The next morning dawned in utter splendor with an insultingly brilliant blue sky and bright sun. Paris wanted it to be rainy and gloomy outside, as she turned over in bed and remembered what had happened the night before. And as soon as she did, she began to cry and looked over to find Peter, but he was already in the bathroom, shaving. And she put on a bathrobe and went downstairs to make coffee for both of them. She felt as though she had been trapped in some surreal tragic movie the night before, and maybe if she talked to him coherently in the bright light of day, everything would change. But she needed coffee first. As though she had been beaten, every inch of her ached. She hadn't bothered to comb her hair or brush her teeth, and her carefully applied makeup from the night before was streaked below her eyes and on her face. Wim looked up in surprise as she walked in. He was eating toast and drinking orange juice, and he frowned when he saw his mother. He had never seen her look that way before, and wondered if she'd had too much to drink at the party and was hung over, or maybe she was sick.

"You okay, Mom?"

"I'm fine. Just tired," she said, pouring a glass of orange juice for his father, maybe for the last time ever, with the same sense of unreality she had had the night before. Maybe this was just a bad patch they were going through. It had to be that. He couldn't mean he wanted a divorce, could he? She was suddenly reminded of a friend who had lost her husband to a heart attack on the tennis court the year before. She had said that for the first six months after he died, she kept expecting him to walk through the door and laugh at her, and tell her it was all a joke and he was just kidding. Paris fully expected Peter to recant everything he had said the night before. Rachel and her sons would then vanish politely into the mists, and she and Peter would go on with their life as before. It was temporary insanity, that was all, but when Peter walked into the kitchen fully dressed and looking grim, she knew it wasn't a joke after all. Wim noticed how serious he looked too.

"Are you going to the office, Dad?" he asked, as Paris handed Peter the glass of orange juice, and he took it from her with a stern expression. He was hardening himself for the ugly scene he expected when Wim left, and he wasn't far wrong. She was planning to beg him to give up Rachel and come home. There was no sense of humiliation with their shared life on the line. And it was a strain for both of them to have Wim in their midst, sharing their final moments. Wim sensed that something was wrong, and wondered if they'd had an argument, although that was rare for them, and a minute later, taking his toast with him, he went back to his room.

Peter had finished the orange juice by then, and half the cup of coffee she'd poured for him, and he stood up, and started to go upstairs to pick up his things. He was only taking an overnight bag with him. He was going to come out during the week and pack up the rest. But he knew he needed to get out now as quickly as he could, before she broke down again, or he said things he didn't want to say to her. All he wanted to do now was leave.

"Can we talk for a few minutes?" she asked, following him into their bedroom, as he picked up his bag and looked at her unhappily.

"There's nothing left to say. We said it all last night. I have to go."

"You don't have to do anything, You owe it to me to listen at least. Why don't you at least think about this? You may be making a terrible mistake. I think you are, and Wim and Meg will too. Let's agree to go to counseling, and at least try to make this work. You can't just throw away twenty-four years for some girl." But he had, and wanted to. He was hanging on to his affair with Rachel like the life preserver that would save him from drowning in the world that he and Paris had once shared. And right now he wanted to get as far away from her as he could. She was the one thing standing between him and the future he wanted desperately, with another woman.

"I don't want to go to counseling with you," he said bluntly. "I want a divorce. Even if I stop seeing Rachel, I realize now that I want out. I want more than this. Much, much more. And you should too. We've drifted apart. Our life is dead, like an old tree that needs to be chopped down before it falls over and kills someone. And the person it's liable to kill right now is me. Paris, I can't do this anymore." He wasn't crying when he said it, he didn't even look remorseful this time. He looked determined. His survival was at stake, and he wasn't going to let Paris keep him from what he wanted, no matter what she said. He knew she loved him, and he loved her too. But he was in love with Rachel and wanted a life with her. He was going to drive to New York now and spend the rest of his life with her. And nothing Paris could do or say would stop him. And she could see precisely that on his face. It was over for him. As far as Peter was concerned, their marriage was dead. And all Paris had to do now was accept it, as far as he was concerned, and move on. Easier said than done.

"When did all this happen? When you met that girl? She must be fabulous in bed to turn you around like this." She hated herself for saying it, but she couldn't help herself. And without saying a word, he picked up his bag, walked out of the room and down the stairs, while Paris watched him. He turned to look at her when he got to the bottom of the stairs, and she felt her stomach turn over as though she had been kicked.

"I'll call you about the details. I think you should use someone in my office. I can use another firm if you want. Are you going to talk to the kids?" He talked about it like a deal he was making, or a trip, and she had never seen him look as cold. There was no sign of the guilt and tenderness he had shown her the night before. The door to the magic kingdom was closing forever. And she knew as she looked at him that she would forever remember that moment, as he stood in khaki slacks and a crisply starched blue shirt, with the sunlight streaming across his face. It was like remembering the moment when he had died, or the way he looked at the funeral parlor. She wanted to fly down the stairs and cling to him, but she didn't. She just looked at him, and nodded. And without another word, he turned, and walked out the front door, as she continued to stand there, feeling her knees shaking. And seconds later she heard him drive away.

She was still standing there, when Wim walked out of his room in shorts and T-shirt with a baseball cap on. He looked puzzled when he looked at her.

"Are you okay, Mom?" She nodded, but couldn't say anything. She didn't want him to see her cry, or get hysterical, and she couldn't tell him yet. She didn't feel up to it. She couldn't imagine when she ever would. And she knew she had to tell Meg too. "Did Dad leave for work?" She nodded again, and smiled eerily at him as she patted his arm, and walked back into her room.

She lay on their bed, and could still smell Peter's cologne on the pillow. Her friend whose husband died said she hadn't changed the sheets for weeks, and Paris wondered if she would do that too. She couldn't imagine a life without Peter. And she wondered why she wasn't angry at him. She didn't feel anything except terror, as though she knew something terrible had happened, and she couldn't remember what. But she knew. At the core of her, she knew. Every fiber of her being knew that she had lost the only man she'd ever loved, and as she heard the front door close when Wim went out, she rolled over onto Peter's side of the bed, buried her face in his pillow, and sobbed uncontrollably. The world she had known and loved for twenty-four years had just ended. And all she wanted was to die with it.

Chapter 3

The phone rang several times that weekend, and she never answered it. The answering machine was on, and she knew later that the calls were from Virginia, Natalie, and Meg. She was still hoping that Peter would call and tell her he'd been insane and was coming home, but he never did. Wim came in and out of her room several times to tell her his plans. She stayed in bed and told him she had the flu.

On Sunday night she had to get up to cook dinner for Wim. He'd been doing homework in his room all afternoon, and he came downstairs when he heard her rattling pots and pans. She was standing in the kitchen, looking confused. She didn't know what she was doing, or what to cook for dinner, and she looked up with an anguished expression when he walked into the room.

"Are you still sick? You look terrible. I can make something if you want." He looked worried about her, he was a sweet boy, and he could see how rotten she felt, what he didn't know was why. And then he looked at her with a puzzled expression. "Where's Dad?" He had come home from a date at one in the morning, the night before, and hadn't seen his father's car in the garage. "He's really working late these days." Paris just stared at him, and sat down at the kitchen table in her pajamas. She hadn't combed her hair in two days, or showered since Friday night, which was more than unusual for her. She always looked immaculate, and even when she wasn't feeling well, she made the effort to get dressed and come downstairs. Wim had never seen her look so distraught. "Mom?" he said, with a worried expression, "is something wrong?" All she could do was nod, as her eyes met his. She had no idea how to tell him what had happened.

"Your father and I had a pretty serious talk on Friday night," she said as he sat down at the kitchen table across from her, and she reached for his hands and held them tight. "I didn't realize it, and I guess that was stupid of me," she said, fighting back the tears that she had wallowed in all weekend, but she knew she had to do this right for Wim. He would remember this moment for the rest of his life.

"But I guess your father has been unhappy for a long time. This isn't a very exciting life for him. Maybe it's been too comfortable, or too boring. Maybe I should have gotten a job once you and Meg got older. Hearing about carpools and how the garden is growing isn't much fun after a while. Anyway, your father has decided," she said, taking a deep breath, and looking gently at her son, not wanting to let Peter off the hook, but feeling she had to for their son's sake, "that he doesn't want to be married to me anymore. I know that's a shock. It was to me too. But we're going to keep the house, or I am, and you and Meg can come here and live here whenever you want. And the only thing that will be different is that Daddy won't be here." She didn't even notice, nor did Wim, that she had called him "Daddy" for the first time in years. Wim looked as though he were going into shock.

"Are you serious? He's leaving us? What happened? Did you guys have a big fight over something?" He had never known them to do that before, and they never had. They had never come close to this in all their years together. There had never been more than a few ruffled feathers, and hardly ever any harsh words. Wim looked as stunned as she had been at what she had just told him.

"He's not leaving you," Paris said carefully. "He's leaving me. He feels this is something he has to do." As she said it, her lip trembled, and she started to cry again. And Wim came around the table to put his arms around her. And when she looked up, she saw that he was crying too.

"God, Mom, I'm so sorry. Was he mad about something? Do you think he'll change his mind?" She hesitated for a long moment, wishing she could answer differently, but she knew she couldn't. Barring a miracle, Peter wouldn't be coming home to her again.

"I wish he would," she said honestly, "but I don't think he will. I think he's made up his mind."

"Are you getting a divorce?" he asked through tears, looking like a little kid again, as they clung to each other, and he hovered over her.

"That's what he wants." She choked out the words as Wim wiped his eyes and stood up.

"That sucks. Why would he do a thing like that?" It didn't even occur to him that there might be another woman in his father's life, and Paris did not volunteer. If Rachel stuck around, and she assumed she would, Wim would find out soon enough. That part of it was up to Peter to explain, and she wondered how he would, without looking like a bastard to his children.

"I guess people change sometimes. They grow apart without even knowing it. I should have seen how he was feeling, but I didn't."

"When did he tell you?" he asked, looking devastated, and still trying to understand what had happened. It wasn't easy for either of them, and the worst part was that there had been no warning.

"Friday night, after our dinner party."

"That's why you both looked like that on Saturday morning. I thought you were hung over." He grinned, and Paris looked moderately insulted.

"Have you ever seen either of us hung over?"

"No, but I figured there's always a first time. You looked awful.

And then you said you had the flu when I saw you later." And then he thought of something. "Does Meg know?" His mother shook her head. She still had that to go through, and dreaded telling her on the phone. But Meg had no plans to come home all summer. They had to tell her.

"I'm going to call her." She'd been thinking of doing it that night, and now that she had told Wim, she knew she had to. "I'll call her later."

"Do you want me to tell her?" Wim offered generously, and was silently angry at his father that he hadn't come home to break the news to him in person. He thought that was lousy of him, but didn't say it to his mother. The truth was, Peter couldn't face it and was relieved to leave that grim duty to Paris. Telling her had been more than enough drama for him for one weekend. And he knew she'd do a good job of it with the kids. And whatever she said that he didn't like, he could always clean up later. He was used to having her take full responsibility for their children, no matter how heavy a burden it was for her this time.

"You don't have to do that," Paris said, looking at him gratefully, just for the offer to call his sister, "that's my job." She wanted to be the one to tell her daughter.

"Okay, then I'll cook dinner." It suddenly occurred to Wim that there was no one to take care of his mother now, and when he left for college, she would be alone in Greenwich. He couldn't believe his father had done that to her, it seemed so unlike him, and tarnished him as Wim's hero. He had another thought then as he took out lettuce and tomatoes and some cold chicken. "Do you want me not to go to Berkeley, Mom?" He had been accepted at a number of eastern schools, who would probably still be happy to have him. He had only just accepted Berkeley and hadn't even responded yet to some of the others. He had been planning to do it that weekend, and hadn't.

"I want you to do exactly what you wanted to do, before all this happened. If your father really goes through with the divorce, then

I just have to get used to it. You can't sit here and take care of me forever." That was the frightening part. She had been lying in bed, thinking about it all weekend. She was on her own now. Forever. And even more so, once Wim left for college. It had been comforting having him stick his head in her doorway all weekend. At least it was another human being in the house, and he loved her. That was the most terrifying thought of all now. Wondering who would be there for her if she got sick, or something happened to her. Who was going to care about her? Who would even know if she was sick? Who would she go to movies with, or laugh with? What if no one ever kissed her again, or made love to her? What if she was truly alone forever? The prospect of all of it was so huge as to be beyond understanding. The reality of it was devastating. Even Wim seemed to understand that. Why didn't Peter?

She sat in the kitchen, trying to make small talk with Wim while he made their dinner, and when he put the chicken and salad on their plates, they both pushed it around without eating. "I'm sorry, sweetheart," she said apologetically. "I'm not very hungry."

"That's okay, Mom. Are you going to call Meg now?" He wanted her to, so he could talk to his older sister about it. They had always been close, and he wanted to know what she thought, and if she thought there was a chance their father might come to his senses. Wim still couldn't understand it. Maybe she would have some insights. He hoped so. He had never seen their mother like this, and it scared him. She looked as though she had a terminal illness.

"I guess so," Paris said sadly, and finally dragged herself upstairs to call her while Wim put the dishes in the dishwasher. She wanted to be alone when she called her daughter. Not that she was going to tell her anything different than she had told Wim, but she didn't want an audience while she did it.

Meg answered on the second ring, and she sounded in good spirits. She had just come home from a weekend in Santa Barbara, and told her mother she had a new boyfriend. She said he was an actor.

"Are you alone, sweetheart, or do you want me to call later?" Paris asked, trying to put some life in her voice, so she didn't sound as dead as she was feeling.

"I'm alone, Mom. Why? Do you have something to tell me?" She sounded as though she thought it was funny, and couldn't imagine what her mother was going to tell her. And a moment later, she could imagine it even less. She was almost shrieking when she responded. She felt as though their entire family had been gunned down in a drive-by shooting. "Are you kidding? Is he crazy? What is he doing, Mom? Do you think he means it?" She was more angry, than sad or frightened. But if she had seen her mother's face, she might have had the same sense of terror Wim had. With her uncombed hair and black circles under her eyes, their mother looked scary.

"Yes, I do think he means it," Paris said honestly.

"Why?" And then there was a long silence. "Is he seeing another woman?" She was older and more worldly wise than her brother. In her months in Hollywood, she had been approached by several married men, and the same thing had happened to her before that. Although she couldn't imagine her father cheating on her mother. But she couldn't imagine him divorcing her either. This was crazy.

Paris didn't want to confirm or deny it, about another woman. "I'm sure your father has his reasons. He said that he felt like he was dead here. And he wants more excitement in his life than I can give him. I guess it's not very exciting coming home to Greenwich every night and listening to me talk about the garden," Paris said, feeling humiliated and disheartened, and responsible somehow for the boredom he felt while he was with her. She realized now that she should have gotten a job years before and done something more interesting with her life, like Rachel. She had won him in the end because she was more exciting. And younger. Much, much younger. It cut Paris to the quick to think about it, and made her feel old and unattractive and boring.

"Don't be stupid, Mom. You're a lot more fun than Dad is, you always have been. I don't understand what happened. Did he say anything before this?" Meg was trying to make sense of it, but there was no sense to make, it was what he wanted. Rachel was what he wanted. Not Paris. But Meg had no clue about it.

"He never said anything until Friday night," Paris said, relieved to be talking to her daughter. Between her and Wim and their unfailing support, she felt a fraction better than she had all weekend. And at least neither of them had blamed her. She had been afraid that they might, thinking she had done something dreadful to their father. But Meg was very clear about her feelings, and where to put the blame. She was furious with her father.

"He sounds like a nutcase. Will he go to counseling with you?"

"Maybe. Not to put the marriage back together. He said he'd only go if it would help me adjust to his divorcing me. Not to save the marriage."

"He's crazy," Meg said bluntly, wishing she were at home with her mother and brother. She hated being this far away at a time of crisis. "Where is he? Did he tell you?"

"He said he was going to stay at a hotel in the city, and he'd call me tomorrow about the details. He wants me to use one of his lawyers." It was more than she had told Wim, but Meg was older, and of considerable comfort. Her outrage somehow made Paris feel more human. "I suppose he must be at the Regency. He usually stays there, if he's in town, because it's close to the office."

"I want to call him. Was he planning to tell me, or did he just expect you to do it?" Meg was both heartbroken and fuming, but her anger kept all the other emotions she felt from coming to the surface. She hadn't even begun to deal with the loss and grief yet. Wim, possibly because he was younger and could see the state his mother was in, was more frightened.

"He knew I'd tell you. I think that was easier for him," Paris said sadly.

"How's Wim doing?" Meg asked, sounding worried.

"He cooked me dinner. Poor kid, I've been in bed all weekend."

"Mom," her daughter said sternly, "you can't let this destroy you. I know it must be tough, and it's been a terrible shock. But weird things happen. He could have died too. I'm glad he didn't. Sometimes people just go crazy. I think he did. I don't know why, but this doesn't sound like him. I thought you guys would be married forever."

"So did I," Paris said, as tears stung her eyes again. She felt as though she hadn't stopped crying since Friday. "I don't know what to do now. What am I going to do for the rest of my life without him?" She started to sob then, and it was half an hour later before Meg asked to talk to her brother. When he got on the line, Paris got off, and the two siblings talked to each other for an hour. Their conclusion at the end of it was that their father had gone temporarily insane, and hopefully would recover. Wim still had some faint hope that he would come to his senses. Meg was less certain, and she was still wondering about another woman.

She called the Regency after she hung up, but he wasn't registered there, and she tried several other hotels, and never found him. He was of course staying with Rachel, but none of them knew that. And she got up at six o'clock the next morning to call him at nine New York time, in his office.

"What's going on, Dad?" she asked, for openers, hoping to get him to tell her honestly what had happened. "I didn't know you and Mom were having problems." She tried to sound sane and rational, and not accusatory, so he would talk to her. But he seemed more than willing, and surprisingly honest.

"We weren't," he said fairly. "I am. How is she? Did you talk to her?" But he knew she had, since she had called him to inquire about their "problems."

"She sounds terrible." Meg didn't pull any punches, and wanted him to feel guilty. He deserved to. "Did you just have a fit or something, and fly off the handle?" But that wasn't like him either.

He sighed before he answered his daughter. "I've thought about this for a long time, Meg. I guess I was wrong not to say anything to her sooner. I thought I might feel differently if I waited, but I don't. This is just something I need to do, for me. I feel like I'm buried alive with her in Greenwich, and my life is over."

"Then get an apartment in New York, and move. Both of you. You don't have to divorce her." She was beginning to feel hopeful. Maybe there was a solution, and she felt as though she owed it to her mother to help him find it. Maybe he would actually listen to her.

"I can't stay married to her, Meg. I'm not in love with her anymore. I know that's awful to say, but it's honest." Her hopes were dashed in an instant.

"Did you tell her that?" Meg held her breath as she waited, realizing the full weight of the blow her mother had taken. It was beyond thinking.

"As tactfully as I could. But I had to be honest with her. I'm not going to put our marriage back together. I wanted her to know that."

"Oh. Now what? Where do you both go from here?" She was fishing, but not brave enough to ask yet. She felt sick for her mother. This was not what she deserved after twenty-four years of marriage.

"I don't know, Meg. She'll find someone eventually. She's a beautiful woman. It probably won't take long." It was an incredibly insensitive, cavalier thing to say, and Meg wanted to hit him for it.

"She's in love with you, Dad," she said sadly.

"I know she is, baby. I wish I were still in love with her. But I'm not." Rachel had changed that. Forever.

"Is there someone else, Dad?" She was old enough for him to be honest with her, but he hesitated. Just long enough to arouse his daughter's suspicions.

"I don't know. There might be. Eventually. I have to sort things out first with your mother." It was an evasive answer, and spoke volumes to her.

"That's such a rotten thing to do to Mom, she doesn't deserve this." All her sympathies lay with her mother, as Wim's did. He had done the damage, and he didn't have to pick up the pieces. She did. And they did. And he couldn't just assume that she'd find someone else, like changing hats or shoes or dresses. She might never find someone else, nor want to. She might be in love with him forever. In Meg's opinion, and her mother's, it was tragic.

"I know she doesn't deserve this," he said sadly. "I care about her a great deal, and I always will. I'll try to make this easy for her," if for no other reason than to soothe his conscience. He had felt sick with guilt all weekend, but his passion for Rachel was undimmed. If anything, now that he was free to pursue it, it was stronger.

"How easy can it be to lose your husband and everything you care about? It's going to be awful for her when Wim goes away to college. What's she going to do, Dad?" There were tears in Meg's voice as she asked him. She was worried sick about her mother.

"I don't know. She'll have to figure that out, sweetheart. This happens to people. Things change. Lives go in different directions. People die, and get divorced, and fall out of love. It just happens. It could have happened to her, instead of me."

"But it didn't," Meg insisted. "She would never have left you. She could never have done that," she said loyally. She still loved her father, but she was heartbroken for her mother. Meg no longer understood him. He sounded like a stranger. A selfish, childish, spoiled stranger. She had never before seen him as self-centered.

"I suspect you're right," Peter admitted. "She's incredibly loyal and decent. I don't deserve that."

"Maybe not, Dad," she said, sounding disappointed in him. "How soon are you going to do this?" She was hoping he'd take some time to think about it, and with luck, change his mind.

"I think we're going to proceed in good order. There's no point dragging it out, or raising false hopes, and making it even more painful than it is. A quick, clean break will be a lot simpler." For him, but not necessarily for Paris. And he didn't tell Meg that he had called an attorney the moment he got into the office, and told him to file the papers. He wanted to be divorced by Christmas. He had promised Rachel they'd be married by the end of the year, and it was what he wanted too. He also knew that Rachel wanted another baby, before the boys got much older.

"I'm sorry, Dad. I'm so sad for both of you, and me, and Wim. This is so awful," Meg said, and started to cry. She hadn't meant to, but she couldn't help it. And a few minutes later, they hung up. She felt as though in a single night she had lost not only her family, but all her illusions. Her father had turned out to be someone she didn't even recognize, and she was terrified that her mother would sink into a deep depression. There was nothing to stop her. She had no job, no children at home in a short time, and now no husband. All she had was an empty house, and her friends in Greenwich. It wasn't enough to keep her going. Or to keep the demons of darkness from her. It was all Meg could think about all day, and she called that night to report to Wim about her conversation with their father.

"There's no way he's coming back," she said somberly. "For whatever reason he flipped out, he's planning to stay there." And after thinking about it, she added, "I think he's seeing another woman." She had come to that conclusion when he dodged her question.

"Did he say that?" Wim sounded horrified. It hadn't even occurred to him. Their father was so proper and upstanding, it seemed totally unlike him. But so was divorcing their mother. Overnight, he had become a stranger to his wife and children.

"No. But I got that impression. We'll see what happens." If he was seeing someone else, and she was important to him, she would surface sooner or later. It would certainly explain why he had walked out on their mother so abruptly.

"Do you think Mom knows?" Wim asked sympathetically. Paris had gone to sleep at eight o'clock, long before he and Meg were talking.

"I don't know. I don't want to upset her. This is bad enough without adding another woman to it. We're just going to have to do whatever we can to help her. Maybe I should come home next weekend." But she had plans that would be hard to cancel. "Let's see how she is. I'll be home for your graduation anyway. What are you doing this summer?"

"I'm going to Europe with four of the guys from my class," he said, sounding glum about it. He didn't want to give up the trip he'd been looking forward to all year, nor did he want to abandon their mother.

"She might be better by then. Don't change anything for now. I'll invite her out here for a visit. She doesn't sound like she wants to go anywhere right now." Meg had called her that morning from work, and Paris sounded too depressed to even talk to her. Meg had suggested she call her doctor, but Paris didn't want to. This was not going to be easy, for any of them, except their father. "Call me if anything happens," Meg told Wim. It was certainly an ugly end to his senior year, and a trauma none of them would forget or recover from quickly.

"I don't think she got out of bed today," he confided to her.

"I'll call her tomorrow," Meg said, as her doorbell rang. It was her boyfriend, and she promised to call Wim the next day. He had her cell phone number if anything untoward happened. But at this point, the roof had already fallen in. What more could happen?

Chapter 4

It was Thursday before Virginia and Natalie got through to Paris. They had been trying all week, and were having lunch together when they called her on Virginia's cell phone. And for the first time in days, Paris answered. She sounded hoarse and groggy, and she had been sleeping. Virginia had heard the news from her husband on Monday night when he came home from the office. Peter had told him discreetly that he and Paris had separated over the weekend and were divorcing. Peter wanted to get the word out as quickly as he could, so that within a reasonable amount of time, he could be seen openly with Rachel. But they weren't the secret he hoped they were. Virginia's husband, Jim, told her about Rachel that night over dinner. And she shared the information with Natalie over lunch, before they called Paris. Within days, Paris had become what she most feared, an object of concern and pity. Both of her friends were horrified to realize what had happened. It was a reminder to each of them that no one was exempt from lightning striking when you least expected. No one could ever know what would happen. And just when you thought you could coast forever and were safe, you discovered that you weren't.

"Hi, babe," Virginia said, sounding sympathetic. All she wanted to do was put her arms around her and hold her. "How're you feeling?" she asked, and Paris could hear that she knew. She hadn't had the guts to call and tell her. She just couldn't. It was too awful. Instead, she had retreated into her bed, and sought refuge in sleep. She was only waking up when Wim came home from school, and he was cooking dinner. She had done nothing since Peter left the house on Saturday morning. She kept telling Wim she'd be fine soon, but he was beginning to doubt it.

"Jim told you?" Paris asked, as she rolled over in bed and stared at the ceiling.

"Yes, he did," but Virginia still didn't know if Paris knew about the other woman, and she wasn't going to ask her. She had been through enough heartache. "Can we come over? Nat and I are just sitting here, worrying about you."

"I don't want to see anyone," she said honestly, although she had finally showered on Monday, and again that morning. "I look awful."

"We don't care how you look. How are you feeling?"

"Like my life ended last Friday night. Life as I know it anyway. I wish he had just killed me. It would have been so much simpler."

"I'm glad he didn't. Have you told Meg yet?"

"The kids have been great. Poor Wim, he must feel like he's running a psych ward. I keep promising him I'll get up, and I mean to, but it's just too much trouble."

"We're coming over," Virginia said in a determined voice, frowning meaningfully at Natalie across the table, and shaking her head, trying to give her a clue as to how Paris was doing. She wasn't.

"Don't. I need some time to catch my breath before I see anyone." She felt humiliated and broken. And even her best friends couldn't fix it. No one could. She had gotten a message on the answering machine from the lawyer Peter had retained for her on Tuesday. And when she called him back, she had thrown up after their brief conversation. It didn't bode well for the future. He told her that Peter wanted to file the papers soon, and get the show on the road quickly. And as he said it, she had been overwhelmed by a wave of panic. It was like free-falling out of a plane without a parachute. The only way she could explain the feeling was terror. "I'll call you when I feel better."

In the end, they left a bouquet of flowers, a note and some magazines on her doorstep. They didn't want to intrude, but they were worried about her. They had never known a marriage as seemingly solid as the Armstrongs' to come apart at the seams as quickly. It was shocking. But they all knew it happened. Like death. Sometimes after a long illness, and sometimes with no warning. But always just as final. They all agreed that it had been a rotten thing for Peter to do to her, and none of them were anxious to meet Rachel. It was going to exclude him from the group that had been his friends for years, but Jim assured his wife it didn't seem to matter to him. He had a beautiful young woman on his arm, and a new life. He suspected that Peter wouldn't look back, or think twice about what he was doing. All Peter wanted now was Rachel. And all their friends could think about was Paris.

It was a month before Paris came out of seclusion finally, in time for Wim's graduation. Virginia saw her there, and nearly cried when she did. She was thin and pale, impeccably dressed as always, in a white linen dress and coat, her hair in a French twist, with pearls at her ears and around her neck, and dark glasses to conceal dark circles and the ravages of the past month. The hardest of all for her was seeing Peter there, she hadn't seen him since the morning he had left her. He had had her served with papers three weeks before, and she just stood there and sobbed, in her nightgown, when she took them. But there was no sign of her distress when she saw him. She stood tall and proud and poised, said hello to him, and walked away to stand with a handful of people she knew, and left him to congratulate his son. Peter seemed to be in surprisingly good spirits. The only one not surprised by it was Paris. She had fully understood in the past month that she had been totally and completely defeated. And all she wanted now was for no one to see it. Her friends were solicitous, and she managed to get through a dinner for Wim at a restaurant. He had invited a dozen of his friends, and Meg had come from Los Angeles. She had agreed to have dinner with her father in the city, and he had had the grace not to come to Wim's dinner. And by the time she got home that night, Paris was exhausted. She lay on her bed feeling as though she had had open heart surgery, as Meg watched her from the doorway. Wim had gone out with his friends, and she had come home to keep an eye on her mother. She was incredibly thin these days, and seemed frailer than Meg had ever seen her. The word Natalie had used that day was *brittle,* as though Paris would break in half at any moment.

"You okay, Mom?" Meg asked softly, and came to sit down on the bed next to her, looking worried.

"I'm fine, sweetheart. Just tired." It was like recovering from an accident, or a major illness. It had been her first time out in public, and it had cost her. She had had to dredge up every ounce of courage she had just to be there. She couldn't even enjoy it. The strain of seeing Peter, so estranged from her, was almost too much for her, and he had barely spoken to her. He had been civil, but distant. They weren't even friends now. She felt like her own ghost as she got through it, returning after her death to haunt the people she once knew. She no longer felt like the person she had been. Even to herself now, she felt like a stranger. She wasn't even married now, or not for long anyway, and her marriage had been such a major part of her identity. She had given up everything she once was to be Mrs. Peter Armstrong, and now she felt like no one. A faceless, unloved, unwanted, abandoned single woman. It was her worst nightmare.

"How was Dad when he talked to you?" Meg had been talking to Wim at the time, but she had seen them together, albeit briefly.

"Okay, I guess. He didn't say much. I just said hello, and then went to talk to Natalie and Virginia. It seemed simpler. I don't think he's too anxious to talk to me now. It's too awkward." He

was sending her a constant flood of papers to sign, settlement of-
fers, which included the house, as he had promised. But just seeing
the papers depressed her. She hated to read them, and sometimes
didn't.

"I'm sorry, Mom," Meg said sadly. She had been shocked by
how thin her mother was, and teased her that it was obviously due
to Wim's cooking. But at least for once he wasn't worried about
her, he could leave her in Meg's hands, and celebrate his graduation. He was leaving for Europe over the weekend. Paris had insisted he stick to his plans. She said she had to get used to being
alone at some point. She was beginning to feel like a patient in a
psych ward, and knew she had to deal with it before it killed her.

"It's all right, sweetheart," Paris reassured her. "Don't you want
to go out and see your friends? I'm just going to go to bed in a few
minutes." It was all she did now.

"Are you sure you don't mind if I go out?" Meg hated to leave
her. But by Sunday, she'd be truly alone. Meg had to go back to
L.A., and Wim would be in England. He was planning to travel
around Europe until August, come back for a few weeks, and then
leave for college. These were her last days with him at home, the
last with both him and Meg under one roof. Their life of living together as they had once known it was already over.

And when she took Wim to the airport on Saturday, Paris felt as
though someone had finally cut the umbilical cord when he left
her. She had made him promise to buy a cell phone as soon as he
got to Europe, so she could keep track of him and call him, but she
finally had to let him go, and have faith in his ability to take care of
himself, and be responsible. She felt as though she had lost yet another huge chunk of her life as she drove back to Greenwich. And
she was utterly bereft the next morning when Meg left, although
she tried not to show it. She wandered around the house like a
ghost afterward, and nearly jumped a foot when she heard the
doorbell. It was Virginia, whose son had left for Europe with Wim
the previous morning. She looked faintly embarrassed when Paris

opened the door, and felt she had to apologize for showing up without calling.

"I figured if you were as nervous as I am about them, I'd better come over. Have they called you?"

"No," Paris said with a smile. She was dressed, her hair was combed, and she had put on makeup for Meg's benefit that morning. But she still looked as though she were recovering from a severe case of tuberculosis, or something equally unpleasant. "I don't think they'll call us for a few days. I told Wim to get a cell phone."

"So did I." Virginia laughed, as Paris went to make coffee. "Where's Meg?"

"She left half an hour ago. She couldn't wait to get back to her new boyfriend. She says he's an actor. He's been in two horror pictures, and half a dozen commercials."

"At least he's working." Virginia was glad to see her up and dressed, but the toll of the last month and Peter's perfidy was all too visible. It was the look of despair in her eyes that was so haunting. As though she no longer believed in anything or anyone and had lost hope and faith in everything she had once believed in. It was brutal.

They chatted over coffee for a while, and Virginia finally looked at her, fumbled in her bag, and pushed a piece of paper at her. It had a name and phone number on it, and an address in downtown Greenwich.

"What's that?" Paris looked startled as she read it. She didn't recognize the name. It just said Anne Smythe, with a Greenwich number.

"My shrink's phone number. I couldn't survive without her." Paris knew that she and Jim had had their ups and downs too. He was a difficult man, had suffered from chronic depression at one time, and had improved immeasurably with medication. But the dark years he'd spent before that had been hard on Virginia and their marriage. Paris knew she saw someone but had never thought much about it, nor asked her.

"Do you think I've gone crazy?" Paris asked sadly, as she folded the piece of paper with the number and slipped it into her pocket. "Sometimes I think so." It was almost a relief to say it out loud and admit it.

"No, I don't," Virginia said honestly. "If I did, I'd have the guys here with butterfly nets and a straight jacket. But I think you will end up that way, if you don't get out of this house, and talk to someone about what happened. You've had a hell of a shock. What Peter did to you is about as traumatic as it gets, short of having your husband drop dead in his dinner. And that's probably a lot easier to survive than what he did. One minute you're married, think you're happy, have a husband and a life you've known and loved for twenty-four years, and the next minute he's gone, he's divorcing you, and you don't know what hit you. And to make matters worse, he's living an hour from here, and dating someone twenty years younger. If that doesn't kick your self-esteem and psyche in the ass, I don't know what will. Shit, Paris, most people would be sitting in a corner, drooling."

"Well, I've thought of it," she said with a grin, "but it's so messy."

"I'd be a basket case, in your shoes," Virginia said, with profound respect for her. Even Virginia's husband had admitted to her that he wouldn't have survived the blow, with or without medication. And her friends realized that there was always the possibility that she could get suicidal over it. With the exception of the comfort of knowing that her children were out in the world somewhere, she had very little to live for. She definitely needed someone to talk to. And Virginia thought Anne Smythe might be just the person. She was warm, down to earth, sensible, and combined just the right amount of sympathy with all-right-fine-now-what-are-we-going-to-do-about-this? She had gotten Virginia back on her feet and out of the doldrums after Jim's depression. After he was fine again, Virginia had suddenly felt depressed and without purpose. She had been so used to centering all her attention on him that when he no longer needed her as much, she started to feel use-less. "She saved my ass, and several of my friends whom I referred to her. I think she's terrific."

"I'm not so sure my ass is worth saving," Paris said as Virginia shook her head.

"That's exactly what I mean. You think there's something wrong with you because he left you, instead of seeing that this is about him, not you. He should be feeling like hell about himself, for what he did to you, not you feeling like that because he left you." All Virginia wished was that Paris would get angry, and even hate him, but she didn't. It was obvious to anyone who knew her that she still loved him. As devoted as she had been to him, it would take a long time for love to die, longer than it would take for him to get the papers he wanted to free him. The divorce could dissolve their marriage, but not her feelings. "Will you call her?"

"Maybe," Paris answered honestly. "I'm not sure I want to talk about it, particularly to a stranger. Or to anyone. I don't want to go out, because I don't want to watch everyone feeling sorry for me. Christ, Virginia, it's so pathetic."

"It's only pathetic if you let it be. You don't even know what life has in store for you. You might wind up with someone a hell of a lot better."

"I've never wanted anyone except Peter. I never even looked at another man, or wanted to. I always thought he was the best of the breed, and I was so damn lucky to be with him."

"Well, it turns out he isn't, and you weren't. He did a rotten thing, and he should be strung up for it. But to hell with him. All I want is to see you happy." Paris knew that Virginia meant it.

"What if I'm never happy again?" Paris asked, looking worried. "What if I'm in love with him forever?"

"Then I'll shoot you," Virginia said with a grin. "Try Anne first. If that doesn't work, I'll find an exorcist. But you've got to get this out of your system, and get over it. If you don't, it'll kill you. You don't want to be sick and miserable forever."

"No, I don't," Paris said thoughtfully, "but I don't see how she can change that. No matter what I say to her, Peter will still be gone, we'll be getting a divorce, the kids will be grown up, and he will be with a woman fifteen years younger than I am. It isn't pretty."

"No, but other people have survived it. I'm serious, you may wind up with a guy ten times nicer than he is. People lose their husbands, they die, or walk out on them, they find other people, they remarry, they have good lives. You're forty-six years old, you can't give up on your life now. That's just plain stupid. And wrong. And not fair to you or your kids, or any of the people who love you. Don't give Peter that satisfaction. He has a new life. You deserve to have one too."

"I don't want one."

"Call Anne. Or I'm going to tie you up and drop you on her doorstep. Will you see her once? Just once? If you hate her, you don't have to go back. Just try it."

"All right. I'll try it. Once. But it's not going to make a difference," Paris insisted.

"Thank you for the vote of confidence," Virginia said, and poured herself another cup of coffee. She stayed until nearly four o'clock, and by the time she left, Paris looked tired, but better. And she had promised Virginia again before she left that she would call Anne Smythe in the morning. She couldn't imagine what difference it would make, and was sure it would make none, but if only to get Virginia off her back, she said she would call her.

Chapter 5

The waiting room looked like a library, full of books and comfortable leather chairs, and a small fireplace that Paris sensed would keep the room warm and cozy in winter. But on a warm June day, the windows were open, and down below, Paris could see a manicured well-kept garden. The address Virginia had given her turned out to be a pretty little wood-frame house painted white, with yellow trim, and quaint-looking blue shutters. The word that came to mind as soon as you walked in was *cozy.* And the woman who greeted Paris minutes after she sat down and thumbed through a magazine was nothing like what she'd expected. She had somehow expected to see Anna Freud come through the door, or someone cold and stern and intellectual. Instead, the doctor was a good-looking, well-dressed, fairly sophisticated woman in her mid-fifties. Her hair was well cut, she had makeup on, and the khaki pantsuit she wore was impeccable and looked expensive. She looked like a well-heeled matron, or the wife of an important executive. She was someone you'd expect to see at a dinner party, and not at all Paris's idea of a psychiatrist.

"Is something wrong?" She smiled at Paris as they walked into her inner sanctum, which was a well-decorated airy room, done in beige and white with handsome windows, and some very interesting modern paintings. "You look startled."

"I just expected all this to be different," Paris admitted.

"Different how?" The doctor was intrigued, as she looked warmly at Paris.

"More serious," she said honestly. "This is very pretty."

"Thank you." She laughed and shared a piece of her history. "I worked for a decorator while I was in med school. I always figure if everything falls apart, I can go back to that. I loved it." Paris didn't want to, but she already liked her. There was a straightforwardness and honesty about her, and a lack of pretension, that was very appealing. She could easily imagine being friends with her, if she hadn't met her for this purpose. "So what can I do to help you?"

"My son just left for Europe." Even to Paris, it seemed an odd thing to start with, given everything else that had happened. But it was what had come out of her head first. And the words were out of her mouth before she thought about them.

"To live there? How old is he?" She had been assessing Paris since she walked in and guessed her to be in her early forties. In spite of the agonies of the past month, she looked no older than she had before it happened, just sadder. And still pretty, despite a certain lackluster quality the doctor correctly recognized as depression.

"He's eighteen. And no, he's only going for two months. But I miss him." She could feel tears sting her eyes just talking to her, and was relieved to see a box of tissues sitting near them. She wondered if people cried there often, and could guess easily they must have.

"Is he your only child?"

"No, I have a daughter. She lives in California, in Los Angeles. She works in the film industry as a production assistant. She's twenty-three."

"Is your son in college, Paris?" the doctor asked personably, trying to gather the pieces of the puzzle Paris was presenting to her somewhat piecemeal. Anne Smythe was used to that, it was her business, and she was good at it.

"My son Wim is starting Berkeley at the end of August."

"And that leaves you . . . alone at home? Are you married?"

"I . . . no . . . yes . . . I was . . . until five weeks ago . . . my husband left me for another woman." Bingo. Anne Smythe sat quietly with a sympathetic look on her face as Paris started to cry, and she handed her the box of tissues.

"I'm sorry to hear that. Did you know about the other woman before that?"

"No, I didn't."

"That's an awful shock. Had there been problems in the marriage before?"

"No, it was perfect. Or I thought so at least. He told me when he left that he felt like he was dead living with me. He told me on a Friday night, after a dinner party we gave, that he was leaving me the next morning. I thought everything was fine before that." She stopped to blow her nose, and then, much to her own surprise, Paris repeated everything he had said to her that night verbatim. She told her about Wim going off to school, the MBA degree she had never used, and the feelings of panic she had been getting, about who would be there for her now? What was she going to do with the rest of her life? And she told her as much as she knew about Rachel. The hour spilled into two, which was what the doctor had planned for. She liked starting with long sessions so she knew what they were going to try to do together. And Paris was shocked to see how the time had flown when the doctor asked her if she'd like to make another appointment.

"I don't know. Should I? What difference is it going to make? It's not going to change what happened." She had cried a lot in the two hours, but for once she felt neither drained nor exhausted. She felt relieved after talking to this woman. They hadn't solved anything, but the boil had been lanced and was slowly draining.

"You're right, it's not going to change what happened. But over time, I hope it's going to change how you feel about it. That could make a big difference to you. You have some decisions to make about what to do with your life. Maybe we could work on that together." It was a new concept to Paris, and she wasn't sure what decisions the doctor meant. So far, Peter had made all the decisions. Now all she had to do was live with them.

"All right. Maybe I'll come back again. When do you think?"

"How's Tuesday?" It was only four days away, but Paris liked the idea of seeing her sooner rather than later. Maybe they could get the "decisions" taken care of quickly, and she wouldn't have to come back again. The doctor wrote the appointment on a card, and handed it to her, and she had written a cell phone number on it. "If things get tough over the weekend, Paris, call me."

"I'd hate to bother you," Paris said, looking embarrassed.

"Well, as long as I haven't gone into decorating, for now at least, this is what I do for a living. If you need me, call me," she said, smiling, and Paris smiled gratefully at her.

"Thank you." She drove home feeling better than she had in weeks, and she had no idea why. The doctor had solved none of her problems. But she felt lighter and less depressed than she had since Peter left her, and when she got home, she called Virginia to thank her for introducing her to Anne Smythe.

"I'm so glad you like her," Virginia said, sounding relieved. But she would have been surprised if she hadn't. She was a terrific woman, and the best gift she could give Paris after everything that had happened to her. "Are you seeing her again?"

"I am," Paris admitted, sounding surprised. She hadn't planned to go back again. "Once anyway. We made an appointment for next week." Hearing that made Virginia smile. That was how Anne had done it with her too. One appointment after another, until in the end she had gone for a year. And she had been back for "refreshers" several times since. Whenever a problem came up, she went to see Anne a few times to hash it out with her, and it always helped.

It was nice just having an objective person to talk to sometimes, and someone to hang on to in a crisis.

The next time Paris saw her, she was surprised by a question the doctor asked her halfway through the session.

"Have you thought of moving to California?" She asked it as though it were a perfectly normal thing to do.

"No, I haven't. Why would I?" For a moment, Paris looked confused. It hadn't even occurred to her. They had lived in Greenwich since Meg was born, and she'd never thought of moving. She had established firm roots. Until recently. But even now, the house was hers, and she'd never thought of selling it. She was glad that Peter was giving it to her.

"Well, both your children live there. You might like living closer to them, and being able to see them more often. I just wondered if you'd thought of it." But Paris only shook her head. She had no idea what either Meg or Wim would think of it. And the idea had never once occurred to her. She mentioned it to Meg on the phone that night, and she said she thought it was a great idea.

"Would you come to L.A., Mom?"

"I don't know. I didn't think I was going anywhere. This doctor I've seen a couple of times suggested it today."

"What kind of doctor? Are you sick?" Meg sounded instantly concerned.

"A shrink actually." Paris sighed, feeling embarrassed, but she never kept secrets from Meg. They were confidantes and had been for years. It was a relationship Paris cherished. It was easier talking to Meg than Wim, mostly because she was a girl, and that much older. "Virginia recommended her. I've only seen her twice. But I'm going again in a few days."

"I think that's a very smart thing to do." Meg wished her father would do the same, he had certainly screwed up everyone's life with no prior warning, and Meg was still wondering what had prompted it. He hadn't said anything about Rachel to either of his children yet, and wanted to let the dust settle first. Rachel said she was anxious to meet them, and Peter had promised her she would.

"She can't change anything," Paris said, wondering what the point was of going to a psychiatrist. The divorce was going forward, and Peter was in love with another woman. There wasn't anything Anne Smythe could do to stem the tides or bring Peter back to her.

"No, but you can change things, Mom," Meg said quietly. "What Daddy did was terrible, but now it's up to you what you make of it. And I think it would be terrific if you came out here. It would do you good."

"How do you think Wim would feel about it? I don't want him to think I'm following him to school."

"I think he'd probably like it, particularly if you were close enough for him to stay with you once in a while, and bring friends. I loved coming home to you when I was in college." She laughed then at the memory of duffel bags full of laundry she'd brought home. "Particularly if you do his laundry for him. You should ask him when you talk to him."

"I can't imagine leaving Greenwich. I don't know anyone out there."

"You'd meet people. Maybe you should look for a place in San Francisco. Wim could come over and see you anytime he wants. And I can always go up on the weekends. I think it would do you good to get out of Greenwich, even if you only do it for a year or two. You'd love it out here. The weather's great, the winters are easy, and we would see a lot more of you, Mom. Why don't you think about it?"

"I can't just walk away and leave this house," she said, resisting the idea. But it came up again in her next session with Dr. Smythe, and she told her what Meg had said when she'd mentioned it. "I can't believe it. She actually liked the idea. But what would I do out there? I don't know anyone. Everyone I know is here."

"Except Wim and Meg," Anne Smythe said quietly. She had

planted a seed and was waiting for it to take hold and grow. She was counting on Paris's children to water it. And if it was the right thing for Paris, she would nurture the seed herself. And if not, there were other things she could do to climb out of the hole she'd been in since Peter left. Anne was planning to help her discover and explore all her options for a better life.

They talked about a vast number of things, her childhood, the early years with Peter, the years she had so loved when the children were small, her friends, the MBA program she'd been so successful at and done nothing with. And in late July they talked about Paris getting a job. She was comfortable with Anne by then, and she liked the time they spent together. It always gave her something to think about when she left and went back to the silent house. Paris was still avoiding her friends. She wasn't ready to see them yet.

It was a lonely summer for her, with Wim gone, and Meg in Los Angeles. She and Peter had come to an agreement about the settlement. She was getting the house, as Peter had promised, and a respectable amount of support. He'd been generous with her, to buy off his conscience, and she didn't have to work. But she wanted to do something. She didn't want to just sit around for the rest of her life, particularly if she was going to be alone, which she assumed she would. Anne Smythe tried to talk to her from time to time about going out with men, and Paris didn't want to hear about it. The last thing in the world she wanted to do was date. It was a door she refused to open. She didn't even want to peek inside, and Anne always let it go, but she continued to suggest it from time to time.

The only people Paris saw that summer were Virginia and Natalie. She didn't go to any dinner parties or social events. She had no desire to go anywhere, except lunch with her two friends occasionally, but by August she was looking better again. She had been working in the garden, reading a lot, and sleeping less during the day, and better at night. She had a deep tan, and had never looked better, although she was still very thin. But by the time Wim came home from Europe, she looked more herself again, and he was relieved to see a familiar twinkle in her eye when she picked him up at the airport and threw her arms around him. He had been very good about calling her, and he had had a fantastic time in France, Italy, England, and Spain, and all he could talk about was going back again next year.

"I'm going with you, if you do," she warned him, with a look of mischief in her eye, which delighted him. She had looked like a dead person when he left. "You were gone for way too long. I don't know what I'm going to do when you go away to school." And then she told him about the suggestion Anne Smythe had made, about moving to California. Paris was curious about his reaction.

"Would you really move?" He looked startled by the idea, and not as enthusiastic as she'd hoped at first. Meg had been much more excited about it. He was looking forward to being independent when he went away to college, and he had visions of her bringing his lunch to him on campus in the little Batman lunch box he'd had when he was in first grade. "Would you sell this house?" It was the only home he had ever really known, and he hated that possibility too. He liked thinking of her in the home he loved, waiting for him, just as he had imagined her all summer while he trotted around Europe.

"No. If I did anything, I'd rent it, but I'm not even sure I'd do that. It's just a crazy notion I had." She wasn't sold on the idea herself.

"How'd you come up with that?" he inquired, looking intrigued.

"My shrink suggested it," she said blithely, and he stared at her.

"Your shrink? Are you okay, Mom?"

"Better than I was when you left," she said calmly, and smiled at him. "I think it helps."

"Whatever works," he said valiantly, and then mentioned it to his sister that night on the phone. "Did you know Mom was going to a shrink?"

"Yes, I think it's done her a lot of good," Meg said sensibly. Her mother had seemed less depressed in the last two months since she had started seeing Anne Smythe, which Meg thought was a good thing.

"Is Mom losing it?" he asked, sounding worried, and his sister laughed.

"No, but she has a right to, after what Dad did to her." She was still angry at her father for disrupting all their lives, and Wim didn't like it either. "A lot of people would have lost it after a shock like that. Did you call Dad while you were in Europe?" He had, but his father hadn't had much to say. He had called his mother more often, and his sister frequently. But most of the time, he just had fun with his friends.

"Do you think she'll really move to California?" Wim was still surprised by the idea, but he could see some benefits in it, as long as she didn't turn up in Berkeley constantly. He was still concerned about that.

"Maybe. It would be a big change for her. I'm not sure she really wants to, I think she's just playing with the idea right now. What do you think?" Meg was curious about his reaction.

"It might be okay," he said cautiously.

"It would be a lot better for her than sitting around in Greenwich in an empty house by herself. I hate to think of her sitting there alone after you leave."

"Yeah, me too." It made him think about what that would be like for his mother, and he didn't like that either. "Maybe she should get a job and meet some people," he said thoughtfully.

"She wants to, she just doesn't know what to do. She's never really worked. She'll figure it out eventually. The shrink will help."

"I guess." He was still surprised by that. He had never thought of his mother needing anyone to solve her problems, but he had to admit, she had had her share of surprises in the last three months. It had been a big adjustment for him too. It felt strange to come home and have his father not be there. He drove into the city to see him two days after he got home, and they went out to lunch. He introduced him to several lawyers in his office, including a girl who hardly looked older than Meg, and she had been very warm and friendly to him. He mentioned her to his mother when he got home, and she looked instantly stressed. All he could think of was that it upset her now to hear about his father, so he didn't say much about it after that.

Peter had promised to fly out to San Francisco, to help settle him in school. And Paris didn't look pleased about that either, although she didn't say anything to Wim. But she was planning to go out and settle him in the dormitory too. And having Peter there was going to be hard for her. But above all, she didn't want to make it a problem for Wim. And it didn't seem fair to Peter or Wim, to ask Peter not to come. But she discussed it with Anne the next time they met.

"Do you think you'll be able to handle being out there with him?" Anne asked her sympathetically, as they sat in her office peacefully one afternoon, and Paris looked uncertain as she considered it, and then finally looked at her, feeling stressed. Even thinking about it was hard.

"To be honest, I'm not sure. It's going to be so strange being there with Peter. Do you think maybe I shouldn't go?" Paris looked worried.

"How would your son feel about that?"

"I think he'd be disappointed, and so would I."

"What about asking Peter to pass on it?" she suggested, and Paris shook her head. She didn't like that idea either.

"I think Wim would be sad if Peter doesn't go."

"Well, you have my cell number. You can always call me, if things get tough. And you can always leave the dormitory, if it's too uncomfortable for you. You and Peter can agree to go there in shifts." Paris hadn't thought of that, and she liked that as a fallback position if it was too awkward being there with him.

"How bad can it get?" Paris asked her hesitantly, trying to sound braver than she felt.

"That depends on you," Anne said quietly, and for the first time, Paris realized that was true. "You have every right to walk away, if you want to. Or to not even go out there. I'm sure Wim would understand, if you don't think you can handle it. He doesn't want you to be unhappy either." And she had been very, very unhappy, and he knew it, ever since Peter left.

"Maybe I'll look at houses while I'm there," Paris said thoughtfully.

"That might be fun for you," Anne said, encouraging her. Paris hadn't made any decision yet about moving west. It was just something they talked about from time to time, but she still thought she wanted to stay in Greenwich. It was familiar, and she felt safer there. She wasn't ready to make any drastic moves. But it was yet another option that she had. She hadn't solved the job issue yet either. And for lack of a better idea, she had signed up for volunteer work at a children's shelter in September. It was a start. It was all a process, a journey, rather than a destination, at this point. And for now, Paris still had no idea where she was going, or where she would land. Peter had tossed her out of the plane without a parachute three months before, and given everything that had happened, Anne told her that she thought she was doing well. She was getting up in the morning, combing her hair, getting dressed, seeing her two best friends for lunch occasionally, and she was bracing herself for Wim to leave for college. It was all she could manage for now.

He was leaving in three days, and Paris was going with him, the last time she saw Anne before the trip. She was braced to see Peter, and she kept telling herself she could handle it. And after she dropped Wim off at school, she was going to L.A. to see Meg. It was something to look forward to, and as she left Anne's office, Paris turned to look at her with a worried expression.

"Am I going to make it?" she asked, feeling like a frightened child, and the doctor smiled.

"You're doing fine. Call if you need me," Anne reminded her again, and Paris nodded, and hurried down the stairs, as she left, reminding herself over and over again of what the doctor had said to her . . . you're doing fine . . . you're doing fine. The words echoed in her head. All she could do now was keep on going, and do the best she could, and hope she landed on her feet one day. It was the only choice Peter had left her when he threw her out of the plane. And one day, maybe, if she was very lucky, and the fates were smiling on her, her parachute would open finally. She wasn't even sure yet if she was wearing one, and all she could do was pray she was. But there was no sign of a parachute yet. The wind was still whistling past her head at a terrifying rate.

Chapter 6

Paris and Wim flew to San Francisco with all his bags and treasures and computer. Peter was flying out on his own later that night. And all the way out on the flight, as Wim watched the movie, and slept for a while, Paris worried about what it would be like seeing Peter again. After twenty-four years of marriage, he almost felt like a stranger to her now. And the worst of it was that she was aching to see him again, almost like a drug she needed to survive. After three months, and all he had done in leaving her, she was still in love with him, and hoping that some miracle would occur and he'd come back. The only person she'd been able to admit that to was Anne Smythe, who told her it wasn't unusual to feel that way, and that one day, she'd be able to let go, and ready to move on, but apparently not yet.

The flight took just over five hours, and they took a cab to the Ritz-Carlton, where Paris had reserved two rooms, for Wim and herself. And she took Wim out to dinner in Chinatown that night. They had a nice time together, as they always did, and when they got back to the hotel, they called Meg. Paris was flying down to see her in two days, after she got Wim settled in his dorm. She assumed it would take two days, and she was in no rush to leave him there. What she really dreaded now was going home.

She had rented a small van to take his belongings across the bridge to the university, and the following morning they left the hotel by ten, and followed all the instructions they'd been given to sign in. And as soon as they got there, Wim took control. He gave his mother the slip of paper with his dorm address, told her he'd meet her there in two hours, and set off on foot. It took her a full half-hour just to find the address. The UC Berkeley campus was huge. She walked around for a little while, and then sat on a rock in the sunshine outside the dorm, waiting for him. It was pleasant just sitting there. The weather was warm, the sun was hot, and it was at least fifteen degrees warmer than it had been in San Francisco an hour before. And as she sat there, enjoying the sun on her face, she saw a familiar figure in the distance, a slow rolling gait she had seen a million times before, and would have recognized with her eyes closed, just from the pounding of her heart. It was Peter, walking straight toward her with a determined look, and he stopped a few feet away from her.

"Hello, Paris," he said coolly, as though they'd scarcely met before. None of their time or history together showed in his eyes or on his face. He had braced himself for that. And so had she. "Where's Wim?"

"Signing up for classes, and getting his dorm room key. He should be here in another hour." He nodded, looking uncertain about what to do, wait with her, or leave and come back. But he had nothing else to do either, and the campus was so overwhelming in its enormity, it was a little daunting to wander off. Like her, he preferred to stay and wait, although he felt awkward being with her. He hadn't been looking forward to the trip either, and had steeled himself for it, for Wim's sake.

They sat in silence for a while, lost in their own thoughts. He tried to keep his mind on Rachel. She kept remembering the things she had discussed with Anne Smythe about seeing him again. And in the end, it was Peter who spoke first.

"You look well," he said formally, without commenting on the fact that she looked beautiful, but very thin.

"Thank you. So do you." She didn't ask how Rachel was, or how he liked living in New York, presumably with her. Paris had suspected for months that the hotel room he was keeping was only a front, for the children's sake, and the proprieties prior to the divorce. She didn't ask him if he was happy to be nearly divorced. The divorce was going to be final between Thanksgiving and Christmas, which would add a new dimension to the holidays for her this year. "It was nice of you to come out," she said politely, feeling an ache in her heart just being this close to him, and having to engage in small talk with him, which seemed so absurd. "It means a lot to Wim."

"I thought it might, that's why I came. I hope you don't mind that I'm here." She looked up at him, and he was more handsome than ever. She had to brace herself just to look at him. It was still nearly impossible to believe how totally and suddenly and irreversibly he had rejected her. It was the single greatest blow of her life. She couldn't even imagine recovering from it, or daring to care about someone again. All she could imagine was loving him, and hurting like this, for the rest of her life.

"I think we both have to get used to doing things like this," she said practically, trying to sound healthier than she felt. "There are going to be a lot of events that are important to the kids, and we've got to be able to manage it for them." Although this was in very close quarters, and over several days, which made it harder for her, particularly on unfamiliar turf. She couldn't go home to safe, familiar surroundings afterward to lick her wounds. All she could do was go back to a hotel, which wasn't the same. He nodded, in silent agreement with her, and all she could feel was the future stretching forever in front of them. A future in which he had Rachel, and she was alone.

He sat on a bench in silence for a while, as she sat quietly on the rock, both of them wishing that Wim would hurry up. And finally, Peter looked at her again. He seemed to be growing increasingly uncomfortable, and whenever she glanced at him, she could almost see him squirm.

"Are you all right?" he asked her finally, and she opened her eyes. She'd been holding her face up to the sun, trying not to feel the proximity of him, which was nearly impossible. She was aching to get up and throw herself into his arms, or at his feet. How was it possible to spend more than half a lifetime with someone and simply have them get up one morning and walk away? It was still nearly impossible for her to accept or even fathom.

"I'm fine," she said quietly, not entirely sure of what he meant. Did he mean now, while waiting for Wim and sitting on a rock in the sun, or in a broader sense? She didn't want to ask.

"I worry about you," he said, looking at his shoes. It was too painful to look at her. Everything he had done to her was in her eyes. They looked like pools of broken green glass. "This has been hard for us both," he offered finally, which was hard to believe.

"It's what you want, isn't it?" she whispered, praying he would say no. This was her last chance to say it to him, or so it felt.

"Yes." He spat the word out like a rock that had been caught in his throat. "It is. But that doesn't mean it's easy for me either. I can only imagine how you must feel." To his credit, he looked sad and worried about her.

"No, you can't. I couldn't have imagined it either, until it happened to me. It's like a death, only worse. Sometimes I try to pretend that you are dead, which is easier, then I don't have to think about where you are, or why you left." She was being excruciatingly honest with him. But why not at this point? She had nothing left to lose.

"It'll get better with time," he said gently, not knowing what else to say, and then mercifully, they both saw Wim running down the road toward them. He arrived like a burst of summer wind, hot and perspiring and out of breath. For an instant, Paris was sorry he had come when he had, and then just as quickly, she was relieved. She had heard all she needed to know. Peter was firm in his decision, and only sorry for her. She didn't want his pity but his heart. The conversation could only have gone downhill from there.

It was easier to focus on Wim, and from then on, they were both busy carrying his belongings upstairs. Once they got into the room, Paris stationed herself in the area of Wim's bed, to unpack what they brought up, and Peter and Wim lugged boxes and bags, a trunk, a small stereo, his computer, and his bicycle up three flights of stairs. They had rented a microwave and a tiny refrigerator from the school. He had everything he'd need, and it was four o'clock before everything was set up. Two of his roommates had arrived by then, and the third appeared just as they left. They all looked like healthy, young, wholesome boys. Two were from California, and the third was from Hong Kong. And they seemed a good mix. Wim had promised to have dinner with Peter that night, and he said he'd be back at six, and then turned to Paris as they walked slowly down the stairs. They both looked tired, it had been a long day, and emotional in every way. She was not only watching her youngest child fly the nest, and helping him do it as she lovingly made his bed and put his clothes away, but she was setting Peter free at the same time, or trying to. It was a reminder of her double loss. Triple, when she thought of Meg. All the people she counted on and loved were now gone from her daily life, and Peter far more than that. He was gone for good.

He turned to her as they reached the main hall, which was graced with a huge bulletin board covered with fliers and messages, and posters of concerts and sports events. It was the essence of college life.

"Would you like to join us for dinner tonight?" Peter asked generously, as she shook her head. She was almost too drained to talk, as she brushed back a lock of blond hair, and he had to fight the temptation to do it for her. She looked like a young girl herself in jeans and T-shirt and sandals. She hardly looked older to him than the girls moving in to the neighboring dorm, and seeing her that way brought back a wave of memories for him.

"Thanks. I'm wiped out. I think I'll go back to the hotel and get a massage." She was even too tired for that, but the last thing she wanted was to sit across a dinner table from him, or worse, next to him, and see what she could no longer have. As tired as she was, she knew all she would do was cry. She wanted to spare them all that. "I'll see Wim tomorrow. Are you coming back?"

He shook his head in answer. "I have to be in Chicago tomorrow night. I'm leaving in the morning, at the crack of dawn. But I think he's pretty well set, by this time tomorrow he won't want anything to do with either of us. He's off and running," Peter said with a smile. He was proud of their son, and so was Paris.

"Yes, he is," she said with a sad smile. It hurt so damn much, no matter how right it was. It was painful for her. "Thanks for carrying all the heavy stuff," she said, as he walked her to the van. "It didn't seem like that much when we packed." It had grown exponentially somehow on the flight out.

"It never does," he said with a smile. "Remember when we took Meg to Vassar? I've never seen so much stuff in my life." She had even brought wallpaper and curtains, and a rug, and insisted her father put up the wallpaper with a staple gun she'd brought. She had her mother's gift for transforming a room, and fortunately her roommate had liked what she'd brought. But Peter had never worked so hard in his life. Putting up the curtains to her satisfaction had been agony, and Paris laughed at the memory with him. "Whatever happened to all that stuff? I don't recall it coming home, or did she take it to New York?" It was the trivia of which lifetimes are made. A lifetime they had shared and never would again.

"She sold it to a junior when she left." He nodded, and they looked at each other for a long moment. So many memories they had shared were irrelevant now, like old clothing left to disintegrate quietly in an attic. The attic of their hearts, and the marriage he had destroyed. She felt as though her entire life had been deposited in a dumpster like so much trash. All things that had once been cherished and loved and belonged to someone, and now had no home. And she along with it. Tossed out, forgotten, unloved. It was a depressing thought.

"Take care of yourself," he said somberly, and then finally let himself say what he'd been thinking all day. "I mean really take care. You look awfully thin." She didn't know what to answer him, she just looked at him, nodded, and looked away so he wouldn't see the tears in her eyes. "Thanks for letting me be here today."

"I'm glad you were," she said generously. "It wouldn't have been the same for Wim if you weren't here." He nodded, and she got into the van without looking at him, and a moment later she drove away, as he watched her for a long time. He believed in the choice he had made, and there were times when he had never known such happiness as what he and Rachel shared. And there were others when he knew he would miss Paris forever. She was a remarkable woman. And he hoped that one day, she would get over what he had done to her. He admired her for her dignity and courage. He knew better than anyone that she was a woman of great grace. More than he felt he deserved.

Chapter 7

When Paris showed up at the dormitory to see Wim the next day, he was on his way out with his friends. He had a thousand things to sign up for, people to meet, worlds to discover, things to do, and she realized within minutes that if she stuck around, she would be in the way. Her job was done. It was time to go.

"Do you want to have dinner tonight?" she asked hopefully, and he looked awkward and shook his head.

"I can't. I'm sorry, Mom. There's an assembly for the athletic department tonight." She knew he wanted to get on the swimming team. He'd been on the varsity team all through high school.

"It's all right, sweetheart. I guess I'll head down to L.A. to see Meg. Will you be okay?" She half-wished he would throw his arms around her neck and beg her not to leave, as he had done at camp. But he was a big boy now, and ready to fly. She hugged him for a long moment, and he looked at her with an unforgettable smile.

"I love you, Mom," he whispered, as the others waited for him in the hall. "Take care of yourself. And thanks for everything." He wanted to thank her for the day she had been willing to spend with his father the day before, in spite of everything, but he didn't know how. His father had spoken respectfully of her the night before, which almost made Wim ask him why he had left if he thought so highly of her. It was impossible to understand, but more than he wanted to know. He just wanted them both to be happy, whatever it took. Especially his mom. Sometimes she seemed so frail. "I'll call you," Wim promised.

"I love you. . . . Have fun . . ." she said, as they walked out of his room, and he hurried down the stairs with a wave, and then he was gone, and she walked slowly down, wishing for only a second that she was young again, and starting all over. But what would she have done differently? Even knowing what she knew now, she would have married Peter anyway. And had Wim and Meg. Other than the last disastrous three months, she had no regrets about their marriage.

She drove back to San Francisco in the van on a brilliantly sunny day, and went back to the hotel to pack. She had thought of looking at some houses and apartments, in case she ever decided to move out, but she wasn't in the mood. Having left one of her chicks at Berkeley, she was now anxious to see the other in L.A. She booked a three o'clock flight, arranged for a car to get her to the airport, and asked the hotel to return the van, since they had rented it for her anyway. And at one-thirty she was on her way to the airport. She was due to arrive at LAX just after four o'clock, and had promised to pick Meg up at work. Paris was staying at Meg's apartment that night, which sounded like fun and would be less lonely than a hotel.

And on the flight down she thought of Peter again, the way he had looked, the things he had said. She had gotten through it at least, and managed not to humiliate herself, or embarrass Wim. All things considered, she had done well. She had a lot to talk about with Anne Smythe. And after that, she closed her eyes for a few minutes, and slept until they landed in L.A.

The moment they arrived, she could sense that she was in a bustling metropolis and not a small provincial town like San Francisco, or a bohemian intellectual suburb like Berkeley. The atmosphere in Los Angeles, even at the airport, felt more like New York, with looser clothes and better weather. It was fun just being there.

And when she got to the studio, she could see why Meg loved it. Her job was crazed. There were a thousand things going on at once. Actors and actresses with beautiful hair and perfect makeup were scurrying across the set or making frantic demands. Technicians were everywhere, with lighting fixtures in hand or coils of wire drapped around their necks. Cameramen were shouting to others to set up scenes that still had to be lit. And a director had just told everyone to call it a day, which left Meg free to leave.

"Wow! Is it like this every day?" Paris asked, fascinated by the action swirling around them. Meg smiled, looking relaxed and poised.

"No." Meg laughed. "Usually it's busier. Half the actors were off today."

"I'm impressed." Her daughter had never looked happier. She looked gorgeous, and just like her mother. They had identical features, the same long blond hair, and these days Paris was even thinner than Meg, which gave her an ever more youthful appearance.

"You two look like sisters!" a lighting technician commented with a grin as he walked by, having just heard Meg call her "Mom." And Paris smiled. It was an intriguing world, and a lively scene.

And when she saw Meg's apartment, she was pleased. It was a small pretty one-bedroom unit in Malibu, with a view of the beach. It was a lovely place. She had recently moved from a smaller one in Venice Beach, a raise in salary had allowed her to come here, along with a small subsidy her parents sent her every month. They didn't want her living in a dangerous neighborhood, and this was anything but. Paris would have been happy there herself, and seeing it made her think again of living in California, to be close to them.

"Did you look at any houses in San Francisco?" Meg asked her as she poured each of them a glass of iced tea from a pitcher she kept in the fridge, just as her mother did. It was a nice reminder of home for Paris, and comforting as they sat on the small deck, and enjoyed the last of the day's sun.

"I didn't really have time," Paris said vaguely, but it was more about spirit than time. It had saddened her to say good-bye to Wim, not to mention Peter, and all she wanted to do after that was leave, and see Meg to bolster her mood. She had felt lonely when she arrived, but she was feeling better now.

"How was it with Dad?" Meg asked with a look of concern, pulling her hair out of the ponytail she'd worn all day at work, and letting her long hair fall over her shoulders and down her back. It was even longer than her mother's, and made her look like a little girl to Paris once she let it loose. She was a spectacular-looking girl, every bit as beautiful as the actresses on the set, but she had no interest in that. She was wearing a halter top, flip-flops, and jeans, her uniform for work. "Was he decent?" Meg asked, looking worried. She was sure it had been a strain on her mom, even though when he'd called, Wim had said they'd been fine. But he was only eighteen, and missed the subtleties sometimes.

"It was okay," Paris said, looking tired, and taking a sip of the iced tea. "He was very nice. It was good for Wim."

"And for you?"

Paris sighed. She could be honest with Meg. She always was. As much as mother and daughter, they were friends, and had always been. They had had almost none of the strife that comes with the teenage years. Meg had always been reasonable and willing to talk about things, unlike most of her peers. Paris's friends said she didn't know how blessed she was, but she did, even more so now. Meg had been her greatest source of support since Peter left, almost like a mother instead of a child. But she was no longer a child. She was a woman, and Paris respected her opinions.

"To be honest, it was hard. He looks like he always did. I see him, and part of me thinks we're still married, and technically we are. It's so weird, and so hard to understand that he's not part of my life anymore. It was probably hard for him too. But this is what he wants. He made that clear again. I don't know what happened. I wish I did. I wish I knew where I went wrong, where I failed, what

I did or didn't do. . . . I must have done something. You don't just wake up one day and leave. Or maybe you do. I don't know. . . . I don't think I'll ever understand it. Or get over it," she said sadly, as the sun glinted on her golden hair.

"You were a good sport to let him go to Berkeley with you." Meg admired her a lot, and especially the dignity with which she was facing the divorce. Paris felt she had no other choice. She didn't hate him, even now. And she knew she had to survive it, whatever it took. For the moment, it was taking every ounce of courage she had.

"It was right for him to be there. It made Wim really happy." And then she told Meg about the college scene at Berkeley, his roommates, his dorm. "He looked so cute when I left. I hated to go. I'm going to hate it even more when I go back to Greenwich. I'm starting some volunteer work in September."

"I still think your shrink is right, and you should move out."

"Maybe," Paris said thoughtfully, but she didn't sound convinced. "So what about you? What's the new boyfriend like? Is he cute?" Meg laughed in answer.

"I think he is. Maybe you won't. He's kind of a free spirit. He was born in a commune in San Francisco, and he grew up in Hawaii. We get along pretty well. He's coming over later, after dinner. I told him I wanted some time alone with you first." Meg loved spending time with her mother, and she knew she wouldn't be in town for long.

"What's his name? I don't think you told me." So much had happened lately, they hadn't talked about the new boyfriend much, and Meg smiled.

"Peace."

"Peace?" Paris looked startled, and Meg laughed.

"Yeah. I know. Actually, it suits him. Peace Jones. It's a great name for an actor. No one ever forgets it. He wants to do martial arts movies, but he's still stuck in horror films for now. He's got a great look. His mother is Eurasian, and his father was black. He is the most incredible mix of exotic-looking people. He looks sort of Mexican, with big sloping eyes."

"He sounds interesting," Paris said, trying to keep an open mind. But even at its most open, her mind was not prepared for Peace Jones when he arrived. He was everything Meg had said, and less. He was exotically beautiful, with a spectacular physique that showed to perfection in a tank top he was wearing and skin-tight jeans. He rode in on a motorcycle you could hear for miles, and he wore Harley-Davidson boots that left black marks all across Meg's beige carpet, which she seemed not to notice or mind. She was enthralled by him. And by the time he'd been there for half an hour, Paris was panicked. He talked freely about all the drugs he had done as a teenager in Hawaii, half of which Paris had never heard of, and he was oblivious to Meg's attempts to change the subject. But he said he had given them all up when he got serious about martial arts. He was a black belt in karate, and said he spent four hours a day, if not five, working out. And in response to Paris's motherly inquiries, he looked blank when she asked where he'd gone to college. He said he took physics regularly to keep his system pure, and was on a macrobiotic diet. He was a complete health nut, which was a relief at least, since he had given up drugs and alcohol as a result. But the only subject he seemed to be inter-ested in talking about was his body. And he talked in rhapsodic terms to Paris about her daughter, which was at least something. He was crazy about her. And even Paris could sense that the physi-cal attraction between them was powerful. It was as though all the life had been sucked out of the room when he kissed Meg passion-ately, and then left them. And Meg laughed when she came back into the room and looked at her mother, whose silence spoke vol-umes.

"Now, Mom, don't panic."

"Give me one reason not to," Paris said, looking sheepish. She and Meg were too close to hide anything from each other.

"I'm not going to marry him, for one thing. We're just having a good time with each other."

"What do you talk about? Other than his herbal enemas and his workout program?" Meg nearly collapsed in hysterics at her mother's expression. "Although, I'll admit, it's certainly a fascinating topic. For God's sake, Meg . . . who is he?"

"Just a nice guy I met. He's sweet to me. We talk about the film industry. He's wholesome, he's not into drugs, or an alcoholic in training, like most of the guys I met when I got here. You don't know what dating's like, Mom. There are a lot of weirdos out there, and a lot of losers."

"It's not very reassuring, if he is what qualifies as a nonweirdo. Although he was polite, and he seems to be nice to you. Meg, can you imagine your father's face if he met him?"

"Don't even think about it. We haven't been going out for that long, and we probably won't for much longer. I need to get out more, and his diet keeps him pretty limited. He hates clubs and bars and restaurants. He goes to bed at eight-thirty."

"That's not much fun," Paris admitted. Meeting Peace Jones had been a whole new experience for her, and made her worry about what Meg was doing. But the fact that he didn't drink or do drugs was at least something, though in Paris's eyes, not enough.

"He's very religious too. He's a Buddhist." Meg was lobbying for him to her mother.

"Because of his mother?"

"No, she's Jewish. She converted when she married some guy she met in New York. Because of his karate."

"I'm not ready for this, Meg. If this is what it's like out here, I'm staying in Greenwich."

"San Francisco is a lot more conservative. Besides, everyone's gay there." Meg was teasing her, but it was certainly a large portion of the population, and famous for it. The girls Meg knew who lived there complained constantly that all they met were gay guys who were better looking than they were.

"That's comforting. And you want me to move there? At least I'll find a decent hairdresser, if I ever decide to cut my hair and get it done," Paris said, and Meg wagged a finger at her.

"Shame on you, Mom. My hairdresser is straight. Gay guys run the world. I think you'd like San Francisco," she said seriously. "You could live in Marin County, which is like Greenwich, with good weather."

"I don't know, sweetheart. I have friends in Connecticut. I've been there forever." It seemed too frightening to just uproot herself and move three thousand miles away because Peter had left her, although it was tempting to be closer to her children. But California seemed like a whole different culture, and even at her age, she felt too old to adjust to it. It was perfect for Meg, but didn't seem like the right move to her mother.

"How often do you see those friends now?" Meg challenged her.

"Not very often," she confessed. "Okay. Never. At the moment. But when things settle down, and I get used to this, I'll go out again. I just haven't felt like it," she said honestly.

"Are any of them single?" Meg cross-examined.

Paris thought for a moment. "I guess not. The single ones, if their wives die, or they get divorced, move to the city. It's a pretty married community, at least among the people we know."

"Exactly. How do you expect to start your life over, among a lot of married people you've known forever? Who are you going to date, Mom?" It was a valid question, but Paris didn't want to hear it.

"I'm not. Besides, I'm still married."

"For three more months. And then what? You can't stay alone forever." Meg was firm, and Paris avoided her gaze.

"Yes, I can," Paris said stubbornly. "If what's waiting for me out there is an older generation of Peace Joneses, I think I'd rather just stay single and forget it. I haven't dated since I was twenty, and I'm not going to start now, at my age. It would depress me profoundly."

"You can't give up on life at forty-six, Mom. That's crazy." But so was being single after twenty-four years of marriage. It was all crazy. And if sanity was going out with a grown-up version of Peace Jones, Paris would rather have been burned at the stake in the parking lot of a shopping mall, and said so to her daughter.

"Stop using him as an excuse. He's unusual, and you know it. There are plenty of grown-up respectable men out there who've gotten divorced or lost their wives, and would love to find a new relationship. They're as lonely as you are."

Paris was heartbroken as much as lonely, that was the real problem. She hadn't gotten over Peter, and didn't expect to in this lifetime. "At least think about it. For the future. And think about moving to California. I'd love it," Meg said warmly.

"So would I, sweetheart." Paris was touched by her daughter's concern and enthusiasm. "But I can always fly out more often. I'd love to see more of you." Meg was planning to come home for Thanksgiving, but they had no plans to see each other sooner, which was going to be hard for Paris. "Maybe I can fly out once a month for a weekend." She had nothing else to do now, but the truth was that Meg was busy on weekends. She had her own life. And eventually, Paris would need one too, she just wasn't ready to deal with it yet.

They cooked dinner together that night in the small cheerful kitchen. And slept in the same bed. And the next day, Paris wandered up and down Rodeo Drive in Beverly Hills, window shopping, and then went back to the apartment to wait for Meg. She sat in the last rays of sun on the deck, thinking about what Meg had said, and wondering what to do about her life. She couldn't even imagine what the rest of her life would be like now, and she wasn't even sure she cared. She really didn't want to find another man, or date. If she couldn't have Peter, she would rather be alone, and spend time with her children and friends. Just the health risks of dating someone these days, and sleeping with them, seemed far too terrifying to her. She had said as much to Anne Smythe. It was far simpler to be alone.

Meg had a problem on the set that night, and didn't get home till ten o'clock. Paris made dinner for her, and was grateful to climb into bed with her. There was something so comforting about just lying next to another human being and feeling her warmth. She slept better than she had in months. And they had breakfast on the deck the next day. Meg had to be back on the set by nine, and Paris was taking a noon flight back to New York.

"I'm going to miss you, Mom," Meg said sadly when she left. She had loved the two nights they had spent together. And Peace had said he thought her mother was great and a real babe, which she duly reported to her mother. Paris had laughed and rolled her eyes. He was harmless, she hoped, but definitely strange. And hopefully a temporary departure for Meg.

"I want you to come back and visit soon, even if you don't go up to see Wim." They both knew that he wanted to spread his wings at last, and be independent from both of them.

As soon as Meg left for work, Paris felt a wave of sadness engulf her. As loving and welcoming as her daughter was, she was a grown woman, with a demanding job and a busy life. There was no room for Paris in it, except for a few days and brief visits. She had to make her own way now, and adjust to the realities of her life. The reality was that she was alone, and would stay that way. And she cried when she wrote Meg a note of thanks before she left. She was sad all the way to the airport in a cab, and on the flight back to New York. And when she walked into the silent house in Greenwich, the emptiness of it hit her like a bomb. There was no one. No Wim. No Meg. No Peter. There was no way to hide from it anymore. She was totally alone, and she thought her heart would break as she lay in bed that night, thinking of Peter, and how beautiful and familiar he had looked in California. It was hopeless. And as she drifted off to sleep in the bed they had once shared, she felt despair engulf her until she felt as though she were about to drown. It was still hard to believe sometimes that she'd survive. At night, alone in her bed, it seemed as though everyone she had ever loved was gone.

Chapter 8

The sessions with Anne Smythe seemed to get more difficult once Paris got back from California. The therapist was pushing her harder, making her look deep into herself, and bringing up a lot of painful issues. She cried in every session now, and the volunteer work she was doing in Stamford with abused kids was depressing. Her social life was nonexistent. She was relentlessly stubborn about it. She went nowhere and saw no one, except for the occasional lunch with Natalie and Virginia. But she seemed to have less in common with them now. Although their children were the same age as hers, they both had husbands, busy lives, someone to share their days and nights with, and take care of. Paris had no one. All she had were calls to Wim and Meg in California. She stubbornly insisted to Anne that she was staying in Greenwich. As Paris saw it, she belonged there, and didn't want to move west.

"What about a job?" Anne pushed her about it again one morning, and Paris looked hopeless.

"Doing what? Arranging flowers? Giving dinner parties? Driving carpool? I don't know how to do anything."

"You have a master's degree in business administration," Anne said sternly. She held Paris's feet to the fire with great regularity, but in some ways Paris loved her for it, although there were times when she hated her for it too. The bond of friendship and respect seemed to grow stronger between the two women week by week.

"I wouldn't know how to run a business if my life depended on it," Paris replied. "I never did. All I learned in business school was theory. I never practiced any of it. All I've done since then is be a wife and mother."

"A respectable pursuit. Now it's time to do something else."

"I don't want to do anything else." Paris sank down in her chair with her arms crossed and looked like a pouting kid.

"Are you enjoying your life, Paris?" Anne said quietly with a calm expression.

"No, I'm not. I hate every minute of it." And she felt certain she always would from now on.

"Then your assignment, before we meet again, is to think about what you'd *like* to do. I don't care what it is. But something you really enjoy doing, even if it's something you've never done before, or haven't done in years. Knitting, needlepoint, ice hockey, a cooking class, photography, hand puppets, painting. Whatever it is. You decide. Forget about a job for now. Let's find some things you like to do."

"I don't know what I like to do," Paris said, looking blank. "I've been taking care of everyone else for the last twenty-four years. I never had time for me."

"That's exactly my point. Now let's take care of you. Fun time. Think of two things or even one that you *want* to do. No matter how silly it sounds."

Paris was still looking baffled when she left, and even more so when she tried to put pen to paper. She couldn't think of a single thing she liked to do, except that something Anne had said in her office had struck a chord with Paris, and she couldn't remember what it was. She was already in bed that night, in the dark, thinking about it some more, when she suddenly thought of it. Ice hockey. That was what Anne had said. Ice skating. She had loved it as a child, and always loved watching figure skaters in pairs. She went back to Anne victoriously three days later. She was still see-ing her twice a week, and didn't feel ready yet to reduce it to one.

"Okay, I found something," she said with a cautious smile. "Ice skating. I used to love it as a little girl. And I took Wim and Meg skating when they were small."

"All right, then your assignment is to get yourself to an ice skat-ing rink as soon as you can. By the time we meet again, I want to hear that you've been out on the ice, having some fun."

Paris felt utterly ridiculous, but the following weekend she went to the Dorothy Hamill Skating Rink in Greenwich, and was out gliding around the ice on a Sunday morning. It was still early, and there was no one on the ice, except a few boys in hockey skates, and a couple of old ladies, who were surprisingly decent skaters, and had been skating for years. And by the time Paris had been out there for half an hour, she was having a ball.

She skated again the following week on a Thursday morning, and amazed herself by hiring an instructor to teach her to do spins. It was becoming her favorite pastime of the week, and by the time the kids came home for Thanksgiving, she had gotten pretty good. What she hadn't done yet was go anywhere socially. She had not been out for dinner, or an evening, or even a movie, since Peter left. She told Anne that it was too embarrassing to go out socially, with everyone knowing what had happened to her, and it was too de-pressing to go to the movies alone. The only place she had fun was on the ice. But at least she had that. And Wim and Meg were vastly impressed by her newfound expertise when she talked them into going skating with her on Thanksgiving morning. She felt like a kid again, and even Wim said he was proud of her when he saw what she could do.

"You look like Peggy Fleming, Mom," Meg said admiringly.

"Hardly, sweetheart. But thanks anyway." They skated together till almost noon. And then they went home to eat the turkey Paris had left in the oven while they went out. But in spite of the pleasant morning they'd shared, and the fact that she was thrilled to have them home, it was a difficult afternoon. The holiday seemed to underscore everything that had changed in the past year. It was agonizing for Paris, and Wim and Meg were scheduled to have dinner with Peter in the city the following night. He was anxious to see them too, but had understood that they wanted to be with their mother on Thanksgiving, and hadn't pressed the point with them.

Wim and Meg both looked very nice when they caught the five o'clock train into the city on Friday afternoon. It was snowing, and neither of them wanted to drive. He was taking them to Le Cirque for dinner, which seemed very festive and generous of him. They were both looking forward to it. Meg was wearing a little black dress of her mother's, and Wim had decided to wear a suit, and looked suddenly older than his years. He seemed to have matured noticeably in the three months since he'd left for school. And Paris was undeniably proud of him.

Peter was waiting for them at the entrance to the restaurant in a pin-striped suit, and Meg thought he looked very handsome, and said as much to him. He was pleased, and happy to spend an evening with them. He had invited them both to stay at the hotel with him, and had reserved rooms for each of them. And on Saturday morning, they were planning to go home to Greenwich. They were both returning to the West Coast on Sunday morning. And on Saturday night, they were both planning to see their friends. It was hard now, with separate parents to satisfy, to fit it all in, although both of them had seen friends the night before, after Thanksgiving dinner, as well. Paris was just grateful to have them sleeping there, she didn't expect to monopolize their time, nor did Peter. And they were glad to come into the city. There were already Christmas trees everywhere, and with the snow falling, there was a festive air and it looked like a Christmas card scene.

Peter seemed a little tense to Meg at first, as though he didn't know what to say to her, and he seemed a little more at ease with Wim. He had never been an easy conversationalist, and he had always counted on their mother to keep the conversational ball rolling. Without her, things were a little stiffer. But eventually, after a glass of wine, he seemed to loosen up. Neither of his children had seen Peter very often since he left, although he made a point of calling them often. And Meg was touched and surprised when he ordered champagne for dessert.

"Are we celebrating something?" she asked, teasing him. It was legal for her to drink, and she pushed her glass over to Wim so he could take a sip too.

"Well, yes, actually," he said, looking uncomfortable, as he glanced from one of his children to the other. "I have a little announcement to make." It was hard to imagine what it would be. Meg wondered if he had bought a new house or an apartment, or better yet, maybe he was thinking of going back to their mother. But in that case, she reasoned, he would have invited Paris to join them, and he hadn't. They waited expectantly as he put down his glass and seemed to be waiting for a drumroll. This was turning out to be harder than he'd expected, and he was feeling extremely nervous and it showed. "I'm getting married," he blurted out finally, as both of his children stared at him in amazement. There had been nothing in their conversations with him to even remotely suggest it before this. He had thought he was giving them time to adjust to the divorce, and protecting Rachel from their inevitable conclusions. It had never even occurred to him what kind of damage he would do to his relationship with them by dropping her into their lives as a fait accompli, a surprise.

"You're kidding, right?" Meg was the first to respond. "You can't be." She looked shocked, and her face went instantly chalk white.

All Wim could think about was his mother. This was going to kill her. "Does Mom know?"

They both looked crestfallen, and Peter looked panicked. "No, she doesn't. You're the first to know. I thought you should know first." Who was he marrying? They hadn't even met her. All Meg could think was, how could he do this? And she couldn't help thinking that the woman he was marrying must be the reason he had left their mother. They weren't even divorced yet. How could he think of getting married? Their mother wasn't even dating, and had barely left the house.

"When did you meet her?" Meg asked sensibly, but she felt as though her head was spinning. All she wanted to do was jump up and hit him and run out of the restaurant screaming, but she knew that would be childish. She felt she owed it to him to at least listen. Maybe he had just met her. But if that was the case, marrying her this quickly was insane. Meg wondered if he was.

"She's worked at my law firm for the past two years. She's a very nice, very bright young woman. She went to Stanford," he said to them, as though that would make a difference. "And Harvard Law School." So she was intelligent and educated. They had established that much. "And she has two little boys, Jason and Thomas, who are five and seven. I think you'll like them." Oh my God, Meg thought to herself, they were going to be her stepbrothers. And she could see in her father's eyes that he meant this. The only thing she was grateful for, as she listened to him, was that he had the good taste not to bring the woman to dinner. At least it showed a certain sensitivity that he hadn't.

"How old is she?" Meg asked, with a sinking stomach. She knew she would always remember this as one of the worst moments of her life, second only to the day her mother had called her to tell her they were getting divorced. But this was running a close second.

"She'll be thirty-two in December."

"My God, Dad. She's twenty years younger than you are."

"And eight years older than Meg," Wim added with a somber expression. He wasn't enjoying this either. All he wanted was to go home to his mother. He felt like a frightened child.

"Why don't you just go out with her? Why do you have to get married so soon? You and Mom aren't even divorced yet." As she said it, Meg was near tears. And her father didn't answer the question. He looked right at her with a stern expression. He was not going to justify this to them. That much was clear. Meg couldn't help wondering if he'd lost his mind.

"We're getting married on New Year's Eve, and I'd like both of you to be there." There was an endless silence at the table, as the waiter brought the check, and Wim and Meg just stared at their father. New Year's Eve was five weeks away. And this was the first they'd heard of it. It was already a done deal, which didn't seem fair, to say the least.

"I was planning to go out with my friends," Wim said as though that would excuse him from an event he would do almost anything not to attend. But he didn't see how he was going to get out of it, judging by the look on his father's face. Peter was actually foolish enough, under the circumstances, to look stern.

"I think you'll have to skip that this year, Wim. It's an important day. I'd like you to be my best man." There were tears in Wim's eyes as he shook his head.

"I can't do that to Mom, Dad. It would break her heart. You can make me come, but I won't be best man." Peter didn't answer for a long moment, and then nodded and looked at Meg.

"I assume you'll be there too?" She nodded, and looked as devastated as her brother.

"Are we going to meet her before the wedding, Dad?" Meg asked in a choked voice. She didn't even know the woman's name, and in his anxiousness, he had forgotten to tell them, and then took care of it in the next breath.

"Rachel and I are going to have breakfast with you tomorrow. She wants you to meet Jason and Tommy too. They're adorable little boys." In a single breath, he had a new family, and it occurred to Meg instantly that his new bride was young enough to want more babies. The very idea of it made her sick. But at least he was including them in the horror. It would have been worse if they'd been excluded, or he'd told them after the wedding.

"Where are you getting married?"

"At the Metropolitan Club. There will only be about a hundred

people there. Neither of us wanted a big wedding. Rachel is Jewish, and we didn't want a religious wedding. We're going to be
married by a judge friend of hers." It was beyond thinking. The vision of her father marrying someone else nearly reduced Meg to
hysterics, no matter how smart or nice the woman was. Like Wim,
all she could do now was think of how it would affect her mother.
She was going to be heartbroken. But hopefully not suicidal. If
nothing else, Meg was glad that she and Wim were in town to
bring her comfort.

"When are you going to tell Mom?" Meg asked cautiously. Wim
hadn't said a word in minutes and was playing with the napkin in
his lap.

"I'm not sure," her father said vaguely. "I wanted both of you to
know first." And then Meg understood what he was doing. He
wanted them to tell Paris. It was going to be their job to break the
news to her.

He paid the check after that, and they rode back to the hotel in silence. He said goodnight to them, and left them alone in the con-
necting rooms he had taken for them for the night. And it was only
after he had left that Meg flew into her brother's arms, and the two
stood there and hugged, crying loudly, like children lost in the
night. It was a long time before they finally let go of each other,
blew their noses, and sat down.

"How are we going to tell Mom?" Wim said, looking as devastated as Meg felt.

"I don't know. We'll figure it out. We'll just tell her, I guess."

"I guess she'll stop eating again," he said, looking grim.

"Maybe not. She's got her shrink. How can he be so stupid?
She's practically my age, and she's got two little kids. I think that's
why he left Mom."

"You do?" Wim looked stunned. He still hadn't made the connection, but he was naïve, and young.

"He wouldn't be getting married this fast otherwise. The

divorce isn't even final for another week or two. He didn't lose any time. Maybe she's pregnant," Meg added with a look of panic, and Wim laid on the bed and closed his eyes.

They called their mother after that, just to check in, but neither of them said a word about their father's plans. They just said they'd had a nice dinner at Le Cirque, and were going to bed at the hotel.

And that night, for the first time in years, they slept in the same bed, clinging to each other in innocent despair, just as they had when they were children. The last time they'd done that was when their dog died. Meg couldn't remember being as miserable since. It had been a very, very long time.

And in the morning, their father called their rooms to make sure they were awake, and reminded them that they were meeting Rachel and her sons in the dining room downstairs at ten o'clock.

"I can hardly wait," Meg said, feeling as though she was hung over. And Wim looked as though he felt worse. He looked sick.

"Do we really have to do this?" he asked as they went down in the elevator. Meg was wearing brown suede pants and a sweater of her mother's. And Wim was dismissively casual, wearing a UCB sweatshirt and jeans. It was all he had brought with him, and he found himself hoping they'd throw him out of the dining room, but they didn't. Their father and a very attractive young woman were already waiting for them at a large round table, and two little towheaded boys were squirming in their seats. And Meg noticed as soon as they got there that Rachel looked like a taller, younger, sexier version of their mother. The resemblance was striking. It was as though her father had turned back the clock and cheated time, with a woman who was a younger version of his soon-to-be-ex-wife. It was a compliment of sorts, but the irony of it somehow made it all seem that much worse. Why couldn't he have just re-signed himself to getting older with their mother, and left things as they had been? And Wim realized as he looked at her, that Rachel was the girl his father had introduced him to casually in his office months before. Seeing her again now made Wim curious about how and when she had come into his father's life, and if they had already been involved back then.

Peter introduced both of his children to Rachel, and to Jason and Tommy. And Rachel made a considerable effort with both Meg and Wim. And finally at the end of breakfast, she looked at both of them and spoke cautiously to them about the wedding. She had disagreed violently with Peter about telling them so late, and was well aware of how hard it was going to be on them. But she wasn't willing to postpone it either. As far as she was concerned, she had waited long enough. She just thought Peter should have told them a lot sooner than he did. His idea about letting the dust settle after he left their mother seemed more than foolish to her. The one thing she had done before the fateful breakfast was to warn Jason and Tommy not to say that Peter was living with them, and they had agreed.

"I know it must be hard for both of you to know that we're getting married," she said slowly. "I know this has been a big change for you, and probably comes as a shock. But I really love your father, and I want to make him happy. And I want you both to know that you're welcome in our home anytime. I want you to feel it's your home too." He had bought a beautiful co-op on Fifth Avenue, with a splendid view of the park, and two guest rooms for them. And there were three rooms for the boys and a nanny. Rachel had said that if they had a baby, which she hoped they would, the boys could share a room.

"Thank you," Meg said in a choked voice after Rachel's little speech. After that they talked about the wedding. And at eleven-thirty, after never speaking once during the entire breakfast, Wim looked at his sister and said they had to catch the train.

They both hugged their father before they left, and they seemed in a great hurry to leave. Peter reminded Wim that the wedding was black tie, and he nodded, and with rapid strides, they were out of the hotel and into a cab after a hasty good-bye to Rachel and the boys. Wim didn't say a word to his sister, he just stared out the window, and she held his hand. New Year's Eve was going to be a killer, they both knew, not only for them, but for their mother too. And they still had to break the news. But Meg wanted to do it, she didn't want her father upsetting her again. She'd been through enough.

"How do you think it went?" Peter asked Rachel as he paid the check, and she helped the boys put on their coats. They'd been very well behaved, although neither of Peter's children had said a word to them until they left.

"I think they both look like they're in shock. That's a big bite for them to swallow all at once. Me, the boys, the wedding. I'd be pretty shocked too." And she had been when her own father had done the same thing. He had married one of her classmates from Stanford the year she'd gotten out of school. And she hadn't spoken to him for three years, and very little since. It had created a permanent rift between them, particularly when her mother died five years later, officially of cancer, but presumably of grief. It was a familiar story to her, but hadn't dissuaded her from what she was doing with Peter. She was desperately in love with him. "When are you going to tell Paris?" she asked, as they walked out onto the street and hailed a cab, to go back to the apartment on Fifth Avenue.

"I'm not. Meg said she would. I think that's best," he said, succumbing to cowardice, but nonetheless grateful he didn't have to do it himself.

"So do I," Rachel said, as he gave the driver the address, and they sped uptown. Peter put an arm around her, tousled the boys' hair, and looked relieved. It had been a tough morning for him. And all he could do now was force Paris out of his mind. He had no other choice. He told himself, as he had for six months now, that what he was doing was right, for all of them. It was an illusion he would have to cling to now, for better or worse, for the rest of his life.

Chapter 9

Paris walked into Anne Smythe's office looking glazed. She looked like a phantom drifting through the room as she sat down, and Anne watched, assessing her again. She hadn't seen her look like that in months. Not since June, when she'd first come in.

"How's the ice skating going?"

"It isn't," Paris said in a monotone.

"Why not? Have you been sick?" They had only seen each other four days before, but a lot could happen in four days, and had.

"Peter's getting married on New Year's Eve."

There was a long silence. "I see. That's pretty rough."

"Yes it is," Paris said, looking as though she was on Thorazine. She didn't scream, she didn't cry. She didn't go into any details, or say how she had heard. She just sat there looking dead, and she felt like she was. Again. The last hope she had harbored was gone. He hadn't come to his senses or changed his mind. He was getting married in five weeks. Meg and Wim had told her as soon as they got back from the city on Saturday afternoon. And afterward Meg had slept in her bed that night. And both of them had gone back to California the next day. Paris had cried all Sunday night. For them, for Peter, for herself. She felt doomed to be alone for the rest of her life. And he had a new wife. Or would, in five weeks.

"How do you feel?"

"Like shit."

Anne smiled at her. "I can see that. I'll bet you do. Anyone would. Are you angry, Paris?" Paris shook her head and started to cry silently. It took her a long time to answer.

"I'm just sad. Very, very sad." She looked broken.

"Do you think we ought to talk about some medication? Do you think that would help?" Paris shook her head again.

"I don't want to run away from it. I have to learn to live with this. He's gone."

"Yes, he is. But you have a whole life ahead of you, and some of it will be very good. It will probably never be as bad as this again." It was a reassuring thought.

"I hope not," Paris said, blowing her nose. "I want to hate him, but I don't. I hate her. The bitch. She ruined my life. And so did he, the shit. But I love him anyway." She sounded like a child, and felt like one. She felt utterly lost, and couldn't imagine her life ever being happy again. She was sure it wouldn't be.

"How were Wim and Meg?"

"Great, to me. And upset. They were shocked. They asked me if I knew about her, and I lied to them. I didn't think it was fair to Peter to tell them the truth, that she was why he left me."

"Why are you covering for him?"

"Because he's their father, and I love him, and it didn't seem fair to him to tell them the truth. That's up to him."

"That's decent of you." Paris nodded, and blew her nose again. "What about you, Paris? What are you going to do to get through this? I think you should go skating again."

"I don't want to skate. I don't want to do anything." She was profoundly depressed again. Despair had become a way of life.

"What about seeing friends? Have you been invited to any Christmas parties?" It seemed irrelevant now.

"Lots of them. I turned them all down."

"Why? I think you should go."

"I don't want people feeling sorry for me." It had been her mantra for the past six months.

"They'll feel a lot sorrier for you if you become a recluse. Why not make an effort to go to at least one party, and see how it goes?"

Paris sat staring at her for a long moment, and then shook her head.

"Then, if you're that depressed, I think we should talk about meds," Anne said firmly.

Paris glared at her from her chair, and then sighed deeply. "All right, all right. I'll go to one Christmas party. One. But that's it."

"Thank you," Anne said, looking pleased. "Do you want to talk about which one?"

"No," Paris said, scowling at her. "I'll figure it out myself." They spent the rest of the session talking about how she felt about Peter's impending marriage, and she looked a little better when she left, and the next time she came, she blurted out that she had accepted for a cocktail party that Virginia and her husband were giving a week before Christmas Eve. Wim and Meg were coming home for two weeks the next day. Wim had a month's vacation, but he was going skiing in Vermont with friends after Peter's wedding. All Paris wanted to do now was get through the holidays. If she was still alive and on her feet on New Year's Day, she figured she'd be ahead of the game.

The one thing Paris had agreed to do, other than going to the party she was dreading, was to baby herself as much as she could. Anne said it was important to nurture herself, rest, sleep, get some exercise, even a massage would do her good. And two days later, like a sign from providence, a woman she had known in her car-pool days ran into her at the grocery store, and handed her the business card of a massage and aromatherapist she said she'd tried, and said was fabulous. Paris felt foolish taking it, but it couldn't do any harm, she told herself. And Anne was right, she had to do something for her own peace and sanity, especially if she was going to continue to refuse to take antidepressants, which she was determined to do. She wanted to get "well" and happy again on her own, for some reason that was important to her, although she didn't think there was anything wrong with other people taking medication. She just didn't want it herself. So massage seemed like a wholesome alternative, and when she got home that afternoon, she called the name on the card.

The voice at the other end of the line was somewhat ethereal, and there was Indian music playing in the background, which Paris found irritating, but she was determined to keep an open mind. The woman's name was Karma Applebaum, and Paris forced herself not to laugh as she wrote it down. The massage therapist said she would come to the house, she had her own table, and she said she would bring her aromatherapy oils as well. The gods were with them apparently, because Karma said she had had a cancellation providentially just that night. Paris hesitated for a beat when Karma offered to come at nine o'clock, and then decided what the hell. She had nothing to lose, and she thought she might sleep better. It sounded like voodoo to her, and she had never had a massage in her entire life. And God only knew what aromatherapy involved. It sounded ridiculous to her. It was amazing what one could be driven to, she told herself.

She made herself a cup of instant soup before the "therapist" arrived, and when Meg called, she admitted sheepishly what she was about to do, and Meg insisted it would be good for her.

"Peace loves aromatherapy," Meg encouraged her. "We do it all the time," she said cheerfully, and Paris groaned. She'd been afraid of something like that.

"I'll let you know how it goes," Paris said, sounding cynical as they hung up.

When Karma Applebaum arrived, she drove up in a truck with Hindu symbols painted on its side, and her blond hair was neatly done in cornrows with tiny beads woven into them. She was dressed all in white. And despite Paris's skepticism, she had to admit that the woman had a lovely, peaceful face. There was an otherworldly quality to her, and she took her shoes off the minute she came into the house. She asked where Paris's bedroom was, and went upstairs quietly to set up the table, and put flannel sheets on it. She plugged in a heating pad, and brought a small portable stereo out of a bag, and put gentle music on. It was more of the same Indian music Paris had heard in the background on the phone. And by the time Paris emerged from her bathroom in a cashmere robe that she seemed to live in these days, the room was nearly dark, and Karma was ready. Paris felt as though she was about to participate in a séance.

"Let yourself breathe away all the demons that have been possessing you. . . . Send them back to where they came from," Karma said in a whisper as Paris lay down on the table. She hadn't been aware of being possessed by demons lately. And without a word, breathing deeply herself, Karma moved her hands several inches above Paris's somewhat anxious, rigid body. This felt silly. Karma waved her hands like magic wands, and said she was feeling Paris's chakras. And then she stopped abruptly just above Paris's liver. She frowned, looked at Paris with concern, and spoke with genuine worry. "I feel a blockage."

"Where?" She was beginning to make Paris nervous. All she wanted was a massage, not a news flash from her liver.

"I think it's lodged between your kidneys and your liver. Have you been having a problem with your mother?"

"Not lately. She's been dead for eighteen years. But I had a lot of trouble with her before that." Her mother had been an extremely bitter, angry woman, but Paris hardly ever thought about her. She had far bigger problems.

"It must be something else then . . . but I feel spirits in the house. Have you heard them?" She'd been right in the first place, Paris decided, trying not to let the "therapist" unnerve her. It was a séance.

"No, I haven't." Paris's philosophies were generally firmly rooted in fact, not fiction. And she wasn't interested in spirits. Just in surviving the divorce, and Peter's impending marriage. She would have preferred dealing with spirits. They might have been easier to get rid of. Karma had begun moving her hands again by then, and she stopped with a look of horror two inches above Paris's stomach.

"There it is, I've got it," she said with a victorious look. "It's in your bowels." The news was getting worse by the minute.

"What is?" Paris asked, torn between a sense of the ridiculous and a wave of panic. The idea of this woman finding something in Paris's bowels did not reassure her.

"All the demons are in your intestines," Karma said with a look of certainty. "You must be very angry. You need a high colonic." Whoever this woman was, she was obviously from the same planet as Peace, Meg's vegan boyfriend. "You're really not going to get what you need out of the massage until you clean all the toxins out of your system." This was getting more frightening by the second.

"Could we just do what we can this time, without the high colonic?" It was the last thing Paris wanted to contemplate. All she had wanted was a massage and a decent night's sleep immediately thereafter.

"I can try, but you're really not going to get my best work without it." It was a sacrifice Paris was willing to make, despite the fact that Karma looked extremely discouraged. "I'll do what I can." And then, finally, she pulled a bottle of oil out of her bag, basted Paris liberally with it, and began rubbing it into Paris's arms and hands and shoulders. She worked on her chest after that, her stomach and legs, and made unhappy clucking sounds of despair each time she passed her hands over Paris's stomach. "I don't want to make the demons comfortable," she explained. "You have to flush them." But by then the music, the oil, the dark room, and Karma's hands had begun to work their magic on Paris. In spite of the alleged demons in her bowels, she was finally relaxing. And she already felt better, by the time Karma whispered to her to turn over. And what she did on Paris's tense back and shoulders was the best part. In spite of the demons and bad karma she was now lying on, she was so relaxed, she felt as though she were melting. It was exactly what she had needed. And as she lay there with her eyes closed, it felt heavenly—until suddenly she felt as though she'd been hit between the shoulder blades by a tennis ball flying at a hundred miles an hour, and then felt as though Karma had ripped a piece out of one shoulder.

"What are you doing?" Paris said, opening both eyes in panic.

"Cupping you. You'll love it. It'll pull out all the demons in your body along with the toxins." Not them again. Apparently, the demons had moved from her bowels to her upper body, and Karma was determined to get them. She kept hitting Paris's back with a hot cup, which created a suction, and then she ripped it off with a loud popping sound. It hurt like hell, and made Paris squirm, but she was embarrassed to ask her to stop it. "Great, isn't it?"

"Not exactly," Paris said, daring to be honest finally. "I liked the other part better."

"So do your demons. We can't let them get too comfortable, can we?" Why not? Paris was tempted to ask. Because when they were comfortable, so was she. The cupping seemed to go on forever, and then mercifully stopped. And with that, she began kneading and slapping Paris's bottom. It was obvious to Paris now that the demons were sitting on her buttocks. But if so, they were getting a hell of a beating at Karma's hands. And then with no warning, she took hot rocks, almost beyond bearing, and laid them on Paris's shoulders, took two more from her bag of tricks, and kneaded the soles of Paris's feet with them until they felt like they were on fire. "This will clear your intestines and your head until you do the high colonic," she explained, and while she was still torturing the soles of Paris's feet, the smell of something burning filled the room. It was a cross between seared flesh and burning tires, and it was so pungent that Paris began to cough, and couldn't stop. "That's what I thought. Breathe deeply now. They hate this stuff. We need to get all the dark spirits out of the room." It was a smell Paris feared would be in the room forever, and she was beginning to worry that she had set fire to the couch, as she opened her eyes and looked around. There was a small heater with a votive candle under it, and a bottle of oil poised over it in a clamp.

"What is that stuff?" she asked, still choking from the fumes, as Karma smiled. And the purity of her face reminded Paris of Joan of Arc as she was engulfed by the final flames.

"It's a potion I mix myself. It works every time."

"On what?" It was going to wreak havoc with the carpet and the curtains. The pungent, oily smell seemed to permeate the entire room.

"This is great for your lungs. See how you're starting to clear everything out." Paris was beginning to fear she might throw up. It was starting to clear the instant soup she'd eaten before Karma arrived to massage her. And before she could ask the woman to put the votive out and get rid of her magic potion, Karma put a different bottle over the flame, and within seconds there was a smell so powerful in the room that tears had filled Paris's eyes. It was a smell somewhere between rat poison, arsenic, and cloves, and was so overwhelming Paris could hardly breathe.

"What does this one do?" It was becoming something of a challenge just to survive in the room while Karma continued the massage. Paris was still lying on her stomach, and the small of her back was now on fire from the hot, oily rocks. It was agony, and yet in a funny way, both the heat and the weight of them felt good. She was beginning to understand the philosophy that led some sects to sleep on beds of nails, or swallow flames. It turned the mind away from its many ills and made you concentrate on all the places in your body that were either burning, in agony, or simply hurt. And when Karma told her to turn over again, and Paris did, without warning she spilled a cup of salt onto her abdomen, covered her belly button, and dropped a hot ball of incense on top of it, while Paris watched in fascination.

"What is that going to do?"

"Suck all the poisons out, and bring you inner peace." The incense was an improvement over the burning oils at least, but the next one Karma put on over the flame was like instant spring, and the flower scent was so powerful that Paris sneezed violently, and it sent the incense on her stomach flying across the room. "They're hating this," Karma smiled, referring to Paris's demons again. But Paris couldn't stop sneezing for the next five minutes, and finally conceded defeat. The oils had done her in.

"So am I, I think I'm allergic to that stuff," Paris said, and Karma looked as though she had been slapped.

"You can't be allergic to aromatherapy," she pronounced with absolute certainty. But by then, Paris had had enough. The massage, what there had been of it, had been nice, but the oils and burning rocks and pungent smells had been too much. And it was after eleven o'clock.

"I think I am allergic to it," Paris said firmly, "and it's getting late. I feel guilty keeping you out at this hour." As she said it, she sat up and swung her legs off the table, and reached for her robe.

"You can't get up yet," Karma said insistently. "I have to settle your chakras down before I leave. Lie down. If you don't, it's like leaving all the faucets open, and you'll lose all your energy as soon as you stand up." A daunting thought, so with a look of suspicion, and in spite of her better judgment, Paris lay down again. And Karma ran her hands above her, chanting something unintelligible with her own eyes closed. It only took five minutes, mercifully, and then she was done. But the smell in the room was so overpowering that Paris couldn't imagine how she would ever be able to sleep there again.

"Thank you so much," she said as she hopped off the table, and Karma warned her not to bathe or shower until the morning. It would be too great a shock, both for her demons and for her. But Paris knew there was no way she would lie in her bed all night, covered in oil.

It took Karma another half-hour to wrap up, she charged one

hundred dollars, which was reasonable at least, and by midnight she was gone. Paris walked back into her bedroom after letting her out, and all she could do was laugh. Some of it had been relaxing, but most of it had been ridiculously absurd. And she had nodded dutifully when Karma warned her that she'd have to have a high colonic and clean her system out before she came back again, or the therapy would never work.

Paris was still smiling to herself as she walked into the bathroom, turned on the shower, and dropped her robe, and then she saw her back in the mirror. There were round symmetrical bruises all over it, from the cupping. It was terrifying looking, and given the deep purplish-red colors of the marks, it was easy to guess that the result of the "cupping" would be deep blue by the next day. It was terrifying to see, and it looked every bit as painful as it had been while the woman did it. Whatever it had done to her demons, it had made a mess of Paris's back. And when she checked again in the morning, her worst fears were confirmed. She looked as though she had been severely abused during the night, and there were two red burn marks on her shoulders from the hot rocks. And the room it had all happened in smelled like someone had died. But if nothing else, it had made Paris laugh. That was something at least. And what did it matter anyway? There was no one to see her back. When Meg called to inquire about it, all Paris could do was laugh.

"How was it, Mom?"

"It was certainly interesting. Sort of a modern form of neo-masochism. And by the way, I have demons in my bowels."

"Yeah, I know, so does Peace. He got them from his father."

"I hope you don't," Paris said, sounding concerned. "She said I got mine from my mother."

"Peace will be really impressed you did that, Mom," Meg said, grinning at the thought of it. Her mother had been a good sport if nothing else.

"You'd be even more impressed if you could see the bruises on my back."

"They'll be gone in a few days, Mom. Maybe you should try Rolfing next time," Meg said, laughing at her.

"Never mind. My demons and I are just fine the way we are."

The day after the Christmas party she'd agreed to go to at the Morrisons', Paris strolled into Anne's office, looking pleased.

"Did you have fun?" Anne asked her hopefully. It was the first time she'd been to a party in seven months. The last one she'd attended was her own, the night Peter told her he wanted a divorce.

"No, I hated it." She looked smugly at her psychiatrist, as though she had proved her point. She had done everything Anne had told her to do, from massage to party, and detested every minute of it.

"How long did you stay?"

"Twenty minutes."

"That doesn't count. You have to stay at least an hour."

"Seven people told me how sorry they were that my husband left me. The husbands of two of my friends asked me if I would meet them on the sly for a drink sometime. And five people told me they were invited to Peter's wedding. I am not going out again. I felt like a pathetic fool."

"Yes, you are going out again. And you're not a pathetic fool. You're a woman whose husband walked out on her. That's tough, Paris, but it happens. You'll survive it."

"I'm not going out," Paris said, with a look of iron determination. "I'm never going out again. And I had a massage. The woman was a nutcase, and I had bruises for days. I have demons in my bowels. And I am never going to another party. Ever, "she said, looking determined and very stubborn.

"Then you'll have to meet some people who don't know about Peter. That's a possibility too. But you can't stay home for the rest of your life like Greta Garbo. If nothing else, you'll worry your children, and you'll be bored out of your mind. You can't just sit at home. You need more in your life than that."

"I'll go out after Peter gets married," Paris said vaguely.

"What difference will that make?" Anne asked, looking startled.

"At least people won't be talking about the wedding. One of them was even stupid enough to ask if I was invited."

"And what did you say?"

"That I could hardly wait, and I was going to New York to buy a new dress for the occasion. What was I supposed to say? No, I'm planning to commit suicide that night."

"Are you?" Anne shot right back at her.

"No," Paris said with a sigh. "Even if I wanted to, I wouldn't do that to my kids."

"But do you want to?"

"No," she said sadly. "I'd like to die, but I don't want to do it myself. Besides, I don't have the guts."

"Well, if you ever reconsider that, and think about it, I want you to call me immediately," Anne said sternly.

"I will," Paris promised, and meant it. She was miserable, but not miserable enough to kill herself. She didn't want to give Rachel the satisfaction.

"What are you doing on New Year's Eve?"

"Crying probably."

"Is there anyone you'd like to see?"

"I guess everyone I know is going to Peter's wedding. That's pretty depressing. I'll be okay. I'll just go to sleep." They both knew it was going to be a tough night. There was no other way it could be.

Christmas was quiet that year. Wim and Meg spent Christmas Eve with her, and Christmas Day with their father and Rachel. Paris had gone out and gotten a tree, and decorated it before they got home from California. And five days before Christmas, her final divorce decree arrived, and she just sat and stared at it for a long time, and then put it away in a locked drawer. It was like reading a death certificate. She had never thought in her entire life that she would see her name on one of those. She didn't even tell the children it had come. She couldn't bring herself to say the words. It was over. Seven months after he had walked out on her, almost to the day. And now he was marrying Rachel. Paris had a sense of unreality about it all. Her life had become surreal.

And on the afternoon of New Year's Eve, Wim and Meg drove into the city. Paris kissed them good-bye, and said nothing to them as she saw them leave. She thought of calling Anne after that, but she had nothing to say. To anyone. All she wanted was to be alone. She made some soup for herself, watched television for a while, and at nine o'clock she went to bed. She didn't even allow herself to think about what was happening. She knew that the guests had been invited at eight o'clock. And she also knew that when she turned out the lights that night, Peter and Rachel had exchanged their vows and were man and wife. The life she had known for twenty-four years and nine months was over. He had a new wife, a new life. She didn't exist anymore, as far as he was concerned. He had blown everything they'd ever had to smithereens. And as she drifted off to sleep, she told herself she didn't care anymore, about him, or Rachel, or anything. All she wanted was to forget she had ever loved him, and go to sleep. They were leaving for a honeymoon in the Caribbean the next day, and a new life would be starting for them. It was a new year, a new life, a new day. And for Paris, whether she wanted it that way or not, it was going to be a new life too.

Chapter 10

The week after Peter's wedding became a blur for her. When Paris woke up on New Year's Day, she had the flu. By the time the kids came back from New York, she had a raging fever, she was sneezing and coughing, and all she wanted to do was sleep. Wim left to go skiing with his friends, and Meg went back to Los Angeles to see Peace. They were still seeing each other, but Meg had admitted to her mother she was tired of him. If nothing else, his health regimen, his strange eating habits, and his intense workout program were getting to her. She was bored out of her mind with Peace.

"Every time I see him, all I want to do is eat a hamburger at Burger King. If he takes me to another vegetarian restaurant, I'm going to go insane."

Paris was relieved. And it was a week after they both left before she felt human again. It was her first morning out of bed after the flu when Natalie called, and said she had had the same flu. She was having a dinner party the following Saturday, she said, just a few old friends, and she wondered if Paris would like to come. There was nothing special about the occasion, and she didn't say a word about Peter's wedding. For a moment, Paris was tempted to decline, and then she remembered her promise to Anne Smythe. She hadn't seen

Natalie since Thanksgiving. It sounded easy and agreeable, so she accepted. And when she told Anne about it, she was pleased.

"Good for you. I hope it'll be fun," she said, sounding sincere, and Paris said that she didn't really care. But as she was getting dressed that night, for the first time in months, she realized that she was looking forward to seeing her friends. Maybe Anne was right, and she was ready. Natalie had told her that there wouldn't be more than a dozen people, which seemed comfortable to Paris. She wasn't in the mood for fancy affairs. And Natalie had said that Virginia and Jim would be there too.

She put on a pair of velvet slacks and a cashmere sweater, and did her hair in a bun for the first time in months. And she was about to put on high heels when she saw that it was snowing. In the end, she stuck them in her coat pockets and put on boots.

And as she looked out the window right before she left, she realized that she was going to have to shovel snow out of her driveway to get out. She thought about calling the Morrisons to hitch a ride with them, but didn't want to be a nuisance. If she was going to go out alone, she had to get used to taking care of herself. She put on a heavy coat, with a hood, donned mittens, and went outside with a shovel. It took her twenty minutes to get the snow out of the driveway, and the ice off her windshield, and she was twenty minutes late by the time she left for dinner. But only four of the guests were there when she got to Natalie and Fred's. The other guests had had the same problem too. It was turning out to be a heavier snowfall than expected. And when Fred found out she'd driven herself, he told her if she had called, they would have been happy to come and get her. But she laughed, and felt surprisingly independent.

By the time the last of the guests arrived, she realized that she was the only single person there, which was more or less what she had expected. They had invited four couples, and Paris. It was what she was going to have to get used to. Being the odd man out. She was relieved that she knew everyone there, and no one had the bad taste to mention Peter's wedding, although she knew some of them had been there, like Virginia and her husband.

"So how's it going?" Virginia asked her quietly. They had had lunch the week before, and Virginia said she was getting over the same flu. Nearly everyone they knew had had it. And they were discussing home remedies when the doorbell rang again, and Paris realized they had invited yet another couple. But when she turned, she saw a man walk into the room whom she didn't recognize. He was tall and had dark hair, and looked faintly like Peter, except on closer inspection, she saw that he was older and had a major bald spot. But he looked pleasant as he walked in.

"Who's that?" Paris asked Virginia, who said she didn't know him. And although she didn't tell Paris, she knew about him. He was Fred's new stockbroker, and they had invited him to introduce him to Paris. They thought it was high time she got out in the world and met someone. And although she was unaware of it, the entire dinner party had been planned around her. It was a mercy dinner, as she told Anne later.

The new addition strolled into the room wearing a blazer, a red plaid turtleneck, and a pair of plaid pants that Paris couldn't help but stare at. They were the loudest pants she had ever seen, and it was obvious almost from the minute he sat down that he had been drinking. He introduced himself to everyone, before Fred could take care of it, and pumped people's hands until their arms ached. And the moment he turned to Paris, she knew exactly why he'd been invited.

"So you're the gay divorcée of Greenwich," he said, grinning at her, and this time he didn't pump her hand, he held it. She had to make a visible effort to get him to loosen his grip so she could reclaim her right hand. "I hear your husband just got remarried," he said bluntly, and Paris nodded, and turned back to Virginia.

"How charming," she whispered as Virginia winced, and saw Natalie glaring at her husband across the room. Fred had sworn that the guy was terrific. But he had only met him twice in the office. All he knew was that he was divorced, had three kids, and was, according to his own reports, a fantastic skier. It seemed enough to inspire Fred to invite him. They didn't know anyone else single, and Fred had assured Natalie he was intelligent and decent looking, didn't mishandle their account, and said he didn't have a girlfriend.

By the time they went in to dinner, he had told a series of lewd jokes, most of which were inappropriate in mixed company, and some of which were actually funny. Even Paris laughed heartily at one of them, but when he sat down next to her at the dinner table, he stepped up the volume. He had had two more scotches by then, and he was starting to slur before he got to the soup course.

"Christ, don't you hate soup at a dinner party?" he said to her, more loudly than he was aware of. "I always get it all over myself, used to get it on my tie, that's why I don't wear them." And she could only assume that he didn't want to get it on his blazer either, since he tucked his napkin into his turtleneck, and asked Fred where the wine was. "Must be a dry state here. You still in AA, Fred? Where's the wine, boy?" Fred hastened to pour him the first glass, while Natalie looked as though she wanted to kill him. She was all too aware of how fragile Paris had been, and the fact that this was the first time she had gone out to dinner. She had wanted to be subtle about introducing her to this man. And he was about as subtle as a flood in a farmhouse, and considerably less attractive. He had a habit of taking his glasses on and off, and in doing so, messed up his hair. The drunker he got, the wilder he looked, and the lewder his jokes got. He had mentioned every possible body part by the end of the first course, every possible sexual position by the end of the second, and by the time dessert came, he was pounding the table and laughing so loudly at his own jokes that Paris couldn't keep a straight face when she looked across the table at Virginia. It was awful.

And as they got up from dinner, Natalie took Paris aside and apologized profusely.

"I'm so sorry. Fred swore he was a nice guy, and I thought you might like to meet him."

"It's fine," Paris said graciously. "He's actually kind of funny. You don't have to introduce me to anyone, you know. I'm perfectly happy being on my own among good friends. I'm not interested in dating."

"You should," Natalie said sternly. "You can't be by yourself in that house for the rest of your life. We have to find you someone." But their first attempt had certainly been disastrous. The lone wolf had settled onto the couch by then, and was swilling brandy. He looked as though he was about to pass out, and Paris commented to Virginia that they were going to have to let him stay the night, or drive him back to wherever he came from. He was in no condition to drive, particularly in a snowstorm. It was snowing much harder than at the beginning of the evening, and even Paris was feeling cautious about driving home, but she wouldn't have admitted it. She was determined to be self-sufficient, and not a burden.

"I really think you should be a good sport, and put him up in your guest room," Virginia said to Paris with a rueful grin. It had been quite an evening. And she was glad that Paris was still smiling. She was sure she wouldn't have been, and she and Jim had exchanged cryptic looks several times during the evening. The stockbroker was definitely not what the doctor would have ordered. And as the stockbroker patted her behind as Paris walked past the couch, her heart sank. It had reached a point where it was no longer funny. And her friends' sympathy, however well meant, was somehow degrading, as though she couldn't take care of herself, and they had to do it for her. She had to have a consort at any price, under any circumstances, so they wouldn't feel sorry for her. He was, without a doubt, the perfect nightmare escort.

"Hi, sweetie. Come and sit next to me, and let's get to know each other." He leered at her.

Paris smiled wanly at him, and went to say goodnight to her hostess. She told her she wanted to slip out quietly, so as not to break up the party. And after looking at her carefully, Natalie didn't argue with her. Paris had taken good sportsmanship to new heights that evening.

"I'm really sorry about Ralph. If you like, I'll just shoot him, before he drinks any more of the brandy. And after that, I'm going to shoot Fred when everyone goes home. I promise, we'll do better next time."

"Next time, just invite me on my own. I'd much prefer it," Paris said softly.

"I promise," Natalie said, giving her a hug, and watching her as she put her boots on. She was so damn beautiful, and she looked so incredibly lonely. It broke Natalie's heart to see it. "Are you going to be all right, driving in the snow?" Natalie asked, looking worried.

"I'll be fine," she said with a wide smile and a confidence she didn't feel. She would have walked home in the snow rather than spend another minute in their living room, with Revolting Ralph, and her friends who obviously felt sorry for her. She knew their intentions were good, but the reality of the situation was enough to bring tears to her eyes. This was what she had been reduced to. Men like Ralph, who wore plaid pants, told crude jokes, and drank enough to qualify for an AA meeting. She just couldn't stand it a minute longer. "I'll talk to you tomorrow, and thank you!" She waved as she flew out the door, praying her car would start. She would have hitchhiked rather than stick around. All she wanted to do was go home now, and take off her clothes. She had had more than enough of the evening.

And as Natalie walked back into the living room with a defeated air, Ralph looked around expectantly for Paris.

"Where's London . . . or Milan . . . or Frankfurt . . . or whatever her name is?"

"Her name is Paris, and she went home. I think she had a headache," she said pointedly, looking daggers at her husband, and he retreated looking sheepish. The evening had definitely not turned out as they'd hoped.

"Too bad. I like her. She's a real looker," Ralph said, taking another swig of brandy. "That reminds me of the story about . . ." And by the time he had finished, Paris was halfway home, driving faster than she should have in a snowstorm, but all she wanted was to run into her house and lock the door, and forget the evening. It had been a nightmare. She knew that whatever else happened in her life, she would remember Ralph forever. She was playing the evening out in her head, as she rounded a bend, and the car skidded. She stepped on the brake, which made it worse, as she hit a patch of ice, and slipped right off the road before she could stop. And the back end of the car got lodged firmly into a snowbank. She tried to gently ease herself out of it, but everything she did made it worse, and she sat there, feeling frustrated and helpless. She waited, and tried again, but there was no moving the car. Even her snow tires didn't help her. She needed to be towed out.

"Shit," she said out loud, and then sat back against the seat, wondering if she had brought her AAA card with her. She looked in her purse and all she had brought was a five-dollar bill, her house keys, her driver's license, and a lipstick. She looked in the glove compartment then, and almost shouted with glee when she saw the AAA card. Peter had always been meticulous about things like that. And she would have been grateful, if she hadn't been so angry at him. It was his fault that she had just spent the evening she had. It was thanks to him that she was being used as fodder for men like Ralph, while he spent his honeymoon in St. Bart's with Rachel. This was all his fault.

She found the emergency number in the glove compartment too, called, and told them what had happened. They told her they would be there as soon as they could, somewhere between half an hour and an hour. And then she sat there. She thought about calling Meg to pass the time, but she didn't want to worry her by telling her she was stuck in a snowbank at midnight. So she just sat there and waited, and the tow truck showed up forty-five minutes later.

She got out of the car, while they lifted it out of the ditch, and got her on the road again. And she was home an hour and a half after she had left the dinner party. It was nearly one-thirty, and she was exhausted. She walked into her house and closed the door, and leaned heavily against it. And for the first time since Peter had left she knew that she was angry. She was so angry she wanted to kill someone. Ralph. Natalie. Fred. Peter. Rachel. Any and all of them. She dropped her coat on the hall floor, kicked off her boots, stomped up the stairs, and took off her clothes. She left them strewn on her bedroom floor, and it didn't matter anymore. There was no one to see it. No one to shovel the driveway or drive her home, or keep her from skidding in her car, or sliding into the ditch, or from assholes like Ralph. She hated all of them, but more than anyone, she hated Peter. And when she went to bed that night, she lay there and looked at the ceiling, hating him almost as much as she had once loved him. And she knew just exactly what she was going to do about it. It was time.

Chapter 11

Paris stormed into Anne's office Monday, and looked at her in amazement. "I'm leaving."

"Leaving where? Therapy?" It was obvious that Paris was angry.

"No. Yes. Well, eventually. I'm leaving Greenwich."

"What brought that on?"

"I went to that damn dinner party Saturday night, and they fixed me up with a total jerk, without even asking me how I felt about it. You wouldn't believe what it was like. First, I had to shovel my driveway, then he showed up in plaid pants and told filthy jokes. He got blind drunk, and patted my ass after dinner."

"And that's why you're leaving?" Anne wasn't sure if Paris was serious or not.

"No. I got stuck in a snowbank after dinner. My car skidded off the road, because Peter always drove in the snow and I don't know how to. And I had to call AAA to drag me out of the ditch at midnight. I got home at one-thirty. That's why I'm leaving."

"Because of the snowbank or the jerk?" Anne had never seen her look better. There was color in her face, and her eyes were blazing. She looked very healthy, and finally alive. She was back in control of her own life, as never before.

"No. Because of Peter. I hate him. This is all his fault. This is what he left me to. He left me for that little shit, and now I have jerks like Ralph to contend with, and my stupid goddamned friends who feel so sorry for me they think they're doing me a favor. I'm moving to California."

"Why?" Anne narrowed her eyes as she watched her.

"Because I have no life here."

"And you will in California?" She wanted her to leave for the right reasons, not just to escape what she wasn't doing in Greenwich. If that was the case, she would take all her troubles with her. A geographic cure was not the answer, unless she did it for the right reasons.

"At least I won't get caught in a snowbank on the way home from dinner."

"And will you go out to dinner?"

"I don't know anyone to invite me," Paris said, slowing down a little. But she was serious about moving. She had made her mind up. "But I could get a job, and meet new people. I can always come back here later. I just don't want to be around friends who feel sorry for me. It makes it all worse. Everyone here knows about Peter. I want to meet people who don't know anything about him, or what happened."

"That sounds reasonable. What are you going to do about it?"

"I'm flying out to San Francisco tomorrow. I've already booked a reservation. I called a realtor this morning. I'm going to see some houses and apartments. I called Wim and he sounds pretty busy, but he said he could see me for dinner. I don't know how long I'll be out there. It depends if I find something or not. But I'm going to try at least. I can't go to another one of those dinners." That had done it. But Anne thought she was ready, she had thought so for months, but the impetus to do it had to come from Paris. And it had now. She was ready to move on.

"Well, it sounds like we've turned a corner, doesn't it?" Anne looked pleased with her patient, although she was going to miss her. They had worked well together, but this was the end result she wanted. Paris on her feet again, and up and running. It had taken her eight months to get there, but she was there now.

"Do you think I'm crazy?" Paris asked, looking worried.

"No. I think you're extremely sane. And I think you're doing the right thing. I hope you find something you like."

"So do I," Paris said, sounding sad again for a minute. "I hate to leave. I have so many memories here."

"Are you going to sell the house?"

"No. Just rent it."

"You can always come back then. You're not doing anything that can't be reversed if you don't like it in California. Give it a chance, Paris. There's a whole world out there for you to discover. You can do anything you want, go anywhere you want. The door is wide open."

"That's pretty scary."

"And exciting. I'm very proud of you." She told Anne then that she had decided not to tell her friends yet. She wanted to find a house first. She didn't want anyone trying to talk her out of it. The only ones she had told were Anne and her children, and all three were pleased with Paris's decision to move.

She left Anne half an hour later, and went home to pack, and Natalie called to apologize again about dinner.

"Don't worry about it," Paris said breezily, "it was fine."

"Do you want to have lunch this week?"

"I can't. I'm going out to see Wim in San Francisco."

"Well, that'll be fun for you." Natalie was relieved to hear that she was moving around at least. She knew how tough the last months had been, and she didn't see a solution for her, unless she found another husband. And with candidates like Ralph afoot, it was beginning to look less than likely. But there had to be someone. She and Virginia had made a solemn vow to find a man for her, whatever it took.

"I'll call you when I get back," Paris promised, and then finished packing.

The next morning she was on the plane to San Francisco. She

was flying first class, and there was an attractive businessman sitting beside her. He was wearing a suit, working on a computer, and looked about fifty. And after glancing at him, she read a book, ate lunch, and then watched the movie. They were only an hour out of San Francisco by the time it was over, and by then her seatmate had put away his computer. He glanced over at her with a smile as the flight attendant offered them cheese and fruit or milk and cookies. Paris took a piece of fruit, and he asked for a cup of coffee, and the flight attendant seemed to know him as she filled his cup.

"Do you go to San Francisco often?" Paris asked him benignly. He was a good-looking man.

"Two or three times a month. We work with a venture capital firm out there, on biotech investments in Silicon Valley." It sounded fairly impressive, and he looked prosperous and solid. "What about you? Are you going out for business or pleasure?" he inquired.

"I'm going to visit my son in Berkeley. He goes to school there." She had seen him glance at her left hand, and she was no longer wearing her wedding ring. She had worn it until the divorce came, and taking it off had nearly killed her. But there was no point wearing it anymore. Peter was married to someone else. But she still felt naked without it. She had never taken it off since the day they were married, she'd been both sentimental and superstitious about it. She noticed that her seatmate wasn't wearing a wedding band either. Perhaps a good sign.

"How long will you be staying?" he inquired with growing interest.

"I don't know. I'm going to look for a house or an apartment. I'm thinking of moving out."

"From New York?" He looked intrigued. She was a very good-looking woman. And he guessed her to be around forty. She looked young to have a son in college.

"From Greenwich."

"Divorced?" He seemed practiced at this.

"Yes," she said cautiously. "How did you know?"

"There aren't a lot of single women in Greenwich, and if you're thinking of moving, it sounds like you're on your own." She nodded, but didn't ask him any of the same questions. She wasn't sure she wanted to know, and she didn't want to look anxious. And when the pilot announced that it was their last chance to get up and move around, she left her seat and waited for the bathroom. She was standing right outside the galley, as the flight attendant looked at her. It was the one who had just served them, and she smiled at Paris and approached to speak in a subdued voice.

"It's none of my business, but you may want to know. He's married, and has a wife and four kids in Stamford. Two of the women on this flight have gone out with him and he doesn't share that information. He commutes out here. I saw him talking to you, and we girls have to stick together. Of course, maybe it doesn't bother you. But it's good to know anyway. He won't tell you himself that he's married, at least he never tells us. We found out from another regular on the flight, who knows his wife."

"Thank you," Paris said, looking stunned as the bathroom became vacant. "Thanks a lot," and then went in to wash her hands and comb her hair, and as she did, she looked at herself in the mirror. It was a big bad world out there full of creeps and jerks and cheaters. The likelihood of finding a good one seemed about as great as finding a needle in the proverbial haystack. Nothing was impossible, but to Paris at least, it seemed extremely unlikely, and she didn't want a man anyway. The last thing she wanted was to get involved with anyone. She knew without a shadow of a doubt that she would never remarry. Peter had cured her. All she could do now, in her opinion, was get used to being alone.

She went back to her seat with freshly combed hair, neatly done in a braid down her back, and carefully applied lipstick, and her seatmate looked at her appreciatively. A moment later he handed her his business card, and she took it from him and held it in her hand.

"I'm staying at the Four Seasons. Call me if you have time for dinner. Where are you staying?" he asked pleasantly.

"With my son," she lied. But after what she'd just heard, she wasn't planning to give him any information. She knew more than enough about him. "I think we'll be pretty busy," she said casually as she put the card in her purse.

"Call me in New York when you go back," he said, and as he did, they landed with a thump and taxied down the runway at SFO. "Do you need a ride into town?" he asked helpfully, and she smiled, thinking with empathy about his wife.

"No, thanks, I have friends waiting. But thanks for the offer," she said blithely. And as he saw her climb into a cab alone twenty minutes later, he raised an eyebrow and caught her eye. She waved, as they took off for the city, and as soon as she got to the hotel, she threw away his card.

Chapter 12

For the next four days, Paris felt as though she saw every house in town. She saw four apartments, and decided in short order that an apartment wasn't what she wanted. After years in a fairly substantial house, with plenty of room to roam around, she wasn't ready for an apartment. In the end she narrowed it down to two houses she liked. One was a large stone house in Pacific Heights reminiscent of the house in Greenwich, and the other was a quaint Victorian with a mother-in-law apartment on Vallejo Street in Cow Hollow. It had the advantage of being close to the water, had a view of the bay, and the Golden Gate, and what she liked most about it was that Wim could use the mother-in-law apartment whenever he wanted, and still feel as though he had a certain amount of independence from her. He could even bring his friends there. It was perfect. The price was right, and the owners were willing to rent it. And she was an ideal tenant. She was solvent and a responsible adult. The whole place had been freshly painted and looked cheerful, clean, and bright.

There were beautiful hardwood floors, and the main part of the house had three bedrooms, one on the top floor with a spectacular view, and two just below it, which she could use for Meg, and whoever else came to visit, or they could just stand empty. There was a pleasant country kitchen, and the living room looked out on a small, well-manicured garden. Everything was on a smaller scale than she was used to, but she liked that about it. She was going to have to pick and choose among her furniture, and send the rest to storage. And the realtor told her that he could rent furniture for her until her own arrived. They settled it in one afternoon. She signed the lease, and the realtor dropped off the keys to her that night at the Ritz-Carlton. She had paid the first and last months' rent, and a sizable security deposit. All she had to do now was rent the Greenwich house, but even if that took a while, there was no reason for her to wait around in Greenwich. She could move anytime she chose.

She had dinner with Wim on the last night, and then drove him over to see it. She had rented a car, and was getting used to driving around the hills. And he fell in love with the mother-in-law apartment.

"Wow, Mom! Can I bring my friends to stay sometime?"

"Anytime you want, sweetheart. That's why I took it." There were two small bedrooms in the downstairs unit, and he shared the garden with her. It was everything she had wanted. It had charm and privacy for her, and more than enough space, and would provide Wim a nest to come home to, although she didn't expect him to come often. He was having a ball in Berkeley. From everything he had told her, he had made a lot of friends, and was even enjoying his classes, and doing well.

"When are you moving in?" Wim looked excited, and Paris was pleased.

"As soon as I pack up Greenwich."

"Are you going to sell the house?"

"No, just rent it." For the first time in months, she had something to look forward to, and was excited about her life. Suddenly something good was happening, instead of disaster and trauma. It had taken her eight months to get here, but she had.

She drove him back to Berkeley that night, and the next morning she flew back to Greenwich. Her seatmate this time was a very old woman who said she was going to see her son, and slept from take-off to touchdown. And Paris felt as though she'd been gone for months when she walked into the house in Greenwich. She had accomplished a lot in a short time.

She called Natalie and Virginia the next morning, and told them what had happened. Both of them were shocked, and saddened by her news. They hated to see her go, but said they were happy for her if that was what she wanted. She didn't tell Natalie that her dinner party had done it. She had already called a realtor, and they were starting to show the house that weekend. They told her it might take a while to rent it. It was a dead time of year, as people were more likely to rent, move, or buy in spring or summer. She had already called movers, and was planning to start packing over the weekend. She had a lot of decisions to make over what to take with her, and what to put in storage. And Virginia called her later that morning. She had told Jim the news, and they wanted to give her a farewell party. And Natalie made the same offer the next morning. By the weekend, at least four people had called and said they wanted to see her before she left, and wanted to have her for dinner. Suddenly people weren't feeling sorry for her, they were excited about what she was doing, though sorry to see her go, and she loved it. It was as though she had finally managed to turn the ship around by deciding to move to California. It never dawned on her that the change in attitude and outlook was more on her part than anyone else's. But overnight the whole atmosphere of her life had changed.

And much to her amazement, by Sunday afternoon, the house had been rented. They were only the second people who had seen it, and the first ones called an hour later, and were severely disappointed that it was gone. The family who were renting it wanted it for a year, with an option for a second year. They were being transferred to New York from Atlanta, and had three teenage children. The house was perfect for them, and they were relieved that Paris didn't object to the children. On the contrary, the thought of her house coming alive again and being well lived in made her happy. And she was astounded by the rent she was able to get for it. It was going to cover the house in California and then some. So the move made sense in every way. She spent the next weeks packing and sorting, seeing friends, and saying good-bye. She was planning to be in San Francisco by the end of January, and when the movers came, she was ready.

She had booked a room at the Homestead Inn for the last weekend, and had her last lunch with Virginia and Natalie before she left. She had actually enjoyed the parties they had given her. They had invited only old friends, and no more strangers to woo her. It felt like old home week. She had never realized how many people she knew and genuinely liked in Greenwich, and for a minute or two she was almost sorry she was leaving. But in her last session with Anne, she knew she had made the right decision. There was a kind of carnival atmosphere to everything she was doing. But she knew it would have been different if she'd stayed. She would have been sitting alone in her house, depressed and in the doldrums. Although she was going to be alone in San Francisco. She still had to find a job, and meet new people. And she promised to call Anne, they were going to have phone sessions twice a week until she got settled.

She left for the airport at eight in the morning on Friday. And as the plane took off for San Francisco, she forced herself not to think of Peter. Although he knew from Wim and Meg that she was moving, he never called her. He was busy with his new life, and she had to make her own now. And if it was a disaster, and she found that she had made a mistake, she could always come back to Greenwich. Maybe she would one day. But for the next year, she was going to spread her wings and fly, or try to at least. And this time, she knew she had her parachute well in place. She wasn't free-falling through space, and no one had pushed her out of the plane. She had jumped, and she knew what she was doing and why. Moving to San Francisco was the bravest thing she had done so far. Wim had promised to come and see her that weekend. And when the plane touched down in San Francisco, she was smiling broadly to herself.

She gave the cab driver the address of her new home, and the realtor had done as he'd promised. He told her he had rented enough furniture for her to tide her over until hers came. She had a bed, and dressers, a dining table and chairs, and a couch and coffee table and some lamps in the living room. It all looked respectable when she got there. She carried her suitcase upstairs and set it down in the bedroom, as she looked around. It was early afternoon in San Francisco, and she could see the Golden Gate Bridge from her bedroom window. And as she saw herself in the mirror hanging over the dresser, she smiled. There wasn't a sound in the silent house as she whispered "Honey, I'm home!" to her own reflection, and then as she stood there, feeling giddy and hopeful for the first time in months, she sat down on the bed and laughed. Her new life had begun.

Chapter 13

There was very little for Paris to do in the new house until her furniture arrived from the East. The rented furniture was spare but adequate, and although the view was spectacular, without her own furniture and paintings and decorative accessories, it looked somewhat impersonal and cold. The only thing she could think of to do was to go to a florist and buy armloads of flowers. So on Saturday, after doing some laundry, and a long conversation with Meg, she got in her rental car and drove around. She wanted the place to look as nice as possible when Wim came for dinner with a friend on Sunday night.

She was thinking of her conversation with Meg, as she drove south on Fillmore Street, and turned right onto Sacramento, where she had seen a number of small antique shops she wanted to browse. Meg had told her that she and Peace had decided to stop seeing each other the previous weekend. She was upset but not distraught over it, and although maybe not for the same reasons, she agreed with her mother that the relationship wasn't right. They had both come to the conclusion that their interests and goals were different, although Meg herself said that he was a very decent guy. And she didn't feel the months she'd spent with him had been a waste of time.

"So what now?" Paris had asked her quietly. She liked staying current with her daughter's life, and always had. "Anyone else in the picture yet?" Paris asked blithely, and Meg laughed.

"Mom! It's only been a week! What kind of slut do you think I am?" Even though it had been a minor relationship in the scheme of things, she needed time to let go and mourn. He had been nice to her, and they had shared a lot of good times, in spite of what Paris thought of him.

"I don't think you're a slut. I think you're beautiful and young, and men are going to be lined up ten deep at your door."

"It's not as easy as that. There are a lot of crazy guys down here. The actors are all in love with themselves, although Peace wasn't, but he was more into martial arts and health than acting," and he himself had said he was thinking of teaching karate instead of taking roles in horror films. He had begun to realize that acting wasn't for him. "Half the guys I meet are heavy into drugs, a lot of them want to go out with starlets and models. Everybody's got an agenda here. And the regular ones I meet, like lawyers and stockbrokers and accountants, are so frigging dull. The men my age are so boring and immature." That about summed it up, in Meg's opinion.

"There's got to be someone, sweetheart. At your age the world is full of eligible young men."

"And what about at yours, Mom? What are you going to do about meeting people?" Meg was worried about that for her. She didn't want her sitting in yet another empty house, getting depressed in a town where she didn't know anyone.

"I just got here yesterday. Give me a chance. I promised my shrink I'd get a job, and I will. But I'm not sure where to look."

"Why don't you teach? You have a master's, could you teach econ at a business school, or at college level? Maybe you should look for a job at Stanford or UC Berkeley."

It was a possibility certainly, and she had thought of it, but teaching jobs of the kind Meg was suggesting were highly competitive, and she no longer felt qualified. She'd have to go back to school herself, and the prospect didn't appeal much to Paris. She wanted to do something more amusing. And thanks to Peter's guilt and generosity, and the small inheritance she had managed well over the years, she didn't have to let salary be the main consideration. "Wim will kill me if I get a job at Berkeley. He'll think I'm stalking him. If I did that, it would have to be Stanford." In spite of the fact that there were thirty thousand students on the UC Berkeley campus, she wanted to respect the newfound autonomy that Wim was so proud of.

"What about an office job? You'd meet a lot of guys there," Meg said, trying to be helpful.

"I'm not looking for a man, Meg. I just want to meet people." Her daughter had other aspirations for her. She wanted her to find a husband to take care of her emotionally, or at the very least, a serious romance. She hated knowing her mother was lonely, and there was no question, she had been ever since Peter left.

"Well, men are people," Meg insisted, and her mother laughed.

"Not always. Some are. Some aren't." Peter had proved that, but what he had also proved was that he was human, with the same foibles as anyone else. No one was perfect. She just hadn't expected him to do what he had. She thought they were married forever. It made it almost impossible for her to trust anyone again. "I don't know, something will come up. I was thinking about taking one of those crazy job-placement tests that tell you what your strengths are. I think they do them down at Stanford. They'll probably tell me I should be an army nurse, or a dental hygienist, or an artist. Sometimes those tests come up with some pretty crazy suggestions. Maybe they give you truth serum to do them."

"I think you should do it," Meg said firmly. "What do you have to lose?"

"Just time and money. I guess I ought to. When are you coming up to see me, by the way?" It was so wonderful that they had the option to see each other more easily now. It was ninety percent of why she had moved to San Francisco, but Meg told her with regret that she had to work for the next few weekends. She was hoping to come up as soon as they wrapped the current movie, but for the moment she was still up to her neck in it.

Paris was still thinking about the job situation, and her recent conversation with Meg, when she parked the car she was renting, and wandered into an antique shop on Sacramento. Her own car was on a truck on its way out from Greenwich, and was scheduled to arrive around the same time as the rest of her belongings. She bought a pretty little silver box, and then went next door to another shop, and found a pair of antique silver candlesticks she liked. She was having a great time just walking from store to store and browsing. And next to the last one, she discovered a very elegant, but small florist in an elegant little Victorian house. There were three spectacular arrangements of spring flowers in the window. She had never seen anything like them. The colors were dazzling, the combination of flowers unusual and magnificent, and the silver urns they were in were the most elegant she'd ever seen. And as she walked in, a very well-dressed young woman was taking orders on the phone. She looked up at Paris when she hung up, and Paris noticed that she was wearing a very large diamond ring. This was no ordinary florist shop by any means.

"May I help you?" the woman asked pleasantly.

Paris actually wanted to buy some flowers for the house, but it was the three arrangements in the window that had drawn her in. "I've never seen such lovely flowers," she said, staring at them again.

"Thank you." The woman at the desk smiled at her. "They're for a party we're doing this afternoon. The pots belong to the client. We can do flowers in your own bowls, if you like, if you want to bring one in."

"That would be wonderful," Paris said pensively. She had an antique silver samovar that was actually very similar to the one in the middle. She and Peter had bought it at an antique show in

England. "I'm not going to have anything for a while, or a few weeks anyway. I just moved out from the East."

"Well, just bring them in any time. And if you're doing a dinner party, we'll be happy to set you up with caterers too." It was a very unusual florist indeed, or maybe the woman was just being helpful. Paris wasn't sure. "Actually"—she smiled again—"that's my end of things. I run a catering service, and I do a lot of work for the owner of the shop. I'm just baby-sitting for them today. The girl who usually works here is out sick. And Bixby's assistant is at a baby shower, she's having a baby next week." The shop was called Bixby Mason.

"Is this actually a florist shop?" Paris asked, looking confused. As she glanced around, she could see that the decor was very high end, and there was a narrow marble staircase to the upper floors at the back of the room.

"It started out as one. But it's actually a lot more now. The man who owns it is an artist and a genius. He does all the best parties in town, from soup to nuts. He provides the music, caterers, decides on the theme, or works with his clients to create the atmosphere they want, from small dinner parties to weddings for eight hundred. He's pretty much cornered the market on entertaining in San Francisco. The flowers are just the tip of the iceberg now, so to speak. He does parties all over the state, and around the country sometimes."

"Very impressive," Paris said quietly, as the woman reached into a bookcase behind her and pulled out three huge leather-bound albums. There were at least two dozen more on the shelves.

"Want to take a look? These are just a few of the parties he did last year. They're pretty fabulous." If the flowers in the window were any indication of his work, Paris was sure they were. And as she sat down to thumb through the books out of curiosity, she was enormously impressed. The homes he worked in were spectacular, the settings more elegant than any she'd ever seen. Mansions, gardens, beautifully manicured grounds on large estates with tents specially designed to accommodate the guests in fabrics she would never have thought of using. The weddings she saw in the book were exquisite. And there were a handful of small dinner parties he had photographed that were any hostess's dream. There were hand-painted gourds on the table in one for a Halloween party, a profusion of brown orchids in another, with tiny Chinese vases holding little sprigs of herbs, and a fifties party with so many funny decorations on the table that she smiled as she turned to the last page, and finally handed the books back, with a look of awe.

"Very, very impressive." And she meant it. She wished she had had the imagination to do something like that in Greenwich. She had done some lovely dinner parties, but nothing in these leagues. Whoever the owner was, he really was a creative genius. "Who is he?"

"His name is Bixby Mason. He's actually an artist, well, a painter and a sculptor. And he has a degree in architecture, but I don't think he's ever used it. He's just a very, very creative man, with incredible imagination and vision, and a nice person. Everyone he works with loves him." Paris also realized, from what she'd seen, that he probably charged a fortune. But he ought to. What he created for his clients was obviously unique in all aspects. "Somebody called him a wedding planner once, and he almost killed them. He's a lot more than that. But he does a lot of weddings. I cater a lot of them, and I love working with him. Everything goes off like clockwork. He's a master control freak. But he has to be. That's why people come back to him, because everything he touches is perfect. And all the hosts have to do is enjoy the party." He was worth his weight in gold to the people he worked for.

"And sign a hefty check afterward, I'll bet," Paris added. It was easy to see that the events he coordinated for them had cost a fortune.

"He's worth it," the woman who was baby-sitting the shop said without apology. "He makes their events unforgettable. Sadly, he even does funerals. And they're beautiful and tasteful. He never skimps on flowers, food, or music for parties. He flies in bands from everywhere, even Europe if he has to."

"Amazing." It was embarrassing now to think of bringing her silver samovar in to have them put flowers in it. He was operating on such a grand scale that any business she could give them seemed pointless. And since she didn't know anyone yet, she wasn't planning to do any entertaining. "I'm glad I came in," Paris said, with open admiration. "I was looking for a florist. But I don't think I'm going to be doing much entertaining for a while, since I just moved here."

The girl handed her a card and told her to call them whenever she felt they could help her. "You'd love Bixby. He's a riot. The poor thing is going nuts right now. His assistant is having a baby in a week, and we've got weddings booked every weekend. He told Jane she may have to work anyway. I don't think he knows much about babies." They both laughed, and as Paris looked at her, she had an outrageous thought, and wasn't sure if she dared to ask her. But as she put the card in her pocket, she decided to throw caution to the wind and try it.

"I'm looking for a job actually. I've given a lot of dinner parties, but not on this scale. What kind of assistant is he looking for?" It seemed ridiculous, even to her, to think he would want her. She had no experience in the workforce, and certainly none in his line of work, except for her own rather staid dinner parties, although some had been very pretty.

"He needs someone with a lot of energy, and a lot of spare time at night and on weekends. Are you married?" She looked as though she might be. She had that quiet, respectable, well-kept look of wives who were well cared for.

"No, I'm divorced," Paris said quietly. She still said it as though admitting to having been convicted of a felony, and saw it as the public announcement of a failure. It was something she and Anne were still trying to work on.

"Do you have children?"

"Yes, two. One lives in Los Angeles, and the other one is at Berkeley."

"Well, that sounds interesting. Why don't I talk to him? He's supposed to call in, in a few minutes. Leave me your number, and if he's interested, I'll call you. He's down to the wire with Jane now. The baby's going to come any minute, and her husband wants her to stop working. I thought she was going to have it at the last wedding. She looks like she's having triplets. Thank God she isn't, but it's going to be a big one. And I don't know what he's going to do if he doesn't replace her. He hasn't liked anyone he's interviewed. He's a perfectionist, and a tyrant to work for, but he does such a beautiful job, and he's basically such a decent person, we all love him." It sounded like nothing but fun to Paris. "Is there anything else you want him to know? Job experience? Languages? Special interests? Connections?" She had none of those, particularly in San Francisco. All she had been for the past twenty-four years was a mother and a housewife. But she thought that if he gave her a chance, she could do it.

"I have an MBA, if that's of any use to him." And then, having said it, she was afraid he'd think she was overqualified and unimaginative. "I know a lot about gardening, and always arrange my own flowers"—she glanced at the window then—"but not on that scale," she said humbly.

"Don't worry, he has a Japanese woman who does those for him. Bix couldn't do that either. He's great at rounding up people who can though. That's what he does best. Orchestrating the whole event. He's the conductor. The rest of us play the music. All you'd have to do is pick up the pieces and follow him around with a notebook, and make phone calls. That's what Jane does."

"I'm a genius with a phone," Paris said, smiling. "And I have time on my hands. And a decent wardrobe, so I won't embarrass him with his clients. I've run a fairly decent house for the past twenty-four years. I don't know what else to say, except that, if nothing else, I'd love to meet him."

"If this works out," the woman said encouragingly as Paris jotted down her name and number, "he'll be your best friend. He's a lovely man." And then as Paris handed her the piece of paper, the woman who said she was a caterer looked Paris in the eye with a sympathetic smile. "I know what it's like. I was married for eighteen years, and when my marriage fell apart, I had no job experience and no skills. All I knew how to do was fold laundry, drive carpool, and cook for my kids. That's how I got into the catering business. It was the only thing I thought I knew how to do. It turns out that I had a lot more skills than I knew. I have offices in Los Angeles, Santa Barbara, and Newport Beach now. Bixby helped me do it. You have to start somewhere, and this may be it for you." What she said brought tears to Paris's eyes, as she thanked her. "My name is Sydney Harrington, and I hope I'm going to be seeing more of you. And if this doesn't work out, give me a call. I've been there, and I have a lot of ideas." She handed Paris her own card, from her catering business, and Paris thanked her again. She felt as though she were floating on air when she walked out of the shop. Even if she didn't get a job out of it, she felt as though she had made a new friend. And Sydney Harrington was a good contact to have. Working for her in the catering business would have been fine too. Working for Bixby Mason sounded like a dream come true. She realized she was unlikely to get a shot at it, she had no experience in the job market, and even less with elaborate events like the ones he did. But at least it was a place to start, and she was proud of herself for speaking up and asking about the possibility. This was a whole new world for her.

Paris spent the next two hours wandering in and out of shops on Sacramento Street. She bought a set of salad plates in a pretty store down the street, and a needlepoint to do on lonely nights. And by four o'clock she was home again, made herself a cup of tea, and sat looking at the view. It had been a nice afternoon. She was still enjoying it, when the phone rang and she answered it. It was Sydney Harrington, and she had exciting news.

"Bixby asked if you could be here at nine on Monday. I don't want to get your hopes up, I have no idea what his take will be, but I told him I thought you were terrific. And he's really desperate. He rejected everyone the agency sent. He thought they were just too dull and unimaginative, and he didn't like the way they looked. You'd have to go to all the events with him, and some on your own, if he has two at the same time. He always stops in, but he can't be in two places at once, particularly if one of them is out of town, so you have to be pretty much at ease with the clients and the guests and fit in. That's important to him. As he says, his assistant is like an extension of him, his representative in the world. He and Jane have been working together for six years. This is going to be a big change for him. He should have hired someone for her to train months ago. I think he had denial about the baby."

"Is she leaving or going on maternity leave?" Not that it mattered, Paris would have been happy to work for him, from all Sydney had said, for months or even weeks until she came back. The experience would be valuable, and the job would surely be fun.

"She's out for good. He did her wedding, and her husband says if she doesn't quit now, Bix can do their divorce. Paul says he hasn't seen Jane for more than ten minutes at a time for the last five years. He wants her at home, and she agreed. I think she's ready for it. Bix is terrific, but it's an incredible amount of work. I hope you're ready for that if you get the job." Sydney was trying to be as honest as possible with her, there was no point being otherwise, and she had liked Paris when they met.

"It sounds fabulous," Paris said enthusiastically, and meant it, and then asked nervously, "what'll I wear? Is there anything he likes or hates?" She wanted to maximize her chance of getting the job, and was grateful for all the information Sydney had shared with her.

"Just be you. That's what he likes best. Be open, honest, and yourself. And be ready to work an eighteen-hour day. He likes that too. No one on the planet works as hard as Bixby Mason, and he expects no less from anyone else." He sounded like an interesting man.

"Sounds great to me. I have no kids at home, no husband, no big house to take care of. I don't even know anyone here. I have nothing else to do."

"He'll love that. And I told him about your MBA. I think he was intrigued. Good luck," she said with a warm tone in her voice. She had so much empathy for the situation Paris was in. She had been there herself five years before, and Bixby had turned it around for her. She was forever grateful to him, and if she could help someone else in the same boat now, she was pleased. "I'll check in on Monday and see how it went."

"Thank you," Paris said gratefully and meant every word of it. "Keep your fingers crossed!"

"I will. You'll do great. I have a good feeling about this. I think it was meant to be that you walked into the shop today. He was going to keep it closed because he didn't have anyone to be there, and I volunteered to keep it open for him, but it was just a fluke. Destiny. Now let's see what comes of it. And if this doesn't pan out, something else will. I'm sure of that." Paris thanked her again, and they hung up, and she sat staring at the view from her living room with a smile on her face. All of a sudden, good things were happening. Better than she'd ever dreamed. She just hoped she didn't make a fool of herself on Monday, or say the wrong thing. She had so little to offer him, she thought, but if he gave her a chance, she was going to put her heart and soul into it. This was the best thing that had happened to her in years.

Chapter 14

Paris parked her car on Sacramento Street on Monday morning at ten to nine, and went to the black door with the brass knocker next to the shop, where Sydney had told her to go. And she noticed with embarrassment that her hands were shaking when she rang the bell. She was wearing a trim black suit, and high-heeled black shoes, her hair was neatly pulled back in a bun, and she had small diamond studs at her ears. She felt a little overdressed, but she wanted him to see that she would look proper at parties, and this was an interview after all. She hadn't wanted to underdress or overdress, and she was carrying a small black classic Chanel shoulder bag that Peter had given her for Christmas several years before. She had so little occasion to wear it in Greenwich that it looked brand new. She wondered if she should be carrying a briefcase, but she didn't own one. All she had to offer him was her brain, her energy, her time, and her organizational skills. She hoped it was enough for him.

A buzzer sounded, and when she pushed the door, it opened, and revealed a short flight of marble stairs leading upward, just like the staircase in the shop. The house was beautifully done. She heard voices on the floor above, and followed them, and found herself in an elegant hallway, with original modern art by well-known artists, and ahead of her was a large wood-paneled room lined with books, and in it were seated a strikingly handsome blond man in his mid- to late thirties in a black turtleneck and black slacks, and a young woman who was so pregnant, Paris almost smiled thinking of Agnes Gooch in *Auntie Mame*. She got out of the chair with diffi- culty, and came to greet Paris in the hall and lead her into the room.

"You must be Paris, what a terrific name. I'm Jane. And this is Bixby Mason. We've been expecting you." He was already looking Paris over with eyes that felt like X rays as he checked her out. She could feel him taking in everything, from her hair and earrings to the Chanel bag and the high-heeled shoes she had worn, but he seemed to approve, and smiled as he asked her to sit down.

"Great suit," he said, as he reached behind him and grabbed a phone that was ringing. He answered a rapid-fire series of ques- tions, and then turned to sum it up for Jane when she sat down.

"The truck is late with the orchids. They're about halfway here from Los Angeles, they should arrive before noon, which means we have to hustle when they get here. But they're going to knock some- thing off the price to make up for the delay. I think we'll make it. The party isn't till seven, and if we get into the room by three, we should be fine." He turned his attention back to Paris then, and asked her how long she'd been in San Francisco and why she had come. She had already thought about how she would answer him. She didn't want to sound depressed or pathetic, he didn't need to know all the gory details, just the fact that she was divorced and on her own.

"I've been here for three days," she said honestly. "I'm divorced. I was married for twenty-four years, ran my home, took care of my kids, didn't work, gave a fair number of dinner parties. I love deco- rating and entertaining and gardening. And I came to San Fran- cisco because my son is at UC Berkeley, and my daughter lives in L.A. And I have an MBA." He smiled at the rapid recital, and although he looked sophisticated and elegant, there was some- thing warm in his eyes too.

"How long have you been divorced?"

She took a breath. "About a month. It was final in December, but we've been separated since last May."

"That's tough," he said sympathetically, "after twenty-four years." He didn't ask what happened, but she could see that he felt sorry for her, and she tried not to give way to tears. It was always harder when people were nice to her. Their kindness always made her cry, but she forced herself to think of what she was doing there, and kept her eyes firmly on his. "Are you doing okay?"

"I'm fine," she said quietly. "It's been an adjustment, but my kids have been great. And my friends. I just wanted a change of scene."

"Were you living in New York?" He was interested in her.

"Greenwich, Connecticut. It's a fairly opulent bedroom community, and has kind of a life of its own."

"I know it well." He smiled. "I grew up in Purchase, which isn't very far away, and is pretty much the same idea. Tiny little communities full of rich people who know each other's business. I couldn't wait to get the hell out after college. I think you did the right thing coming out here." He smiled approval at her.

"So do I." She smiled broadly at him. "Particularly if I get a job working for you. I can't think of anything I'd like more," she said, almost shaking as she made her brave little speech.

"It's a lot of very, very, very hard work. I'm a pain in the ass to work for. I'm totally manic, and obsessive about everything. I want everything perfect. I work a million hours a day. I never sleep. I'll call you in the middle of the night to tell you something I forgot and that you have to do first thing in the morning. Forget having a love life. You'll be lucky if you see your kids for Thanksgiving and Christmas, and probably not then either, because we'll have parties to do. I promise to run you ragged, drive you crazy, teach you everything I know, and make you wish you'd never laid eyes on me at least ninety percent of the time, if not more. But if you can stand all that, Paris, then we'll have a hell of a lot of fun. How does that sound to you?"

"Like a dream come true," she said honestly. It was all she wanted to do. It would keep her busy and distracted, make her feel useful, the parties and events they did had to be exciting, she would meet new people, even if they were his clients and not her friends. She couldn't think of a better job for her, and she didn't care how hard she worked. She wanted to. "I think, I hope I can do a great job for you."

"Want to try it?" he asked with a look of excitement in his eyes too. "We're only doing four dinner parties this week. One tonight, two tomorrow, and a good-sized fortieth-anniversary party on Saturday night. If you survive all that, you're on. Let's see how we both feel about it by the end of the week." Then he looked at Jane with a stern expression. "And if you have that baby before that, I'm going to spank it and strangle you, do you understand, Mrs. Winslow?" He wagged a finger at her, and she laughed, rubbing the enormous Buddha belly that looked like it was going to explode out of her dress at any minute.

"I'll do my best. I'll have a talk with him and tell him that if he shows up before the weekend, his godfather will be extremely pissed."

"Exactly. No inheritance from me, no trust fund, no graduation party, no presents for Christmas or birthdays. He's to stay where he is until Paris and I figure out if we can work together, understood? And in the meantime, I want you to teach her everything you know." In a mere five days. Jane didn't flinch.

"Yes, sir, Captain Bly, Your Honor. Absolutely." She saluted him, and he laughed at her as he stood up. And Paris was startled by how tall he was. He was at least six foot four, incredibly handsome, and she was almost certain he was gay.

"Oh, shut up," he said to Jane, laughing at her as she stood up too, though with considerable difficulty. She needed a crane to get her out of the chair. And then he turned to Paris with a mock-severe expression. "And if you get pregnant, in or out of wedlock, you're fired on the spot. I can't go through this again." He looked meek and boyish then, and they both laughed. "This has been very hard on me. You may have stretch marks," he said to Jane, "but my nerves are stretched a lot tighter than your stomach!"

"Sorry, Bix," she said, looking anything but contrite. She was thrilled about the baby, and she knew he was happy for her. In six years of working for him, he had become her mentor and best friend.

"On second thought," he said to Paris then, "have your tubes tied. How old are you, by the way?"

"Forty-six. Almost forty-seven."

"Really? I'm impressed. If I didn't know you had kids, I would think you were in your late thirties. When you said you had a son at Berkeley, I figured you for forty, tops. I'm thirty-nine," he said easily, "but I had my eyes done last year. You don't need a thing done, so I won't bother to give you his name." He was very generous with his praise, and she was touched by what he said. And then he looked serious as he glanced at the mountain of papers on his desk. There were files scattered everywhere, photographs, fabric swatches, blueprints, designs, and Jane's desk in the next room looked considerably worse. One entire wall of her office was cork, and there were a million notes and messages pinned to it. "When can you start?" he asked Paris bluntly, seeming to rev his engines suddenly. She could see what a dynamo he was. But he had to be. He had a lot on his plate.

"Whenever you like," she said calmly.

"All right then, now. Will that work, or do you have plans today?"

"I'm all yours," she said, and he beamed, and Jane invited Paris to come into her office with her.

"He loved you," she whispered when they sat down across the desk from each other. She was going to show her everything she could. She thought this was going to work. "I can tell. Everyone else he's seen was out the door in about two minutes. 'Hello, good-bye, thank you very much, get lost.' He hated them all. But he liked you. You're just exactly what he needs. Also, no husband, no kids, you're new in town. You can follow him around everywhere, if that's okay with you." Jane looked as hopeful as she felt.

"It sounds like a custom-made job for me. It's everything I wanted. And I like him too. He seems like a nice man." Beyond the elegance and the good looks, and the sophisticated style, she could sense that he was decent, real, and down-to-earth.

"He is," Jane reassured her, "he's been incredible to me. I was supposed to get married right after I came to work here, and my fiancé walked out on me, literally while I was standing in the church. My parents were furious, they had spent a fortune on the wedding. I was a mess for about a year, but it worked out for the best. The marriage would never have worked. And as Bix says, he did me an enormous favor, although it didn't feel like it at the time. Anyway, then I met Paul, and we got engaged in about four months, which shocked everyone, and my parents refused to pay for the wedding. They said I was marrying him on the rebound and it would never work, and they had already paid for one wedding, so to hell with me. So Bix put on the most sensational wedding you've ever seen. He flew in a band from Europe, Sammy Go, who is fabulous. He gave it at the Gettys' house, with their permission of course. It was incredible, and he paid for everything himself. My parents were embarrassed, but they let him do it anyway. Things were pretty tense between us for a while. And now Paul and I have been married for five years, and we're having this baby. I put it off as long as I could, because I hated to leave Bix in the lurch, but Paul finally put his foot down, so here we are. And Bix just hasn't wanted to face it. He couldn't find anyone he liked, and he didn't really look. And I swear, I don't think the baby will hold out till the weekend, so you'd better learn everything quick. I'll do whatever I can to help you." It was a lot of information in one short speech, and when she said she was thirty-one a few minutes later, Paris realized that she was the same age as the girl who had married Peter. And Jane seemed almost like a child to her, although she was obviously extremely capable. It made Paris wonder briefly if Peter and Rachel would have a baby too. The very thought of it made her feel ill, but she didn't have time to worry about it now, she had far too much to do.

They spent the whole morning going over files, important details about their best clients, how their resource system worked, who to count on and who not to, and who to use anyway. And then they went over a seemingly endless list of upcoming events. Paris could barely fathom that many parties in one town within a short span of months. There were several in Santa Barbara and L.A. as well, and there was a large wedding tentatively planned in New York in the fall, but the couple was not yet officially engaged. The bride's mother had already called, just in case.

"Wow!" Paris said as they sat back after a few hours. There was enough there to keep ten assistants busy, she couldn't begin to imagine how Jane had done it all. "How do you keep it all straight?" Paris asked, looking worried. She was beginning to wonder if the job was too much for her after all. She didn't want to turn his business, or his parties, into a mess. It was a herculean job. And she had huge respect for both of them.

"You get used to it after a while," Jane said reassuringly. "It's not magic, it's just work. The key is using really good resources that don't let you down. It happens sometimes anyway, but very rarely. And Bix only lets it happen once. If they screw up, or let him down somehow, he never gives them a second chance. Our clients just won't put up with it. Perfection is the secret to his success. And when something goes wrong, the client never knows about it. We work our butts off to fix it, or improvise so it still works."

"He really is a genius," Paris said admiringly.

"Yes," Jane said simply, "but he also works like a dog. And so do I. Are you okay with that, Paris?"

"Yes, I am." And she meant it.

They spent the rest of the afternoon going over more files, the orchids for the dinner party that evening arrived, as promised, and

by three o'clock, Jane and Paris were at the site of the dinner. It was
a large imposing house on Jackson Street in Pacific Heights. And
Paris had heard of the client, he was the head of an internationally
known biotech firm in Silicon Valley. It was a formal dinner for
twenty. The house itself was exquisitely done by a well-known
French decorator, and the entire dining room was done in bright
red lacquer.

"Bix doesn't like to do the obvious," Jane explained. "Anyone
else would have done red roses in here, and I think a lot of people
have. That's why he went with brown orchids." Their own staff
was doing the cooking that night, and Bix had bought perfect little
silver bells with each guest's initials engraved on them as party favors. His ingenious party favors, from teddy bears to copies of
Fabergé eggs for each guest, were one of his trademarks. People
loved coming to his parties.

He had arranged for a dance band afterward, and some of the
furniture had been cleared out of the living room to accommodate
it. And as Jane and Paris stood by, a truck arrived with a baby
grand piano. There was not a single thing he did by half measures.

Bix arrived himself about half an hour later, and he stayed until
nearly dinnertime. By the time he left, everything was set up and in
perfect order. He had pulled and tugged and tucked and tweaked
the flowers himself, and at the last minute he changed one of the
silver bowls they were in because he didn't like it. But one thing
was certain, the evening would be one that all the guests would remember.

Jane ran home herself then to put a black cocktail dress on, and
she was planning to be back before the first guest arrived. She liked
to be on hand to be sure that everything went smoothly. With small
dinner parties, she usually stayed until the guests sat down, with
larger more complicated ones, she stayed until they were dancing
after dinner. It made for long workdays and longer evenings. She
had told Paris she didn't have to be there that night, but Paris had
insisted that she wanted to join her, and see how she coordinated

the evening. When caterers were used, she kept an eye on them, and made sure the service was impeccable. She made sure the guests were greeted properly when they arrived, their escort cards were handed to them, the musicians were at their stations, the flowers still looked right, and the valet parkers knew what they were doing with the cars. There was not a single detail overlooked by Bixby Mason or any of his employees. And when press coverage was appropriate, they wrote the releases.

Paris drove home as quickly as she could, and ran a bath, as she pulled a short black dress out of her closet, and let her hair down to brush it. She hadn't stopped since nine o'clock that morning. And this was only the beginning.

She dialed Meg quickly as she foraged for something to eat. She had less than an hour to dress and meet Jane back at the party, before the first guests came. Meg was still at the studio when she answered her cell phone.

"I think I have a job," she said excitedly, and then told Meg all about Bixby Mason.

"That sounds terrific, Mom. I hope you get it."

"So do I, sweetheart. I just wanted to tell you, I'm working. This is so exciting!" She told her about what she'd done all day, and then Meg got called back to the set. And Paris called Anne Smythe in Greenwich.

"I found the perfect job, and I'm trying out this week," she said excitedly when she reached Anne at home. She felt like a kid who had just made the team, or was at least trying out for it. "I love it!"

"I'm proud of you, Paris," Anne said, beaming on her end. "That was fast work. What did it take you? Three days?" As quickly as she could, Paris told her all about it. "If he has any sense, he'll hire you in a hot minute. Call and tell me."

"I will," she promised, and then slipped into the bath and closed her eyes for five minutes. She had really enjoyed what she'd done all day, and one of the things she liked about it was that they could see their concepts and hard work executed and completed. There was a tremendous sense of accomplishment in watching the events unfold. Paris could already see that.

She arrived back at the house on Jackson Street five minutes before Jane did, and they left at precisely ten-thirty, once the guests were dancing. Everything had gone smoothly. And the hosts had been pleasant and welcoming when they met Paris. She looked every bit as elegant as the guests in a simple black cocktail dress. She had been careful to wear something covered up and distinguished. The idea was to blend in, not to draw attention to herself, which she understood completely. Jane thought she was perfect, mature, sensible, capable, hardworking, resourceful. When one of the valet parkers had created a problem with one of the guests, Paris had told the head of the team quietly and firmly to call their base and replace him. She hadn't waited for Jane to give her directions. She'd been busy in the kitchen working out the schedule with the chef, to make sure the soufflés they were having for the first course wouldn't fall before they got the guests to the table. Every piece of the puzzle had to fit, and like a corps de ballet, they all had to move with infinite precision, even more so when they managed enormous weddings. This was just a taste of what the rest was, but Paris had stepped right in and handled it with grace and competence. Jane knew she was exactly what Bixby needed.

"You must be exhausted," Paris said to her sympathetically as they left the house on Jackson Street. She was nine months pregnant and had been on her feet for fourteen hours. It was not exactly what her doctor recommended, or her husband wanted.

"I told the baby I don't have time for him to be born this week," Jane said, looking tired as they stopped at her car and she smiled at Paris.

"When's your due date?" Paris asked warmly, she genuinely liked her. Jane gave her all and then some to Bixby. It was definitely time for her to pass the baton, Paris just hoped that Bix would let her take it from her.

"Tomorrow," Jane said with a rueful smile. "I'm trying to pretend I don't know that. But he does," she said, rubbing her belly. The baby had been kicking her all night, and she'd been having contractions for two weeks now. They were just practice runs, she knew, but the final performance was coming. "I'll see you in the morning," she told Paris, as she slid behind the wheel with difficulty, and Paris felt sorry for her. This was no way to put your feet up and wait for a baby. Her schedule would have killed most women who weren't pregnant, and it was easy to see why her husband had insisted she quit and stay home with her baby. She'd done this for six years, and it was time to stop now. For her sake, and the baby's. "You did a great job today," she told Paris, and then drove off with a wave, as Paris got in her car and drove home to the house on Vallejo. And she realized as she walked in, and set down her handbag, she was exhausted. It had been a long, interesting day, followed by a successful evening. She had been acutely aware during all of it that she was concentrating constantly in order to learn everything she needed to know as quickly as possible. But nothing she had done that day seemed out of the ordinary to her, or impossible to accomplish. She knew that she could do this. And as she stretched out in her bed that night, all she wanted was to land this job as Bixby Mason's assistant. And God willing, if it was meant to be, she would do that.

Chapter 15

The next two days, as Paris learned the ropes from Jane, were a whirlwind. They had two parties to do on Tuesday night. Bixby spearheaded one of them, the more important of the two, and Jane handled the other, for a slightly less demanding client. One was a remarkable event in an art gallery, which involved a light show and a techno band, and a lot of complicated technical details. The other was a black tie dinner party for old friends of Bixby's. And Paris went back and forth between the two, helping where she could, and learning whatever they could teach her. She had fun at the art gallery, but she enjoyed being with Jane at the black tie dinner party too. Jane wasn't feeling well that night, and halfway through the evening, Paris sent her home and handled the remainder of the dinner party for her. And Jane still looked a little rough the next morning. There was no question, the baby's arrival was coming closer. She was a day past her due date.

"Are you all right?" Paris asked her with a look of concern, as they settled down across the desk from each other in her office.

"I'm just tired. I couldn't sleep last night I had so many contractions. And Paul is mad at me. He said I shouldn't be working. He thinks I'm going to kill the baby." Paris didn't entirely disagree with him, at least in that she thought Jane should be resting, and not pushing herself as hard as she was, but Jane wanted to give Paris a chance to settle in, and she had promised Bix she'd finish the week, if she didn't have the baby.

"You won't kill the baby, but you might kill yourself, at this rate. Here," she said, pushing a velvet stool toward her, "put your feet up."

"Thanks, Paris." They went over the rest of the files then. And bookings for two more weddings came in that morning. Paris saw how she handled the details, who she made notes to call. It was a very carefully done setup. There was a secretary who came in twice a week to type things up for them, and a bookkeeper who did the billing. But the responsibility for all the rest of it was on Bixby and Jane's shoulders, and hers if he hired her. And Paris knew she was going to really miss this, if he didn't. She was loving every minute of it, and by Thursday afternoon, she felt as though she'd been there forever.

On Friday they handled the last details of the Fleischmann anniversary party. It was their fortieth, and they were having a black tie dinner party for a hundred on Saturday in their home in Hillsborough. It was apparently a palatial estate on a hilltop, and Mrs. Fleischmann said she had looked forward to the event for an entire lifetime. Bixby wanted everything to be perfect for her. She had an unfortunate weakness for pink, and he had convinced her to have a tent made that was so pale, it almost wasn't. And they had flown in the palest of pink tulips from Holland. He had managed to rescue the celebration from bad taste and metamorphose it into something exquisite. Mrs. Fleischmann was planning to wear pink, of course, and her husband had given her a pink diamond ring for the occasion.

When Paris met her on Saturday, she was an adorable little round woman in her late sixties, who looked ten years older. She had three sons, and thirteen grandchildren, all of whom were coming, and it was obvious that she was crazy about Bixby. He had done one of her grandsons' bar mitzvahs the year before, and Jane told Paris they had spent half a million dollars on it.

"Wow!" Paris said, impressed.

"We did one for two million in L.A. a few years ago, for a famous producer. They hired three acts from the circus, and literally had a three-ring circus, and a skating rink for the kids. It was quite something."

By the time the guests arrived for the Fleischmanns' anniversary party, the Bixby Mason team had everything in full control, as usual. Mrs. Fleischmann was beaming from ear to ear, and her husband looked thrilled with the party Bixby had created for them. And when Oscar Fleischmann led his wife onto the floor for the first dance, a waltz, Paris stood there with tears in her eyes, smiling.

"Cute, aren't they?" Bix whispered to her. "I love her." He loved most of his clients, which was how he was able to create such magic for them. He had to really care about them to do it. There were those he didn't like, of course, and he did his utmost for them too, but it never had quite the same feeling as it did when he liked them, or had a special fondness for them.

Paris was standing near the buffet, watching the scene, in a simple navy blue silk evening gown, as a man walked over to her, and began chatting. The dress was pretty on her, and she'd worn her hair in a French twist, but she was being careful not to look showy, or wear bright colors when she was working. She tried to blend into the woodwork, the way Bix and Jane did. Bix almost always wore black, like a puppeteer or a mime artist, and he had a quiet elegance about him. Jane was limited to one black cocktail dress these days, and one black evening gown that was straining at the seams. But she'd been in good spirits all day, and seemed to get a second wind halfway through the evening. By then, the baby looked beyond enormous, and the doctor had said he was going to be a ten-pounder. She looked it.

"Nice party, isn't it?" a gray-haired man in a dinner jacket commented, as Paris glanced over her shoulder. He was standing just behind her. And when she turned, she couldn't help noticing that he was very handsome. He looked to be somewhere in his late forties, and seemed very distinguished.

"Yes, it is." She smiled at him blandly, trying not to pick up the conversation, while still being polite to him. She didn't want to encourage him. She was working. She just didn't look it. She was better looking than most of the guests, most of whom were a great deal older. But the Fleischmanns' sons were there, and a handful of their friends. Paris assumed the man with the gray hair was one of them.

"Fabulous buffet." There was an entire table devoted to caviar, which had been doing a considerable business. "Do you know the Fleischmanns well?" he asked conversationally, determined to engage her. He had bright blue eyes the color of Peter's, and much as she hated to admit it, he was better looking. He looked lean and athletic and in good shape. And he was so handsome he could have been an actor or male model, but in this crowd, she was sure he wasn't.

"I just met them today," she said quietly.

"Really?" he said, assuming she was someone's date. He had checked out her left hand for a wedding ring, and there was none. "They're lovely people." And then, with a smile that was nearly dazzling, he turned to her. "Would you like to dance? My name is Chandler Freeman. I'm a business associate of Oscar Junior's." He had taken care of the full introduction as she smiled at him, but made no move toward the dance floor.

"I'm Paris Armstrong, and I work for Bixby Mason, who organized this spectacular event. I'm not a guest. I'm working."

"I see," he said, not missing a beat, as his smile grew broader. "Well, Cinderella, if you dance with me until the stroke of midnight, I promise to look for you all over the kingdom, until I find the matching glass slipper. Shall we?"

"I don't really think I should," she said, looking amused but embarrassed. He was very appealing, and very charming.

"I won't tell if you don't. And you look far too beautiful to be standing out here on the sidelines. One dance won't hurt anything, will it?" He already had an arm around her, and without waiting for a response, he was leading her toward the dance floor. And much to her own amazement, she followed. She caught Bix's eye along the way, and he smiled at her and winked, which seemed to suggest he had no problem with it. So she let Chandler Freeman lead her onto the floor and sweep her away. He was an expert dancer, and it was three songs later when he led her to his table. "Would you like to join us?" He was there with several friends, and was in fact sitting with Oscar Fleischmann Jr., who was a handsome man about Paris's age with a very pretty wife, who was covered in diamonds and emeralds. The family had made their fortune in oil in Denver, and then moved to San Francisco. It was Oscar Jr.'s son who had had the bar mitzvah, Jane told her later.

"I'd love to," Paris said, in answer to his invitation to join them. "But I have to get back to my team." She didn't want to be inappropriate and overly familiar with the guests, and make a bad impression either on their client, or on Bixby. She had no problem keeping her place, and had no intention of picking up the guests, however handsome. And there was no question, Chandler Freeman was a knockout. She wondered who his date was, and how she had felt about his dancing with Paris. But she couldn't identify anyone at the table who looked as though she was with him. As it turned out, his date had canceled at the last minute.

"I had a great time dancing with you, Paris," he said, nearly in her ear so no one would hear him. "I'd love to see you again."

"I'll leave my number in the glass slipper," she said as she laughed. "I always wondered why the prince didn't at least get her name. It has to make you wonder about him." Chandler laughed at what she said.

"Paris Armstrong. And you work for Bixby Mason. I think I can remember that," he said, as though he fully intended to call her and see her again. But she wasn't counting on it. He was just a very

charming, very handsome man. It was good for her ego, for a
minute or two, but she didn't expect or want more than that.

"Thank you again, have a lovely evening," she said to the table
in general and drifted off, and as she did, she could hear Oscar's
wife say in a loud voice "Who was that?" and Chandler answer
"Cinderella," and everyone at the table laughed. Paris was still
amused when she got back to Bixby and Jane.

"Sorry," she said to Bixby apologetically. "I didn't want to insult
him by not dancing with him, and I escaped as soon as I could."
But Bixby didn't look in the least concerned, except about Jane,
who was finally sitting down, and looked as though she were
about to pop.

"Part of the secret of our success is knowing when to mix with
the locals, and when to back off and work. You did it just right.
People like it sometimes if we mingle with them for a while. I do.
And I think it's just fine if you do a bit of that too. As long as we
keep an eye on how the event is going. There are plenty of parties
we do where I'm on the guest list," he said, smiling at her. As far as
he was concerned, Paris was not only efficient and competent, but
she was socially adept, and he wanted her to know that. "By the
way," he said with a gleam in his eye, "that looked like a good
one," he said mischievously, referring to Chandler. "He's very nice
looking. Who is he?"

"Prince Charming," she said blithely, and then looked down to
notice Jane rubbing her lower back.

"Are you okay?" Paris asked her, looking worried.

"I'm fine. The baby is just in a weird position. I think he's sitting
on my kidneys."

"How pleasant," Bix said, rolling his eyes in mock horror. "I
don't know how women do it. That would kill me," he said, pointing at her stomach.

"No, it wouldn't, you get used to it," Paris said, smiling.

"Your son is very well behaved, by the way," he said to Jane, as
some of the guests finally started leaving. It had been a long

evening, and they had nearly an hour's drive back to the city. Bix had hired a crew to take down the tent, and oversee the undoing of the party, so they didn't have to stay there. "I told him not to come until after the Fleischmann anniversary, and there's no sign of him yet. Excellent manners, Jane, I commend you. My godson is a little prince. I would have spanked him if he'd come any sooner." They all laughed, and Bix went to chat with Mrs. Fleischmann until the last of her guests had collected their cars, and she was finally alone with her husband, Bix, Jane, and Paris.

"It was everything I had dreamed it would be," she said happily, looking like a vision in pink, as she gazed adoringly at her husband, and then gratefully at Bixby. "Thank you, Bix. I'll never forget this."

"It was beautiful, Doris, and so were you. We had a good time too."

"You all did such a good job," she said warmly. She liked Paris too, and thought she made an excellent addition to the team.

Bix went to get his briefcase, and the clothes he had changed out of when he put on his tuxedo. He had been working there all afternoon. The Fleischmanns went into the house arm in arm, and Paris was walking to the car, when she heard Jane give a soft moan. She didn't know what it was at first, and when she turned to look at her, Jane suddenly bent over, and there was a rush of water that splashed onto the grass where she stood.

"Oh my God," she said, looking at Paris with wide eyes, "I think my water just broke," and within seconds, she was doubled over with a terrible pain.

"Sit down," Paris said firmly to her, and helped her to sit down on the grass so she could catch her breath. "You're okay, it's going to be fine. Well, it looks like the baby did just what Bix said. He waited till after the party. Now let's get you home." Jane nodded, but the contraction she was having was too strong for her to speak. And when it ended, she looked up at Paris miserably.

"I think I'm going to be sick." Paris had had labors like that, fast and hard, vomiting everywhere, and too many things happening all at once. But in her experience, it had meant that the baby came quickly too. Jane was throwing up when Bix came back to look for them.

"Good lord, what happened to you? What did you eat? I hope it wasn't the caviar or the oysters, people were gobbling them up, saying how good they were." But Jane just looked up at him, mortally embarrassed.

"I think she's in labor," Paris said quietly to him. "Is there a hospital near here?"

"Now? Here?" Bixby looked horrified, and Jane interrupted immediately.

"I don't want to go to a hospital here. I want to go home. I'm okay. I feel better now."

"Let's discuss it in the car," Paris said sensibly, and helped Jane into the backseat so she could lie down. There was a towel in the trunk, and Paris set it next to her, and got into the front seat. Bix had driven them, and he took off his tuxedo jacket, put it in the trunk, and a moment later they took off. By then Jane had called Paul, and told him what was happening. She promised to call him back in five minutes. "I think you should call your doctor too. When did the contractions start?" Paris asked, as Jane dialed her obstetrician's number.

"I don't know. I've been feeling weird all afternoon. I thought it was something I ate." She got through to her doctor's exchange then, and they patched her through to him. He told her to go straight to California Pacific Medical Center in the city. He thought driving back would be fine. And if anything changed dramatically, he told her to stop and go to a hospital along the way, or at the very worst, call 911. He was relieved to hear that she wasn't driving back alone, and she was lying down. She called Paul back then and told him where to meet her, and to bring her overnight bag. It had been sitting in the front hall for three weeks. And as soon as she finished talking to him, another contraction hit. It was another major one, and she couldn't talk for three or four minutes.

"If memory serves," Paris said to Bix as she held Jane's hand. Jane was nearly breaking her fingers, and gripping Paris's hand in a vise as she squeezed her eyes shut and made a moaning sound that terrified Bix. "As I recall, once you can't talk during contractions, it's time to be in the hospital. I think she's further along than she thinks."

"Oh my God," Bix said, looking panicked. "I'm a homosexual, for chrissake. I'm not supposed to see these things, or even know about them. What am I supposed to do now?"

"Drive back to the city as fast as you can," Paris said, laughing at him, and feeling better again, Jane was laughing weakly in the backseat too.

"Your godson wants to see you, Bix," Jane teased, and he groaned louder than she had a moment before.

"Well, tell him I do *not* want to see him. Yet. I want to see him neatly wrapped in a blue blanket, in a hospital ward, and not until his hair has been combed. And that goes for you too," he said, glancing at Jane in the rearview mirror, but he was genuinely concerned. The last thing he wanted was for something untoward to happen to her, or the baby, while he drove them into town. "Are you sure we shouldn't stop at a hospital along the way?" he asked both women, and Jane insisted she was fine. She had several more contractions, and Paris was timing them. They were still about seven minutes apart. They had time, but not much, she knew.

The two women talked softly between contractions, and Jane had a horrific one just as they cruised past the airport, going at full speed.

"Are you okay?" Bix asked, and Jane's voice was hoarse when she spoke again.

"Yeah. I think I might get sick again." But this time she didn't, and she told Paris as they reached the outskirts of the city that she felt like she wanted to bear down.

"Don't!" Paris said firmly. "We're almost there. Just hang in."

"Oh my God," Bix said, "this isn't happening." And then he turned to Paris with a nervous look. "Do you deliver babies too?"

"Is that part of the job description?" she asked, keeping an eye on Jane and her hand in hers.

"It may have to be. I hope not. And by the way . . ." he began as they flew through a red light on Franklin Street, and narrowly missed being hit by a car. He had never driven as fast, or as recklessly in his life. "You're hired, Paris. In case I haven't told you yet. You've done a great job this week. And you in the backseat," he said jokingly to Jane, "you're fired. I don't want to see you in the office on Monday. Don't come back again!" They were on California Street by then, and Jane was making horrible sounds. Paris was trying to get her to pant like a dog so she wouldn't push.

"Can we stop?" Jane asked feebly. The motion of the car was making her feel sick.

"No!" Bix nearly screamed. The hospital was only a few blocks away. "I am not stopping, and you will not have that baby in this car! Do you hear me, Jane?"

"I will if I want," she said, lying back with her eyes closed. She had broken out in a sweat and let go of Paris's hand to hold her belly. Paris knew that they would be lucky if they got there in time. The baby was definitely coming. And just as she thought it, Bix screeched to a halt outside the hospital, in the parking slots reserved for emergency vehicles. Without asking either of them, he jumped out of the car, and ran inside to find a doctor. "I think the baby's coming," Jane said to Paris in staccato breaths, and all she wanted to do was scream.

"It's okay, sweetheart, we're here," Paris said, as she jumped out of the car, and opened the back door to get to Jane, but just as she did, two attendants rushed out with a gurney, and Paul was with them. They got her onto the gurney as she cried, and she was sobbing as she reached for Paul with both hands. She had been very brave, but now she was frightened, and so relieved to see him.

"I was so worried about you," he said, as he held her hand and they wheeled her inside at full speed, while Paris and Bix watched, and followed her inside. They didn't even try to get her upstairs, but took her straight into the emergency room, and Paris and Bix were still trying to catch their breath when they heard her scream. It was a long horrifying howl that was so primeval, so deep and so profound that it went to one's very soul. Bix looked at Paris in terror, and clutched her hand.

"Oh my God, is she dying?" He had tears in his eyes. He had never heard anything like it. It sounded as though someone had sawed her in half.

"No," Paris said quietly, as they held hands in the waiting room, "I think she just had a baby."

"How awful. Was it like that for you?"

"With one of them. I had a C-section with the other."

"You're a remarkable breed, all of you. I could never go through it."

"It's worth it," she said, as she wiped a tear from her eyes too. Thinking about it reminded her of Peter.

And a moment later one of the emergency room nurses came out to tell them that the baby was healthy and weighed ten pounds three ounces. Half an hour later they wheeled Jane past them, as Paul followed proudly, holding the baby. They were all going upstairs to a room.

"Are you okay?" Paris asked as she bent to kiss her. "I'm so proud of you. You were terrific."

"It was pretty easy," Jane said gamely. They had just given her something for the pain, and she was looking very woozy. And at ten pounds three ounces, Paris knew it couldn't have been easy.

"We'll come back and see you tomorrow," Paris promised, as Bix leaned over and kissed her too.

"Thank you for not having it at the Fleischmanns' party," he said solemnly, and all three of them laughed. He took a peek at the baby, and remarked to Paul that he looked enormous. "He looks like he should be smoking a cigar and carrying a briefcase. That's my godson," he said proudly to one of the nurses. And a moment later, the little family they had become went upstairs to get to know each other.

"What a remarkable evening," Bix said to Paris, as they stood outside in the starry night. It was three o'clock in the morning.

It had been an extraordinary week. She had gotten a job, made two new friends, and nearly delivered a baby.

"Thanks for the job," she said as he drove her home. She felt as though they were old friends now.

"We'll have to put midwifery in the brochure after tonight," he said solemnly. "I'm awfully glad we didn't have to deliver that baby."

"So am I," Paris said with a yawn, as she smiled at him. She knew the night had created a bond between them that might not have been there otherwise. Neither of them would ever forget it. Nor would Jane, she was sure.

"Would you like to come to breakfast tomorrow?" Bix asked as he dropped her off at her house. "I'd like you to meet my partner." It was a compliment and an honor for him to bring her into his private world, but he felt she had earned it. She was a lovely person.

"I didn't know you had a business partner," she said sleepily, looking puzzled, but pleased to be invited.

"I don't. I was referring to the man I live with," he said, laughing at her. "You have led a sheltered life, haven't you?"

"Sorry, I wasn't thinking." She giggled. "I'd love it."

"Come at eleven. We can get drunk thinking about tonight. It's a shame he wasn't with us. He's a doctor."

"I can't wait to meet him," she said sincerely, and then got out and waved as she unlocked her front door, and stepped inside.

"Good night," he called as he drove away, thinking of the events of the evening. A baby had come into the world, and he'd nearly had to deliver it, and he had a new assistant. It had been quite a day.

Chapter 16

After sleeping as late as possible, Paris took a shower, put on khaki slacks and an old cashmere sweater and her favorite pea coat, and turned up at the door next to the shop at eleven. She knew Bix and his friend lived on the two floors above the office. He had bought the building years before, and the private quarters, when she entered them, were lovely. The rooms were cozy and warm. There were books everywhere, and there was a roaring fire, where Bix and an older man had been sitting and reading the Sunday paper. The older man was wearing a tweed jacket and slacks and an open blue shirt, and Bix was wearing jeans and a sweatshirt. The older man had white hair, but looked youthful and very rugged. They were a handsome couple.

Bix introduced her to Steven Ward, and Steven greeted her warmly. He looked to be in his early sixties.

"I hear you two had quite an evening last night, and you almost delivered Jane's baby."

"It was very close," Paris said with a grin, as Bix handed her a Bellini. It was champagne with a splash of peach juice, and when she tasted it, it was delicious. "I didn't think we'd make it."

"Neither did I," Bix said honestly. "I figured if I didn't kill us in the car, we might all live through it. Pretty hairy."

"Very," Paris agreed, taking another sip of the Bellini, and turning to Bix's partner. "Bix tells me you're a doctor," she said easily, and he nodded.

"I'm an internist," he said discreetly.

"Specializing in HIV and AIDS," Bix corrected, looking obviously proud of Steven. "The best in the city."

"That must be hard," Paris said sympathetically.

"It is, but we're doing much better these days with medications."

Paris learned as she talked to him that he had come to San Francisco from the Midwest, to work with AIDS patients in the early eighties, and he'd been there ever since. And as Bix made omelettes for them, Steven told her that his previous partner had died of AIDS ten years before, and he and Bix had been together for seven. He was sixty-two years old, and it was obvious that he admired Bix greatly, and they were very happy.

They sat in the dining room, eating omelettes and croissants, as Bix poured them each a cappuccino. He was a fabulous cook, and informed her that it was a good thing, because Steven couldn't boil water. He could save lives, or make people more comfortable, but he was hopeless in the kitchen.

"He tried to cook for me once, when I was sick, and he damn near killed me. I had stomach flu, and he made me tomato soup, out of a can thank you very much, and a can of chili. I do the cooking," Bix said firmly. Their relationship appeared to be interesting and lively, based on mutual respect and deep affection. Steven talked openly about how traumatic it had been for him when his previous partner died. They had been together for twenty-seven years before that.

"Learning to live without him was a tremendous adjustment. I didn't even go out for two years. All I did was work, read, and sleep. And then I met Bix, we dated for a year, and we've been living together for six. I've been very lucky," he said with a grateful look at Bix.

"Yes, you are," Paris said quietly. "I was married for twenty-four, and I never thought we'd get divorced. I'm still reeling from the shock. Sometimes I think about it, and I just can't believe it happened. He's married to someone else now."

"How long has it been since he left you?" Steven asked sympathetically. He could see easily why Bix liked her. She was a very nice woman, bright, interesting, fun to be with, it was hard to imagine why her husband had left her. She seemed to him like everything a man could want.

"It's been nine months," Paris said sadly.

"And he's already remarried?" Bix looked shocked, and was more inquisitive than his partner. "Is that why he left you?" She nodded, but managed not to cry for once, which was at least something. Things were looking up. She was feeling better.

"She's thirty-one years old. I guess that's hard to compete with."

"You shouldn't have to," Bix said bluntly. "I hope she was worth it. What a rotten thing to do to you, Paris. Have you dated yet?" he asked with interest.

"No, and I don't intend to. I'm too old for that. I'm not going to make a fool of myself competing with girls my daughter's age. And there's no one I want anyway. I really loved him." This time her eyes did fill with tears, and Steven touched her shoulder.

"I felt that way too. I swore I'd never date again. And you're a lot younger than I was when John died."

"I'm forty-six years old, and I'm too old for dating."

"No one is too old to date," Steven said sensibly. "I have survivors of patients I see who are seventy-five years old and fall in love, and get married."

"Not all his patients are gay," Bix said by way of explanation.

"I'm serious, Paris. You have a lifetime ahead of you. You just need time. Nine months is nothing. For some anyway. Others seem to find someone in weeks or months. But no matter how you do it, grieving the loss of a loved one or a relationship is never easy. It took me three years to find Bix, and I never thought I'd feel this way again. We're very happy," he said, and Paris was touched by their honesty and compassion. What they were sharing with her was valuable information. It made no difference to her if they were gay or straight. The feelings about relationships were the same.

"And it's a lot harder to find someone worth having in the gay world," Bix said bluntly. "Everything is about looks and beauty and youth. There's nothing harder than getting old alone in gay life. If you're not young and beautiful, it's all over. I was back out in the dating world for two years after my last relationship, and I hated every minute of it. And I was only thirty, and I already felt then as though it was all over for me. I met Steven when I was thirty-two, and I couldn't wait to settle down with him. I'm not a dater," Bix said honestly, but he could have been. At thirty-nine, he was still dazzlingly handsome. In his youth, after college, he had been a model. But his values were based on something far more solid.

"I'm not a dater either," Paris said with a sigh. "Can you imagine anything more ridiculous than being out there on dates at my age? It's so humiliating, and so depressing." She told them about the night of the dinner party in Greenwich with the drunken stockbroker who had told dirty jokes and was wearing plaid pants. It had been the decisive moment in her moving to San Francisco, if only to escape evenings like that among her friends.

"I think I dated his gay brother," Bix said, laughing, and then told her some stories that made her laugh even more. "I have had some of the worst blind dates on the planet. My last partner dumped me for a younger guy, he was twenty-two, I think, and everyone felt sorry for me. So in order to prove it, they fixed me up with the worst people they could think of. Preferably multi-addicted, or better yet, psychotic. I dated one guy who'd been sleep deprived for two years, and he was so nuts, he kept hallucinating and thinking I was his mother. I came home and found him passed out on the couch in pink hot pants and a black bra one afternoon, ripped out of his mind on Quaaludes, and I told him he had to go. That was nothing compared to the nature lover, who must have been related to the Hillside Strangler. He had five snakes and let them loose in my house. He lost two, and it took him a month to find them, and I nearly gave up the apartment. I had some lulus! I promise you, Paris, I will never fix you up on a blind date. I like you too much. You'll have to do your own shopping. I have too much respect for you to even try."

"Thank you. How did you and Steven meet?" she asked, curious about them. She really liked them. And the breakfast Bix prepared had been delicious. He said Sydney had taught him how to make the omelettes.

"It was pretty straightforward. I needed a new doctor. We liked each other. It took him about two months, and a lot of sinus problems and headaches and mysterious backaches I kept making up, but he finally got the message, and invited me to dinner." Steven smiled at the memory, and Bix looked adoringly at him.

"I was a little slow on the pick-up," Steven apologized. "I thought he was looking for a father figure."

"Nothing that kinky," Bix said simply. "Just a boyfriend."

They were far more than that now, they were more like a comfortable married couple, from what Paris could see, and she respected the relationship they shared. In a funny way, it reminded her of her closeness to Peter, and when she went home that afternoon, she found that it had made her feel lonely. They were so close and at ease with each other, and so comfortable. It reminded her of how nice it was to have someone to share your life with.

She called Meg and she was out. And at six o'clock Wim showed up with one of his roommates. She had promised to fix him dinner, and they had a lovely evening. It had been a nice day, and she was enjoying her California life. Even the weather had been cooperating since she arrived. She had been there for ten days, and although it was February, it was warm and sunny. According to reports from Virginia and Natalie, it was snowing in Greenwich. Paris was delighted that she'd left.

"So how do you like your new job, Mom?" Wim asked with interest as he stretched his long legs out across the couch, and recovered from an enormous dinner. He and his roommate had thanked her profusely, and had eaten as though they were starving.

"I love it," she said, beaming.

"What exactly do you do?" He couldn't remember. When she had first described it, it sounded confusing. It was some kind of wedding planner, he thought, which was close enough, as long as it made her happy.

"We plan events and parties. Weddings, dinner parties, openings. The man who does the conceptual work is very creative."

"Sounds like fun," he said, relaxing in her new home. And he loved the downstairs apartment. He and his friend had checked it out, and he said he was going to visit often. She hoped he would, but knew enough about kids his age not to count on it. He was going to be busy in college.

They stayed until after ten o'clock, and then drove back to Berkeley. And by eleven o'clock, she had cleaned up, and gotten into bed in her nightgown. It had been a delightful Sunday. Weekends were what she feared most, and what she had most disliked in Greenwich. It felt as though everyone else in the world had someone to be with, and she didn't. But here it seemed easier somehow. She had enjoyed her morning with Steven and Bix, and her evening with Wim and his roommate. Meg called her just as she was about to fall asleep, and told her about the day she'd spent at Venice Beach, and she'd had a good time too. All was well in the world, at least in California, in Paris's new world.

Chapter 17

Monday was a busy day. Paris no longer had Jane to counsel her, she was happily at home with her husband and her new baby. They had called him Alexander Mason Winslow, and she said he was an easy baby.

Paris and Bix worked closely together. The following Saturday was Valentine's Day, and they had two events planned. As he had with Jane, he planned to be at one, and wanted Paris to be at the other. But neither was an enormous party. And it was late afternoon when the phone rang, and the secretary who had come in to clean up their paperwork for them told Paris it was for her, and it was a Mr. Freeman.

"I don't know one," she said briskly, and she was about to tell her to take a message for her, when she suddenly remembered. It was Prince Charming. "Hello?" she said cautiously, wondering if it was the man she had danced with at the Fleischmanns' anniversary. And as soon as she heard his voice, it sounded like him, as closely as she could remember.

"I hope you don't mind my calling you," he apologized smoothly. "I got your number from Marjorie Fleischmann, who got it from her mother-in-law. Rather a circuitous route, but apparently effective. How are you, Cinderella?"

"Fine." She laughed at him, impressed by the effort he'd put into locating her, and wondering why he had bothered. She hadn't been all that friendly, in spite of the dance they'd shared. "We've been busy. We had a lot of cleaning up to do today. And I nearly delivered a baby on the way home from the party the other night." She told him about Jane, and he sounded amused. And then she waited to hear the reason why he had called her. Maybe he wanted to give a party himself.

"I thought we might have lunch tomorrow. How does that sound to you, Paris?" *Silly* was the first word that came to mind, but she didn't say it. And *why* was the second. She was definitely not in the right mind-set for dating. It was the last thing she wanted.

"That's very nice of you, Chandler." She remembered his name. And she didn't want to have lunch with him. "I don't usually go to lunch. We're awfully busy."

"Your blood sugar will plummet if you don't. We'll make it a quick one." He was not in the habit of taking no for an answer. And he didn't intend to in this case. He was so forthright that she didn't know what to say to him, other than to be rude, which didn't seem appropriate either. He was a perfectly nice man.

"Well, very quick then," she conceded, and then was annoyed at herself for being pushed into a lunch she didn't want to go to, with a man she didn't know. "Where shall I meet you?" She was going to make it in and out and businesslike, no matter what he had in mind.

"I'll pick you up at your office at noon. And I promise I'll have you back in an hour."

"It'll be easier if I meet you," she insisted stubbornly. "I don't know where I'll be in the morning."

"Don't worry about it. I'll pick you up. That way you don't need to worry if you're late. I can return calls from my car while I wait." It was exactly what she didn't want, to drive off with a total stranger in his car. "See you at noon, Cinderella," he said blithely, and hung up as she sat at her desk and stewed as Bix walked in.

"Something wrong?" he asked as he saw the expression on her face.

"I just did something really stupid," she said, annoyed at herself. The man on the phone had been in complete control.

"Did you hang up on a client?" he asked with a blank expression. He couldn't imagine what it was.

"Nothing like that," she reassured him. She had already thanked him for brunch the previous day, and told him how much she had enjoyed meeting Steven Ward, and what a nice man he was. Bix had been pleased. He wanted the three of them to be friends. "I let some guy talk me into having lunch with him, and I didn't even want to. But before I knew it, he had spun me around and told me he'd pick me up at noon." Bix smiled.

"Anyone I know? The guy at the Fleischmanns' anniversary party?"

"How did you know?" She looked surprised.

"I figured he'd call. That type usually does. What's his name again?"

"Chandler Freeman. He's an associate of Oscar Fleischmann Jr. I don't know what he does."

"I've read about him here and there. Sounds like a professional dater to me. Buyer beware."

"What does that mean?" She was an innocent lost in the woods of a brave new world.

"It's a particular breed. Some of them have never married, others have had ugly divorces that cost them a lot of money, from women they hated anyway. They have a chip on their shoulder as a rule. And for the rest of time, they date and they date and they date and they date, and tell everyone what a bitch their ex-wife was. And according to them, the reason they never remarried is because they haven't found 'the right woman' yet. And the key is they never will. They don't want to. They just want to date. To them, temps are more fun."

"Well, that certainly takes care of them," Paris said with a broad smile. "I'll see how much he'll tell me about his history, and I'll let you know if any of it matches up."

"Unfortunately, it probably will." Bix felt sorry for her. Dating was something he hoped never to have to do again. Gay or straight.

"Do you mind if I go out to lunch tomorrow?" she asked him as an afterthought, and he laughed.

"Do you want me to say yes?"

"More or less." She wasn't entirely sure. He had been a good-looking man, seemed like fun, and it was only lunch, she told herself.

"Go. You'll have fun. You have to get your feet wet. He looks like a decent guy."

"Even if he's a professional dater?"

"So what? It's not marriage. It's lunch. You'll be safe. It's good practice for you."

"For what?"

"The real world," he said honestly. "You're going to have to get out there one of these days. You can't stay home forever. You're the kind of woman who deserves to have a good man in your life, Paris. And you aren't going to find one if you don't go out."

"I thought I had one," she said sadly, and Bix nodded.

"It turned out he wasn't as good as you thought."

"I guess not."

Half an hour later he showed her a four-foot white teddy bear made of roses that he was sending to Jane, and it was so spectacular it took Paris's breath away. "How on earth did you do that?"

"I didn't. I designed it. Hiroko did the rest. Cute, don't you think?" He was proud of it, and pleased that Paris liked it too.

"It's incredible. She's going to fall in love with it." He took it back downstairs to the shop at street level and sent it off to Jane with a note, which reminded Paris that she wanted to get a baby present for her, maybe over the weekend, when she had time, if she did. She had to work one of the Valentine's Day parties, but she was free for most of the day before that. She couldn't believe how busy her life had gotten in barely more than a week. And she said as much to Anne Smythe when she called her that night when she got home. They had to do their sessions now at night or on weekends, in spite of the time difference, and Anne said she didn't mind. She was happy to hear from her, and delighted that things were going so well. They had already agreed to reduce their sessions to once a week. Paris didn't have time for more. Except, in an emergency, she knew she could always call.

She told Anne she was having lunch with Chandler the next day, and what Bix had said about him, about being a professional dater possibly.

"Keep an open mind," Anne reminded her. "You might have fun. And even if he's a 'professional dater,' as Bix says, he might be an interesting person to know. You were going to meet people, remember. You don't have to love them all. He might introduce you to a whole circle of his friends." It was a good point. She was starting from scratch, and she had known when she left Greenwich that it would be hard work. This was only the beginning.

At five minutes before noon the next day, Paris heard a roar beneath her office window, and when she looked down, she saw that it was a silver Ferrari. And seconds later she saw Chandler Freeman get out in a blazer, gray slacks, blue shirt, and yellow tie. It looked like Hermès. He looked very chic, and extremely prosperous. He rang the bell, came upstairs, and a moment later, was standing in front of her desk, with a dazzling smile.

"I'm very impressed. This is quite an office."

"Thank you. I've only worked here for about five minutes." She didn't want to take credit for it. Bix had done all the decoration himself.

"How so?"

"I moved out from Greenwich, Connecticut, less than two weeks ago. This is only my second week in the job."

"You look like you've been here forever."

"Thank you." She smiled.

"Shall we go?" he said with a wide smile. He had perfect teeth, and looked like a toothpaste ad on TV. He was an incredibly good-looking man. It was impossible not to notice, and she felt flattered somehow that he was taking her out.

She followed him down the stairs and out to his car, and seconds later the silver Ferrari roared off. "Where are we going?" she asked nervously, and he smiled at her.

"I'd like to tell you I'm kidnapping you, but I'm not. I know you're pressed for time, so we're going very nearby." He took her to a tiny Italian restaurant in a Victorian house, with a garden out back, only blocks from her office. "This is one of the city's best-kept secrets." And the owners seemed to know him well. "I go out to lunch a lot," he explained, "and I hate to get stuck inside." The weather was even warmer than the week before. Spring had arrived.

The waiter offered her a glass of wine, and she asked for iced tea instead. Chandler had a Bloody Mary, and they ordered salads and pasta for lunch. And the food was extremely good. Somewhere, halfway through lunch, as he chatted with her, she started to relax. He was actually a very interesting man, and he seemed like a nice guy.

"How long have you been divorced?" he asked her finally, as she realized she was going to be hearing this question a lot. Maybe she should hand out leaflets with all the details.

"Two months. I've been separated for nine." She didn't offer any further information. For now at least, it was none of his business. She didn't owe him any explanations.

"How long were you married?"

"Twenty-four years," she said simply, and he winced.

"Ouch. That must have hurt."

"A lot," she said, and smiled, and turned the tables on him. She wanted information too. "What about you?"

"What about me?" he asked with an evasive smile.

"Same questions. How long have you been divorced? How long were you married?" She was learning the ropes.

"I was married for twelve years. I've been divorced for fourteen."

"That's a long time," she commented, thinking about it.

"Yes, it is," he agreed.

"You've never remarried?" Maybe he was hiding one from her, but not if Bix was right.

"Nope. I haven't."

"Why not?"

"Never found the right woman, I guess." Oh shit. Maybe Bix was right. "Or maybe being single has just been too much fun till now. I was thirty-four when I got divorced. And I was pretty badly burned. My wife ran off with my best friend. It was a lousy trick. Turns out they'd been having an affair for three years before she left. Things like that happen, but it hurts like hell when they happen to you." More data. The ex-wife as supreme bitch. And slut.

"That sounds pretty rough," she said sympathetically, but he no longer looked upset. It had been a long time. Maybe too long. "Do you have kids?"

"One. My son is twenty-seven, lives in New York, and has two little girls. I'm a grandfather, which I still have trouble believing sometimes. But the girls are awfully cute. They're two and four. With another one on the way." At forty-eight and as good-looking as he was, he didn't look like a grandfather to her.

They chatted about other things then, traveling and favorite cities, languages they spoke and wished they did. Paris spoke a smattering of French. Chandler said he was fluent in Spanish. He had lived in Buenos Aires for two years as a young man. Favorite restaurants in New York. He even asked about her name, which had always seemed silly to her. Her parents had honeymooned in

Paris, and had conceived her there. So they had named her after their favorite city. He said it was exotic and looked properly amused. With a practiced hand, he kept the conversation light. He was good company, and on the way back to the office in the Ferrari, he told her he flew his own plane, with a copilot of course. It was a G4. And he offered to take her up in it sometime. He told her when he dropped her off that he'd love to see her again, maybe they could have dinner later that week, and she told him that she had to work. He just smiled, and kissed her on the cheek before he left. And then in a roar from the engine, he sped away as Paris walked up the stairs. Bix was doing sketches at his desk.

"Well?"

"I think you're right. I don't even know why I went. I don't want to date. So what's the point?"

"Practice for when you grow up. You will one day. Unless you want to be a nun."

"It's a thought."

"So?"

"He was married for twelve years, has been divorced for fourteen. And he just hasn't met the right woman to make him want to marry again. How do you like that?"

"I don't," Bix said, looking cool. After knowing her for a week, he already felt protective of her. She needed it, more than anyone he knew. And he wanted to do that for her. She was a babe in the woods. And by all rights she should still have been happily married in Greenwich, but she wasn't. Thanks to Peter. Who had Rachel. Now Bix wanted her to have someone too.

"He has one son, and two granddaughters and another one on the way. He lived in Buenos Aires for two years. And he flies his own plane. Oh, and his wife had an affair with his best friend while they were married, and ran off with him, hence the divorce. And that was about it."

"Very good." Bix smiled at her. "Did you take notes, or did you remember all that?"

"I recorded it on a device in my shoe," she said, grinning. "So what do you think? My shrink says it doesn't matter if he's a shit, he could introduce me to his friends."

"Who are probably shits too. Professional daters stick together. They hate married couples, they think they're bourgeois and dumb."

"Oh. So? Is he? A professional dater, I mean."

"Maybe. Be careful. Did he ask you out again?"

"He suggested dinner later this week. I said I had to work."

"Do you like him?"

"Sort of. He's interesting and intelligent, and very sophisticated. I just don't know if he's nice."

"Neither do I, that's what you have to watch. Give him a chance, but a very small one. Protect yourself, Paris. That's what counts."

"This is a lot of work."

"But it's worth it. Unless you want to be a nun."

"I'll give it some thought."

"The habits are ugly these days, remember that. No more Audrey Hepburn and Ingrid Bergman in flowing robes. They're short and polyester, and the hairdos suck." She laughed, shook her head, and went back to her desk. And later that afternoon Chandler sent her flowers. Two dozen red roses, with a note. "Thanks for taking the time off from work. I had a great lunch. See you soon. CF." Bixby looked at the flowers and read the note and shook his head.

"He's a pro. Nice roses though." Bixby was tough on her behalf. She sent Chandler a thank-you note and forgot about him. For the rest of the week, in anticipation of Valentine's Day, they were swamped. Every client they had wanted to send someone something creative, even if it was their mother, or their sister in Des Moines. And the romantic ones were the worst. He had to come up with some stroke of genius for each one of them, but he always did. And they still had two parties to work on.

On Thursday Chandler called again. And asked her for dinner on Saturday night.

"I'm sorry, Chandler, I can't. I have to work."

"Do you know what day that is?" he asked pointedly.

"Yes, I do. Valentine's Day. But I still have to work." If she hadn't been in this business now, she would have been trying to forget. She was glad she'd be working. She and Peter always went out to dinner, and had the year before, although he'd been seeing Rachel, she knew now. She wondered how he'd handled that. However he had at the time, he had taken care of it permanently in May. This year he'd be with Rachel.

"What time will you finish work?"

"Late. Probably around eleven." She was working a small dinner, and according to the house rule, could leave when the guests sat down. She was giving herself leeway when she said eleven. And trying to discourage him.

"I can wait until then. How about midnight supper with me?"

She hesitated a long beat, not sure what she was doing. She did not want to date. But she was talking about it to him as though she might. She didn't know what to do. He was backing her into it. And she was allowing it to happen. But there was something about him that was very appealing.

"I don't know, Chandler," she said honestly. "I don't think I'm ready for that. Valentine's Day is a big deal."

"We'll make it a small one. I understand. I've been there too."

"Why me?" she asked plaintively, and he sounded very gentle when he answered.

"Because I think you're terrific. I haven't met anyone like you in fourteen years." It was a heavy statement, and what's worse, he sounded as though he meant it. She had no idea what to say.

"You ought to go out with someone who doesn't have to work."

"I'd rather go out with you. Why don't we say midnight? We'll do something simple and not scary. And if you finish earlier, you can call me. We'll do something easy like a hamburger. No pressure. No memories. Just good friends on a silly day." He made it sound palatable, and she was tempted to accept. "Why don't you think about it, and I'll call you tomorrow. How does that sound?"

"Okay," she said weakly, somewhat under his spell. He was so reasonable and so easy and so convincing, he was hard to resist.

And although she thought about it that night, she had come to no decision. She half wanted to see him and half didn't. And when he called her on Friday morning, she was busy and distracted, and before she knew it, she'd agreed. She said she'd call him after the party, when she finished, and they would go out for hamburgers in jeans. It was the perfect solution for Valentine's Day. She didn't have to be alone, but she wasn't going to have a romantic dinner either. And that suited her just fine.

As it turned out, they sat down to dinner at nine o'clock at the dinner she was working. She left at nine-thirty, and he picked her up at ten, in jeans, as promised. She was wearing jeans and a red cashmere sweater and an old white duffle coat she'd had for years.

"You look like a Valentine, Cinderella," he said, smiling at her, as he kissed her on the cheek, and they were halfway through dinner at a quiet restaurant he'd chosen, when he pushed a small box toward her, and two cards. She didn't have anything for him.

"What's that?" she asked, looking embarrassed. From the pink and red envelopes, it was easy to see what they were. They were Valentines for her, and when she opened them, they were funny and very cute. And in the wrapped box there was a small heart-shaped silver box filled with candy conversation hearts. It was a very thoughtful gift. "Thank you, Chandler, that was very sweet. I don't have anything for you."

"You don't have to. You came to dinner with me. That's enough." He looked as though he meant it, and she was very touched. It was an easy evening. She was home at midnight, and when he walked her to her door, he kissed her chastely on the cheek.

"Thank you, it was perfect," she said, and meant it. She hadn't felt uncomfortable or pressured. And he'd been very good company.

"That's how I wanted it to be. What are you doing tomorrow? Can I talk you into a walk on the beach?" She hesitated for a moment and then nodded. "Great. I'll pick you up at two."

And when he did, they were both wearing running shoes and jeans. They spent two hours walking on the beach and Crissy Field, all the way to the Golden Gate Bridge. It was a glorious afternoon with a gentle breeze. She had worn her hair down, and he looked at her admiringly as her long blond hair flew in the wind. And when he brought her home, she invited him upstairs for a drink. She drank iced tea as usual, and he had a glass of white wine, as he admired the view.

"I love your place," he said pleasantly.

"So do I," she said, as she joined him on the couch. She was beginning to feel comfortable with him. "I can't wait for my furniture to arrive." It was due in another week.

They sat there for an hour, talking about their children, and why their marriages had gone awry. He said he had probably taken his wife for granted and been too cavalier.

"I guess I trusted her too much," he said calmly. "I just assumed I could."

"You have to be able to trust someone, Chandler."

"I don't think I have since. I guess that's why I'm not married."

"You have to trust the right person."

"Did you trust him?" he asked, looking hard at her, and she nodded. "What did you learn from that?"

"That even people you love make mistakes. People change their minds. They fall out of love. It happens, I guess. It's just bad luck that it happened to me."

"You're very naïve. Luck doesn't make things like that happen, or it would have happened to you and me too. I didn't cheat on her. You didn't cheat on him. Did you?" Paris shook her head, that was true. "So maybe the correct conclusion is that he wasn't trustworthy. My guess is that he's not as decent as you think. That wasn't an accident. He let it happen, just like my wife did. Maybe he even pursued it, with total disregard for what it would do to you. That didn't matter to him."

"I don't think it's as simple as that," she said fairly. "I think things happen, and people get tangled up in relationships they can't get out of. They get confused. And people change. Peter did. He said he was bored with me."

"Boredom is part of marriage. If you get married, you have to expect to be bored."

"Not always," she said, hearing Bix's words ring in her head. *Professional daters think married people are boring and bourgeois.* "I wasn't bored."

"Maybe you didn't know you were. I'll bet your life is a lot more interesting now," he said with a smile as he took a sip of his wine. He had very definite ideas.

"In some ways," Paris conceded. "But this isn't what I'd have chosen to do with my life. I was happy the way things were."

"I'll bet a year from now you'll be happy he left." That concept was inconceivable to her. She knew that whatever happened, she would never be happy Peter left. All she would have wanted was to stay married to him. But since she couldn't have that, she was willing to acknowledge the blessings in her new life. But even now they were second best, and she suspected they would always be.

Chandler stayed until six o'clock, and then he left. He said he was going to L.A. in his plane the next day, and he would call her when he got back. And the next morning, she had flowers from him again.

"I see Mr. Freeman is in hot pursuit," Bixby commented drily as he came into her office to go over some sketches for a wedding they were doing in June. "Having fun?"

"I think so," she said cautiously, but she wasn't sure. He was easy and pleasant and very charming, but under the surface there was something bitter and angry. He had a chip on his shoulder the size of his ex-wife.

It was Thursday before she heard from him again, and by then he was in New York. He had business there, and said he wouldn't be home till Sunday night, not that she cared. But it had been thoughtful of him to call. And the following week he called her, and asked if she'd like to go to L.A. with him, on his plane. She hesitated, but only for an instant. She had no intention of going away with him, or more specifically, sleeping with him. She wasn't ready to cross that bridge yet. And as delicately as she could, she said as much to him, and he laughed.

"I know that, silly. I was planning to get two rooms at the Bel-Air. I wanted to take you to one of the pre-Grammy parties with me. I have a friend in the music business, and he invites me to come down every year. It's quite a show. Would you like to come?"

She hesitated and then realized she could see Meg. She could have seen her anyway, if she went down on her own. But she had to admit that the party he was suggesting sounded like fun.

"I'm not sure I can get the time off from work. Let me talk to Bixby, and I'll let you know." She wasn't sure what she wanted to do about it, but she was stalling for time. And that afternoon she asked Bixby about it when she was sitting in his office working with him.

"I can spare you for a day, if that's what you want," he said generously. "Are you sure you want to go?"

"No, I'm not," she said, looking as confused as she felt. "He's a nice man, but I'm not ready to sleep with him or anyone," she admitted candidly. "He said he'd get me my own room. It might be fun. I don't know."

"Hell, Paris, why not?" Bixby said with a grin. "I'd like to go too."

"Then you go with him," Paris teased.

"Wouldn't he be surprised?" Bixby laughed. "Was he all right about your having your own room?" He was curious.

"He seemed to be," she said pensively.

"He sounds pretty smooth." It was precisely what Bixby didn't like about him. He sounded like a pro to him.

By the end of the afternoon she called Chandler, and taking a deep breath, she said she'd go with him. He said they were going to fly down Friday morning. The party he was inviting her to was that night. And fortunately, by sheer luck, Bixby didn't have any major events scheduled for that weekend. Just a small dinner party Sydney Harrington was catering for them, and she would handle that on her own. The following weekend they were doing a huge wedding, and Paris couldn't have gone to L.A.

Paris called Meg that night and told her she was coming down. She said she didn't know what their plans were for the rest of the weekend, but she was going to find time to see Meg whenever she could. She was planning to tell Chandler that too.

"Sounds pretty glamorous, Mom," Meg said, sounding pleased for her. "What's he like?"

"I don't know. Nice, I guess. He's very good-looking, and very well dressed. He talks a good game, as Bixby would say. And he's been very nice to me." But she didn't sound enthused. He wasn't Peter, and it was strange being with a new man, stranger still traveling with him to another city. She still wasn't sure she should. But he seemed to understand the ground rules, and accepted them. She was relieved that he had agreed to separate rooms. Otherwise she wouldn't have gone. And she was planning to pay for her own. She didn't want to be indebted to him. Going to the party with him and to L.A. on his plane was more than enough.

"Are you falling for him, Mom?" Meg asked, sounding concerned.

"No, I'm not. I'm not really dating him," she said, kidding herself. "We're just going out as friends."

"Does he think that's all it is?"

"I don't know what he thinks. But he's certainly clear that I'm not going to sleep with him. I think he's a gentleman, and if he's not, I'll come stay with you." Meg laughed at her mother's illusions about dating.

"You'd better take some Mace with you, in case he breaks into your room."

"I don't think he's the type. At least I hope not. If he does, I'll call the police."

"That would be nice," Meg laughed again, and then told her mother she was seeing someone new. He was the first man she'd gone out with since Peace.

"Does this one have a normal name?" her mother teased, and Meg said he did. His name was Anthony Waterston, and he was another young actor she'd met on the set. She said he was very talented, but she didn't know much about him yet.

"It's a lot of work, all this stuff, isn't it?" It reminded Paris of weeding her garden in Greenwich. Sometimes you had to look hard to decide which were the flowers and which were the weeds. And even then sometimes you weren't sure. "I'll see you sometime this weekend," Paris promised, and then she called Wim to let him know she'd be away. He was out, but she left him a message on his machine.

And that night, when she went to bed, she thought long and hard about what she'd wear. She didn't think she had anything glamorous enough for a Hollywood black tie event, and then she settled on a white silk dress Peter had loved. It had been a little racy for Greenwich, but it was the best she could do, and she didn't have time to shop. She was too busy at work. She didn't have another minute to breathe all week. Or to think about Chandler Freeman.

Chapter 18

Chandler picked Paris up in the Ferrari at eight o'clock on Friday morning, and she was ready and waiting for him. Her bag was packed, and she was carrying her dress in a garment bag. She was wearing a black pantsuit and a fur jacket, and he was wearing a dark suit. They made a handsome pair as they drove off. And an hour later, after parking his car, they were boarding his plane.

It was comfortable and sleek, and she was surprised to see that there was a hostess on board when he took his place in the pilot's seat.

She had a cup of tea and read the paper as they flew south, and by the time she was finished, they were ready to land. It had been a short flight, and she was impressed by how expertly Chandler flew the plane. He obviously took it seriously, and he paid no attention to her until they were on the ground. There was a limousine waiting for them. Meg was right. It was turning out to be a very glamorous weekend. More so than she'd thought.

They chatted in the limo on the way to the hotel, and everyone seemed to know him at the Bel-Air. They bowed and scraped, and an assistant manager escorted them to their rooms, and when she saw them, Paris was impressed. He had an apartment of sorts that he said he always had, and he had reserved a huge suite for her, which he had already paid for, in spite of her objections. He said he wanted to do that for her. In fact, he insisted on it.

"Chandler, this is wonderful," she said, looking embarrassed. It was hard to believe he was spoiling her this much. She hadn't expected anything even remotely like it.

They had lunch in the dining room, and admired the swans as they waddled by and swam in the pond. And afterward Chandler asked her if she'd like to shop on Rodeo Drive. He still had the limousine standing by, and she confessed shyly that she would.

"You don't have to come with me. I just want to browse a little bit. I never have time when I come to see Meg," she told him. But they had several hours before they needed to get ready. They didn't have to be at the Grammy party till seven. And it never took Paris long to dress. All she did was bathe, and wind her hair into a sleek knot. And she wore so little makeup, it didn't take long to put on. She was seldom late. She was always perfectly dressed, and impeccably organized. Chandler had already noticed that about her.

He seemed to be enjoying her company considerably, and Paris was finding him easy to be with. He had a nice sense of humor, and an uncomplicated nature. And he seemed to be well versed at shopping with women. He knew all the right shops, and waited patiently while she looked. He didn't even mind when she tried a few things on. And on their way back to the hotel, he astounded her by producing a small shopping bag from Chanel, and handing it to her. He had bought it while she tried on some sweaters and a blouse that were on sale. In the end, the only thing she'd bought on the entire shopping spree was a pair of very simple black shoes that she thought might be good for work. And as she held the bag he had handed her, she looked up at him with hesitation.

"Chandler, you didn't have to do that." Whatever it was, she knew that it was expensive if it was from Chanel.

"I know I didn't. I enjoy spoiling you a little. You deserve it, Paris. I want this weekend to be fun for you, and now you'll remember it whenever you see this gift." She opened the gift box cautiously as they rode back to the hotel, and she was stunned when she saw that it was a beautiful black lizard bag. And much to her amazement, it was one she had admired and walked by. She wouldn't have dared to buy it for herself, and he had noticed that, so he had bought it for her. "Chandler, my God!" she exclaimed with wide eyes when she saw it. "It's so beautiful." And it was also incredibly expensive.

"Do you like it?"

"I love it, but you shouldn't have." She turned and gave him a gentle kiss on the cheek. No one had ever done anything like that for her. She scarcely knew him, and the gesture was as generous as it was spontaneous. It was a lovely gift. But Chandler was accustomed to buying the women in his life extravagant gifts, even when they hadn't slept with him yet. And he seemed to want nothing in return. She knew the bag was going to become a prize possession, and would always remind her of him, which was precisely his intent. It was a good investment for him, and had made a major impression on her.

He had ordered a massage for her when they got back to the hotel. And he disappeared to his own rooms, to have one himself. She didn't see him again until shortly before seven. Until then, she relaxed with the massage, luxuriated in her bath, and admired the handbag he had given her again and again. She called Meg and told her about it, and her daughter sounded concerned.

"Watch out for him, Mom. If he bought you a present like that, he's going to jump your bones." Her mother laughed at the expression.

"I was afraid of that myself. But I don't think he will. He's being very proper and restrained."

"Wait till tonight," Meg said darkly, and then hurried back to work. She worried about her mother with this man. Paris had no idea what she was doing. And the guy was a big spender obviously, and something about him was beginning to suggest to Meg that he was too smooth. Unless he was madly in love with her mother and had never done this before, he sounded like a playboy of some kind to her. But as long as her mother could handle it, if she could, maybe it would be okay. Meg was no longer so sure.

Chandler appeared at Paris's door at five minutes to seven in an impeccably cut tuxedo that had been made for him in London, and he looked better than any movie star, and Paris looked terrific too. The white evening gown clung to her just enough, but not too much, and her figure looked spectacular. She had worn a little more makeup than usual, and she had rhinestone sticks in her chignon, and diamonds at her ears. As they left the hotel, she wore a white mink jacket over her dress. And as she walked, Chandler could just barely see high-heeled silver sandals with rhinestone buckles. She looked exquisite, and he was obviously proud to have her on his arm as they walked into the Beverly Hills Hotel.

The entire hotel had been taken over by his record business friend Walter Frye, who, Paris discovered as they walked in, was easily the most important man in the music business. As they entered, it seemed as if two hundred photographers took their picture.

"You look beautiful, Paris," Chandler whispered to her, as he patted her hand tucked into his arm, and they glided by the photographers. Allison Jones was just ahead of them, and she was nominated for four Grammys, the previous year's major winner, Wanda Bird, was bringing up the rear. They were both Walter's discoveries, and incredible singers. Allison was twenty-two years old, and was wearing a cream lace dress that barely covered her figure, and left little to the imagination.

It was a dazzling evening. There were eight hundred people in the room, among them every major name in the music business, singers, producers, power brokers of all kinds, and the photographers who were wending their way among them were going crazy. And in the midst of it all was Walter Frye, who was delighted to see Chandler, and smiled warmly when he saw Paris.

An hour later they all moved slowly into the dining room, and

Paris was no longer surprised to see that they were at Walter's table, and she was seated between Chandler and Stevie Wonder.

"This is quite an evening," she said to Chandler in a whisper.

"It's fun, isn't it?" he said, looking extremely comfortable.

"Yes, it is," Paris agreed, which was a vast understatement.

And as soon as the dessert had been served, the lights dimmed, and a star-studded group of performers took turns singing for the audience, including most of those nominated for Grammys. All told, they sang for nearly three hours while people shouted and rocked and sang along with them, and by the time it ended, Paris wished it would go on forever. She only wished her children could have seen it. She couldn't even begin to describe it to them. It ended long after midnight, and it was after one by the time they got back to the Bel-Air.

"Would you like a drink at the bar?" Chandler asked her.

"I'd love it," Paris agreed. She hated to end the evening. "What an incredible performance," she said, sipping a glass of champagne, while he drank brandy. "I'll never forget it."

"I thought you might enjoy it." He looked pleased, and he had enjoyed sharing it with her.

"Enjoy it? I loved it." They talked about it for another hour until the bar closed, and then he walked her back to her room, kissed her on the cheek, and said he'd see her in the morning. She had mentioned Meg to him earlier, and he had suggested to Paris that she invite her to have lunch with them. He was incredibly generous and hospitable, and acted as though he was dying to meet her. Paris had never known anyone like him. The whole experience was unforgettable, and as she walked into her room, she saw the black lizard bag again, sitting on the table. She put it on with her white gown, and looked in the mirror. She couldn't imagine anyone doing all this for her. She had no idea how to thank him.

And when she called Meg the next morning, Paris was laughing.

"What's so funny?" Meg asked, rolling over in bed with a yawn. "God, Mom, it's only nine-thirty."

"I know. But I want you to have lunch with us. You have to meet him."

"Did he propose?" Meg sounded panicked.

"No. And he didn't jump my bones either." She'd been waiting all night and since early morning to tell her.

"Did you have fun last night?"

"It was incredible." And then she told Meg all about it.

"I have to meet him."

"He said to meet us at Spago at twelve-thirty."

"I can't wait. Can I bring Anthony?"

"Does he look decent?"

"No," Meg said honestly, "but he has very good manners. And he doesn't talk about high colonics."

"I suppose that's something," Paris said gratefully, and when she met Chandler for breakfast, she warned him that Meg was bringing her current escort.

"That's fine. I'd love to meet him," he said enthusiastically, and she warned him that she couldn't be responsible for how he looked. And then she described Peace to him, and he roared with laughter.

"My son used to go out with girls like that. And then he met 'the one.' She looks like the girl next door, and he married her six months later. And now they have three babies, or almost. There's hope for us all yet," he said good-naturedly. "I just haven't been as lucky as he was. Till now." He smiled meaningfully at Paris, and she ignored it. She wasn't ready to make any commitments, and still didn't think she ever would be. And she said as much to Chandler over breakfast. She didn't want to mislead him. "I know that," he said gently. "You need time, honey. You can't go through all that you did less than a year ago and expect not to have scars. It took me years to get over what my ex-wife did to me." And Paris wasn't sure he had yet. He spoke with thinly concealed venom whenever he mentioned his ex-wife.

"I don't know that I'm ever going to be ready to get involved again," she said honestly. "I still feel like I'm married to him."

"I felt that way too, for a long time. Be patient with yourself, Paris. I am. I'm not going anywhere." She couldn't believe she'd had the good fortune to meet him. He was everything any woman could want, and all he seemed to want was to be with her, whatever the ground rules.

They sat in the garden at the Bel-Air for a little while afterward, and they arrived promptly at Spago at twelve-thirty. Meg and Anthony arrived twenty minutes later, and although Meg looked lovely, Anthony didn't. He was wearing wrinkled black cotton pants and a wrinkled T-shirt, and although Paris tried not to notice, he looked like his hair was dirty. It hung in locks over his eyes and was greasy. But he was a very handsome boy. And he was extremely polite to Chandler and Paris. He had a tattoo of a snake running down one arm, and he was wearing rather large earrings. But Chandler looked completely unaffected by his appearance, and had a very intelligent conversation with him, which was more than Paris could do. Although she had found Peace eccentric and a little zany, she took an instant dislike to Anthony. She thought he was a phony. He name-dropped constantly, and she thought he was condescending to her daughter, as though he were doing her an enormous favor just being with her. And it irritated Paris throughout lunch, so much so that she was still steaming after he and Meg left the table. He had an audition that afternoon, and had promised to drop Meg back in Malibu, and Paris promised to call her later.

"I gather you don't like him," Chandler said to her once they were alone at the table.

"Was it that obvious?" Paris looked embarrassed. She couldn't stand him.

"Not to the untrained eye. But you forget, I'm a parent. I've been through it. You just have to grit your teeth sometimes and pretend not to notice. They usually disappear pretty quickly. I think he's fairly ambitious. Sooner or later, he'll get himself latched on to someone who can help his career." And Meg was only a production assistant. Paris just hoped he didn't hurt her feelings. She didn't want Meg to get her heart broken by some young actor, and Anthony looked like just the guy to do it.

"I thought he was arrogant and pompous, and so narcissistic it's a wonder he can hold a conversation."

"Isn't that a prerequisite for an actor?" Chandler teased. "He's a bright boy. He'll probably go far. Is she madly in love with him?" She didn't look it to him.

"I hope not. The last one was weird. This one is awful."

"I'm sure you'll see lots more before it's all over. I did. I couldn't keep track of my son's dates for a while. But every time I started to panic about one of them, she vanished."

"My kids have been that way too. Or Meg has. Wim is usually a little more constant. Or at least he was before he went to college. I hate worrying about them, but I don't want them to end up with the wrong people."

"They won't. They just need to play first, and experiment a little. My guess is this boy will be gone before you know it."

"I hope so," Paris said as they left the table, and then thanked him for taking them all to lunch. She felt as though they had imposed on him somewhat, but he didn't seem to mind. In fact, he acted as though he liked it, and he said he had been delighted to meet her daughter. Chandler had all the right instincts, and endless thoughtful gestures in his repertoire.

They spent the afternoon looking at art galleries, and went to the L.A. County Museum before going back to the hotel. That night he took her to L'Orangerie for dinner, and ordered caviar for her. There was nothing he didn't do to spoil her. And by the time they got back to the hotel, Paris was happy and relaxed, and had had another wonderful evening. And this time, when he left her at her door, he kissed her long and hard on the mouth, and she didn't resist him. But he made no attempt to go further. And he looked at her with tenderness and regret when he left her.

And as she looked at herself in the mirror as she brushed her hair, she wondered what she was doing. She could feel herself drifting slowly away from Peter. Chandler was the first man she had kissed in twenty-six years other than Peter. And what was worse, she had liked it. She was almost sorry she hadn't stayed in the same room with him. And realizing that kept her nearly sleepless until morning. Although nothing dire had happened yet, she could feel her budding relationship with Chandler slipping slowly out of her control.

Chapter 19

Chandler flew her back to San Francisco at noon on Sunday, after a hearty breakfast at the Bel-Air. And she was home by two-thirty after a magical weekend.

"Now I really do feel like Cinderella," she said as he carried her bag in. "I'm going to turn into a pumpkin any minute."

"No, you won't. And if you do, I'll just spirit you away again," he said, smiling at her. "I'll call you later," he said, as he kissed her in the doorway, and she hoped no one was looking. She felt more than a little racy, having a man bring her home with a suitcase. But she didn't know who she was hiding from. She didn't know anyone in the neighborhood, and no one cared what she was doing.

And just as he had promised, he called her that evening.

"I miss you," he said softly, and Paris instantly had butterflies in her stomach. She hated to admit it, but she missed him too, more than she wanted.

"So do I," she answered.

"When am I going to see you again?" he asked hungrily. "What about tomorrow?"

"I'm working late with Bix," she said regretfully, and it was true this time. "What about Tuesday?"

"That's perfect. Would you like to see my apartment? I could cook you dinner."

"You don't have to do that. Or I can help you."

"I'd love it," he said, sounding happy, and promised to call her in the morning.

And the next day, at work, Bix was waiting for her like a stern father, and wanted a report.

"So how was it?"

"Terrific. Better than I expected. And he was a perfect gentleman."

"That's what I was afraid of," Bix said grimly.

"Why? Did you want him to rape me?" She was in frighteningly good spirits.

"No. But real men aren't perfect gentleman. They get grumpy and tired. They don't take women shopping. Which reminds me, did he?"

"Yes," she said, laughing at him, "and he bought me a Chanel handbag."

"Worse yet. When was the last time a man took you shopping and bought you a Chanel handbag? Did Peter?"

"No. He loathed shopping. He preferred root canal to shopping with me."

"Precisely. This guy is too smooth, Paris. He scares me. And real guys rip off your clothes. They're klutzes. They don't know all the right moves unless they've done that routine a lot, with a lot of women."

"I don't think he's a virgin."

"I hope not. But he sounds like a playboy to me."

"He says he hasn't met the right woman. He's been dating."

"I don't buy that. There are a lot of good women out there, dying to meet straight guys. If he wanted to, he could have found one by now."

"Maybe. From what everyone says, it's not that easy."

"For a guy like him it is. He's got a Ferrari and a plane, and a lot of money. How hard do you think it would be to find the right woman?"

"Good women don't necessarily want all those things. He's cooking me dinner tomorrow."

"I'm getting nauseous," Bix said, sitting back in his chair with a worried look.

"What's wrong with cooking me dinner?"

"Did Peter?" he asked bluntly.

"Not if he could help it." And then she looked serious for a moment. "Peter left me for another woman. How good was he in the end? Not very." It was the first time she had said that. "Chandler was in the same boat as I am. I think he's been cautious," she said fairly. It was beginning to annoy her that Bix was so suspicious of him. Chandler didn't deserve that.

"I think he's been busy. I went out with a guy like that once. He spoiled the hell out of me, and I couldn't understand it. Watches, bracelets, cashmere jackets, trips. I felt like I'd died and gone to heaven, until I figured out that he was sleeping with three other guys, and was the most promiscuous sonofabitch on the planet. He had no soul, no heart, and when he got bored with me, he wouldn't even take my phone calls. I was heartbroken until I figured it out. There was no there there. He was a player. I'm afraid that might be Chandler. Same guy, this one just likes women. Try not to sleep with him too quickly," he said, and she nodded. In a short time, she and Bixby had become amazingly close, and she loved him. Bix was smart, sensible, and he cared about her. All he wanted to do was protect her, and she appreciated it, but she thought he was wrong about Chandler.

They worked as late that night as she had expected, and the following day she left the office at six o'clock, and Chandler picked her up at seven-thirty. She didn't recognize him at first when he drove up, he was driving an old Bentley instead of the Ferrari.

"What a lovely car," she said, admiring it, and he said he almost never used it, but hated to sell it. He had thought she'd like to see it.

But his apartment, when she saw it, was even better. It was a penthouse on Russian Hill with a three-hundred-and-sixty-degree view, and a terrace that nearly made her dizzy. And everything in the apartment was either white marble, black granite, or black leather. It was very striking, and very masculine. The kitchen was a state-of-the-art wonder. And he had everything ready. Oysters on the half shell, cold lobster, and he made a delicious capellini pasta with caviar. There was nothing for her to do, as they sat down to eat at a long granite table in his kitchen. He dimmed the lights and lit candles, and played CDs by some of the artists they had seen perform at Walter Frye's party. And he poured an excellent French white Bordeaux for her. The dinner was far more elegant than anything she would have cooked for him, and she thoroughly enjoyed it.

Afterward they sat in his living room in front of the fire, admiring the view. It was chilly outside, and nice being next to him by the fire. And in a little while, they were kissing. She had only known him for three weeks, but in spite of all her reservations, and Bix's warnings, she knew she was falling for him. She could no longer remember why this was supposed to be such a bad idea, or why she had felt such eternal loyalty to Peter. What difference did it make? He was married to Rachel. She owed him nothing, she told herself, as Chandler continued to kiss her, and ran a hand slowly up her leg, but he was cautious, and didn't want to upset her. He stopped and looked at her, and she melted into his arms, and it seemed like hours later, but suddenly she was lying next to him in bed, and she had her clothes off.

"Paris, I don't want to do this unless you want to," he said gently.

"I want to," she whispered, as he nestled his head against her, where he found her breasts and caressed them. Their bodies seemed to mesh and blend, and he took her expertly and carefully. He gave her pleasures that even Peter had never thought of. She spent the night with him, and they made love again in the morning. Peter had never done that. She felt an odd disloyalty when she got up, but when she sat across the breakfast table from Chandler, she felt better. He looked happy and at peace, and he was smiling at her. This wasn't a dream, it was real.

"That was incredible," he said, and then teased her when she blushed. It was better than she had ever expected.

"Yes, it was," she said, drinking the orange juice he gave her.

He took her home in time to change for work, and promised to call her later. Which he did, and then took her for lunch at their favorite Italian restaurant with the garden. She felt completely under his spell, and this time she didn't say anything to Bix. It was none of his business. The night she had spent with Chandler had changed things. Her loyalty was to him now. They had a relationship.

And she felt awkward with him at lunch, as she struggled to ask him an unfamiliar question, but this was her first venture into new waters. And she wanted to act responsibly. "I . . . should we . . . are we supposed to get an AIDS test before we go any further?" She was grateful that he had used protection, but she knew that if they were going to stop using it, at least some of the time, they should probably get tested. That seemed to be what people did, according to Meg at least.

"As long as we use protection, we don't need to," he said, smiling at her, and she nodded. She didn't want to press the matter further. It was too awkward. And his answer seemed reasonable to her. Besides, it solved the issue of birth control for her.

He picked her up at her house that night after work, and she spent the night in his apartment again, and the next day Meg called her at the office, sounding worried.

"Mom, are you okay? I called you last night and the night before, really late, and you were out. Were you working?"

"No . . . I . . . I was out with Chandler."

"Did something happen?"

"No, of course not. Everything's fine, sweetheart. We were just out late, talking."

"Well, be careful. Don't fall for him too quickly." She sounded like Bix, but Paris thanked her and went back to her office. Poor thing, everyone was so suspicious of him, and he was so good to her. She couldn't remember being this happy. She wanted to call Anne and tell her about it, but she didn't have time until the weekend. They had two weddings on Saturday, and with the time difference, she never called her. And Paris worked so late, she didn't see Chandler all weekend. One wedding went until two-thirty, and the other till after four in the morning, and she didn't want to call and wake him. Weddings were different than dinner parties, a lot more could go wrong. They needed to keep track of each minute detail, and they always stayed to supervise till the bitter end. Chandler said he understood, and she saw him Sunday night for dinner. She wanted him to meet Wim, but when she called him in the dorm, he said he was busy. So she and Chandler ate alone.

They spent a quiet evening at her house watching videos, and this time she cooked him dinner. She made a big bowl of pasta and a salad, far simpler fare than he served, but the wine was good. And after they made love, he went back to his apartment. He said he had an early meeting the next day.

And for the next three weeks, they lived in their own cozy world. Whenever she wasn't working, she was with him. She spent the night at his place more frequently than she did in her own house. But the one thing she no longer was was lonely. She felt as though she were living a fairy-tale existence. She had never known anyone like him. He was attentive to her every need, kind, thoughtful, and funny. And he continued to be very conscientious about using protection. She suggested to him one day that they get AIDS tests, to reassure each other, so they no longer had to, when it was safe for her. But he said it was just as easy to use condoms. And thinking about it later that day somehow set off a bell in her head, and that night she asked him about it again.

"If we get AIDS tests, we don't have to use anything," she said cautiously. It seemed so much simpler to her.

"It's always a good idea to use protection," he said wisely, as he came back from the bathroom and snuggled next to her again. He was in extraordinarily good shape, and had a splendid body. And his sexual skills were beyond impressive. But in spite of that she decided to ask him the question that had popped into her mind that afternoon, although she already knew the answer, or assumed she did.

She propped herself up on one elbow in bed and smiled at him. "You don't sleep with anyone else, do you? Now, I mean, since we've been together."

He looked at her and smiled, and traced her nipples with one finger, which aroused her. "That's a pretty big question."

"I assume it has a simple answer," she said softly. "I'm assuming that this is an exclusive arrangement." She had heard Meg use the term.

"*Exclusive* is a big word," he said, as he lay on his back and stared at the ceiling without expression.

"What does that mean?" She could feel a knot form in her stomach.

"I haven't slept with anyone else since I've been with you," he said, as he looked at her, and she watched him. "But it could happen. It's awfully early in the day for us to make a commitment to each other."

"I don't expect a commitment," she said quietly. "But I do expect to be exclusive, or monogamous, or whatever you want to call it."

"As long as we use condoms, that's not a problem. I'm not going to put you at risk, Paris, I wouldn't do that."

"But you're not going to be monogamous either?"

"I can't promise you that. I don't want to lie to you. We're adults. Anything can happen."

"Are you reserving the right to see other women?" Paris looked stunned. It hadn't even occurred to her that he might, or that he would want to.

"You don't leave me time for that," he said lightly. But he traveled. And there were plenty of nights when she had to work. She had never expected his answer, and she looked deeply upset as she sat up in bed and looked down at him, lying next to her. It had never dawned on her until then that this was not an exclusive arrangement. "You never said that was an issue for you," he said, looking somewhat irritated that the subject had come up.

"I didn't think I had to. I just assumed that was what you wanted too. You said this was special and different."

"It is special. But I'm not going to be put on a leash. We're not married. And we both know how little that means."

"No, I don't," she said plaintively. "I don't know anything of the sort. I was faithful to my husband, and he was faithful to me for more than twenty years of our marriage. And that's beside the point." She looked sad suddenly. Reality had hit her. This wasn't marriage—it was dating. "I don't want to share you."

"You don't own me," he said, sounding angry.

"I don't know that I want to. But I do want to know that while you're sleeping with me, however long that is, you won't sleep with other people."

"It's premature in the relationship to do that, Paris. We're adults, we're free. You might meet someone you want to sleep with."

"Not if I'm involved with you, and if that happens, you'll be the first to know." She was sitting ramrod straight now.

"That's noble of you," he said practically, "but I'm not going to make you the same promise. Things happen, even if you don't plan them."

"Would you tell me afterward if it did?"

"Not necessarily. I don't owe you that. Not after six weeks. In six months maybe, depending on how things go between us. But that's a long way off. We're not there yet."

"Is there a rule book on this? Because if there is, I want to see it. Are there timetables about what happens when, like what happens at six weeks, and then what you can expect at three months, or six, or a year? Who makes these rules?"

"It depends on the arrangement between two people," he said comfortably. He was not going to let her pressure him. It bothered him that she even tried to. Exclusivity was not part of the deal. For him.

"And what arrangement do we have?" Paris asked, looking straight at him.

"None officially for the moment. We're having a good time, aren't we? What more do we need than that?" Paris didn't say a word as she got out of bed and looked over her shoulder at him.

"I need a lot more. I need to know that I'm the only woman in your life, or in your bed at least, for the moment."

"That's not reasonable," he said simply.

"I think it is. I think this is a sad way for people to live. Life is about integrity and caring and commitment, not just playing and having sex."

"Do you have fun with me?" he asked as he rolled over on his side and watched her. She was dressing.

"Yes, I do. But life is about more than just fun too."

"Then give it a chance to get there. It's too early to be talking about things like this. Paris, don't spoil it."

"You just did." But she had to admit, he was honest at least. But not much else.

"If you leave it alone, we might get there eventually, but you can't force it."

"And while we're 'getting there,' you want to sleep with other people?"

"I may never do it. I haven't yet. But yes, I could."

"I don't want to worry about it, and I would. I would always wonder. Now that I know how you feel about it, I'm not sure I would ever trust you. How could I? Any more than you could trust me. You'd never know what I was doing. Except with me, you would know. That's the difference."

"I don't expect that of you. Those are the ground rules."

"What? Every man for himself, and screw whoever you want to? How pathetic. And how sad actually. I want more than that. I want love and integrity between two people."

"I've never lied to you. And I wouldn't."

"No," she said sadly, "you just wouldn't tell me. Would you?" He didn't answer, and she stood and looked at him for a long moment. "If you ever feel differently about this, call me." She wanted to say, if you ever grow up and decide to stop playing. "This has been wonderful. But it wouldn't be if I knew you were cheating on me. And to me, that's what it would be. I'm a very old-fashioned person."

"You just want to be married, and control me, " he said cynically. "And if you're not married, you want to pretend you are. Well, you're not. You might as well enjoy it. And you're not going to control me." It was the ultimate crime to him, a capital offense.

"I was enjoying it . . . for a minute . . . you spoiled it."

"You're wasting your time," he said, looking annoyed, as he got up and stood naked before her. "People don't play by those rules anymore. They went out with the Dark Ages."

"Maybe so," she said quietly, "but if so, I'm going out with them. Thanks for everything," she said, and then walked out and closed the door. She stood in the hall for a minute, and then rang for the elevator. Part of her hoped that he would open the door and beg her to come back. And the rest of her knew that would never happen. She had learned a painful lesson. And whatever the ground rules were in Chandler Freeman's version of modern dating, Paris knew they weren't for her, and neither was he. Bixby had been right.

Chapter 20

It was the third week in March when she stopped seeing Chandler, and a full two weeks later before Bix questioned her about it. He had the feeling somehow that he was no longer calling. She had been quiet for a few days, and then seemed to be keeping unusually busy. He finally asked her about it on an evening they were working late, planning a wedding.

"Have I missed something? Or is Chandler no longer calling?"

She hesitated for a moment, and then nodded. "That would be correct. He isn't."

"Did you two have a falling out? Or did you get tired of caviar and Ferraris?" He had a way with words, and she smiled at him. She had been upset for the first week, and she was beginning to feel better. But as well as hurt, she felt extremely foolish. She should have known better, but she hadn't. And he had never called her. He had vanished in a puff of smoke. She had learned something, but she hadn't enjoyed it. And she hated to admit it, but she missed him. He had been wonderful to her, and if nothing else, the sex had been terrific. For the first time in a year, she had felt like a woman, instead of a reject. In that sense, he had been good for her, but he had chipped away at a piece of her. Worse yet, she had given it to him.

"It didn't work out. I made a mistake." She hesitated for a moment, and then she told Bix about it.

"The little shit. How sleazy."

"Was it?" she asked Bix honestly. He was eight years younger than she, but he was far more experienced, and she trusted his judgment. She felt like she was in a time warp and had come from another world. And in some ways, she had.

"Yes, it was sleazy," Bix confirmed to her. "And not very nice. That's a lot of bullshit. But there are plenty of people out there who behave like him. Men and women. It's not exclusive to either sex. They're just not very nice people. And they don't play by very nice rules. You shouldn't have to ask if a relationship is exclusive. Decent people don't want to sleep with several people at the same time. I didn't. Steven didn't. But some of the people I dated were just like Chandler. They're still out there getting laid. So what? The sad thing is they're not getting loved, and most of them aren't capable of loving anyone, not even themselves."

"I always feel like everyone else has the instruction manual, and I don't. It made sense to him, and he was very convincing. The only problem was I wasn't convinced. I would hate myself if I lived like that. The one thing it taught me is that I don't ever want to sleep with someone again who doesn't love me. I thought he did. Or I thought he was falling in love with me, and I was falling in love with him. I don't think it was love. I think it was lust. And look what I got."

"You got a hell of a nice handbag out of it," he reminded her, and she laughed.

"Yeah, I did. That's a hell of a trade. My integrity for a purse."

"You didn't sacrifice your integrity. You didn't know what was going on."

"I thought I did. I assumed, that was the mistake."

"Well, you won't do it again. And it broke the ice. You lost your virginity. Now you can go out there and find a nice guy." Bix smiled at her. He admired her honesty, and was sorry Chandler had been such a horse's ass, but he wasn't surprised.

"How many frogs am I going to have to kiss first?" she asked, looking worried. She seriously questioned her own judgment.

"A few. We all did. If you get warts on your lips, you can always get them taken off."

"I'm not sure I have the courage to do a lot of this. It really hurts," she said honestly.

"Yes, it does, and it's depressing as hell. Dating is the shits."

"Thank you, Peter," she said, sounding bitter for the first time. "I can't believe he condemned me to this." Bix nodded. That was the way it worked. One person walked off with someone else, and the other guy got tossed into the pit, and had to survive the snakes. It wasn't much fun. "I should hate him for doing this to me, but I'm not sure I do yet, or ever will. I just hope I don't miss him for the rest of my life. I still do every goddamned day," she said, with tears in her eyes. "And I can't believe that at my age, I have to go out there like some dumb kid and date. How disgusting is that? And pathetic."

"It's not pathetic. It's just the way it is. And even if a relationship works, sooner or later, somebody dies, and the other one is left alone, and has to start again. It's rotten, but that's life."

"Like Steven," she said solemnly, thinking of Bix's partner whose lover had died nine years before. "But he got lucky." She smiled at her friend. She felt as though they had been friends for years, instead of months. "He found you."

"Nothing's perfect," he said cryptically, and she looked at him, wondering if they had had a fight too.

"Is something wrong?" She wanted to be there for him too, as he was for her. He had been a good friend since they'd met.

"Could be, someday. Not yet."

"What does that mean?"

"It means no one comes out unscathed. Steven's partner died of AIDS. And he's HIV positive. It may not hit him for years, or ever turn into full-blown AIDS. But it could at some point. I knew it going in. I figured however long we had would be worth it in the end.

And it has been. I don't regret a minute I've spent with him. I just want him to live forever." There were tears in his eyes, and hers, when she came to give him a hug. They held each other for a long moment, and he smiled at her through tears. "I love him so damn much, he is such a wonderful man."

"So are you," she said with a lump in her throat. Life was definitely not fair.

"You know, if I were ever attracted to women, which I'm not, thank God, men are complicated enough thanks a lot . . . you would be my first choice."

"Should I consider that a proposal?" she teased, as she smiled through her tears.

"Absolutely . . . but not exclusively . . . sorry, I'd still have to sleep with boys . . . and I wouldn't tell you about it . . . but you could definitely assume we're not exclusive. Would that do?"

"Where do I sign up?"

They both laughed, and Bix shook his head. He liked talking to her. She felt almost like a sister to him. "I told you Chandler was no good."

"I knew you'd say that eventually. But he talked such a good game. He told me he hadn't felt this way in fourteen years. What was that all about?"

"Snowing you. Guys like that say anything that works. When you meet the real thing, you'll know it. He wasn't."

"Apparently."

They wrapped up for the night, and felt closer to each other for the admissions they'd made, she about her mistake in getting involved with Chandler, and he about Steven having HIV. It had lightened some of the burden for him, as well as for her. And when Paris got home, she called Meg. And much to her mother's chagrin, Meg was in tears.

"What happened? Did you and Anthony have a fight?"

"I guess you could call it that. I found out that he's seeing some other girl. She's not even a girl. She's a woman. She's some big producer, and he's been sleeping with her for weeks." His ambition had gotten him in the end. Another one with no integrity. But in his case, Paris wasn't surprised, nor was Meg. She had known who and what he was. She just hoped he would hang around for a while. He had lasted about as long as Chandler—six weeks.

"I'm sorry, sweetheart. Chandler is out of the picture too." And then she had an idea. "Do you want to come home this weekend?" Her furniture had arrived the month before, and it felt like home to her now. The house was looking great.

"What happened with Chandler?" Meg asked as she blew her nose.

"Same idea. I didn't ask if we were exclusive. I didn't know I was supposed to."

"That happened to me in college," Meg said wisely. "You always have to ask."

"How come no one ever told me?"

"You didn't need to know. Now you do. Next time, ask. And if they say no, hit the door. In fact, make it a deal breaker going in."

"Will you negotiate my next contract for me?" Paris teased her.

"Sure." And then Meg sighed. "Doesn't this just suck? I wonder if I'm ever going to meet anyone decent. Probably not down here." She sounded discouraged, even at twenty-four. That wasn't good news to Paris. She was turning forty-seven in May.

"They don't seem to be much better here."

"Or anywhere else. My friends in New York meet the same guys. They're all players or liars, or commitment phobics. And when you meet a really nice guy, he tells you he's gay. I give up."

"Not at your age. The right one will come along, for you, if not for me. I'm not sure I care. I'm too old."

"Don't be stupid, Mom. You're still young. And you look great. Maybe I will come home this weekend. I'm depressed."

"Me too. We can sit in bed and eat ice cream together, and watch TV."

"I can't wait."

Paris picked her up at the airport on Friday night, and she didn't have to work all weekend. They did exactly what they said they were going to do. They sat in bed and hugged each other, and watched old movies on TV. Neither of them got dressed or combed their hair, or put on makeup, and they loved it, and Wim came over for lunch on Sunday, and looked startled when he saw them both. Fortunately, he had come alone.

"Are you two sick?" he asked, surprised. "You look like shit," he told his sister.

"I know," she said, grinning at him. She had had a great weekend hanging out with their mother.

"We had a mental health weekend," Paris explained.

"What's that?"

"We watched old movies and cried and stayed in bed, and bashed boys. My boyfriend cheated on me." Meg gave him the details.

"That's a bummer," he said sympathetically.

"What about you?" Meg asked, as Paris handed each of them a cup of soup, and sat down on the couch. She loved being with them. "Are you going out with any cute girls?"

"Dozens of them," he said proudly. "We had a contest in the dorm, to see how many of them we could each get. I had twelve in two weeks," he said, looking innocent, and his sister looked like she was going to throw something at him.

"You are a pig. That is the most disgusting thing I've ever heard. Christ, with all the shit guys loose in the world, we don't need you to turn into one too. Get real."

"What do you expect me to do? Get married freshman year? I'm a kid." He was all innocence and good humor.

"Then be a decent one, for God's sake," Meg scolded him, as Paris approved. "Be a nice guy, who treats women with kindness and respect. The world needs more nice guys like you."

"I don't want to be a nice guy yet. I want to have some fun."

"Not at someone else's expense, I hope, Wim," Paris chided him.

"People have a responsibility to each other, to treat each other well."

"Yeah, I know. But sometimes you just have to be a little funky. You can't be responsible all the time."

"Yes, you can," his sister insisted. "Start now. You're nearly nineteen years old." His birthday was two days after his mother's in May. "It's never too early to be a decent man. I'm counting on you, Wim."

"Do I have to?" he asked, as he finished his soup. His mother and sister both seemed to be in a weird mood.

"Yes, you do," Paris said. "Because if you aren't, you're going to hurt someone one day." And in spite of herself, she was thinking of their father as she said it. It went over Wim's head, but Meg understood.

Chapter 21

Paris didn't even think about dating after she broke up with Chandler. As May rolled around, they had a thousand details to take care of for the weddings they were doing in June. There were seven. And Meg flew up for the night to celebrate her birthday with her, and then flew back on a six A.M. plane. It was a sweet thing to do. Bix had given her a cake in the office, and a lovely turquoise cashmere stole. He said it would look fabulous on a black dress. And two days later she drove over to Berkeley to celebrate Wim's birthday with him. It was a busy month.

But the anniversary of the day Peter had left her was a hard one for her. She woke up with a bleak feeling, and remembered instantly what date it was. She was quiet and solemn all day. Bix asked her about it finally, and she told him what it was. And when she got home from work, she went to bed and cried. A lot of good things had happened to her in the last year, but if anyone had asked, or given her a magic wand, all she would have wanted, in an instant, was to have Peter back. No questions asked. Her life was forever changed, and not always for the best. But some nice things had happened too. The move to San Francisco, the house she was living in, and the job that had been her salvation, thanks to Bix, his friendship and Steven's. There were a lot of things she was grateful for. But she still missed Peter terribly, and was beginning to suspect she always would. It was just the way it was. She no longer expected anyone to fill that void, and didn't imagine that they could. She was relieved when she fell asleep finally, and the hideous day was over at last.

It was a few days afterward when Sydney Harrington called. She'd had an idea. She had an old friend coming into town, and she wanted to give a little dinner party for him. But her real reason for calling was that she said she wanted to introduce him to Paris first. He lived in Santa Fe, and was an artist. Sydney said he was a lovely man, and if nothing else, Paris would enjoy him. He was a sculptor, and worked in clay.

Paris tried to be polite about it, but she was noticeably vague. And finally, after Sydney rhapsodized endlessly, she agreed to meet them for lunch. She felt she owed Sydney one for recommending her for the job nearly four months before. And Sydney was a sensible, intelligent woman, with a fine mind, sound judgment, and good taste. How bad could her friend be?

Paris mentioned it to Bix that afternoon, and he laughed and rolled his eyes.

"Do you know something I don't?" she asked, looking worried.

"No. But you know how I feel about blind dates. One of my favorites was the eighty-two-year-old man who was dropped off for lunch with me by his nurse. I was twenty-six at the time, and the friend who'd set me up thought I would put a little spark back in his life. I would have, except the poor old guy just sat there and drooled. He could hardly talk, and I burst into tears when I left. But there were others that were worse."

"You're not encouraging me," Paris said, looking unnerved. "I couldn't get out of it. Sydney twisted my arm. He's an old friend of hers."

"We're all blind about our friends. Where does this guy live?"

"Santa Fe. He's an artist."

"Forget it. He's geographically undesirable. What are you going to do with a guy in Santa Fe, even if he's great?"

"How did I get myself into this?" Paris complained. "Three months ago I said I'd never date. Now I've become cannon fodder for visiting artists, and God knows who else. What am I going to do?"

"Go to lunch with the guy. It'll make Sydney happy. And we're going to kill her in June with all these weddings." She was catering five of them, and making a hell of a lot of money.

But when the day of the blind date came, Paris was tired and in a rotten mood. Her blow dryer had short-circuited and nearly set the house on fire. Her car had broken down on the way to work. And she was coming down with a cold.

"Can't I just commit suicide and forget lunch?" she asked Bix. She had waited an hour for AAA. They'd had an emergency on the bridge.

"No. You promised Sydney. Be nice."

"You go, and tell him you're me."

"That would be cute." He laughed at her. "You got yourself into this, now go play."

They had agreed to meet at a Mexican restaurant, which was four blocks away, and Paris didn't even like Mexican food. And when she got there Sydney was waiting at a table. Her friend was parking the car. He must have parked it in another county, because it was another half-hour before he showed up. And when he came through the door wearing an Indian poncho and a cowboy hat, he seemed to be staggering, and Paris thought he was drunk. Sydney was quick to explain.

"He has a problem with his ears. It affects his balance. He's a really great guy." Paris smiled wanly as he approached, and he smiled at her hesitantly and sat down. He took the cowboy hat off and set it down on a chair, and as he did, Paris couldn't help noticing that he looked like he had ten years of clay under his nails. But there was no denying, he was an interesting-looking man. He looked almost Native American himself, but said he wasn't when she asked. He said he hated them, and they were the scourge of Santa Fe.

"They're all drunks," he said, as Paris recoiled. And after that he went on a tirade about blacks. He somehow forgot to mention Jews. He managed to make racial slurs on just about everyone else, including their Mexican waiter, which the man heard, and he turned around to give all three of them an evil look. Paris was sure he would spit in their food, and she didn't blame him a bit.

"So, Sydney tells me you're an artist," Paris managed to say sweetly, trying not to worry about the waiter and their food. But she had to get through this somehow. It was not going to be easy, and all respect for Sydney's judgment had vanished when the man appeared.

"I brought you some pictures of my work," he said proudly. His name was William Weinstein, which may have explained why he left Jews off his hate list. He had been born in Brooklyn, and moved to Santa Fe ten years before. He took an envelope out of his pocket, rifled through some pictures, and handed them to Paris. They were ten-foot phallic symbols made of clay. The man had penises on the brain.

"It's very interesting work," Paris said, pretending to be impressed. "Do you use live models?" she asked more in jest, and he nodded.

"Actually, I use my own." He thought that hysterically funny and laughed so hard he almost coughed himself to death. Along with the clay under his nails, enough of it to create another sculpture, his fingers were stained with nicotine. "Do you like to ride?"

"Yes, but I haven't in a long time. Do you?"

"Yes, I do. I have a ranch, you ought to come down. We have no electricity and no plumbing. It's a two-day ride to my ranch."

"That must make it very hard to get in or out."

"I like it that way," Bill said. "My wife hated it. She wanted to go back to New York. She died last year." Paris nodded, paralyzed with astonishment that Sydney had wanted her to meet him. She didn't know what to say.

"I'm sorry about your wife."

"So am I. We were married for nearly fifty years. I'm seventy-three." And with that, mercifully, their food arrived. Paris had ordered a quesadilla, which was as bland as she could get. The artist had ordered some evil-looking concoction covered with a mountain of beans, which he seemed to like and said he ate almost every day. "Beans are the best thing you can eat. Healthiest food there is. Even if they do make you fart. Do you like beans?" Paris made a choking sound, and Sydney seemed not to notice. She said he had been a friend of her father's, who had also been an artist, and had had a great fondness for Bill's wife. Paris couldn't even imagine what the poor woman's life had been like, trapped on a ranch with him. She could only assume she had committed suicide, as her only avenue of escape. And as she thought about it, Paris excused herself, and went to the ladies' room. And as soon as she got there, she locked the door and reached for her cell phone. She got Bix at the office.

"Is he cute?"

"If you don't get me out of here, I may have to kill Sydney before the end of lunch. Or myself."

"Not cute, I guess."

"Beyond belief. He's a Neanderthal in a cowboy costume, who makes ten-foot sculptures of his dick."

"Listen, if his dick is that big, it might be worth going to Santa Fe. I might even come with you."

"Will you shut up? Call me in five minutes. I'm going to tell them you have an emergency at the office."

"What kind of emergency?" He sounded vastly amused. Paris wasn't.

"I don't care what kind of emergency. The emergency is this goddamn lunch."

"You're being very expressive. Did he show you pictures of his dick?"

"More or less. The sculptures are the worst thing I've ever seen."

"Don't be such an art critic. Maybe he's a nice guy."

"Look, he's worse than your drooler. Does that paint a picture for you?" She was getting more desperate by the minute.

"He can't be." Bix sounded skeptical. "That was the worst blind date I ever had."

"So is this. Now call me on my cell phone in five minutes."

"Okay, okay, I'll call you. But you'd better think up a good emergency. Sydney's no fool. She'll see right through it."

"Sydney is a total fool if she wanted me to meet this guy. In fact, she must be psychotic. Maybe she hates me."

"She doesn't hate you. She told me last week how much she likes you. And Paris?"

"What?" She was ready to kill someone. Bix if need be.

"Bring me a picture of his dick."

"Just call me . . . I mean it! Or I quit."

She went back to the table with fresh lipstick on, and the artist looked up from his lunch. "You look nice with lipstick. It's a good color."

"Thank you," she said, smiling at him, and as she started eating again, her phone rang.

"I hate those things," he commented as she answered it, and she immediately frowned. It was Bix, saying every lewd thing he could think of over her phone.

"You did *what*?" she said, looking horrified, as she glanced at Sydney with concern. "Oh Bix, how awful. I'm so sorry . . . now? I . . . well, I'm at lunch with Sydney and her friend . . . oh all right, all right, calm down . . . I'll be back in five minutes. Don't try to move till I get back." She clicked off the phone, and looked at Sydney with distress.

"What happened?" She looked worried too.

"It's Bix. You know what a wimp he is." She glanced over at Bill with a smile, to create a little mischief before she left. "He's gay," she explained.

"I hate fags," he said, and burped.

"I thought you might say that." She turned back to Sydney then. "He threw his back out."

"I didn't know he had a bad back." She looked instantly sympathetic, because Paris knew she had a bad back herself, and wore a brace when she worked.

"He's on the floor and can't even move. He needs me to get him to the chiropractor. He says if I don't come back now, he'll call 911."

"I know just how he feels. I have a herniated disk, and when it acts up, I can't walk for weeks. Do you want us to come too?"

"Don't worry. I can manage him. But I've got to get back."

"All fags should be shot," the artist declared, and then burped again.

"I'm so sorry to run," she apologized to them both, and then shook Bill's hand. "Have a wonderful time while you're here. I enjoyed meeting you very much. And good luck with your work."

"You mean with my dick?" He laughed out loud, and then coughed.

"Absolutely. Good luck with your dick. 'Bye, Syd. Thanks for lunch." She waved and ran out the door, fuming all the way back, and when she got to the office, Bix was waiting for her with a grin.

"So where is it?"

"Where is what? I may have to kill someone I'm so mad."

"My picture of his dick."

"Don't even talk to me. Ever again. I'm never speaking to you or Sydney. For the rest of my life. The guy was a total nutcase. And for your information, he hates fags, and thinks they should all be shot. But he hates blacks and Native Americans too."

"I love this guy. What did he look like?"

"A zombie. He lives on a ranch with no electricity or plumbing."

"No wonder he makes ten-foot sculptures of his dick. The poor bastard has nothing else to do."

"Don't talk to me. Just don't talk to me. Ever again. And I am never, ever, never for the rest of my whole goddamned life going on a blind date again."

"Yeah, yeah, I know," Bix said, leaning back in his chair, laughing at her. "I said that too. And you know what? I did. And so will you."

"Fuck you," she said, marched into her office, and slammed the door so loudly the bookkeeper came out of her cubbyhole and looked around with a frightened expression.

"Is Paris all right?"

"She's fine," he said, still laughing. "She just had a blind date."

"It didn't work out?" she asked, looking sympathetic, and Bix grinned widely and shook his head.

"I think not, Mrs. Simpson. I think not. And that is the story of blind dates."

Chapter 22

Paris and Bix were enormously busy in May, and managed to survive all seven weddings in June, much to their own amazement. Paris had never worked as hard in her life, and Bix said he hadn't either. But all of the weddings were gorgeous, all the brides ecstatic, all the mothers proud, and all the fathers paid the relatively astronomical bills. It was a great month for Bixby Mason, Inc. And the weekend after the last wedding, Meg came up from L.A. It was their only moment of respite, since they were doing two mammoth Fourth of July parties on the following weekend.

They were relaxing quietly in Paris's garden, talking about work, and life, and Wim's trip to Europe. He had left with friends the day before, when Meg turned to her mother cautiously, and seemed to be weighing something. And Paris saw it.

"What are you chewing on?" Paris asked her. "What's up?"

"I wanted to ask you something, but I wasn't sure how."

"Uh-oh. Sounds important. Someone new in your life?"

"Nope." Neither of them had dated in two months. And Paris was emphatic that she didn't want to. The blind date Sydney had set up had been the icing on the cake. But she knew Meg would meet someone at some point, and she hoped she would. "I ran into a friend from Vassar the other day. I haven't seen her in a while.

She's married and having a baby, which seems weird, but she also told me a sad story. I haven't seen her since we graduated, and her mother was very sick then. Apparently she died that July. She's been gone for two years, breast cancer, I think. I didn't want to ask." Paris was trying to figure out where Meg was going with all this, she couldn't see what she could do to help. Or maybe the girl needed a motherly figure to talk to, especially now that she was pregnant. And if so, Paris was willing.

"How's she doing?" Paris sounded concerned.

"She seemed okay. She's a very strong girl. And she married a very nice guy. I had a crush on him myself." She smiled at the memory, and then turned to her mother with serious eyes. "Anyway, she says her father's doing fine, but he's lonely. I just wondered if . . . well . . . actually, I met him a few times, and he's a really nice man. I think you'd like him, Mom."

"Oh, for God's sake . . . Meg, don't start. I told you, I'm not going out anymore." She sounded not only firm, but emphatic. Chandler Freeman and the sculptor from Santa Fe had been enough to last a lifetime, or at least several years. Paris was no longer interested in dating.

"Mom, that's silly. You're forty-seven years old. You can't just quit for the rest of your life, and give up. That's not right."

"It's extremely right for me. I don't need a man in my life. And furthermore, I don't want one." The truth was she did, on both counts, but it was just too damned hard to find one. And the only one she'd ever wanted was gone.

"What if you're passing up the opportunity of a lifetime? He's a banker, and an extremely decent person. He's not some kind of swinging singles wild man."

"How do you know?"

"Because I've met him," Meg insisted. "And he's even handsome."

"I don't care. You haven't dated him. Men turn into sociopaths when they date."

"No, they don't. Some are just weirder than others. Like Peace." Paris grinned, and Meg laughed.

"Exactly. How do you know this man isn't Peace's father?"

"Trust me. He looks like Dad. Same type. Shirt, tie, pin-striped suit, good haircut, nice manners, polite, smart, and he's a good father. Everything you like."

"I'm not doing this, Meg."

"Yes, you are," her daughter said with a wicked smile.

"No, I'm not."

"The hell you aren't. I told her we'd have dinner with them tonight. She was coming home for the weekend too, to see her dad."

"You *what*? I can't believe you did that! Meg, I won't!"

"You have to, or you'll make a liar out of me. This is how nice people meet. They get fixed up. This is what parents used to do, now kids do it, they introduce their divorced parents to new mates." It sounded sensible to Meg.

"I don't intend to 'mate' with this man." Paris was incensed, but Meg wouldn't budge an inch, and Paris didn't want to embarrass her, so under great protest, in the end, she agreed. "I should have my head examined," she muttered as they drove downtown. They were having dinner at a steakhouse Meg's friend had suggested. His name was Jim Thompson, and apparently he liked steak. At least he wasn't a vegan. And Paris intended to make it the shortest evening possible. She had worn a grim black suit, her hair in a ponytail, and no makeup.

"Can't you at least try a little bit?" Meg had complained while she watched her dress. "You look like a funeral director, Mom."

"Good. Then he won't want to see me again."

"You're not helping things," Meg chided her.

"I don't intend to."

"This is how a lot of women meet their second husbands."

"I don't want a second husband. I haven't gotten over my first one. And I am positively allergic to blind dates."

"I know. I remember the last one. He must have been an exception."

"No, he wasn't. Some of Bix's stories are worse," she muttered darkly, and on the way downtown, Paris sank into a sullen silence.

Both Thompsons were there when they got to the restaurant. Jim was a tall, thin, gray-haired man with a serious face, in gray slacks and a blazer. He was with his very pretty, very pregnant daughter, who was Meg's age. Her name was Sally, and Paris remembered her as soon as she saw her. She didn't even let herself look at Jim, until they sat down. There was something very kind and decent looking about him, Paris had to admit, and she thought he had beautiful, sad eyes. You could tell that something terrible had happened to him, just as it had to her, but you could also tell that he was a very nice man. And without meaning to, Paris felt herself feeling sorry for him. And halfway through dinner, they started to talk. They spoke quietly while the girls caught up on old times, and laughed about their friends. And all the while, Jim was telling her about when his wife died. And before she knew it, she was telling him about Peter leaving. They were trading tragedies like baseball cards.

"What are you two talking about?" Sally asked, as the two elder members of the group looked suddenly guilty. It wasn't exactly cheerful dinner conversation, and they didn't want to share it with their children. Sally and his son always told Jim he had to stop talking about their mother, particularly to strangers. He did it often. She'd been gone for nearly two years now. And to Jim, it seemed like minutes.

"We're just talking about our children," Paris said blithely, covering for him, and herself. Sally's brother was a year older than Wim, and was at Harvard. "What rotten kids you are and how much we hate you," Paris teased, with a conspiratorial look at Sally's father, for which he was grateful. He had liked talking to her, more than he'd expected. He had been as reluctant as she to come to dinner, and he had done everything he could to dissuade his daughter. But now that he was here, he was delighted he hadn't succeeded. Both girls were very stubborn, and loved their parents.

They talked about their respective Fourth of July plans then. Sally and her husband were going away for the weekend, probably their last one alone before the baby came. Jim said he was in a sailboat race with friends, and Paris said she would be working, on two holiday picnics. Jim thought her job sounded like great fun, although he admitted that personally he wasn't fond of parties. He seemed like a quiet, somewhat withdrawn person, but it was hard to tell if that was from circumstance or nature. He admitted to Paris that he had been depressed since being widowed. But he also had to admit that once he was out, he felt better.

The girls kissed each other good-bye when they left, and Jim asked Paris quietly in a discreet aside if he could call her. He seemed very old-fashioned, and very formal, and she hesitated for a moment, and then nodded. If nothing else, maybe she could help him. She wasn't physically attracted to him, but he obviously needed someone to talk to, and he wasn't unattractive. His circuits just seemed to be disconnected at the moment, and she wondered if he was on some kind of medication. They shook hands when they separated, and Jim whispered to her that he'd call her, and then he walked briskly down the street with his daughter. He looked like a man without a country. Even the slope of his shoulders suggested that he was unhappy.

"So," Meg asked, as they got in the car, "what did you think?" She had the feeling her mother liked him, even if she wasn't willing to admit it. And Sally had whispered to Meg as they hugged good-bye that she hadn't seen her father so animated since her mom died.

"I like him. Not the way you think, or the way you and Sally plotted, evil children that you are." Paris smiled. "But he's a lonely man who needs someone to talk to. And obviously a very decent person. His wife's illness and death were very hard for him."

"It was hard on Sally too," Meg commented, and then looked

sternly at her mother. "He doesn't need a psych nurse, Mom, he needs a girlfriend. Don't be so codependent."

"I'm not codependent. I feel sorry for him."

"Well, don't. Just enjoy him." But there wasn't much to enjoy yet. He had spent the entire dinner talking about her doctors, and her disease, her death, her funeral and how beautiful it had been, and the monument he was still building for her. All roads had led to Rome, and whatever subject she brought up had led right back to the late Phyllis. Paris knew he needed to get it out of his system, just as she had needed to with Peter. And obviously it took longer to mourn a death than a divorce or a betrayal. As far as she was concerned, Jim was entitled, and she was willing to listen. Besides, she could relate to a lot of it. In some ways, she still felt less divorced and more widowed, because of the suddenness of Peter's departing, and the fact that she had no voice in it. He might as well have died.

"He said he'd call me," Paris volunteered, and Meg looked pleased. Particularly when she answered the phone and it was he the next morning. After saying hello pleasantly to Meg, Jim asked to speak to her mother. And Paris took the phone from her quickly. They chatted for a few minutes, and Meg saw her mother jot a note down, nod her head, and say she'd be delighted to have dinner with him.

"You have a date?" Meg asked with a look of astonishment. "Already? When?" She was grinning from ear to ear as Paris looked nonplussed, and insisted it wasn't romantic. "Tell me that in three weeks when you're sleeping with him," Meg teased. "And don't forget, this time remember to ask if it's exclusive." Although they both agreed that with Jim Thompson that wasn't likely to be a problem, at least not for the moment. Sally said he hadn't even looked at another woman since his wife died. And Paris believed it. She wasn't sure he was looking at her either. He just needed someone to listen, while he talked about his late wife. "So when are you seeing him?" Meg asked anxiously. She felt like a little mother. She wanted this romance to work. They all did.

"Tuesday, for dinner."

"At least he's civilized, and won't take you to the kind of places mine take me. I either get to go to bottom-of-the-barrel sushi places where I get food poisoning, vegetarian, or diners so scary I'm afraid to walk into them. The men I go out with never take me any-place decent."

"Maybe you need someone a little older," Paris suggested sim-ply, although Meg had never liked older boys even when she was growing up. They just didn't appeal to her. She always liked them her own age, and once in a while, a year or two younger. But then she had to put up with all the immature games that went with it.

"Call and tell me how it goes with Mr. Thompson," Meg re-minded her when she left, and Paris spent the rest of the evening doing laundry, which wasn't glamorous, but useful. And on Mon-day she and Bix got in high gear over the Fourth of July picnics they were doing that weekend. By Tuesday night Paris was up to her ears in details, and almost forgot she had a date with Jim Thompson. She ran home from the office at six, after flying out of a meeting with Bix, and telling him she had to go out for dinner.

"Do you have a date?" He looked startled. She hadn't said a word about meeting someone new, and she'd been emphatic lately about not dating. She was still bitching about the blind date from Santa Fe, and used him as ample reason to remain a born-again virgin.

In answer to his question, Paris looked vague and said, "Not really."

"What does that mean?"

"I'm acting as a psych tech to the father of a friend of Meg's who lost his wife to breast cancer two years ago."

"That's tough," Bix said, looking sympathetic. "What's he look like?"

"Proper, uptight, nice looking. Normal."

"Excellent. How old?"

"About fifty-nine or sixty."

"He sounds perfect. We'll take him. Go."

"Don't get yourself excited. All he does is talk about his late wife. He's obsessed with her."

"You'll change all that. Steven was just like that when I met him. I thought if I heard one more time about how his lover had died in his arms, I would scream. It takes a while, but eventually, it goes. Give him time. Or maybe Prozac. Or maybe Viagra."

"Never mind that. I'm just having dinner with him. This is grief counseling, not sex therapy, Mr. Mason."

"Whatever, have fun. G'night!" he called after her as she hurried down the stairs, and half an hour later she had washed and blow-dried her hair, woven it quickly into a braid while it was still damp, and put on charcoal-gray slacks and a matching sweater, and she had just put on shoes when the doorbell rang. She was still breathless when she opened the door and invited Jim in.

"Am I early?" Jim Thompson asked hesitantly. She had that look of what-are-you-doing-here-so-soon?, but she was just harassed and in a hurry, and tried to relax as she smiled at him and he walked in.

"Not at all. I just got home from work a little while ago. It's a crazy week, it always is. If it isn't Fourth of July, it's Valentine's Day, or Thanksgiving, or an anniversary, or a birthday or a wedding or 'just a little dinner party' for forty on a Tuesday night. It's fun, but it keeps us on our toes."

"It sounds like a happy business you're in. Lucky you. Banking isn't a lot of fun, but I suppose it's useful too." He sat down on the couch in the living room, and she poured him a glass of wine. It was a beautiful night, and the fog hadn't come in that afternoon, so it was still warm. Often it was colder in the summer than in the spring. "What a lovely house you have, Paris," he said, looking around. She had beautiful antiques, and obviously excellent taste too. "Phyllis loved antiques. We used to go antiquing in every city we went to. She preferred English, just as you do." As she had the first night, Phyllis had joined them once again. And Paris tried to steer the conversation toward their kids, by asking him about his son. Like Wim, he had just left for Europe to travel with friends. "I don't see enough of him, now that he's on the East Coast," Jim complained. "He doesn't seem to like to come home anymore, and I can't say I blame him. It's not a very happy place."

"Are you taking any trips this summer?" Paris asked, determined to turn the conversation around, and genuinely trying. If she could just get him off the subject of his loss, he might actually have a good time, or even be one. There was nothing obviously wrong with him. He was solvent, intelligent, educated, employed, good-looking, almost handsome, and he had children the same age as hers. It was certainly more than enough to go on, if she could just get Phyllis out of the room. It was becoming something of a challenge to her, and Paris was determined to win, for his sake as well as her own. As Bix had guessed from her thumbnail sketch, he was the most likely candidate she'd seen. And the most like Peter in some ways. All they had to do was ease Phyllis gently back into her grave, where she belonged.

They chatted for a while, and then Jim drove her to dinner, at a little French bistro with a sidewalk café. It was an adorable place, and brought back a flood of memories for Jim. He and his late wife both loved France, and had spent a lot of time in Paris. In fact, Phyllis had spoken nearly flawless French. It seemed hopeless to stem the tide as they limped awkwardly through dinner, and not knowing what else to do, Paris found herself pulling out memories about Peter. What their marriage had been like, how close they had been for all those years, and the immense shock it had been when he left. They seemed to alternate war stories with each other, and by the time Paris got home, she was exhausted. She hadn't talked about Peter that much since he left her.

"I'd like to see you again," Jim said cautiously when he took her home after dinner. Paris didn't ask him to come in. She just didn't want to hear another story about Phyllis, nor to talk about Peter yet again. She wanted to bury them both. And she was dying to make a pact with Jim that if they saw each other again, neither of them could speak of their previous spouses. But she didn't feel she knew him well enough to say that to him. "I'd love to cook you dinner," he volunteered.

"I'd love that." Paris smiled at him, although she was a little leery of having dinner in what he clearly perceived was his late wife's house, as much as his own. She still thought he was a lovely person, but it had been an uphill battle for neutral conversation all night. Whatever they did, wherever they went, Phyllis seemed to peek around the corner at them, whether talking about children, antiques, or trips. Or anything else that came to mind. And Peter had been running a close second all night. More than anything, Paris wanted to bury their dead. "I have to work this weekend," she reminded him.

"What about Sunday night?" he said, looking hopeful. He really liked her a lot, and she was a wonderful listener. Sensitive, and sympathetic. He hadn't expected to like her as much as he did.

"That would be perfect," Paris said, giving him a warm hug, and she waved at him as she closed the door. She had had a nice evening, but she had to admit that being alone in her house again, without Phyllis or Peter, was an immense relief.

"So? How was it?" Bix asked as she walked in the next morning, looking distracted. "Wild sex all night? Are you addicted yet?"

"Not exactly." She grinned. "I'm still doing grief counseling on a fairly major scale," she confessed, and he shook his head.

"Enough of that. If you let it go too far, you'll never get him off it later. He'll start to associate you with her." He had eventually made a deal with Steven that he could only mention his late partner once a day. And it had worked. Steven said it had helped him get control of himself again, and it had helped the relationship no end. Now all these years later, he hardly mentioned him at all, and when he did, it was in a healthy way. Jim Thompson was still in the deep grieving phase, even after two years.

"Great," Paris said, looking discouraged. "I don't know why I'm working so hard at this, or why I care. What do you suggest?"

"It becomes a challenge just to unseat the dead person and take their place. No one wants to be outranked by a ghost. I'd say, if gentle conversational hints don't do it, then maybe a blow job is in order," Bix said, looking serious, while sitting at his desk, and Paris laughed.

"Terrific. I'll suggest it to him the next time he comes to the door."

"You might want to wait till he gets inside. The neighbors might start lining up." Bix smiled mischievously at her, as the phones started to ring, and they didn't stop all day, or even all week. But both picnics went off without a hitch, as planned. Bix did the one in Palo Alto, and Paris did the one in Tiburon. There was no way, given the distance, that they could go back and forth. But Bix was completely confident that she could handle anything by now. Sydney Harrington had worked the Tiburon party with her, and she started to apologize again for her friend in Santa Fe, and Paris told her not to worry about it, he was probably a nice man.

"You know, sometimes you don't realize how wacky your friends are, till you set them up with someone for a date. I thought he was a little off that day." Paris didn't tell her that she thought he was about as off as it could get. But without saying more about it, they both went back to work.

Paris slept nearly all day Sunday. It was a lazy day, and she had been working hard for weeks. Between their heavy schedule in May, the June weddings, and the Fourth of July picnics, she felt as though she hadn't slowed down in two months. It was nice to have a day to sleep. And at six o'clock, she drove to Jim's address. He lived in a handsome, rambling old house in Seacliff. The weather tended to be foggier out there and, because of that, sometimes more depressing than it was farther east, where Paris lived. But the house had been designed by a famous architect, and had a breathtaking view of the Golden Gate Bridge and the Bay. She admired it as soon as she walked in. And below the house there was a slice of China Beach, where Jim said he often liked to walk. Phyllis had loved to walk there too. She was with them even before Paris had taken off her coat. And Peter was close on her heels.

"Peter and I always loved the beach." Paris couldn't believe what she was doing. As much as she liked Jim Thompson, he seemed to bring out the worst in her. Or the worst of her memories at least. She tried to remember what Bix had told her, and made a deal with herself to only mention Peter once a day. It was weird, because for all intents and purposes, she had stopped talking about him months before. And now, thanks to Jim, and Phyllis, he was back in her conversation full force. It hadn't been this bad since he left.

Jim had been busy in the kitchen. He was making roast beef for her, with purée of asparagus, and little fluted potatoes. She knew what was coming before he said it, he and Phyllis had loved to cook. And Paris almost shuddered when she saw Phyllis's tired old faded straw hat hanging on a hook near the back door. It was still there after two years, and she wondered how many of her belongings were still around. Probably most or all. Jim had a lot of mopping up to do, and he didn't seem to have done any of it yet, nor want to.

"It's a big house for me alone," he admitted, as he sat down to dinner. "But the children love it, and so do I. They grew up here, and I can't bring myself to give it up." No Phyllis, Paris noticed as she held her breath. Now she was counting the times he didn't mention her, as much as she was counting the times he did. It was sick, but she couldn't seem to stop herself from keeping track of how often he spoke of his late wife.

"I had the same problem with the house in Greenwich," she countered. "I felt lost in it after Peter left. And when Wim left for Berkeley, it damn near killed me. That's why I moved out here."

"Did you sell it?" he asked with interest. The meat was delicious, and the vegetables better yet. He was a surprisingly good cook. Though Phyllis was probably even better.

"No, I rented it for a year, with an option for a second year. I wanted to buy time to see how I felt out here."

"And how do you feel?" he asked with genuine interest, as they sat in a cozy corner of the large kitchen that also shared the view. It would have been an ideal house, if it hadn't been quite so dark. There was a lot of dark wood paneling everywhere, which seemed to fit Jim's mood.

"I love it here," Paris said, smiling at him, and beginning to relax, as she felt the dual ghosts recede, although it was a little odd being in Phyllis's house, with her hat hanging only feet away. "I love my job. I never worked in all the years I was married. And this isn't brain surgery, but it's wonderfully creative. And the man I work for has become a dear friend. He's incredibly good at what he does. Coming out here has turned my life around just as I hoped it would."

"What did you major in in college?" he asked, wanting to know more about her. But he was already impressed by what he did know.

"Econ. I was practically the only girl, except for two sisters from Taiwan. I got an MBA, but I never used it. I just took care of Peter and the kids."

"So did Phyllis. She had a Ph.D. in art history, and she wanted to teach, but she never did. She stayed at home with our children. And then of course, she got sick." Paris tried not to wince. They had already been there.

"Yes, I know. What about you? Tell me about your sailing." She knew he had been out on the bay in a regatta the day before, and said they'd come in third place. "Do you have your own boat?"

"Not anymore. I sold it years ago. It was just a little thirty-footer." She knew what was coming next, before she heard the words. "Phyllis and I used to take it out on weekends. She was the best sailor I've ever seen. My kids love it too."

"Maybe you should get another boat. You could have a lot of fun with it on weekends." She was trying to think of constructive things for him to do, instead of sitting in the house thinking of Phyllis.

"Too much work," he said, "particularly all alone. I couldn't do it. At my age, I'd rather crew on someone else's boat." By then, she knew that he was sixty-one years old. But unlike other men she knew, even those like Bixby who hadn't had surgery, Jim looked older than his years. It was more than likely what grief had done to him. It was a powerful force, and even killed people sometimes, usually when they had been married forever and ever, and lost each other when they were very old. He was young enough to recover, if he wanted to. Paris wasn't sure he did. That was the key. "Do you like to sail?" he asked her.

"Sometimes. Depends on the circumstances. Yes, in the Caribbean. No, in rough waters like these. I'm a big chicken," she said honestly, smiling at him.

"You don't look it to me. Maybe I can teach you to sail one day."

He said he was going to visit friends in Mendocino later in the summer. He'd been invited to Maine too, but it was too far away and he didn't want to go. And then he talked about the summer he and Phyllis had spent with the children in Martha's Vineyard. And the next thing Paris knew, she was chronicling every trip she, Peter, and the children ever took. She was about to suggest a pact with Jim, a ban on talking about their late and ex-spouses, but she didn't dare.

And in spite of it, she had a nice evening with him, helped him do the dishes, and left around ten. But as she had the last time she saw him, she felt drained when she got home. There was something so profoundly sad about him. And she noticed that he drank a lot of wine at dinner. Given how he was feeling, it was hardly surprising, but alcohol wasn't going to help buoy his spirits. On the contrary, the more he drank, the sadder he got, and the more he talked about his late wife. It was beginning to seem hopeless.

Jim called her at the office the next morning, and they made plans to go to a movie later that week. He suggested a particularly sad one, which had had excellent reviews, and she countered with a funny one she wanted to see. And after they saw it, they went out for pizza, and he smiled at her.

"You know, my daughter was right to introduce us, Paris. You're good for me." He had laughed nonstop at the movie, and they were both smiling when they came out. He seemed to be in a particularly buoyant mood. And for once Peter and Phyllis hadn't come with them. Neither of them had mentioned their absent spouses all night. But Paris knew it wouldn't be long before one or both of them reappeared. "You seem like a very happy person," Jim said admiringly. "I envy you. I've been depressed now for two years."

"Have you thought about taking medication?" she said helpfully, remembering Meg's warning not to be codependent, but it was hard to resist with him. Being sympathetic was okay, rescuing wasn't. Sometimes it was hard to distinguish between the two.

"I did. It didn't help. I took it for a week."

"It takes longer than that for it to work," Paris said quietly, wishing she had met him a year or two later. But she wasn't sure if he'd be any healthier then, unless he made some serious efforts to get there. "I think you have to be patient about those things. I've been in therapy since Peter left." Although she was only talking to Anne now about once a month, just to check in. And she hadn't called her in about six weeks. She hadn't felt the need or had the time. Although lately, she'd been wanting to call. After talking about Peter constantly with Jim, he was more on her mind than he had been in a year.

"I admire you for that," Jim said, commenting on her mention of being in therapy. "But it's not for me. I went to a grief group for the first few weeks, and it just made me feel worse."

"Maybe it was too soon. Maybe you should try it again now."

"No," he said, smiling at her, "I'm fine. I've made my peace with things." Paris had a mouthful of pizza when he said it, and she looked up and just stared at him. "Don't you think? I've pretty much accepted Phyllis's death." *Are you kidding?* Paris wanted to scream. He had her propped up in a corner and took her everywhere he went. It was *Weekend at Phyllis's*, instead of *Weekend at*

Bernie's, although even thinking it seemed disrespectful of him. But it was true. He hadn't even begun to make peace with it, and was in complete denial over the state he was in.

"You're the best judge of how you feel," she said politely, and then talked about the film they'd seen again, to keep the subject light.

And that night, when he took her home, he surprised her by kissing her tenderly on the front steps. She was surprised by what a passionate man he was, and she melted toward him when they kissed. He was either lonelier than even she thought, or the old adage was in fact true that still waters run deep. But he was far more sexual than she had thought, and she could feel as he held her close to him that he was aroused, which was a hopeful sign. At least Phyllis hadn't taken that with her too.

"You're a beautiful woman, Paris," he said gruffly. "I'm hungry for you . . . but I don't want to do anything we'll both regret. I know how you felt about your husband, and I . . . I haven't been with any-one since my wife . . ." She had suspected as much, and she didn't want to tell him that she'd already had one affair since Peter left. She didn't want to seem like a slut. But both her psyche and the rest of her machinery seemed to be working fine. She wasn't sure about his. Intense grief did strange things. And as he himself admitted, he had been depressed for two years. Men, and their elaborate inner works, were fragile beings. She didn't want to frighten him.

"We're in no rush," she said in a soothing tone, and he kissed her again before he left. She thought it was a hopeful sign, and she was beginning to like him better and better. She liked what he stood for, and how he felt about his children, he had a lot of integrity, and a good heart. If they could just get Phyllis out of the way, maybe everything would be fine. But thus far, she seemed reluctant to leave. Or rather, Jim was reluctant to let her go. He was still hanging on tight. Though maybe, judging by the kiss he and Paris had exchanged, not quite as tight.

For the next several weeks, they continued to see each other, go to movies, and dinner. They even cooked dinner at her house, which Paris thought was easier for him. There were no memories of Phyllis there, and no hat hanging in the kitchen. There was just Paris. And things got rather heated between them late one night when they were first sitting, and then lying on the couch. It was early August by then. And she had put on a stack of CDs he liked. He seemed happy with her, happier than he'd been in a long time. But in the end they decided not to pursue their physical relationship any further that night.

Bix checked in with her later that week. "Are you still a virgin, or has it happened yet?"

"Don't be so nosy." She felt protective of Jim, and was beginning to have stronger feelings for him. As they got to know each other better, she could even imagine falling in love with him. And it was a definite selling point that he was also a very sensual man. His senses had just been asleep for a long time.

"Are you falling for him?" Bix was intrigued.

"Maybe," she said cryptically. "I think I could, with time."

"That's pretty neat." He looked pleased for her. And Meg was pleased too. She could tell from her mother's voice when she called that good things were happening. Sally had had the baby by then, and the two girls had talked and agreed that things were looking good. Sally said her father was crazy about Meg's mother, and couldn't stop talking about how beautiful she was. And if he wasn't in love yet, he had a major crush. And so did Paris, although she was keeping it quiet. But she liked everything he stood for.

And by mid-August, Meg had her own news, which she had been keeping under her hat. She had met someone over the Fourth of July weekend, and they had been seeing each other for five weeks. But she wasn't sure how her mother would feel about it. She was afraid she wouldn't like it. He was considerably older than Meg was, and a year older than her mother.

"What's he like?" Paris asked benevolently. Meg had not yet mentioned his age to her. She hadn't said anything about him for a month until she was sure they were at least minimally compatible with each other. He was a major departure for her.

"Nice, Mom. Very, very, very nice. He's an entertainment lawyer. A big one. He represents some pretty major stars." And Meg had already met several of them, as she told her mother.

"How did you meet him?"

"At a Fourth of July party." She didn't say that he was a friend's father. She was still afraid of her mother's reaction.

"Will I like him, or does he have spiked hair and wear earrings?"

"No earrings. He looks kind of like Dad. Sort of."

And for no reason in particular Paris moved on to the next question. "How old is he?" She was expecting to hear twenty-four or twenty-five, Meg's usual range, or maybe a little younger, but not if he was an attorney. He was probably fresh out of law school, so maybe twenty-six or twenty-seven. And then she remembered that he had important clients. There was silence at Meg's end. "Are you there?" Paris thought the cell phone had disconnected.

"I'm here. He's kind of older, Mom."

"How kind of older? Work back from ninety," Paris said, smiling. To Meg, "older" would be twenty-nine or thirty.

She took it at one gulp and spat it in her mother's lap. "Forty-eight. He's divorced, and has a daughter my age. That's how I know him."

"Forty-eight?" Paris said in disbelief. "He's twice your age? What are you doing? He must feel like a father to you." Paris sounded upset, and was.

"No, he doesn't. I just feel comfortable with him. And he doesn't play all those games and bullshit."

"I should be dating him," Paris said, still sounding shocked, and not sure what to make of it. He sounded like a player, like Chandler, if he was going out with a girl Meg's age. She was instantly inclined not to like him.

"Yes, you should, Mom," Meg agreed. "You'd love him. He's a terrific person."

"How terrific can he be if he's robbing the cradle and going out with children?" Worse yet, *her* children.

"Those things happen. I don't think age matters. All that matters are the people."

"When you're forty-five, he'll be nearly seventy, if it gets to that. That's something to think about."

"We're not there yet," Meg said softly. But they had talked about it.

"I certainly hope not. Maybe I should come down and meet him."

"We've been talking about coming up for Labor Day weekend."

"I think you should. I want this man to know that you're not an orphan, and you have a mother who's keeping an eye on him. What's his name?"

"Richard. Richard Bolen." Paris was stunned into silence. Her daughter was dating a forty-eight-year-old man. And she didn't like it. But she tried not to get too excited about it when she talked to Meg. She didn't want to push her into it any deeper in order to defend him. And she talked to Jim about it that night. He was concerned too, but willing to concede that major age differences weren't always a bad thing, if he was a responsible, decent person.

"See what you think when you meet him," Jim said reasonably.

"I'd like you to meet him," she said, and he was flattered. Other than that piece of somewhat distressing news, they had a nice time that night, and Jim asked her if she'd like to go away for a weekend with him, to the Napa Valley. Given what had been happening between them, it was a major invitation. They had been dating for two months, and hadn't gone to bed yet. A weekend in Napa might make a difference. And Paris looked at him mischievously as he kissed her.

"Two rooms or one, Mr. Thompson?" It was a very bold question.

"What would you like?" he asked gently. She'd been ready for weeks, but she didn't want to scare him.

"Would you be comfortable with one, Jim?" she asked, as she

snuggled against him. The one thing she didn't want was to take Phyllis with them. Or Peter. She was ready for Peter to go back in the closet, where he belonged now, with Rachel. Phyllis was a far different matter. And Jim had to put her in his own closet, when he was ready, and so far he still wasn't. She dropped into their midst like a Murphy bed, as often as he let her. Which was often.

"I think I'd be happy with one room," he said, smiling at Paris. "Shall I make a reservation?" She thought he looked handsome and sexy as he asked her.

"I'd love it." Paris beamed at him.

Two days later they were on their way to Rutherford, in the Napa Valley, to stay at the Auberge du Soleil. What he didn't tell Paris till they got there was that he had spent his last anniversary there, with Phyllis, only months before she died.

"Why didn't you tell me?" Paris looked disappointed when he finally shared that with her. "We could have stayed somewhere else." And should have. She was afraid of their single room now, with the huge king-size bed and the cozy fireplace. There was something sexy and subtle about the room, and she would have had a good time there, minus Phyllis. But she had already joined them, and was settling in as Paris unpacked.

He told Paris all about the final anniversary, where they'd gone, what they'd done, what they'd eaten. It was as though he did it to protect himself from his feelings for Paris. Phyllis was the shield he was using against his own emotions. His guilt was stronger than his libido. He poured Paris a glass of champagne, and drank three himself before they went to dinner. And when they got back, he lit the fire, and turned to Paris, just as two and a half years before, he had turned to Phyllis. He could still see it, although for once he didn't say it. But Phyllis's presence was palpable in the room.

"Tired?" he asked quietly, and she nodded. In fact, she wasn't. She was extremely nervous. And it was hard to tell how he felt. He had seemed nostalgic and quiet all evening. Maybe he was getting ready to let Phyllis go, Paris hoped. Maybe this was going to be the epiphany he needed. She was praying it would be. It was time.

Paris put on the simple white satin nightgown she had brought, which dropped easily over her lithe figure, and clung to it enticingly as she emerged from the bathroom. He was already in bed, wearing crisp linen pajamas. His hair was combed, and he had shaved for her. She felt like a bride and groom on a wedding night, fraught with all the same tensions as old-fashioned couples who had never slept with each other. And she was beginning to wonder if they should have made less of a fuss of it, and just climbed into bed one night at her house. But they were here now, and there was no turning back.

And as she got into bed and he turned off the light, he kissed her, and all the passion they had felt for each other suddenly rushed to the surface. He was instantly aroused and so was she, and they seemed to be starving for each other. It was far more heated than she had hoped for, and she felt relief wash over her along with passion. She dropped her nightgown to the floor, and he peeled off his pajamas and they disappeared somewhere, as they entangled in each other's arms, and their hands and lips discovered each other. And then just as he was about to enter her, she felt everything stop, and everything but the essential part of him went rigid.

"Are you okay?" she whispered in the dark. He had pulled away from her, and she was frightened.

"I was about to call you Phyllis." He sounded as though he was nearly crying, and Paris suspected he was, or would be in a minute.

"It's all right, sweetheart . . . I love you . . . don't worry . . . everything is going to be fine. . . ." She stroked him gently as she said it, but he was slowly backing away, and even in the half light, she could see that he was panicked. She didn't know what to do, she wanted to make this better for him. She cared about him, as a man, and as a person.

"I can't do this to her," he said hoarsely. "She would never forgive me."

"I think she'd want you to be happy," Paris said, rubbing his back gently, and trying to relax him. "Why don't you let me give you a backrub, and not worry about this. We don't have to make love tonight. There's no hurry." And no need for pressure. But all he wanted suddenly was to get away from her. To be as far from Paris as he could get, and as close to Phyllis. It was as though he wanted to crawl back into the womb of time and be with her, and Paris could feel it.

Instead of letting her rub his back, he got up, and walked across the room naked. She could see he had a remarkable body for a man his age, but it did her no good, if he wouldn't share it with her. And he wouldn't. He locked himself in the bathroom without a word to her, and stayed there for half an hour, and when he came out, he was wearing what he had worn to dinner. Paris was shocked, but tried to conceal it. He stood looking down at her in bed with a tragic expression.

"I hate to do this to you, Paris. But I can't be here. I want to go back to the city." He looked as though something in him had died. He had given up.

"Now?" She sat up in bed and looked at him, and the glow of her skin shimmered like pearls in the moonlight. She was every bit as beautiful as he had thought she would be. But he still couldn't do it. To his late wife. He honestly believed Phyllis would never forgive him.

"I know you must think I'm crazy, and I guess I am. I'm just not ready, and I don't think I ever will be. I loved her too much for too long, and we went through too much together. I can't leave her, or betray her."

"She left you," Paris said gently, leaning back against the headboard. "She didn't mean to, and I'm sure she never wanted to, but she had no choice. She's gone, Jim. You can't die with her."

"I think I did. I think I died in her arms that night. I just didn't know it. I'm sorry to do this to you. I can't have a relationship. Now or ever." It was what she had feared from the beginning and had begun to think was all right, but clearly it wasn't. He wasn't willing to recover. He didn't want to. He had opted for death instead of life. And nothing Paris could do would change that.

"Why don't we just spend the night together, and hold each other? We don't need to make love. Let's just be here. You'll feel better in the morning." She patted the bed for him to come closer to her.

"No, I won't." He looked panicked. "I'll walk back to the city if I have to." He didn't want to take the car and leave her stranded, but all he wanted now was to go home. He didn't even want to look at her. And if he had, all he would have seen was his late wife's face. He had blocked Paris out completely.

"I'll get dressed," she said quietly, trying not to think of what was happening. She felt immensely sad, and the rejection was overwhelming for her. She wasn't angry at him, and she knew it had nothing to do with her, but it hurt anyway. She was disappointed that their weekend, not to mention their relationship, had turned out as it had.

Ten minutes later she followed him to the car in blue jeans and a sweater she had brought with her, and her suitcase hastily repacked. Jim put it in the back of his car without a word, as she slid into the passenger seat. And five minutes later they drove away. The hotel had an imprint of his credit card, so he didn't need to settle accounts with them. Only with himself. They were halfway to the city before he spoke to Paris, and all he could say was that he was sorry. He was stone-faced the rest of the way. And when she tried to put a hand on his, he didn't react. She wondered if he'd had too much to drink, and that increased his panic somehow. It was as though he was in the grip of a powerful demon. Or perhaps more simply, and more benignly, Phyllis had simply reclaimed him.

"I'm not going to call you again," Jim said woodenly as he stopped in front of her house at two-thirty in the morning. "There's no point, Paris, I can't do this anymore. I'm sorry I wasted your time." He was angry at himself, but sounded as though he was angry at her.

"You didn't waste my time," she said gently. "I'm disappointed for both of us. I hope one day you work this out, for your sake. You deserve not to be alone for the rest of your life."

"I'm not. I have Phyllis and all our memories. That's enough for me." And then he turned to her, and what she saw in his eyes broke her heart. They were two pools of pain that looked like burning embers. In the white heat of his misery, there was nothing left of him but ash. "And you have Peter," he said, as though to let himself off the hook and draw her into the swamp of despair with him. But Paris shook her head.

"No, I don't, Jim," Paris said clearly. "Rachel does. I have myself." And with that she got out of the car quietly, took her bag, and walked up her front steps. She unlocked the door, and before she could turn to look at him or wave, Jim Thompson drove away. She never heard from him again.

Chapter 23

Just as she had said they might, Meg brought Richard Bolen up to San Francisco for the Labor Day weekend. Richard took a room at the Ritz-Carlton, and although she would have preferred to stay with him, she decided to stay with her mother in the end. Richard thought it would make for a smoother introduction to him than if he was in competition with Paris for her little girl. And it proved to be a wise move, although it was clear from the moment they met that Paris was suspicious of him. She circled him like a dog around a tree, asking questions, looking long and hard, and talking to him about everything from his childhood to his job. After three days in his company, she hated to admit it, but she liked him very much.

And she couldn't help but think that he was exactly the sort of man that she should have been going out with, but he was dating a woman half her age, who in this case happened to be Meg. It was a very odd thought. But she didn't hold it against him, and they were sitting alone in her garden while Meg went upstairs for a few minutes, when Paris turned to him with a concerned expression.

"I don't want to be intrusive, Richard, but do you worry about the age difference between you?" He was twenty-four years older than Meg, exactly twice her age. And a year older than Paris.

"I try not to," he said honestly. "The last woman in my life was older than I am, she was fifty-four. Generally, I've always gone out with women my own age. My ex-wife was, we were college sweethearts. But your daughter is a very special young woman, as you know." He was handsome and rugged and looked younger than his years. And oddly enough, he looked very much like Meg and Paris, with green eyes and sandy blond hair. He looked almost more like Paris than Meg. And the two seemed extremely well suited to each other. In his company, Meg seemed to flourish and relax. She looked as though she felt totally safe with him. They had been dating for exactly two months, and Paris had the feeling it might be getting serious between them, from everything he said.

"I don't want to be terribly old-fashioned," Paris said apologetically, feeling foolish, particularly given the closeness of their age. "It's too soon for either of you to know what your intentions are, but don't play with her, Richard. I don't want a man your age coming along and breaking her heart. She doesn't deserve that." She was thinking about Chandler Freeman as she said it. He would have made mincemeat of a young girl. But Richard didn't look to be cut of the same cloth. And wasn't. "You're a lot older and wiser than she is, and stronger. If you're not serious about her, don't play with her, and don't hurt her."

"I promise you, Paris," he said intently, "I won't. And if I am serious?" He asked the question pointedly, and held his breath. "Would you object?"

"I don't know," she said honestly. "I'd have to think about it. You're a lot older than she is. All I want is for her to be happy."

"Happiness doesn't always respect the boundaries of age," he said wisely. "In fact it often doesn't. Age has nothing to do with this. She is the woman I love," he said simply. "I've never felt like this about any woman, except my ex-wife." What he said rang a bell with her, and she frowned as she looked at him.

"How long have you been divorced?"

"Three years," he said quietly. And Paris was immediately

relieved. At least he hadn't been divorced and playing for fifteen or twenty. She remembered all the warnings she'd had from Bix.

"That's respectable."

"I haven't met anyone important to me yet. Until Meg. And I didn't expect it to be with her. She and my daughter are friends."

"You never know how love is going to walk into your life, or if. And when it does, you don't know what face it's going to wear. In some ways, for both of you, I'm glad it's hers." She liked him a lot. It was just odd to have her daughter's boyfriend be the same age as she was. But it also allowed them to be friends, and far more candid with each other than she ever could have been with Anthony or Peace, who were mere children. Richard was a man, and a good one, and she said as much to Meg when they left. Meg looked peaceful and happy, and thrilled that her mother had liked him. She was madly in love with Richard, and he was equally so with her.

And after they left, Paris couldn't help musing about how strange life was. The kind of man she should have been with was with her daughter. And she was left to damaged goods like Jim Thompson, playboys like Chandler Freeman, and blind dates like the sculptor from Santa Fe. There wasn't a decent one in the lot, except Jim, who was a nice man, but wounded beyond repair. She was beginning to wonder if that was all she would find, and all the good ones belonged to someone else. She wondered if there was another one like Richard Bolen out there somewhere. She doubted it, and if there wasn't, she was better off alone. She had finally come to accept that. It no longer felt like a life sentence to her anymore, but a simple fact of life. If she never found another man to love, she knew she'd be all right. Better alone than with the wrong one. She no longer had the energy for that, or the interest. Love at any price came too dear.

She told Bix about Richard the next day.

"That's too bad," Bix said sensibly. "He sounds like just the kind of guy you need, instead of all these weirdos and freaks running around, and wounded animals with thorns in their paws. Christ, sometimes I wonder if there's anyone normal left."

"So do I. And you're not dating them, I am. Or I could be, if I were crazy enough to try. And the good ones like Richard want women half my age. By the time they want me, they have to be a hundred years old."

"Hardly. A nice fifty-year-old would do you just fine. All we have to do is find one."

"Good luck!" Paris said, looking cynical.

"Do you think he'll marry her?" Bix inquired with interest.

"I don't know. He might. Last week I would have said 'I hope not.' This week I'm not so sure. He's too old for her theoretically, but shit, Bix, if they're happy and they love each other, why not? Maybe age doesn't matter as much as we think."

"I don't think it does. Look at Steven and me. We have almost as much age difference as Meg and Richard, and we couldn't be happier."

"Maybe I need an old one," Paris said with a grin. "If I find a guy twenty-four years older than I am, he'd be seventy-one. Maybe that's not such a bad thought."

"Depends on the guy," Bix said openly. "I've met some seventy-year-olds I would give my right arm for. These days, if they want to be, men can be young into their eighties, and beyond that. I know a woman who's married to an eighty-six-year-old man in Los Altos, and she swears their sex life is better than ever, and two years ago, they had a baby."

"Now, there's a thought." Paris looked amused, although eighty-six seemed a little over the limit, at least for the moment.

"What, an eighty-six-year-old? I can find you one in a hot minute. They'd love to have you!" He was laughing.

"No, a baby. God, I'd love that. It's what I do best, Bix, bringing up children." For just a minute, there were stars in her eyes.

"Please!" he said, and rolled his eyes. "I hired you because you're a grown-up, single, your kids are out of the house, and you're not going to get pregnant, and give birth at our next party. If you go and get pregnant on me, Paris, I'm going to kill you!" But she wasn't thinking of getting pregnant. More and more lately, she had been thinking that she would be alone forever, and she'd love to adopt a baby. But she hadn't said anything to anyone about it, not even Meg, and surely not Bix. He would have had the vapors if she told him. And she didn't know if it was something real she wanted to pursue, or a pipe dream she had to cheat Father Time and delude herself that she was still young. Starting out with a baby at this point would be a major challenge, and she wasn't ready to do more than think about it yet. But the idea had crossed her mind.

And the following week she felt as though she had almost been psychic, when the subject of babies came up again. But it came up very differently this time. Meg called her to tell her that Rachel was pregnant, and expecting a baby in May. She was six weeks pregnant, and Meg admitted to her mother that Peter was thrilled. And when Paris hung up the phone, she sat staring into space for a long time, digesting it. There was no question now. He was really gone. His life was enmeshed with Rachel's forever. And she felt it almost like a physical blow to her heart and soul.

Much to her surprise, Wim called her the next day to tell her how angry he was about Peter and Rachel's baby. He thought it was a terrible idea, and that his father was a complete fool, and too old. Meg was a little more moderate about it, but she wasn't happy either. They both seemed to feel threatened by it, which surprised Paris at their age, since they were both out in the world and had spread their wings, and they would hardly see their father's new child. But it also told them that Rachel was there for good, and important to him. And even if only out of loyalty to their mother, neither of them was crazy about her. She seemed to devour their father's energies and attention, and had him wrapped around her two little boys, who never saw their own father. Meg said he was thinking of adopting them. The landscape of their family had certainly changed in the last year and a half. There was no denying it anymore. And somehow, in spite of the two children she adored, Paris felt like the odd man out. Wim and Meg would go on to their own lives one day, and in fact already had. Peter had Rachel and his new family, and was starting over again. And she was alone. Sometimes it was tough to swallow.

And as always when she was troubled, Paris buried herself in work, with Bix's help. They did the opening of the opera and the symphony, which were the two most major social events of the year, and a slew of parties to mark the beginning of the social season. They were nearly halfway through most of them, when Bix came into her office looking sheepish. By now she knew him well. They spent so much time together that sometimes they seemed like Siamese twins, with one brain. She could hear him in her head.

"Okay, you look guilty as hell," she accused him. "What have you done? From the look of it, I'd say you booked three weddings on one date, or maybe four. Something equally nightmarish, I'm sure." He hated to say no to anyone, and sometimes he booked four or five events in one day, which nearly drove them both insane when they had to pull them together.

"It's nothing like that. I just had a thought."

"Let me guess. You want to go to Carnival in Rio and do the entire event? . . . or . . . you're taking over PacBell Park and turning it into a garden party . . . or you want me to fly the Rockettes in for some event and they won't come. . . ." He was laughing at her, she knew him too well, but he shook his head.

"It's nothing like that. I want to do something I know you won't like." Her eyes opened wide as he said it.

"Is Jane coming back? Are you firing me?" Her only fear these days was of losing the job she loved so much.

"Hell, no. I think she might be pregnant again. She said something about it when we last talked. She's gone forever. I'm never letting you go . . . but I want you to do something for me. Promise you'll do it, and we'll discuss it after."

"Does it involve nudity or lewd acts in public?" she asked suspiciously, but Bix shook his head. "Okay, I promise. I trust you. What is it?"

"I want you to go on a blind date. You know how I hate them, and I don't believe in them. All those people who claim they met their husbands that way have to be lying. I've never met anyone but psychos and drips on blind dates. But this guy is perfect for you. I met him last week. He's a fairly well-known writer, and he hired us to do a birthday party for his mother. He's an incredibly smart guy, and has a lot of style. I think he's just what you want. He's been widowed for five years, but he talks about her sensibly, he's not obsessed. He has three grown kids. He travels between here and England. He has kind of a tweedy look. He just broke up with a girlfriend six months ago who was approximately your age, and he seems surprisingly normal."

"He probably isn't. Did you ask him if he cross-dresses?"

"No, but I asked him everything else. The minute I saw him, I thought of you. Will you meet him, Paris? You don't even have to go to dinner with him. I didn't say anything to him about you. But you could come with me on our next meeting, or go alone. Will you meet him at least?" She had heard him out, and although she didn't want to date anymore, or so she said, she was intrigued. And when Bix told her who he was, she said she had read three of his books. He was very good at what he did, and was always at the top of the best-seller lists. And Bix even loved his house.

"Okay, I'll go with you," she said, more cooperative than usual on the subject. After Sydney's artist friend, she had sworn she would never go on another blind date. But this wasn't a blind date. It was a blind meeting. "When are you seeing him again?"

"Tomorrow morning, at nine-thirty." Bix looked pleased that she'd offered no resistance. He was convinced it was a perfect match.

Paris nodded and said nothing, and the next morning Bix picked her up at nine-fifteen. The writer they were seeing, Malcolm Ford, lived only a few blocks from her. And when they got to his address,

Paris had to admit the house was impressive. It was a solid brick residence on upper Broadway, on what was referred to as the Gold Coast. All the biggest bucks in the city were there. But there was nothing showy about him when he opened the door. He had salt-and-pepper hair and steel-blue eyes, and he was wearing an old Irish sweater and jeans, and as they walked through the house, it was handsome but unpretentious. They settled into a library that was lined with first editions and rare books, and there were stacks of more current books on the floor. He went over the details for his mother's party calmly. He wanted something elegant and nice, but not too showy. And since he didn't have a wife, he had hired them. His mother was turning ninety, and Bix knew Malcolm was sixty. He had a very distinguished look, and he chatted with them for quite a while. Paris told him she'd read his books and enjoyed them very much, and he seemed pleased. There was a nice photo of his late wife on the desk, but he didn't talk about her. There was an equally nice one of his last girlfriend too, who was also a well-known writer. And he mentioned that he had a house in England. But everything about him seemed normal and human, and surprisingly low-key considering how successful he was. He didn't drive a Ferrari or have a plane, and he said he went to Sonoma on weekends, but admitted that his place there was a mess, and he liked it that way. He had absolutely everything going for him, including looks and money, and as they left his house after the meeting, Bix looked at her victoriously. He had found a gem for her, and he knew it, but the expression on Paris's face was blank.

"Was I right?" he asked her in the car, grinning happily as he drove her to the office. "He's great, isn't he?" He was practically in love with him himself, but he also looked a little like Steven.

"Totally," Paris agreed, but she didn't wax poetic about him, and she didn't offer further comment.

"So?" He could see that something was wrong. "What aren't you saying to me?" Bix asked, curious about her silence, and she seemed to be thinking about it herself.

"I don't know. I know this sounds crazy, and you'll think I'm nuts. He's incredibly nice, looks great, he's obviously smart. I like his house. But I don't feel any chemistry for him. Nothing. He doesn't appeal to me or turn me on. I have no vibes at all. If anything, I think he's boring."

"Shit," Bixby said, looking heartbroken. "I finally find you a good one and you don't want him." But he knew himself that if there was no chemistry, there was nothing. And why and when there was, was impossible to explain, but it was crucial.

"It must be me. I just don't feel anything. If I met him at a party, I think I'd probably walk right by him. Just nothing."

"Well, so much for that," Bix said, looking disappointed. "Are you sure? You decided that very quickly." But chemistry was a quick decision. They both knew you either felt it with someone, or you didn't.

"Absolutely. I'm not sure I want anyone anymore. I'm perfectly comfortable the way I am."

"That's when the good ones always come. At least that's what they say. When you don't give a damn anymore, they flock to you like flies to honey. God, if that guy were gay and I was alone, I would leap on him."

"I'm sure he'd be happy to hear it," Paris said, laughing. "I don't think he's gay, by the way. He's just not for me, and I don't think he felt anything for me either. No electricity, no contact."

"Well, back to the drawing board," Bix said cheerfully. He had tried, and Paris was grateful to him for it.

"I think you can put the drawing board away. For now anyway. I think I'm burnt out on men." He could see why. Her little episode with Jim Thompson that summer had really disappointed her. The one thing Paris didn't need was another rejection, and Bix didn't want that for her. She'd had enough heartache for one lifetime.

They went back to the office after that, and got to work. They worked their way through their October events, and it was early October when she and Bix were sitting in his office working out the last details of an October wedding. The bride was French, and her parents were bringing in a photographer from Paris. But other than that, they were using all their usual resources, and so far everything had gone smoothly. The bride looked like a little porcelain doll. And the dress had been made by Balmain in Paris. It was going to be the social event of the season, possibly the decade.

"Do we need to book a room for the photographer?" Paris asked, checking her notes.

"I already took care of it. He's staying at the Sir Francis Drake. I got a good rate. He's bringing two assistants. He's coming out before the wedding, to do family portraits." There were also at least a dozen relatives, and twice as many social friends, many of them titled, coming in from Europe. They were all booked into the Ritz. All the last details were set. And the only last-minute hitch was that the van they had rented for the photographer had to be picked up in the city, and not at the airport.

"He can take a cab," Bix said. The flight was due in an hour.

"I can pick him up," Paris volunteered. "He may not speak English, and all we need is some spoiled-brat French photographer having a tantrum at the airport and kicking our ass for it later. I have time this afternoon. I'll do it." She looked at her watch, and knew she had to leave in a few minutes.

"Are you sure?" She had better things to do, and Bix hated to use her as a chauffeur. But everything was in good order, and she liked to make sure that every last detail and loose end was tied up, even if she had to do it herself.

She left for the airport five minutes later, in her station wagon, and hoped she'd have enough room for their equipment. If not, they could put one of the assistants in a taxi, but at least the photographer himself would feel that they had paid him sufficient homage. She knew how the French were. Or photographers, at least. And it was a nice break to drive to the airport. It was a crisp October day, and San Francisco had never looked better.

She parked her car at the airport, and went to wait while the passengers made their way through customs after an eleven-hour flight that had just landed from Paris. She assumed she would recognize them by their equipment. The photographer's name was Jean-Pierre Belmont. She had seen his work in *French Vogue,* but hadn't a clue what he looked like. She kept her eyes peeled for people carrying cases that looked like photographic equipment. And finally she saw them. There were three of them, a distinguished older man with gray hair, carrying two enormous silver cases, and two younger ones, one of whom had bright red hair and looked about fourteen and another barely older with spiky black hair, an impish smile, and a diamond earring. The younger two were wearing leather jackets and jeans, and the older man wore a proper topcoat and a muffler. And Paris rapidly approached them.

"Hello," she said with a broad smile. "I'm Paris Armstrong, from Bixby Mason. Mr. Belmont?" she said to the older man, and she heard a burst of laughter behind her, and the boy with the red hair chuckled. The older man looked uncomfortable and shook his head. It was obvious that he didn't speak a word of English.

"You are looking for Monsieur Belmont?" the imp with the spiky hair and diamond earring asked her. He seemed to be the only one who spoke English, though with a heavy accent.

"Yes, I am," she said politely. She was wearing slacks and a pea coat and the spiky-haired imp was barely taller than she was. But she saw as she talked to him that he was probably a little older than she'd guessed. She had figured him for about eighteen or twenty, and seeing him at close range, she guessed him to be Meg's age. "Is that he?" She indicated the older man again without pointing directly at him. He had to be. He was the only obvious grown-up in the threesome.

"*Non,*" the imp said, and she wondered if she had mistaken the entire group and they were playing with her. If so, she had missed the right crew completely, and had no idea where they were now. "It is me, Monsieur Belmont," he said with a look of vast amusement. "Your name is Paris? Like the city?" She nodded, relieved at least to have found them, although it was hard to believe that this boy was Jean-Pierre Belmont, who was a considerably well-known photographer in Paris. "Paris is a man's name," he corrected her. "He was a Greek god in mythology," he said with interest.

"I know. It's a long story." She was not going to explain to him, with subtitles, that she had been conceived on her parents' honeymoon in Paris. "Do you have all your bags?" she asked him pleasantly, still trying to figure out who was who. But if he was Belmont, the other two were obviously his assistants, although one of them looked old enough to be his father.

"We have everything," he said in heavily accented but coherent English. "We have very little bag, only cameras," he explained and pointed, and she nodded. There was something vastly charming about him. She wasn't sure if it was the accent or the hair or the earring, or maybe the smile. She kept wanting to laugh every time she looked at him. And the red-headed boy looked like a baby, and was in fact Jean-Pierre's nineteen-year-old cousin. Belmont himself was thirty-two, Paris discovered later, but looked nowhere near it. His whole demeanor and style was that of someone infinitely younger. He was the personification of charming, outrageous youth and totally Parisian.

She told him she would be back in a minute with the car, and left the three of them with a porter, and five minutes later she was back, and the two assistants and the photographer himself proceeded to pack her station wagon with such speed and precision that it looked like some kind of puzzle. And moments later he was in the passenger seat, the two others were behind them, and they were on their way to the city.

"We go to the hotel or to see the bride girl now?" he asked clearly.

"I think they're expecting you a little later. I thought you'd like to go to the hotel first, rest, eat, shower, and get ready." She said it carefully and clearly as he nodded, and seemed very interested in his surroundings. He spoke to her again a few minutes later.

"What do you do? You are secretary . . . assistant . . . to the bride mother?"

"No, I plan the wedding. Bixby Mason. Flowers, music, decoration. We hire all the people to do the wedding." He nodded, having understood what her function was in the scheme of things. He was quick and alert, and extremely lively. And as he looked out the window, he lit a Gauloise, *papier mais,* with bright yellow paper made from corn, and a pungent smell like no other filled her station wagon.

"Ees okay?" he asked politely after it was lit, remembering that Americans weren't nearly as amenable to smoking, but Paris nodded.

"It's okay. I used to smoke a long time ago. It smells nice."

"*Merci,*" he said perfunctorily, and then chatted with the others. Although she spoke a little French, she had no idea what they were saying. They spoke far too quickly. And then he turned to her again. "Ees a good wedding? Beautiful dress? . . . Good?"

"Very good," she reassured him. "Beautiful girl, beautiful dress. Handsome groom. Beautiful party. It is at the Legion of Honor Museum. Seven hundred people." The Delacroix family controlled an enormous French textile industry and had moved to San Francisco during the Socialist regime, and then stayed there, to protect their fortune from French taxes. But they still spent as much time in France as they could get away with.

"Big money, yes?" he inquired, and Paris smiled and nodded.

"Very big money." She didn't tell him, but they were spending two and a half million dollars on the wedding. More than respectable, to say the least.

She drove him to the hotel without further ceremony, and arranged at the hotel desk for someone to pick up their van and deliver it to them. All they had to do was show their driver's licenses and sign the papers. She handed Jean-Pierre Belmont a map of the city, and showed him on the map where they had to be at six o'clock.

"Will you be okay?" she asked, as he blew a cloud of smoke in her face inadvertently, and someone at the desk asked him to put it out. He found an ashtray full of sand a few steps away, and came back to Paris at the desk. "Call me if you need anything," she said, and handed him her card. He was going to be doing portraits of the family and the bride.

He relayed everything to the others then, waved at her, and they disappeared into the elevator to find their rooms, as Paris went back outside to her car. Being around Jean-Pierre was like being in a whirlwind, with arms waving everywhere, hands gesticulating, clouds of smoke, and snatches of conversation with the others that she didn't understand. There were lots of exclamations, facial expressions, and through it all he never seemed to stop moving with his big brown eyes and spiky hair. He looked like one of Meg's friends, except everything about him was so French. And at the same time, although he looked young, he seemed very much in command. She could still smell his corn-wrapped cigarettes when she got back in her car and drove back to the office, to pick up her messages and a last file.

Bix was still there, and he looked up when she came in. "Everything go okay?" She nodded, glancing at her messages. Everything was on track for that night.

"Fine," she reported, and then told him about Jean-Pierre Belmont. "He looks about twelve. Well, not quite, but close."

"I figured he'd be older than that," Bix said, looking surprised, and she nodded.

"So did I. He's very French. Too bad Meg has a boyfriend, he'd be fun for her." But she wasn't sorry really that Meg had Richard. He was so wonderful to her. They'd been dating for almost three months, and Meg was ecstatically happy.

Bix and Paris were both at the Delacroix house that night, overseeing a family dinner for thirty people, as people started arriving from France. And Paris stood in a back corner to watch the portraits being done. Ariane Delacroix looked exquisite when she posed in her wedding dress, which no one else saw. The bride looked like a tiny fairy princess, and laughed when she saw Jean-Pierre smile his outrageously contagious smile. When he caught sight of Paris, he winked at her, and then went back to work, as his assistants alternated cameras, and changed film for him. He took several family portraits. And when the bride went upstairs to change into a dinner dress, to pose for a photograph with her mother, he stopped for a minute to talk to her.

"Would you like a photograph?" he asked Paris formally, since no one else was around, and she shook her head quickly. It would have been terribly unprofessional, and she would never have done that.

"No, no, thanks." She smiled.

"Beautiful eyes," he said, pointing to her green eyes.

"Thank you," she said, and as he looked at her, she could almost feel an electric current run through her. It was exactly the opposite of what she had felt, or hadn't felt, for Malcolm Ford. She couldn't even talk to this man, and he looked about half her age, but everything about him was masculine and electric, and he had a visceral effect on her. She could never have explained it, nor wanted to. There was nothing gentle or subtle or cautious about him. Everything about him was bright and vibrant and bold, from his brilliant eyes to his spiky hair, to the diamond in his ear. And when the bride and her mother came back, he went back to work again and Paris disappeared. But she felt almost shaken as she left the room, as though she had touched something and gotten a severe electric shock.

"You okay?" Bix asked as she walked by. He thought she had an odd look on her face.

"Yes, I am," she said, and they met again once the family and guests had gone into the dining room, and Jean-Pierre and his crew were leaving too. He smiled at her, and she had never had such a flirtatious look from any man. And certainly not one her own age.

"Pretty hot," Bix commented, which was the perfect word for him. "In my youth, I'd have gone berserk over him," he said, and laughed, as Paris did the same.

"In my old age, so would I," Paris said. She was teasing, but nonetheless it would have been impossible not to feel the energy that emanated from the young photographer from Paris.

And for the next few days, their paths crossed constantly. He was always at work, crouching at people's knees, or hanging from somewhere, nearly falling off a staircase, or inching toward a face. He was in constant motion, yet every time Paris was in the vicinity, he made eye contact with her. And as the bride left the wedding, he finally seemed to unwind for an instant, and then walked over to where Paris was standing.

"Very good!" he said. "Very, very good marriage! Beautiful photographs . . . beautiful decor . . . *et les fleurs*!" The flower arrangements Bix had designed were beyond belief. They were all roses and lily of the valley, and exquisite tiny flowers Paris had never even seen before. They had been flown in from Africa and France and Ecuador, at outrageous expense. But the Palace of the Legion of Honor had never looked more beautiful. The lighting Bix had organized was spectacular and worthy of Versailles. And as she and Jean-Pierre stood there under a starry sky at two in the morning, she wasn't even tired. "We go for a drink?" he asked, and she was about to say no and then nodded. Why not? He was leaving in a few days anyway. She knew he was going to stick around to take some shots in San Francisco, although she also knew that his assistants were leaving the next day. "I go in your car?" he proposed, and she told him she'd meet him out front in ten minutes.

She told Bix she was going, and he was about to leave too. All the members of the family had left, and there were only a few stragglers left. Neither he nor Paris needed to stay.

"It was terrific, wasn't it? We did a hell of a job." Bix beamed, tired but pleased.

"No, you did. All I am is the shepherd, and the organizer of details. You're the genius behind all this, Bix." He kissed her and thanked her, and then she left to retrieve her car from the valet, and a moment later she and Jean-Pierre were in it, speeding off into the night. There was nowhere to go at that hour, except an all-night diner she knew, but he was enchanted when he saw it, and immediately started taking photographs at weird angles, including a quick roll of her. And then he settled back in the booth and ordered pancakes and scrambled eggs. He hadn't had time to eat all night.

"I love America," he said with a jubilant look, and he looked more than ever like an elf who had fallen from another planet. He was medium height, and taller than Paris, but he was extremely wiry and lithe. Almost like a young boy. "You are married?" he asked her, although she had a distinct impression that he wouldn't have cared if she were.

"No. Divorced." She smiled at him.

"You are happy or sad?"

"About being divorced?" she inquired, and he nodded. And she thought about it. "Both. Very sad at first. Very, very sad. Now I'm happier."

"You have a little friend?" She looked puzzled, and he wrapped his arms around himself in a passionate hug and looked like he was embracing someone, and she laughed. *"Un petit ami,"* he said in French this time, and she understood.

"A boyfriend! No. No boyfriend." It seemed a funny question for him to be asking, and she pointed a finger at him to ask the same question. Not that it mattered. She was nearly twice his age.

"My little friend . . . my girlfriend . . . she go away . . . I am very, very sad." He made a tragic face and marked tears down his face with his fingers. "Now I am verrrrry happy. She was very much trouble." He managed to get his messages across, and Paris laughed. "You have children?" She loved his accent and his mannerisms, and he was full of life as he conversed with her. Language didn't really seem to be a problem.

"I have two children. A son and a daughter. Maybe older than you. How old are you?" she asked, and he laughed. People never guessed his age correctly, and he found it funny.

"Thirty-two," he said, and she looked surprised.

"You look younger."

"And you? Thirty-five?"

"*Merci*," she said, laughing at him too. "Forty-seven."

He nodded with a very Gallic face. "Bravo. You look very young." She loved his accent and the way his eyes danced. "You are of California?"

"New York. Then Connecticut. Now here for nine months, because of the divorce. My children are here," she explained.

" 'Ow hold?" He had trouble with *h*'s, but she knew what he meant. How old?

"My daughter is twenty-four, and my son is nineteen. He's in college, and she lives in Los Angeles and works for a movie studio."

"Very good. *Actrice?*"

"No. Production." He nodded, and they continued to chat while he ate his pancakes and eggs, and she drank tea and had an English muffin. She wasn't hungry, but she was enjoying him very much. "How long will you be here?" She was curious. It would be fun seeing him again, although it seemed a little silly. Even though he was older than he looked, he was still very young. Too young for her, no matter how attractive he was.

"I don't know," he said in his rolling accent. "Three days. Four. Maybe I go to Los Angeles, and do some work. I have a visa for six months. Maybe I stay a month. I don't know. I want to see Lac Tahoe, Carmel. Los Angeles. Santa Barbara. *En voiture.*" He made the gesture of a steering wheel. He wanted to drive around. "Maybe photo for *Vogue* in New York. I am very tired. Work very much. *Maintenant peut-être des vacances. On verra.*" He lapsed into French, and this time she understood because he spoke slowly. He said he might take a vacation, he would see. When he talked to the others, he spoke so quickly, she didn't get it, but when he spoke to her, it was much easier.

They left the diner well after three o'clock. She dropped him at his hotel, and he kissed her on both cheeks before he left, and then she drove home, peeled off her clothes, and fell into bed. And she lay staring at the ceiling for a few minutes, thinking about Jean-Pierre. It was crazy, but she was incredibly attracted to him. He was a boy, and very talented, but he was so full of life and charm. If she thought she could get away with it, she would have loved to run away with him, just for a day or two. But she knew that was impossible, and would have been very foolish, but even at forty-seven, sometimes it was nice to dream.

Chapter 24

Paris's cell phone rang the next morning, and she rolled over in bed and grabbed it, and was surprised to find it was Jean-Pierre. He said, *"Bonjour,"* and she knew instantly who it was.

"How are you?" she asked with a smile on her face.

"Very good. *Et toi?* And you?"

"Tired," she admitted as she stretched.

"I wake you up? I am very sorry. What do you do today?"

"Je ne sais pas," she said carefully. "I don't know." It was a lazy Sunday and she had no plans, other than to recover from the wedding.

"I see Sausalito. You will like to come?" She smiled as he said it. Crazy as it was, she liked the idea. There was something so joyful and full of life about him. He was playful and high-spirited and full of fun. And she liked being with him. It was the antithesis of the time she had spent with Jim Thompson, who was such heavy furniture and so much work. And even Chandler, who was so sophisticated and so smooth. There was no artifice to this boy, which was the only way she could think of him. He was totally alive, and unfailingly direct, even with his broken English. Something told her that whatever you did with him, or said, you would know where you stood. "We go to Sausalito together?" he asked, and she thought about taking him to Tiburon to lunch at Sam's. It was on the water, and there was an open deck. She had a feeling he would like that very much. She looked at her watch. It was just after eleven.

"I'll pick you up at noon."

"Noon? Where is that?" He sounded confused.

"Twelve o'clock," she clarified, and he laughed.

"Ah bon, midi. D'accord."

"D'accord?" It was her turn not to understand.

"D'accord is 'okay.' " She liked the way he said "okay." She liked everything about him, which was the worst of it. She showered and put on a red sweater and jeans, and grabbed her pea coat out of her closet. She knew that with him, she didn't have to get dressed up. And she told herself they were doing just a little harmless tourism. It didn't hurt anything. They could have fun seeing the sights together, and he'd be gone in a few days.

He hopped in her car when she picked him up, and he had a camera in his pocket. He was wearing jeans, a black sweater, and a black leather jacket, and he looked like a rock star with the diamond earring and the spiky hair. She tried to say as much to him, and he laughed.

"I cannot sing," he said, pretending to strangle himself, and they headed toward the Golden Gate Bridge. He hung out the window and took photographs of the city as they went across. It was a crystal-clear day, and when they got to Tiburon, he was delighted with Sam's. He managed to explain to her, using both languages, that he had been taking pictures since he was a little boy. His parents had died, and he was raised by an older sister whom he loved very much. He had been married at twenty-one, and he had a son ten years old, but the boy lived with his mother, and Jean-Pierre almost never saw him because he and the child's mother were on bad terms.

"That's very sad," Paris said. He showed her a photograph of an adorable child, who looked undeniably French. "Where do they live?"

"In Bordeaux. I don't like at all. Good wine, but very small."

They managed very decently to talk about her children, and the divorce, the work she did with Bix, and the fact that Peter had left her for another woman. He told her that he wanted to take a lot of photographs in the States, and he liked San Francisco a lot.

After that they went to Sausalito, and they walked around, and then he asked her if Sonoma was very far away.

"Not very," she said, looking at him. "Do you want to go?" They had no plans, and it would take less than an hour to get there.

"*Maintenant?* Now?"

"Sure."

"Okay." He looked pleased.

They drove past the vineyards, and roamed around, and then went on to the Napa Valley, and were there by dinnertime, and they stopped at a little bistro for dinner where everyone spoke French, and Jean-Pierre was thrilled. He and the waiter had a long conversation, and they headed back to the city around nine o'clock. They were back in San Francisco at ten-thirty, and had had a terrific day.

"What do you do tomorrow, Paris?" he asked when she dropped him off.

"I work," she said ruefully. But it had been a nice day. "What are you doing?" She was going to invite him to the office, to show him around, but he said he was going to Los Angeles in the morning. He was going to drive the van. "Will you come back?"

"*Je ne sais pas.* I don't know. If I come back, I call . . . *je t'appellerai.*"

"*D'accord,*" she said, and he smiled.

"*Sois sage,*" he said as he looked at her, and she looked puzzled. "It means be very good behaved. You know, be a good girl." It was odd, Paris realized, when she was with him, she didn't feel the difference in their age. She wondered if it was like that between

Richard and Meg. But this was ridiculous. Jean-Pierre was fifteen years younger than she. And he was only there for a minute. It was fine to drive around with him for a day, playing tourist, but she couldn't think of him as a romantic possibility. And he probably wouldn't come back anyway. He kissed her on both cheeks, and hopped out of the car, and she waved as she drove away. When she glanced in the rearview mirror, he was standing outside the hotel, watching her.

And all that night, she was haunted by him. All she could think about were the things they had talked about, and the expressive look on his face. And the French words he had taught her seemed to dance in her head. She was still feeling dazed the next day, as though she had taken a drug and was hung over. Being with him was some kind of strange aphrodisiac she couldn't have explained to anyone. He was such a powerful presence, in an almost sexual way. She could suddenly understand for the first time in her life why older women had affairs with younger men. But that wasn't going to happen to her.

She and Bix worked on a number of projects, and she was aware of a sense of malaise all day, as though some part of her were causing her body to be too big for her skin. She felt raw and uncomfortable all day. And it was crazy, but she actually missed him. She was determined not to give in to it, and she didn't call him on the cell phone he had rented, although he had given her the number. She went to bed early that night, and worked hard again the next day.

She felt better by Wednesday, and Meg called that night about their Thanksgiving plans. They were going to be with their father that year, and with her for Christmas. She never asked Meg how Rachel was doing with her pregnancy, because she didn't want to know. She had never asked if Peter was happy about it, if it was an accident, or planned. She couldn't bear to think of any of it, and Meg very discreetly never volunteered anything her mother didn't ask. She sensed just how painful it was for her, particularly since she was alone.

On Thursday as she drove home from the office at eight o'clock, her cell phone rang. She assumed it was either Bix or Meg. No one else ever called her on her cell. She was just pulling up in front of her house as she answered, and as she did, she saw him sitting there. It was Jean-Pierre both calling her, and sitting on her front steps.

"*Où es tu?*" he said in French, and she knew what it meant. It meant "Where are you?" She stopped the car, and smiled at him, embarrassingly pleased that he was there.

"I'm right here," she answered, and got out of her car with the phone in her hand. She walked up the steps, and was going to kiss him on both cheeks, but he took her in his arms and kissed her searingly on the mouth. And she responded before she could stop herself. She never wanted it to stop, and didn't want him to go. It was as though she was being swept away on a tidal wave of sensuality, and for a moment she felt crazed. She had no idea what she was doing, why, or with whom. She hardly knew him, but all she did know was that she didn't want it to stop.

"I miss you so much," he said simply, looking like a boy again, although he acted like a man, in all the important ways. "So I come back from Los Angeles. I go to Santa Barbara yesterday. Like Bordeaux. Very beautiful, and very small. Too quiet."

"I think so too," she agreed, and her heart pounded as she let them both into her house. He had gotten the address when he called her office and said he had proofs to show her. He followed her inside and looked around, nodding approval, as he took off his leather jacket. It looked as though it had been through the wars. "Would you like dinner?" she asked as he smiled and nodded, and went to look at the view, and then, while she was cooking, he took photographs of her. "Don't, I look terrible," she said, brushing a lock of hair off her face. All she had was soup she had heated, cold chicken and salad she made for them, and she poured them each a glass of wine, while he put on some music. He seemed very much at home, and he came to kiss her from time to time while she organized dinner for them. It was harder and harder to keep her mind on what she was doing.

They sat down at the kitchen table, and talked about music. He had very sophisticated tastes, and was very knowledgeable about classical music. He said his mother had been an artist, and his father a conductor. And his sister was a doctor in Paris. A heart surgeon. He had an interesting background. He asked her what she had studied in school, and she told him economics, and he said he had studied political science.

"Sciences Po," he said, as though he expected her to know it. "It is a very good school. And you? You did more high studies?" She knew what he meant.

"Graduate school. I have an MBA." He didn't understand, and she said it was a very respected business degree, and he nodded.

"I understand. We have a very good school for that. HÉC. It is like Harvard Business School for us. I don't need that to take photographs," he said, and laughed. And after they ate, he kissed her again, and she had to fight back a wave of passion that seemed to overwhelm her. This was crazy. She couldn't just let animal instinct overpower her. Nothing like this had ever happened to her, and she finally looked at him in dismay.

"Jean-Pierre, what are we doing? We don't know each other. This is crazy."

"Sometimes crazy is good, no? I think yes. I am crazy to you."

"For you, or about you."

"Yes, that."

"I feel that way too, but in a few days you'll leave, or sooner, and we'll be sorry if we do something foolish."

He touched his heart and shook his head. "No, then I will always remember you. Here."

"Me too. But maybe later we will be sorry." She was worried

about what they were doing or might do. He was nearly impossible to resist.

"Why sorry?"

"Because the heart can be very easily hurt. And we don't know each other," she said sensibly, but he disagreed.

"I know you very much. I know many thing about you. Where you go to school, your children, your work, your marriage, your *tristesse* . . . your sadness . . . you have lose very much . . . sometimes we must find," he said as he remembered something he wanted to share with her. "You know the book, *The Little Prince*, by Antoine de Saint-Exupéry? There it say, *'On ne voit l'essentiel qu'avec le coeur'* . . . you only see the important thing in life with the heart . . . not the eyes. Or the head. It is a very wonderful book."

"I read it to my children. It is very sad. The little prince dies in the end." She looked touched. She loved the book.

"Yes, but he live forever in the stars." He was pleased that she knew the book. It told him that she was a very special woman, as much so as he had thought. He had seen it in her eyes when he took photographs of her. "You must always see with the heart. And after, you will live forever in the stars." It was a lovely thought, and it touched her.

They spent hours talking that night, and although she sensed that he would have liked to stay, he didn't ask her and she didn't offer. He didn't want to press her, and spoil what they had.

The next day he called her and then showed up at the office, and Bix looked surprised when he walked in.

"Are you still here, Jean-Pierre?" Bix asked with a smile of welcome. "I thought you left on Sunday or Monday."

"I did. I go to Los Angeles." He made it sound like a French city, and Bix smiled. "And then I come back yesterday."

"How long will you be here?"

"Maybe a few week," he said as Paris came out of her office and saw him. And something passed between them, as they looked at each other, like an electrical current of industrial voltage. Neither said anything, but Bix saw it immediately. He invited Jean-Pierre to stay for lunch, and the three of them ate sandwiches and drank cappuccinos in the room where they made presentations to clients. And afterward Jean-Pierre thanked them and left. He said he was going to visit Berkeley. He never said anything obvious to Paris, but he managed to communicate to her without words that he would see her later. And after he left, Bix stared at her.

"Am I imagining things, or is there something going on between you two?" He looked stunned, and turned to Paris, as she hesitated.

"No, there isn't really. We spent the day together on Sunday. I took him to Sausalito and Sonoma. And he dropped by last night. I'm not that foolish." Though it was sorely tempting, and she knew that if he stayed much longer, it would get harder and harder to resist him. But however attracted to him she was, she had managed to keep her resolve so far.

"I would be," Bix said, looking at her. "That foolish, I mean. Hell, Paris, he's adorable, and you don't owe anyone any explanations."

"Yes, I do. I owe myself one. He's a kid. He's fifteen years younger than I am."

"It doesn't look that way. You look like a kid yourself, and he's older than he looks. Hell, if he were giving me looks like that, I'd grab him. He's a hottie."

"You sound like my children." Paris laughed, and she couldn't disagree with him. But having an affair with Jean-Pierre would be total self-indulgence, no matter how attractive she found him. And she did. Very.

"I think you ought to kidnap him, and chain him to your bed-post before he goes back to Paris," Bix said warmly, and Paris laughed.

"Is that what you did with Steven?" she teased him.

"I didn't have to. He did that with me. Well, not really," Bix admitted. "But we were very attracted to each other pretty quickly. You two looked like you were going to set the room on fire with those looks. I could hardly eat my lunch. I thought he was going to grab you and throw you on the table." He would have liked to, but Paris had tried to maintain appearances, at least for Bix. "Are you seeing him tonight?"

"I might," she said, and Bix looked as though he approved, and when he commented on it again before she left, she scolded him for being a libertine.

"Why not, darling? You only live once. And I'd hate to miss a night with him, if I had the chance." But she knew perfectly well he wouldn't have traded anyone on the planet for Steven. They were crazy about each other.

As she drove up in front of her house that night, Jean-Pierre was sitting on the steps again, looking very relaxed, eating an apple, and reading a magazine. The van was in her driveway. And he looked up with pleasure the minute he saw her. She had known him at that point for exactly eight days, and she knew more about him than many people she had known for years. But it still didn't justify the attraction she felt for him. What was happening between them was all about chemistry and hormones and pheromones. It was totally out of their control, except that Paris was trying to do everything she could to keep a harness and muzzle on her feelings.

"I don't have much in the fridge," she said as they walked into the house together. And before she could say another word, he took her handbag and briefcase from her and set them down. He closed the front door with his foot, and kissed her so passionately it took her breath away. She had to fight to catch her breath when he stopped. She had never been kissed like that in her entire life, not even by him the night before.

"I am going crazy, Paris," he said desperately, and then kissed her again, and as he did, he took off her coat and dropped it on the floor, and then her blouse, and her bra, and she did nothing to stop him. She didn't want to. All she wanted was what he was doing. And as he continued undressing her, she began undressing him. She unbuttoned his shirt, undid his belt buckle, and unzipped his trousers. And within seconds, they were both standing naked, and glued to each other in the front hall. And without a word, he swept her into his powerful young arms, and carried her up the steps to her bedroom, as though he had done it a thousand times before. He deposited her on her bed, and looked at her for a long moment, and then gave a soft almost animal moan, as he began kissing her everywhere, and touching her, and making her writhe with pleasure, and she turned to return the favor to him. She put all of him that she could into her mouth, and his head arched back, and the beautiful young head with the spiky hair was thrown backward, as she did all she could to bring him pleasure, and then finally he got on the bed with her, and made love to her as she had never been made love to before. It was a tidal wave that neither could stop, and it seemed to go on for hours, and when she lay in his arms finally afterward, he ran a hand through her long silky hair and told her that he loved her. And although they barely knew each other, she believed him.

"*Je t'aime,*" he whispered hoarsely, and then began kissing her again. He couldn't keep his lips or his hands off of her, or keep his body away from her, and she couldn't keep hers away from him. It was many hours later when they finally fell asleep in each other's arms, and when they woke at sunrise, they made love again, but more quietly this time. It was a night Paris knew she would never forget, and that she would remember for the rest of her life. She was totally under the spell of Jean-Pierre.

Chapter 25

Fortunately the first days of Paris and Jean-Pierre's love affair began over a weekend, because they never got dressed or out of bed for nearly forty-eight hours. All she wanted was to be with him. They ordered pizza on Saturday, and made peanut butter sandwiches, which he said were disgusting and then ate two of them. All he wanted to satisfy him was Paris. They were luxuriating in her bathtub on Sunday night, when the phone rang and it was Meg.

Paris talked to her for a few minutes, and didn't tell her anything, and Jean-Pierre understood immediately, and didn't say a word while she was on the phone. And he did the same again when Wim called half an hour later.

She didn't ask Jean-Pierre what they were going to do, because they weren't going to do anything. He was going to be there as long as he was there, and they would enjoy it for what it was. A brief and blissfully torrid interlude. She had never done anything like it, but she didn't expect anything more. She wasn't going to try to make it into something it wasn't, or extort promises from him, or offer them. She asked no questions, expected no answers. Whatever time they shared with each other was a gift, however brief. She wanted nothing more. And she assumed that he didn't either.

But as she left for work on Monday morning, she asked him what he was going to do all day, and he looked vague.

"I must see a magazine. Someone tell me about it in Paris. I am curious what they do."

"Will you be here tonight when I come home?"

"I try." He smiled at her, and then kissed her. He still had his hotel room but hadn't been there in three days. They hadn't put on clothes since they'd come through the door on Friday. They'd been living in bathrobes and towels, and walking around naked much of the time. She had no sense of modesty with him, and they couldn't get enough of each other's bodies. Before she left, she handed him a set of spare keys, and showed him how to work the alarm. She had no qualms about letting him roam around her house when she wasn't there. She trusted him completely, not only with her house, but with herself. She felt totally at ease with him.

"*Merci, mon amour,*" he said, thanking her for the keys. "*À tout à l'heure.*" See you later, he said, as he blew her a kiss when she left, and he went out only minutes after she did.

"How was your weekend?" Bix asked as she came into the office, and she looked vague as she hung up her jacket.

"It was fine. How was yours?"

"Don't give me that," he said, he knew her too well. "Is Jean-Pierre still here?"

"I think so," she said innocently, and he saw nothing in her eyes this time. She was so tired, she could hardly keep them open.

And when she went home that night, he was there, and had already started cooking dinner for her. He had made a roast leg of lamb and string beans, bought cheese and a baguette. It was a delicious dinner, and she asked him about the magazine he'd gone to see as they ate.

"How was it?" she asked as they devoured the *gigot*. They were both starving, neither of them had had a decent meal in three days.

"Interesting," he said. "It is very small, but they do very good work. It is new."

"Are you going to do some work for them?" He nodded and looked at her, and over the bread and cheese he asked her an honest question.

"Paris, do you want me to stay, or go? Will it make too complicate for you if I stay for one month or two?"

She looked at him long and hard, and was honest with him. "I'd like you to stay." She was stunned by her own words, but it was how she felt.

He beamed at her, he was ready to do whatever she wanted, for as long as he could. "Then I stay. My visa is for six months. But I go whenever you say." It was a pact between them, and entirely comfortable for her. No one knew he was there, and their nights and weekends belonged to them.

Meg was too busy to come up from Los Angeles these days, and Wim had midterms and was busy with his friends. They had a month together, before Meg volunteered to come to spend a night with her before she left for Thanksgiving in the East. Jean-Pierre had long since given up his hotel room, but he told her he'd be happy to leave for the night when Meg came.

"That might be a good idea," Paris agreed. She didn't want to shock her daughter unduly, and she had no idea what she was going to say, if anything.

Meg arrived on the Tuesday night before Thanksgiving, and Wim came over to spend the night as well. Paris loved having both of her children there, and she cooked them a delicious dinner, which was more than she'd done so far for Jean-Pierre. And both Wim and Meg were flying to New York in the morning. Richard was staying in Los Angeles with his daughter.

"Will you be okay for Thanksgiving, Mom?" Meg already knew she was going to Steven and Bix's for the holiday, but she worried about her getting lonely over the weekend. She didn't have a lot of friends in San Francisco yet, and Meg knew she wasn't seeing anyone, or so she thought.

"I'll be fine. I'm just glad you'll be here for Christmas. That's more important." And it was only later, when she and Meg were both getting ready for bed, and Wim was downstairs, that Paris shared her secret, or part of it at least, with her. She rarely kept anything from her daughter. And what had gone on for the last five weeks was unusual for her in every way. She told her she was dating someone, and he was French. But she did not say that he was staying with her, and he was fifteen years younger. That was too much to confess at one gulp.

"What's he like?" Meg looked pleased for her, as she always was when things were going well for her mother.

"Adorable. He's a photographer. He's on assignment here for a few months."

"That's too bad." Meg looked disappointed. "How soon is he going back?"

"I don't know. We're having fun for now." She sounded philosophical about it.

"Widowed or divorced?"

"Divorced. He has a ten-year-old son." She didn't say that he was barely older than that himself.

"It's weird how all these older guys have young kids, isn't it?" Meg was thinking of her father, and her mother's new friend had obviously gotten a late start, she assumed. Paris made a vague mmming sound as she nodded and brushed her teeth. But she knew that sooner or later, if they met him, she would have to at least acknowledge the difference in their age. It didn't bother her or Jean-Pierre, he said it didn't matter to him at all, his ex-wife was older than he was too, though only five years, and not fifteen. But Paris had no idea how her children would react, and she was nervous about it.

She talked to Bix about it in the office the next day. She had felt dishonest not saying something to Meg, particularly after her comment about older guys getting a late start and having kids. There was nothing "older" about Jean-Pierre.

"I don't think anyone gives a damn these days," Bix reassured her. "Older, younger, same age. Fifty-year-old women have twenty-five-year-old boyfriends. Seventy-year-old men marry thirty-year-olds and have babies. The world has changed. A lot of people don't even bother to get married to have kids these days. Single men and women adopt children. None of the old rules hold. I think you can do damn near anything you want. And you're not hurting anyone. I hope your children will be decent about it." But Paris was still unsure.

Paris talked to them on Thanksgiving, they were at their father's. They were staying there, and Rachel answered the phone when she called. Paris just asked to speak to Meg, and didn't say anything to her. But she told Wim to wish his father a happy Thanksgiving. It was the only contact she had had with Peter in over a year, when they took Wim to school. They no longer even talked on the phone, they had no reason to, and it was easier for her this way.

Jean-Pierre was with her when she talked to them, and afterward they went to Bix and Steven's, and had a lovely Thanksgiving. It was Jean-Pierre's first, and he said he liked it. And they went to see two French movies and an American one that weekend. Jean-Pierre loved films.

And for the next month, they lived in their little bubble, like twins in the womb. Everything was protected and happy. She worked a million Christmas parties with Bix, or it felt that way at least, and Jean-Pierre was doing a lot of work for the new magazine. They couldn't believe their good fortune to have him, and he had to do a lot of explaining in Paris and New York as to why he had dropped out of sight for the past two months, and didn't know when he would return. He had until April, and then he either had to do something about getting a permanent resident's visa, which wouldn't be easy to obtain, or go home. But for the moment, everything was easy and simple in their world. And Paris had never been happier in her life. She invited Richard to join her and and the children for Christmas, and realized that she had to say something to Wim and Meg, so Jean-Pierre could be there too, and she wanted him to be. She finally took the bull by the horns with Meg the week before they came. She wanted to give her at least a few days to digest it, but her hands were shaking before she made the call. Their approval and support were important to her, and she wondered if, in their eyes, she had gone too far.

She chatted with Meg for a few minutes, and then decided to drop the bomb. "Something unusual has happened," she began, as Meg waited.

"Are you still seeing that French photographer?" Meg sensed what it was, or so she thought.

"Yes, I am. If it's all right with you, I'd like him to join us for Christmas. He has no one else here he knows, except the people he works with, and Bix and Steven."

"That sounds fine, Mom." She was grateful that her mother had invited Richard. Things had gotten very serious between them.

"I think I should probably mention something before you get here."

"Is there something weird about him?" Meg sounded suspicious as Paris plunged in.

"Not weird," Paris said cautiously. But all she could do now was tell the truth. "Just different. For me at least. He's young." There was a silence at the other end of the phone, and she felt like the daughter instead of the mother.

"How young?"

Paris took a breath. "Thirty-two." There, she'd said it, and Meg didn't answer for a minute.

"Oh. That's pretty young, Mom." Meg sounded a little stunned.

"Yes, it is. He's very mature," and then she laughed at herself. In fact he wasn't. He was totally age-appropriate, and sometimes she felt like his mother, except very certainly not in bed. "No, he's not," she corrected. "He's a perfectly normal thirty-two-year-old, and I'm probably an old fool. But I'm having a wonderful time with him." What she said was honest at least. There was no pretense about what she was doing.

"That's good." Meg was trying to be mature herself, but Paris could hear that she was shocked. It was surely a departure from the ordinary, and not one her daughter had ever expected from her. "Are you in love with him?" Meg sounded concerned.

"I think I am. For now. But sooner or later he'll have to go home. We can't do this forever. He's basically taking some time off from his normal work. He can't do that forever either. He's working for a tiny magazine here, instead of *Harper's Bazaar* and *Vogue*. We're having fun."

"If you're happy, Mom, that's all that counts. Just don't do anything too crazy. Like marry him." Meg didn't think that would work although the age difference between her and Richard was far greater, but that seemed more normal to her, because he was a man. It was a shock to Meg to think of her mother with a much younger man. And later Richard reassured her. He didn't think her mother would do anything foolish, although a lot of well-known women seemed to be involved with younger men these days. And after she talked to him about it, Meg felt better.

It was Wim who was shocked. "How old is he, Mom?" he asked in a suddenly high-pitched voice. She told him again.

"That's like me going out with a four-year-old," he said to bring the point home. Paris got it. He was upset.

"Not exactly. He's a grown man."

"What's he doing with a woman your age?" Wim said in a tone of disapproval. The whole world was going crazy, as far as he was concerned. His father had left his mother and married a woman barely older than Meg, and they were having a baby, which seemed ridiculous to him, and in bad taste. And now his mother had a boyfriend nearly half her age, or close enough. Or actually the same age as his father's new wife. Young was certainly in. And Wim thought both his parents were nuts.

"You'll have to ask him," Paris answered, trying to sound calmer than she felt. She didn't want either of her children to be upset, or to look foolish in their eyes and she was sure she did. But Bix reassured her again the next day. He thought Jean-Pierre was a terrific man. And Jean-Pierre himself seemed unconcerned. Whenever she brought it up, he brushed the age difference away, and she didn't feel it as a problem between them. It just sounded so bad. But in reality, it looked fine. No one ever stared at them, or seemed surprised to see them together, which was a relief for her.

And when her children arrived on the day before Christmas Eve, there was an awkward moment when she introduced them to Jean-Pierre. They all seemed to be circling each other and sniffing the way dogs did, checking each other out. But while Paris checked on dinner, Richard made an effort to break the ice. And before she knew it, everyone was talking and laughing, and teasing each other and making jokes, and by the end of the evening, they were friends. Even Wim. He and Jean-Pierre played squash with each other the next morning, and by the time they sat down to Christmas Eve dinner, he seemed more like their friend than hers. Their objections and concerns seemed to evaporate in thin air. It was a lovely Christmas, and at one point even Paris had to laugh. The world really was upside down. Meg was with a man old enough to be her father, who should have been going out with her mother, and her mother was with a man technically young enough to be her son. She was still thinking about it when she and Jean-Pierre went to bed that night. Her children were in the mother-in-law apartment downstairs.

"I like your children very much," he said with a warm look. "They are very good. And very kind to me. They are not angry to you?"

"No, they're not. Thank you for being so understanding." It couldn't have been easy for him either. He was in a foreign country where he barely spoke the language, working on a magazine that was far beneath his stature, living with a woman old enough to be his mother, or almost, with grown children he had to audition for. And he'd been a terrific sport. It had been a lovely Christmas so far, and when they went to bed, he handed her a small package with a smile. When she opened it, it was a beautiful gold bracelet from Cartier, with the Eiffel Tower on it and a gold heart with her initials on it on one side of the heart, and his on the other, and just above it he had had engraved *Je t'aime.*

"*Joyeux Noël, mon amour,*" he said softly. And then she made him unwrap her present. They had shopped in the same place. She had bought him a Cartier watch. And she knew that whatever happened later, it was a Christmas she would cherish forever in her heart. They were savoring stolen moments, and living in a magic bubble. But it was becoming a little more real. The bubble included her children now, and so far at least, all was well. *Joyeux Noël.*

Chapter 26

Meg and Richard and Wim stayed with Paris for a week, and over the New Year weekend they all went to Squaw Valley to ski, and stayed at a large resort hotel. And Jean-Pierre joined them for the weekend. He turned out to be an Olympic-class skier and had raced in Val d'Isère as a kid. Wim loved skiing with him, and Richard stayed with Paris and Meg and skied more sedately down the slopes. And at night they all went out. It was an ideal vacation for all of them, and on New Year's Eve, Paris forced herself not to think that it was Peter and Rachel's first anniversary and they were having a baby in five months. It was still hard for her to believe. And she could remember all too easily how ghastly the day had been for her a year before, knowing that he was out of her life forever, and in Rachel's arms for good. As she thought about it while she dressed for the evening, Jean-Pierre saw the look on her face.

"*Tu es triste?* You are sad?"

"No, just thinking. I'm all right." She smiled at him. He had understood instantly what it was. She only looked that way when her children talked about their father, and it hurt his feelings sometimes. To him, it meant that she didn't love him as much as he loved her. But it was more complicated than that. It was about history and memories and hearts that were forever intertwined, from her point of view at least, no matter what the legal papers said. She had tried to explain it to him once, and he had been upset for two days. He viewed her feelings about Peter as a disloyalty to him, and no amount of explaining changed that. She had learned that the words were better left unsaid. He didn't seem to understand what the loss of her marriage had meant to her. Maybe he was too young. He hadn't lost enough yet himself. There were times when, in spite of his warmth and charm, she felt the difference in their ages. He saw life as a young person, and preferred to live only in the moment. He hated to think about the future or make plans. He was entirely spontaneous, and did whatever felt good at the time, with no regard for consequences, which sometimes irked her. He had called his son on Christmas Day, but he admitted that the child was almost a stranger to him, and he didn't feel the loss. He had never spent time with him from the first. And had never allowed himself to love him, which seemed wrong to Paris. She felt Jean-Pierre owed him more than that, but Jean-Pierre didn't. He felt he owed him nothing, and it made him furious that he had to send money to support him. He hated the boy's mother, and said so. He and his ex-wife had married to give the child a name, and had divorced shortly after that. He had had no great emotional investment in the mother or the child. They had both been a burden to him, one he tried to ignore. So he avoided the boy, which seemed sad to Paris, and irresponsible. He had no other father than Jean-Pierre, but Jean-Pierre resisted any emotions about him, because he had been manipulated by the boy's mother. Paris always felt, when they talked about it, that his responsibilities to the child should have transcended his feelings about the mother, but they didn't. He had shut them both out years before. And ultimately it was the child's loss, which bothered Paris. But they saw it differently, and probably always would. She had stopped talking to him about it, because they argued over it, which upset her. She felt he owed the child more than he was giving, and she thought his attitude about it was selfish. But perhaps it was only young.

There were other things they saw differently too. He had a more casual work ethic than she, and the people he liked were younger, which made her uncomfortable. She preferred hanging out with people closer to her own age. And the people he brought home from the magazine were in their twenties and made her feel ancient. And one of the important topics they disagreed about was marriage.

Jean-Pierre talked a lot about it. Paris never did. She avoided it discreetly. There were times when she actually thought about it, and wondered if it could ever work with him long term, but there were subtle hints, to her, that it couldn't, that it would be too big a stretch. The people he liked, his boyishness, which translated to juvenile to her at times. And although he wasn't a socialist, he had very definite political ideas that were far more liberal than hers. He thought riches of any kind were offensive. He detested all things bourgeois. He hated old-fashioned ideas, and traditions and obligations that seemed pointless to him. He was very avant-garde and free in his thinking. He believed in high taxes, for the good of the people. And he detested anything elitist with a passion. The parties she and Bix organized always irritated him, because he thought the people were so pretentious. And they were, some of them, but she and Bix loved them, for the most part. And elitism was the essence of their business. Some of his ideas she knew were because he was French. But the essence of it was that he was young. It did make a difference. And the only ancient tradition he believed in was marriage, because he was a romantic, and believed in commitment, which she admired in him. Unlike Chandler Freeman, who was committed to nothing and no one. But Jean-Pierre was the reverse side of that coin, and he often pressed her and asked if she thought she would marry him one day. And threatened that, if she wouldn't, he would move on. She never promised that she would, and she thought about it herself from time to time, but never as often as he did, and she came to different conclusions, on her own. She thought that over time the difference in their age and philosophies would pull them apart, rather than the reverse.

Meg asked her about it before they left Squaw Valley. She had finally taken several runs down the mountain with Jean-Pierre and her
brother, while Richard and Paris skied the easier runs in the afternoon. And that night she questioned her mother about Jean-Pierre.

"Are you thinking of marrying him, Mom?" she asked with a
look of concern.

"No, I'm not. Why?"

"I just wondered. I went up on the chair with him today, and he
said he hoped you would, and maybe next summer we could all
take a trip to celebrate. I didn't know if that was his idea or yours."
She looked worried.

"His," Paris said with a sigh, but it made her sad anyway. She
knew that one day reality would have to be faced. She couldn't
imagine committing the rest of her life to a man his age. A boy, as
she thought of him at times, although he hated it when she said
that. But he was. He was carefree and independent, and very
young. He was a free spirit, detested schedules and plans, and was
always late. It was hard at times to think of him as an adult. He had
never had the responsibilities she had, and had no idea what they
meant. It was hard to explain away time, or change it, to add it or
subtract it at will. It wasn't an easy thing to do, even when the reasons for it were good. Time and history and experience were what
they were, and couldn't be discounted or erased. They had to be
earned, like patina on bronze. It took a long time to get there, and
once it was there, it stayed. She knew it would be years before Jean-
Pierre was responsible or even mature, if he ever was.

"He's terrific, and I like him a lot," Meg said honestly, careful not
to hurt her mother's feelings, but she had her own ideas, and Paris
didn't disagree with them. They were similar to her own. "But a lot
of the time, he reminds me of Wim. A little careless, a little crazy,
they just don't see the whole picture, they're too busy having a
good time. Not like you. You understand a lot more about people,
who they are, what they need, and why they do what they do. He
seems like such a kid." The trouble was, he did to Paris too.

"Thank you," Paris said with a warm look, she was touched. But she saw the same things in Jean-Pierre that Meg did. He was an irresistible, charming, delicious boy. But nonetheless a boy. Tender-hearted and loving, but irresponsible at times. He had never had to be otherwise, but she had, for many, many years. And she also thought he should have children one day, more than just a son he had been estranged from for all his life. And she wasn't going to have babies with him, although he had mentioned it more than once. He thought they should one day. Paris just couldn't see that, even if she could, which she was no longer sure was possible, not with ease anyway. Even if she started now, she'd be forty-eight when they had a child, which was pushing it, in her mind at least. And if they waited any longer, it wouldn't be possible at all. Not in a year or two, or five, when he'd be ready to settle down. There were so many reasons why marrying him didn't make sense, but loving him did. She just didn't have the answers yet. And in four months his visa would run out. That reality was going to force them both to make decisions they probably didn't want to make. And she was trying not to think of it. "Don't worry about it, Meg," Paris reassured her.

"I just want you to be happy, Mom, whatever it takes. You de-serve it. You've earned it after everything Daddy did." She still felt terrible about that, and resentful of Rachel as a result. It had all been so unfair to her mom. "If you think you'd be happy with him forever, then do it, and we'll make the best of it. We all like him. I just don't think he's right for you in the long run." She wanted someone who would take care of her mother, and she doubted Jean-Pierre ever would. It didn't even occur to him, which was part of Paris's appeal to him. She was totally capable of taking care of herself, and him, emotionally, which was all he wanted from her. But even that was a lot. Sometimes Paris felt like he was her third child.

"I don't think he's right for me either," Paris said sadly. "I wish I did." It would be so much simpler than going back out into the big bad ugly dating world again. She couldn't bear the thought. And Jean-Pierre was so sweet to her, sweeter than anyone had ever been. Even Peter. But sweet wasn't always enough. And love wasn't always enough. Sometimes life was just plain cruel, and no one was more aware of that than Paris.

And when she and Jean-Pierre snuggled in bed that night, all she could think of was how devastated she would be if she gave him up. She couldn't imagine that anymore either. There were a lot of decisions to make. But not yet.

And when they all went back to the city, they felt like a family, even Jean-Pierre. But as he cavorted in the snow, and then drove home with them in a van Paris had rented for the occasion, he seemed more like the kids than the adults. She knew exactly what Meg meant. He played tricks, he told jokes, and Paris loved all of that herself. He encouraged her playful side, and made her feel young again, but not young enough. He and Wim had constant snowball fights in Squaw Valley, but just like Wim, he never knew when to stop. They would pelt each other till they dropped, no matter what Paris said. And they came in soaking wet, and left their clothes strewn all over the floor. They were like two boys. Even Meg seemed more mature at twenty-four. And at times Paris and Richard would look over their heads, as they said something, or did something childish, and they seemed like parents to a Cub Scout troop. But there was no question, Jean-Pierre was a delicious cub. And she loved him like one of her own. She couldn't imagine giving him up.

The life Paris shared with Jean-Pierre was magical all the way into spring. On January 6, they celebrated Epiphany, *La Fête des Rois,* with a cake with a lucky "baby" in it, to bring luck all year to the one who found it. He bought the cake on his way home from work and explained it to her, and then they ate the cake, and when Paris found the baby, he cheered.

They drove to Carmel and Santa Barbara, went hiking in Yosemite, and visited Meg and Richard in Los Angeles. And on

Valentine's Day, Meg called her mother, breathless with the news. But Richard had called Paris to ask her the day before, and she had approved. He had proposed, and they were getting married in September. He had given her an enormous ring. And she couldn't wait to show her mother.

And much to her consternation, Jean-Pierre gave her one too, a far simpler one than Richard had given Meg, but with equal meaning, though his came without a proposal, but the implication was clear. It was a gold band with a tiny diamond heart on it, and he put it on her left hand, which had seemed so naked to her for so long. She had missed her wedding ring so much and so often wished that she could still wear it, but it seemed a travesty now, with Peter married to someone else. Paris had loved all it stood for, and had never taken it off till the end. But Jean-Pierre's ring warmed her hand and her heart again, and made her wonder yet again if she should think seriously about spending the rest of her life with him. There were worse fates. She asked Bix what he thought of it, when they were talking about Meg's wedding one day, the week after she'd gotten engaged.

"You have to follow your heart," he said sensibly. "What do you want?"

"I don't know. To be safe, I guess." They were the first words that came to mind. After what had happened with Peter, that meant everything to her. But they both knew that in life everything was possible, and nothing was sure. There were no guarantees. Some risks were greater than others, and they seemed considerable to her with Jean-Pierre. He was undeniably young, though he had just turned thirty-three, which sounded better to her. But she was about to turn forty-eight in May, just over two months away. It sounded so old to her. And everything about him was young, his looks, his mind, his ideas. He was undeniably and irresistibly immature, and even if they had been the same age, their lifestyles and ideas and goals were often worlds apart. His sweetness appealed to her, and they loved each other. But Paris knew better than most that love was not always enough. He might grow up and feel differently one day, and fall in love with someone else. Or maybe not. Peter had. It had shaken her faith in everything, and now Jean-Pierre. It would forever taint whatever she loved or believed in or touched. There was no turning back the clock.

"Do you love him?"

"Yes," she said without hesitation. "I just don't know if I love him enough."

"How much is enough?"

"Enough to grow old together, and put up with all the miseries and disappointments that come your way in life." They both knew that they never failed to come, no matter how much you loved someone. You had to be willing to stick it out. Peter wasn't. Would Jean-Pierre? Who the hell knew? Paris didn't. Nor did Bix. Jean-Pierre probably didn't know himself, but he thought he did. And in March, he proposed. His visa was running out in a month, and he wanted to know what Paris was going to do. She was desperately sorry he had asked. Once he did, there was no turning back. And he was devastated that she did not instantly accept. She gave it a great deal of thought.

He wanted her either to marry him so he could stay in the States and get a green card, or move back to Paris with him, so he could resume his life. But that meant giving up everything she had now. She loved working with Bix, and her life in San Francisco. It meant leaving the States. But Jean-Pierre was more than willing to stay. And he could only stay legally if they got married, so he could work. He felt he couldn't put off his real life any longer. He had given her a six-month gift. But she knew she couldn't hold him back forever. It wasn't fair to him. He had to go back to what he'd been doing before, as a star photographer in a bigger world. Or stay with her forever here, and drum up work on a bigger scale, probably in L.A. But they couldn't live in the twilight zone forever, as he pointed out to her when he told her how much he loved her, and wanted her to be his wife. In some ways, she wanted that too, but she couldn't help but worry about the future, and what would happen when he grew up, because he wasn't a grown-up yet. He was nearly there, but not quite, and his boyishness erupted constantly. It made her feel like his mother. And she hated that. She didn't want to be his mother. She wasn't even sure if she wanted to be his wife. There was no question that she loved him. The question was how much. And in all fairness to him, she felt he deserved someone who was sure.

It took her three weeks to figure it out, and it was already early April when they took a long walk in the Marina, and wound up on the lawn at the Palace of Fine Arts, sitting on the lawn, and watching the ducks. She loved going there with him. She loved going everywhere with him. It took every ounce of courage to say the fateful words to him that he had waited for, for three weeks. She said them in a whisper, and they tore at her heart, and were like a cannonball in his.

"Jean-Pierre, I can't marry you. I love you, but I just can't. The future is too uncertain . . . and you deserve so much more than I can give you . . . kids, if nothing else." And he deserved to be a kid, if he wanted to be. The problem was, she needed an adult, and she wasn't sure he ever would be. Or not for a long time at least.

"Will you live with me in France, unmarried?" he asked in a strangled voice. His heart felt like a rock in his chest, just as hers once had. She knew it only too well, and hated doing it to him. But it was better this way in the long run. Better now than later. Better a terrible pain now than a total disaster later on, for both of them. She silently shook her head, and he walked home alone.

He said almost nothing to her that night, and he slept downstairs. He would not sleep with her again, would not touch her, would not beg her. And in the morning his bags were packed. She did not go to work that day, and they both cried uncontrollably when he left.

"I love you. I will always love you. If you want to come, I will be there. If you want me to come back, I will." She couldn't have asked for more, and she was throwing it away. She felt insane. But right. At a terrible, terrible price. For both of them. *"Je t'aime"* were his last words.

"Moi aussi," she whispered, and sobbed when he was gone. It was almost beyond bearing, but she bore it, because she knew it was right. She loved him. Too much to make a mistake. And enough to set him free, which was the greatest gift of love she could give him, and the right one, she believed.

She didn't go to the office all week, and when she did, she looked like death. She had been there before. She knew it well. She didn't even call Anne Smythe this time. She just gritted her teeth and lived through it. And on the second anniversary of the day Peter had left her, all she could think of was the double loss. And this time she knew that she had learned yet another painful lesson. That she could not give her heart again. Ever. Peter had taken the biggest part of it with him. And when Jean-Pierre had left, it had cost her the rest.

Chapter 27

Peter and Rachel's baby came the day after Wim's birthday, on the seventh of May. Three days after Paris's. She was numb by then, and almost didn't care. Almost. But some part of her still did. All she could think of were the moments she and Peter had shared with their babies. A time when life was beginning, not over for her as it was now. It just added to the bleak landscape she saw all around her, and a sense of utter despair.

Although she said little to them, and never mentioned Jean-Pierre, her children had no idea how to console her, and worried about her. Meg talked to Richard about it every time she spoke to her mother, and finally called Bix.

"How is she really? She sounds awful, but she keeps telling me she's fine. She doesn't sound fine to me." Meg sounded worried, and sad for her mom.

"She isn't fine," he confirmed, much to Meg's chagrin. "I guess she just has to get through it. I think it's a lot of stuff on top of each other. Your father. His new baby. Jean-Pierre. It all hurts like hell."

"What can I do to make it better?"

"Nothing. She has to get through it herself. She'll find the way back. She has before." But the road back was more arduous this time, and seemed to take longer. Although nothing would ever be as bad again as when Peter had left her, except death. This time she did not die. But she crawled back slowly, on her own. And the only thing that kept her going were the plans for Meg and Richard's wedding in the fall. They were having three hundred guests, and she and Bix were handling it all. Meg had total faith in them, and was leaving all the decisions to her mother.

It was in June, two months after Jean-Pierre left, that Paris finally couldn't stand it any longer, and sat for an entire night staring at the phone. She had promised herself that if she still wanted to call him in the morning, she would, and do whatever he wanted her to do, if he still did. She couldn't tolerate the agony anymore. She had been lonely for too long, and she missed him more than she ever knew she would. At eight o'clock in the morning in San Francisco, five in the afternoon in Paris, she called Jean-Pierre. Her heart pounded waiting to hear him, as she wondered if she could be on a flight by that night. If he still wanted her, she knew she would go. Maybe the age difference didn't matter after all.

The phone rang, and a woman's voice answered. She sounded very young. Paris didn't know who it was, and she asked for him. The girl said he was out. Paris spoke to her in French. She was able to now, thanks to him.

"Do you know when he's coming back?"

"Soon," the girl said. "He went to pick up my little girl. I have the flu."

"Are you living there?" Paris dared to ask, fearing some horrible reprisal for her intrusion. She had no business doing that to him, and she knew it, but she wanted to know.

"Yes, I am, with my little girl. Who are you?"

"A friend in San Francisco," she said vaguely, wanting to ask the girl if she loved him, and if he loved her, but that was going too far. And she didn't need to know. They were living together, he hadn't lost much time. None at all. But she had wounded him deeply, she knew, and they each had to put balm on the wounds in their own way. He owed her nothing now.

"We're getting married in December," the girl volunteered. It was June.

"Oh," Paris said, feeling a torpedo shoot through her. It could have been she. But it couldn't have been, she knew. She couldn't do it. And her reasoning had been right at the time, for her, if not for him. Just as Peter had done what he had to do. Maybe they all did, even if others got hurt. It was love at a price. "Congratulations," Paris said in a dead voice.

"Do you want to give me your name and number?" the girl asked helpfully, and Paris shook her head. It took her a moment to find her voice.

"No, that's all right. I'll call back. You don't have to tell him I called. In fact, better not. I'll surprise him when I call. Thank you," Paris said, and hung up, and then sat there for an hour staring at the phone. Just like Peter, he was gone forever, living with this girl. He hadn't wasted any time. She wondered how it had happened, and if he really loved her, or if it was rebound. Whatever it was, it was his. Their lives had come unhooked. Their time together had been a magical moment, but that was all it was. Magic. And like all magic, something of a trick. An illusion. Something that she wanted it to be, but not necessarily what it really was.

She dressed and went to the office, and when Bix saw her, he shook his head. The one thing he was not going to suggest this time was that she start to date. She was in no condition to go out with anyone, and he suspected she wouldn't be for months. It was another two months before she looked human, as far as he was concerned, and by then Meg's wedding was only a month away. Paris hadn't even bought a dress, although Meg's had been hanging in the closet of the downstairs apartment for two months. It was spectacular and had been made according to a design Bix had drawn. There was an endless train, and the dress was white lace.

It was late August by the time Bix heard Paris laugh again, at a joke someone told, and he was so startled, he looked around to see who had laughed. It was she. And for the first time in four months, she looked like herself. He didn't know when it had happened, but when it had, it had happened overnight.

"Is that you?" He looked relieved. He'd been worried sick about her. They all were.

"Maybe. I'm not sure."

"Well, don't go away again. I miss you too much when you do."

"Believe me, I'm not planning to do that again. I can't afford it. I'm done. No more men."

"Oh? Are we doing women now?"

"No." She laughed again. It was a delicious sound. She had done her work for the past four months, but nothing else. She didn't go anywhere, see anyone, and she had only spoken to her children, just to check in. Wim was away for the summer again, on a work program in Spain, and Meg was swamped in L.A. The wedding was in four weeks. "I'm not planning to 'do' anyone. Men or women. Just me."

"That'll do," Bix said, looking pleased.

"I have to buy a dress for the wedding." She looked panicked. Like Rip Van Winkle, who had just woken up. She'd been a zombie for four months. And she had never told him about the call in June to Jean-Pierre, which had only made it worse.

Bix looked sheepish, as he unlocked the door to his locked closet. He had had a dress made for her. If she liked it, she could have it, as a gift from him. If she didn't, he would give it away. It was a beautiful beige lace dress with a pale pink taffeta coat, and it looked perfect with her coloring and hair. "I hope it fits. You've lost a hell of a lot of weight." Again. She had been through it before. But that had been worse. This was bad enough. She felt cured for life. She didn't want to get involved with anyone again. It just hurt too much. And maybe it always would. Maybe there was no way to avoid the price. Paris no longer knew, or cared. She was just glad to be back, and sane again.

"I'll take it home and try it. You're an angel, Bix." They spent the rest of the afternoon going over the last details. Everything was in

order. As usual, Bix had done an incredible job, even without a lot
of help from her. Even though she had done her best. But her best
hadn't been at its top form for a while, since Jean-Pierre left.

And that night when she went home, she tried on the dress.
Even Paris had to smile when she looked in the mirror. She looked
beautiful and young. He had made exactly the right choice. And it
coordinated with the rest of the wedding. The bridesmaids were
wearing beige silk. Seven of them. At the wedding of Meg's
dreams.

The only nightmare for Paris was that Peter and Rachel were going to be there. And their baby. And Rachel's boys. The perfect little
family. And Paris would be alone. It was a condition she accepted
now, as she had once before. But losing Jean-Pierre was different. It
had not been inflicted on her, like a prison sentence she had been
given. It was a choice she had made. She had decided, after much
thought, in the past four months, that she was better off alone. It
wasn't what she had wanted, or how she had envisioned her life
once upon a time. But it was what had happened to her. Her destiny maybe. And she knew without a moment's doubt now that
she could be happy and comfortable without a man. She had come
to that conclusion once before, and then everything had gone
wrong again. But it wouldn't this time. And in the last two months,
she had done a lot of thinking, and she had a plan.

She knew what she wanted. She wasn't sure how her children
would feel about it. But it was her decision, no matter what anyone
else thought. She had made quiet inquiries, and she had two
names. She was going to call them after the wedding, and proceed
from there. And even before she called them, she knew it was right
for her. It was the only avenue that made sense to her now. The one
thing she knew she was good at, and wouldn't break her heart. She
didn't know how she'd get there, but she knew she would if it was
meant to be. Paris wanted a baby, but not a man.

Chapter 28

Meg's wedding was everything Paris wanted it to be. It was elegant, beautiful, done in exquisite taste, not too showy. Unforgettable. Meg wanted it in a garden setting, so they held it at the Burlingame Club. And Paris and Bix agreed it was one of the prettiest weddings they'd ever done, which was what her mother had wanted for her.

She had spoken to Peter a few times over the final details, and estimates about cost, since he was splitting it with her, but their conversations had been cursory, businesslike, and brief. And each time she'd spoken to him, she'd felt shaken, and had to catch her breath afterward, but she knew it would be very different being able to set the phone down and walk away, than having to face him on Meg's wedding day. Paris had been dreading seeing him again. She hadn't in two years, since they'd settled Wim in Berkeley, and she had hardly spoken to him since. Now she had to face not only him but Rachel, her children, and their baby. Her stomach and her heart were in knots over it.

She was so busy with Meg the day of the wedding that she almost didn't have time to think of it, and when she saw Peter finally, he was waiting for his daughter in the back of the church. Richard was secluded in a separate room, with the best man, so he wouldn't see his bride before the ceremony. Meg wanted to do everything according to tradition, and she looked like a fairy princess in the gown Bix had designed for her, with a vast ephemeral cloud of veil, a tiny pearl tiara, and the white lace dress with the seemingly endless train. It was everything Paris had wanted for her. An unforgettably beautiful day, marrying a man who loved her just as much as she loved him. Paris had long since stopped worrying about the difference in their ages, she agreed that Richard was the perfect man for Meg.

And as she walked into the back of the church to check on the last details, she saw Peter standing quietly by himself, waiting for Meg. She was downstairs with her bridesmaids, having a last nervous giggle with the girls as they settled her veil over her face and wished her well. She was anxiously clutching an enormous bouquet of lily of the valley and the tiniest white orchids. Bix had had the lily of the valley flown in from Paris especially for her.

As Paris entered the room, she saw Peter standing there, and they said nothing to each other, just stood there. It was impossible not to think of their own wedding day twenty-six years before. She had never thought it would be this way when their children married. She had fully expected to go to Meg's wedding with her husband next to her, and not to meet him for the first time in two years in a church, knowing he was married to someone else.

"Hello, Peter," she said formally, and she could see in his eyes that he was affected by seeing her. Thanks to Bix, she looked almost as breathtaking as Meg. The pink taffeta coat swirled around her and enveloped her, and underneath it the beige lace dress molded her still youthful figure. He wanted to say something to her about how remarkable she looked, but he couldn't find the words at first, and then he slowly approached her, looking shaken by the emotions of the day, and the sight of her. She was lovelier than he'd allowed himself to remember.

"Hello, Paris. You look beautiful," he said simply. And for a moment, he even forgot that they were there for Meg. Like Paris, all he could think of suddenly was their own wedding day, and how everything had gone awry since then. He was happy with Rachel, and he loved their baby, but seeing Paris seemed to sweep the present away. He felt transported backward into time, and when he hugged her, she could sense in him and herself, everything they had once felt for each other. She pulled away and looked up at him.

"You look very handsome." He always had. She had always loved him, and always would. "Wait till you see our daughter." But it wasn't Meg who filled his heart now, it was Paris, and everything they had once shared, and lost since then. He didn't know what to say. He knew there was no way he could ever make up to her for all he'd done to her. It was so different knowing that at a distance than seeing her face-to-face again. He hadn't been prepared for the flood of emotions and regrets that would overwhelm him when he looked into her eyes. He could see there that she had forgiven him. But the worst of it, he realized, was that he no longer knew if he could forgive himself. It was far harder to do while looking at her. She was so elegant and so dignified, so vulnerable and so proud. Just feeling her stand next to him, his heart went out to her, and he had no idea what to say. He only hoped that one day life made it up to her. And he knew from what his children said that thus far at least it had not.

"They'll be ready in a few minutes," she warned him, and then left the room again. Wim took his mother to her seat in the first pew, and she saw that Rachel was sitting directly behind her with her two boys, and she tried not to stiffen, but wished they had put her a few rows farther back at least. Paris turned to face forward, and Wim took his seat next to her, and an instant later the organist began playing the music that she knew meant the wedding was about to start, and the first of Meg's bridesmaids glided slowly down the aisle.

And when she saw Meg come toward her on her father's arm, Paris could hear her own breath catch, and others murmur. She was such a lovely bride, it tugged at the heart, and was everything a wedding was meant to be. She was all innocence and beauty, and hope and trust. And as she looked into Richard's eyes, there was such joy on her face that Paris thought her heart would burst and she could feel tears fill her eyes. Peter caught Paris's eye as he came back down the aisle toward her, and there was so much tenderness in his expression that she wanted to reach out and touch his hand. But she knew she couldn't. He slipped quietly into the pew behind her, beside his new wife, and Paris had to steel herself not to cry harder. The single gesture and the reality of where he was sitting summed up the entire situation, and Wim looked down at her to make sure she was all right, just as his sister would have. Meg had warned him that morning to be extra nice to Mom, because the wedding would be hard on her, Meg knew, and Wim had understood. And as they sat down again, he patted his mother's hand, and Paris smiled up at him through her tears. Paris knew she was lucky. He was a good boy, and a loving son.

And after the ceremony was over, Paris and Peter stood at the entrance to the church with the bride and groom, the matron of honor and the best man, and they formed a receiving line as people came past to greet and congratulate them. For a fraction of an instant, it felt like being married again, and then Paris looked across the vestibule through the crowd, and saw Rachel watching her. There was a strange look of apology on her face, and not the mask of victory Paris had feared would be there. The two women nodded discreetly to each other, so that no one else could see, and Paris nodded as though to tell her she forgave her. There had been no way of stopping Peter from what he wanted, and Paris knew it. And in some ways it was more about him than either of the women. And Paris was able to accept now that losing him was what was meant to be. A lesson of some mammoth proportion, a loss she had to experience of nearly everything she loved and believed in except her children. It was one of life's enormous cruelties, yet somewhere in it she knew there would be a gift one day. She had not found it yet, but she knew it was there, waiting for her to discover it, and when she did, she would be free. And until then she was struggling to find it, and still growing stronger every day. Rachel had been part of the journey, and Peter, and even Bix, and Jean-Pierre. And one day Paris knew that she would discover why it had happened to her.

But in the meantime, this woman Peter had left her for seemed insignificant suddenly. Paris envied her less for him than for the baby they now shared. Someone handed the baby to Rachel as Paris watched them, and she was mesmerized, and saw her holding the little girl close to her. She was only four months old, and she was everything Paris wanted now. It was all that was left to her. If a man was not going to love her, then perhaps another child would one day, in addition to those she had. She had said nothing to her children, but this was what she hungered for now, it was the path she was taking, or would soon, she hoped. And then she turned away from Rachel to greet the rest of their guests, and Meg and Richard were standing only a few feet away. Paris had never seen a happier couple in her life. Her new son-in-law embraced her, looking far older than his mother-in-law, and he thanked her profusely for everything she'd done for them, and for being so supportive of their marriage. He was grateful to her, and enormously fond of her now.

"I'll always be here for you, Paris," he whispered as he hugged her, and she believed him. She and Richard were friends now, more than just being related by marriage, and she knew he would take wonderful care of Meg. She was a very lucky girl, and she deserved it. Paris knew she'd be a good wife to Richard, and a loving mother to his children. It was wonderful to see them embark on their journey, and to share in it. She wished them an abundance of happiness for the rest of their lives, and hopefully never grief. All her prayers, as Meg's mother, were that life would be kind to them.

The wedding party left for the club a short time later, and they spent an hour posing for photographs while the guests had cocktails and laughed and chatted, and Bix wove expertly through the crowd, greeting people, meeting friends, introducing some guests to others, and keeping an eye on all the details.

All three hundred guests had been seated according to careful seating charts, and there were two long tables with escort cards on them, which Paris had checked herself at the crack of dawn that morning. Two young women were handing them out as guests arrived. Paris and Peter were at separate tables, and were seated as far apart as correctly possible, and Bix and Steven were sitting with her, along with a handful of her friends. There had been three gaps at her table, because she wasn't close to that many people, even after being in San Francisco for nearly two years, but she worked so hard for Bix she had no time to cultivate friendships, except with clients for a brief time until their events were completed. So they had put Richard's business partner at her table, and the matron of honor's parents, whom Paris knew from Greenwich, which made a nice group for her.

Natalie and Virginia had come out for the wedding, and Paris had scarcely had time to see them. They were leaving in the morning, so she still wouldn't, but Meg had wanted them at other tables with a large group of Peter's friends who had come out from Greenwich, so socially it was kind of a lost day. There were too many other things for Paris to do than to sit and catch up on gossip with her friends.

By the time they sat down to dinner, she was breathless. She had said hello to all three hundred people, solved a minor crisis that Bix was unaware of, between a photographer and one of the catering staff, and she introduced herself to the man she knew was Richard's partner, as she slipped off the pink taffeta coat, and caught her breath.

"I'm sorry to be such an inattentive seatmate," she apologized with a smile, as he helped her with the evening coat. "Have you met everyone at the table?" she asked solicitously, thinking that he looked surprisingly like Richard, except that he was older, taller, and his hair was darker. But there was a definite family air, and when she asked him about it, he laughed. His name was Andrew Warren, and Paris vaguely remembered Meg saying that he was divorced and had two daughters, but she couldn't remember more than that, other than that he was an entertainment attorney, like Richard. And when Paris inquired about it, he said that he actually handled writers, and Richard represented actors and directors, which was far more glamorous, he claimed, but also more stressful. He said writers caused far less trouble.

"I deal with all the screenwriters, and authors who sell books into movies. Most of them are a fairly reclusive lot, so I never see them, I just carry a lot of manuscripts around and read their work. And they like it a lot better if they never have to see me. A lot of the time I just stay home and read. I don't have to visit movie sets, and coax actresses out of trailers who are having hysterics, or go to premieres, like Richard. I'd much rather do what I do," he admitted. "I'm a frustrated writer, I've been working on a book myself." He sounded interesting and was nice to talk to, but Paris didn't pay much attention to him. She had to get up every five minutes to talk to someone, and she felt sorry for him. She was very poor company, she knew, and sorry to be so rude. He seemed pleasant enough, although she hardly spoke to him. She whispered to Bix as she left, for about the tenth time, to try and keep him amused. And Bix and Steven said afterward that they'd enjoyed talking to him.

When they played the first dance, Meg danced first with Richard, then her father, and then Peter danced with Rachel while Wim danced with Paris, and Richard danced with his mother, and then the bridal party and everyone else got on the floor, and Paris finally got back to her table, and collapsed in her chair. She hadn't stopped moving all evening.

"You haven't had a bite to eat all night," Andrew chided her, looking fatherly, and they finally had a chance to chat a little. He said he had two daughters in their thirties, one in London, one in Paris, both were married, but neither had children yet. And he mentioned in passing that his ex-wife was remarried and lived in New York. He had lived there when he was married. And then Paris suddenly remembered what Meg had said. His ex-wife was from a famous family, and was now married to the governor of

New York. He had moved in fairly illustrious circles while he was married, but led a quiet life now. And more out of training and habit, thanks to Bix, than out of any real interest, she asked how long he'd been divorced. And he smiled and told her it had been about ten years. He wasn't apologetic, didn't seem angry, spoke fondly of his ex-wife, and seemed very normal and low-key.

"It's been ten years. Both of my girls were in college, and we thought getting divorced made more sense than the way we were living. I had moved out here for business, and she hated California. She stayed in New York when I came to Los Angeles. She's very tied into political circles in New York, and that meant a lot to her. She thought it was too superficial out here, she hated the film industry, and I didn't disagree with her. I just liked what I was doing, and had a great business opportunity. The political arena in the East never meant much to me, but it meant everything to her. We were always very different, and eventually we just ran out of steam. Commuting got too difficult, and our lives had gone in opposite directions. We're very good friends, and I'm very fond of her new husband. He's perfect for her, much more so than I was. We had one of those hopeless romances that we tried to make last forever and couldn't," he said, smiling pleasantly. "But we're on very good terms. When the girls were younger, I used to spend holidays with them and my ex-wife. I think the governor thought we were crazy, but it worked. I went shooting in Scotland with him last year. Modern-day families, they're a lot different than they used to be," he said, laughing, and then invited her to dance, unless she'd rather just sit down and relax. He felt guilty making her get up again. And she didn't really want to dance with him, but she thought it would be rude to refuse. She would rather have sat at the table and chatted with Bix and Steven.

"It sounds very civilized," she said about his relationship with his ex-wife and her husband, as they danced a slow waltz around the dance floor. "I don't think I'd be capable of it," she said honestly. She and Rachel hadn't spoken at the wedding. They had only exchanged a look and a nod in church, acknowledging each other, but neither of them wanted more than that. Particularly Paris. The scar of losing Peter to her was still too raw, and perhaps always would be. Andrew Warren's relationship with his ex-wife seemed infinitely different.

"I'll admit, it's pretty rare. I don't know what the circumstances of your divorce were, but that only works if it was a fairly amicable mutual decision. We were both ready to let go, by the time we divorced. It was a mercy for both of us, and it turned out to be a real blessing for her. I think she's a lot happier with him than she was with me, or was for the latter half of our marriage. We were one of those couples who never should have gotten married, but did anyway, and tried like hell to make it work. It was a long shot at best. She's highly political, I wasn't. She's very social, I hated it. She was a debutante, my father owned a grocery store, and then turned it into a chain, and sold it very nicely, but I didn't grow up with the advantages she did," although Paris knew from Meg he had made up for it since, and like Richard, he was a very wealthy, highly successful man. "She loved horses, I was terrified of them. I wanted lots of kids, she didn't. There was a lot of all that. To tell you the truth, I think I bored her to death." He laughed, it didn't seem to bother him. He seemed very easygoing, so much so that Paris hardly paid attention to him. She was just doing her social duty as they chatted. "At least now we can be friends."

She couldn't imagine being friends with Peter. All they were were strangers with common memories now, and many of them painful. The best she could offer him was peace and distance, and it was all he wanted from her. What Andrew and his ex-wife shared was something very different. And his ex-wife's husband was the leading hopeful for the next presidential election, so it was an interesting connection.

"And you've never wanted to remarry?" Paris pursued the conversation politely when they sat down again. He was an intriguing man, and she was waiting for the line about not meeting the right woman in ten years of looking, but he surprised her again.

"I have, but I don't need to. I've met a lot of wonderful women, most of whom would have made great wives. I'm not so sure about myself. I'm a pretty quiet guy. All I do is sit around reading manuscripts. I don't want to bore someone to death again. According to Elizabeth, my ex-wife, being married to me was about as exciting as watching paint dry. I figured I should spare someone that." What he was saying really was that he didn't want to make another mistake, which was what most divorced people felt. He made a lot of sense and she liked him, not in a romantic sense. But he had the same kind of solid substance her new son-in-law did. She didn't view Andrew as a potential date, but thought he might make a nice friend, and given his close relationship with Richard, she was sure their paths would cross again.

"At my age, I don't need to get married." He continued chatting with her. "I think it's wonderful for Meg and Richard. But I'm fifty-eight years old, I don't have the energy for a young girl, and I'd feel foolish with one. Richard is ten years younger than I am, that makes a difference. He wants kids with her, and to start all over again. I'm enjoying coasting, seeing my kids, being with my friends when I'm in the mood for it. I don't need to start all over again. I like my life fine the way it is." He seemed completely comfortable with himself, and had no interest in impressing anyone, least of all Paris. He asked her about her job then, and she told him about it, and Bix entered the conversation and peppered her accounts with a lot of funny stories about her and their clients. Andrew said he thought it sounded terrific. "You two must have a lot of fun working together," he said pleasantly, and Andrew went on talking to Bix when Paris's son-in-law came and asked her to dance.

"That's my best friend you're talking to," Richard said to her easily, after he thanked her again for the wedding. "He's a great guy. I've told Meg a hundred times I wanted to introduce you two. She didn't think you'd like him, he's usually pretty quiet. But there isn't a better friend on the planet. I think his ex-wife will probably end up being First Lady."

"That's what Meg said. We've had a nice time talking. I just hope Bix doesn't tell him a lot of horrible stories about me while we're dancing." She laughed at the thought, but she didn't really care. She wasn't trying to impress Andrew. He wasn't that kind of person. He was the sort of man you could let your hair down with, and be normal. And she liked that. She could see how he would make a great friend. He didn't appeal to her in any other context. He was a nice-looking man, very handsome actually. But she wasn't interested in dating anymore, and he didn't seem particularly interested in her either. He was just as happy talking to Steven and Bix as he was to Paris, which was one of the things she liked about him.

And when Richard brought her back, Andrew had gone off to talk to someone at another table. Bix tried to tell her what a terrific guy he was, and she brushed him off, and said she had no interest. It wasn't even about chemistry now, or the lack of it. She was no longer interested in dating. At all. She liked her life the way it was, just as he did.

"Don't tell me this is another Malcolm Ford," Bix said with a look of annoyance. She had become absolutely impossible since Jean-Pierre. She had surrounded herself with insuperable walls. "If you have no chemistry with this guy, then you must have an aversion to handsome, intelligent, nicely behaved men. Malcolm Ford is one of the smartest, nicest, best-looking guys I've ever met, and if you'd had the brains to go after him, or even talk to him, instead of that Parisian kid, you'd be married by now, Paris," he scolded her with a stern expression.

"I don't want to be married," she said happily, looking smug about it.

"Am I interrupting something?" Andrew asked as he sat down again, and Bix rolled his eyes and said she was impossible.

"Not at all. I just said I don't want to be married again."

"That's too bad," Andrew said pleasantly, "I don't disagree with you, but it's nice when it works out well. It's hard to get all the pieces of the puzzle lined up just right so they fit. But when they do, there's nothing better. Look at Meg and Richard." They both smiled at the couple kissing on the dance floor.

"She's a lot younger than I am," Paris laughed. "And as you said yourself, it takes a lot of energy. I'm not sure I have it. In fact, I'm sure I don't."

"That's my problem too." He smiled at her, and Bix groaned.

"The two of you need vitamins. If more people felt like you about marriage," Bix said pointedly to her, "we'd be out of business." They all laughed at his comment. He had a point. The lion's share of his business, and the real moneymaker, was weddings.

"Marriage is for the young," Paris said emphatically.

"Marriage is for the young at heart," Bix corrected.

"Marriage is not for sissies," Andrew added, and they all laughed.

"Good point," Steven said, entering the conversation. And a little while later they all left the tables, talked to friends, moved around, and the young people danced for hours. It was three o'clock in the morning when Paris and Bix left the wedding. Peter and Rachel had left hours before, and hadn't even stayed to watch Meg toss the bouquet. Rachel wanted to go to the hotel to nurse the baby, and the boys were exhausted. So Peter went with her, although he would have liked to stay, and have a few moments' conversation with Paris, if only to thank her, but it never happened. And Paris was relieved it hadn't. She had nothing left to say to him. There was too much water under the bridge now, and he didn't need to thank her. They had done it for their daughter. All Paris wanted was healing, and she was getting there. There were scars, she knew, but she could live with them. She was at peace now. It had taken a long time.

And Meg had done a silly thing when she'd tossed the bouquet. She had insisted that her mother get out on the dance floor with the single women. Bix had made her a special, smaller bouquet just for tossing, so Meg could preserve her real one. He did it for all brides. He thought it a terrible waste to let a magnificent bouquet go home with a stranger. And the smaller ones were easier for brides to throw at the single women. Meg had refused to move an inch till her mother was out there. And Paris felt ridiculous standing among girls half her age, or even slightly older, who were leaping and jumping to catch hope, in the form of an ancient tradition. It was a hope Paris no longer cherished, nor even wanted. And she had raised her hands half-heartedly and looked away as the bouquet flew at her and hit her in the chest like a football. Her daughter had taken careful aim and hurled it at her. Paris's first instinct was to let it drop and let someone else get it, and then as though a force beyond herself took over by simple reflex, she reached up and grabbed it before it fell. She thought it might be bad luck for Meg if she let that happen. So she stood there, holding it, with a dazed expression, and everyone cheered, as Meg looked at her lovingly from the chair she'd been standing on when she threw it. And immediately afterward Richard had tossed the garter to the bachelors, most of whom didn't want it, any more than Paris had wanted the bouquet. But she had it, and was still carrying it when she and Bix left the wedding. It had been a memorable celebration, and even Bix looked happy.

"What are you going to do with that?" He nodded at the bouquet as Steven went to get the car. Paris shrugged, as she smiled at him.

"Maybe burn it."

"You're disgusting. I hope you see Andrew again, by the way. He said he has two writers in San Francisco, and comes here fairly often. You should invite him sometime."

"To what? You keep me too busy to entertain. I don't have time to see him." Or the interest, she almost added, but she didn't say it. He was nice. But so were a lot of men. She didn't want one. She'd had enough for one lifetime, she had decided, and had retired from the race.

"If you don't make an effort one of these days, I'm going to have

Sydney dig up one of her blind dates. You can't play grieving widow forever," Bix threatened. Jean-Pierre had been gone for nearly six months, and she had gotten more and more determined to stay by herself, instead of less so. It seemed like a hell of a waste to Bix.

"I'm not grieving. I'm happy," she said, and meant it.

"That's what worries me. You're not lonely?"

"Sometimes. I'm not desperate. That's different. Lonely is the way it is sometimes." She was feeling nostalgic, with her daughter having just gotten married. "I'd love to be married. I thought I always would be. But I don't need to do it again. Maybe I'm too scared to. By the time you figure out it's not going to work, you're up to your neck in alligators and you're drowning. I couldn't survive that again, Bix. The stakes are too high. And the chances of winning the prize at my age are so infinitesimally small. I'd rather buy a lottery ticket, I figure the odds are better."

"Maybe it is time for another blind date," he said, musing, as they waited for Steven. He was taking forever.

"I don't need one. Although it might be entertaining, particularly if you ask Sydney." She still groaned when she thought of the sculptor from Santa Fe. Bix teased her about it often.

"You can't stay alone forever," Bix said sadly. "You're a beautiful woman, and a nice one. Don't waste that." He hated to think she might not find someone, but it certainly wasn't easy. And she was obviously no longer willing to make the effort. And there was no question, it was a lot of work to find someone. And most of the time, the pickings were slim, and the rewards few and far between, or even nonexistent.

"I think your needle-in-the-haystack theory is great," she responded. "But the haystacks get bigger, and the needles get smaller as you get older. And my eyes aren't as good as they used to be. It's easier to just stop looking."

"And when you do," he said philosophically, "you dance over it barefoot, and it pricks you!"

"You sound like the guy from Santa Fe. He was a ten-foot prick if

I ever saw one." She laughed, and Bix grinned as Steven drove up
with the car, and they both got in. She was still holding the bouquet, and she put it in water when she got home. It had been a
sweet gesture on Meg's part. And hopefully, harmless. She hadn't
really caught it anyway, Paris told herself. It had hit her. And damn
near knocked her over, which didn't count. She was safe. But the
bouquet was pretty.

Chapter 29

Just as she had promised herself she would, on the Monday after Meg's wedding, she took both business cards she'd been hanging on to to the office. And when she had a break midmorning, she called them.

The first one called her back in twenty minutes, or his assistant did, and said he was out of town till mid-October. The second one called back at lunchtime, while Paris was eating a yogurt and an apple at her desk. The second one was a woman. Her name was Alice Harper, and her voice sounded young and enthusiastic. Paris told her why she had called, and they made an appointment for Friday morning. It was very exciting.

Alice Harper's office was in a quiet residential neighborhood at the west end of Pacific Heights, on Maple. She had an office in her house, a secretary, and a young attorney working with her. And despite the youthful voice, Paris was surprised to find her to be a motherly-looking woman in her early sixties. She was an attorney specializing in adoption, and she welcomed Paris into her private office. And a moment later the secretary brought the cup of tea Paris had asked for.

"Let's start at the beginning," Alice said pleasantly. She had a worn, comfortable face, short curly hair, and wore no makeup. But her eyes were lively and alert, she was in the business of assessing people constantly, both birth mothers and adoptive parents. The success of her matchmaking depended on how astute she was at listening to what they told her, and if need be, weeding out the weirdos, and those that thought they wanted a baby but didn't, or wanted one for the wrong reasons, just like biological parents who were bored, or didn't know what else to do, or were trying to fix a failing marriage. She assessed the birth mothers just as carefully, so as not to disappoint hopeful would-be parents when a girl decided not to give up her baby. She turned off the phone, and turned her full attention to Paris. "Why do you want to adopt a baby?"

"A lot of reasons," Paris said cautiously. She wanted to be honest with her. She had come to the decision through a circuitous route. But she was almost certain it was the right decision for her. Which was exactly what Alice Harper wanted to know. "I think being a mother is what I've done best in my life. It's what I'm most proud of. I love my kids, and they're wonderful. I can't take credit for that, that's just who they are. But I have loved being part of their lives for every minute I've been there. And I hate the fact that they're gone now."

"Are you married?" There was no sign of a husband, and Alice suspected that there wasn't one. But she wanted to know. She wanted to be sure that there wasn't in fact a husband, who hadn't come because he was either indifferent or hostile to the project. This required full participation, from either one single parent, or both if there was a partner.

"No, I'm not," Paris said clearly. "I was, for twenty-four years. I'm divorced. I've been alone for two and a half. My husband left me." She wanted to be entirely honest about it. "For another woman. They're married, and have a baby."

"Is their having a baby part of this decision?"

"Maybe. It's hard to say what is the overriding factor. I think the strongest one is that I want a baby. I'm not going to get remarried, and I don't want to be alone for the rest of my life. To be crude about it, I guess this would buy me another eighteen or twenty years of cooking dinner, going to soccer or ballet, and driving carpools. I loved that, and I really miss it."

"Why aren't you going to get remarried?" Alice was curious about it. "You can't be sure of that, can you?" She smiled gently.

"I think I am sure," Paris said firmly. "I think the likelihood of my finding someone at this point is slim to none. It doesn't matter to me." That was almost totally true, but not quite, and she knew it. She would have loved to be married, but she had accepted the fact that she wouldn't be, and considered it a reality.

"Why do you think it's so unlikely you'll find someone?" The attorney looked intrigued as she watched her. She wanted to make sure she wasn't unbalanced or suffering from a deep depression. She didn't want to place a baby with a sick woman, but Paris sounded very healthy. "You're a beautiful woman. I would think you could have any man you want."

"It takes too much effort," Paris said, smiling.

"So does a baby," Alice said, and Paris laughed.

"I don't have to go on a blind date with a baby. It won't lie to me, cheat on me, forget to call me for another date, be commitment phobic, have peculiar sexual habits or ideas, it won't be rude to me, at least not until it reaches about thirteen, I don't have to play tennis, golf, ski, or take cooking lessons to meet it, I don't have to audition for it, and it won't get drunk halfway through the first date. I'd rather drive carpool for the next twenty years, and change diapers for the next two or three than go on another blind date. Actually, I'd rather go to prison for ten years, or have my toenails ripped out than go on another blind date."

Alice laughed and looked at her ruefully. "You may have a point. I'd forgotten what it's like. You bring back some memories. I've been remarried for sixteen years. But if it's any consolation, I was about your age when I met my husband. We met in a hospital emergency room when I fell off a ladder and broke my arm, and he had broken a toe. We've been together ever since. But I felt exactly the way you did about blind dates. How old are you, by the way?"

"Forty-eight. I'll be forty-nine in May. Will that be a problem? Am I too old?"

"No," the attorney said carefully, "you're not. It all depends on what the birth mother wants. You're single, and you're a little older, as those things go. If a birth mother wants a couple, then it won't be a match. But you have other things to offer, you've obviously been a good mother," although that would be checked out carefully, with references and a home study by a licensed social worker, as Alice was going to explain to her later. "You're experienced, you've already provided a good home and know-how, you're affluent, you're responsible. Some birth mothers don't care if there's a father or not, and many won't mind your age. Some will. You'll find, when we get further into it, that most birth mothers don't ask a lot of questions, far fewer than you or I would. If they do, we may be in trouble, and what she may really be saying is that she doesn't trust you, and she thinks she'd be a better mother than you would. If we present you, and you've been checked out, and you will be, then it's all about chemistry and instinct. It's the adopting mothers who usually ask all the questions. But for the most part, I hate to say it, adoption is a lot like dating."

Paris grinned at the comparison. "At least there's a reward at the end of it. I'm not sure that's the case in dating, there all you get is a lot of heartache."

"Sounds like you've been dating the wrong guys," she smiled, "but haven't we all! It's the good ones, when you finally find one, that make it all worthwhile. Just like adoption." She smiled.

She explained the entire process to Paris then. She had numerous options, a foreign adoption, a domestic one, private, or closed, the adoption of a special needs child, which Paris said she didn't want to undertake on her own, and Alice nodded, it was all a personal choice. And Paris said she wanted a domestic child. Foreign adoption sounded too difficult and too stressful for her. And she didn't want to spend two months in a hotel room in Beijing or Moscow waiting for a lot of red tape to be cut, and forms to be filled out. She wanted to lead a normal life and go to work every day while she waited for the right baby to be found. And that sounded reasonable to Alice. There had to be a home study, done by a licensed adoption agency if it was going to be a private adoption, which this was. Paris would have mountains of papers to fill out, documents to sign, fingerprints and criminal records to provide, medical exams, as well as references and information about herself.

"Have you told your children yet?" Alice asked.

"No, not yet. My son is in college, and my daughter got married on Saturday. They're pretty much out of the house, and they can't have much objection, it's not going to affect them."

"Don't be so sure. Even grown children have strong opinions sometimes about their parents adopting. Sibling rivalry can happen at any age." Paris couldn't imagine it, but the attorney obviously had more experience than she did.

"What do I do now?" Just listening to her, Paris was excited. She knew more than ever that her decision was right, and she could hardly wait. Alice had told her that they screened birth mothers very carefully. They wanted to be sure that the family background was as sound as possible, the birth father had signed off so there were no problems later, and the match between adoptive mother and baby was as good as it could get, and of course that the birth mother was really going to give the baby up. And there was drug and alcohol screening for the birth mother as well.

"We give you a packet of papers," Alice said, standing up. "And you start filling them out. I'll be in touch in the next week or two. I want to get your home study started, because if a baby comes up on short notice, and they do that sometimes, we can get a call from a hospital or a mother, after the baby has been born, and you want to be able to move forward quickly."

"Does it usually happen that fast?" Paris looked surprised. She had assumed it would take months, or even years.

"It can happen just that fast. Or it can take a lot longer. Realistically, it will probably take about a year. Most of the time it's about that long. If we're lucky, six months. But I think I can tell you reasonably that you should be changing diapers within a year." Paris smiled. It was a hopeful thought. And she liked this woman enormously. Paris had total confidence that she was in the right hands. She had gotten the name from her gynecologist, whom Sydney had referred her to. She did a lot better with doctors and jobs than she did with blind dates.

Paris gave Alice her number at the office, her home number, and the number of her cell phone. And after that, she drove to the office. She was totally excited about what she was about to do, and for the moment she didn't have a single doubt. The only thing she was wondering about now was if Alice was right and Meg and Wim might be upset. She didn't think they would. And it wasn't something she wanted to discuss with them on the phone. Meg and Richard were in Europe for three weeks on their honeymoon, so she had to wait until they got home.

And when she got to the office, Paris saw that Andrew Warren had called. She hesitated about returning the call, and didn't want to pursue anything romantic with him. He was a nice man, but she was serious about not dating. She had no interest in him. She saw that the message was in Bix's handwriting, and stopped in his office, with the message in her hand.

"What did he want?" She didn't look enthused.

"He asked if you'd donate a kidney," Bix teased her. "Don't look so suspicious. He said he had to see a client here next week, and I think he wanted to know if you wanted to have lunch."

"I don't," she said curtly, tossing the message in the trash.

"Don't be such a pain in the ass," Bix said, looking annoyed. "He's a nice man." They had chatted for a few minutes on the phone, and Bix had invited him to stop by sometime. If Paris wouldn't have lunch with him, he would. "What have you got to lose?"

"My sanity and self-respect. I'm fond of both."

"Where were you this morning, by the way?" She usually let him know where she went, and she had left a message on the machine saying she'd be late, but not why.

"I had my teeth cleaned." She smiled at him, but something in her eyes told him it was something else.

"You must have more teeth than I do. You were gone a hell of a long time."

"I had to wait," she said, and went back to her desk. She didn't call Andrew Warren. He was a nice man, but there was no point. She could always see him sometime in L.A. when she visited Richard and Meg. Meg said they saw a lot of him. And she saw no reason to cultivate a friendship. She didn't need or want a male friend. She had Bix.

She heard from Alice Harper, as promised, the following week. Paris had returned as many of the forms as she could fill out. She still had to get her fingerprints done, and a computer check of her criminal record, but she'd been planning to do that in the next few days. And she wasn't prepared for what Alice said.

"I have a birth mother for you, Paris," she said, and Paris could feel her heart pound. This was much better than a date. This was forever, just like a baby of her own. It was like waiting to find out if she was pregnant, in the early days of her marriage. They had been the best years of her life. And this was a way of bringing those days back, without Peter of course. But you couldn't have everything. Not anymore.

"Tell me about her," Paris said, as she closed her office door. Bix glanced out of his office and saw her do it, and had the feeling that something smoky was going on. He hoped she wasn't looking for another job. Paris never closed her door.

"She's nineteen years old, in college in the Bay Area, from a solid family in Mill Valley. She's healthy, anxious to pursue her education. She's very athletic, which is why she didn't know she was pregnant. She didn't find out till she was five months along."

"How pregnant is she now?"

"Seven months. The baby is due on December first. She's not into drugs, and hasn't had any alcohol since she found out. She says only a little beer and wine before that, she's on the tennis team at her school, so she's pretty wholesome. She's been drug tested, and she's clean. And judging from the photographs, she's a very pretty girl, blond hair, blue eyes, she looks a little like you. I'm going to see her myself tomorrow. The birth father is twenty-two, just graduated from Stanford, working in New York. Four point oh GPA all through college, he sounds like a real brain. No drugs. They went out for two years, and broke up six months ago. They don't want to get married, neither of them wants the baby, nor do their parents. His family is pretty well known in the city. I think they just want this to go away. You could be the answer to their prayers."

"How does the birth mother feel about me? Does she mind that I'm single and older?" Paris asked, feeling humble. In a way, it was worse than dating, because there was so much at stake. A child for the rest of her life.

"She's going to talk to two other couples. So this isn't a sure thing. Let's get your home study complete as fast as we can do it. Have you told your kids?" Alice asked.

"My daughter won't be home from her honeymoon for two more weeks."

"That's soon enough. Let's see where this goes." And on Saturday afternoon, she called Paris at home. She was sitting in her living room, in front of the fire, reading a book. And for some odd reason, she'd been thinking of Jean-Pierre, missing him, and wondering how he was. She hoped he was happy and well.

"The birth mother wants to meet you," Alice told Paris. "She's going to see the other couples too." This was auditioning big time. "Are you free tomorrow?"

"Absolutely." She was having dinner with Wim, but she had no other plans. Her life was quiet these days. Quieter than it had ever been.

Alice named a restaurant in the heart of town, where they could meet and talk for as long as they wanted. She said the birth mother was coming alone. They agreed on two o'clock, and Paris said she'd be there. And when she showed up exactly on schedule the following afternoon, the young woman walked in at almost exactly the same time. She was a beautiful girl, with a lean athletic figure, and the baby was a tight neat ball that hardly showed, despite her seven months. The birth mother looked strikingly like Meg.

They were given a quiet corner table, and the girl looked uncomfortable, so Paris spoke first. She asked how she was feeling, and she gave Paris a shy smile.

"Stupid mostly. I should have figured it out. My periods are so irregular, I just missed it." She told Paris afterward that her parents were extremely upset, especially her dad. She was an only child, and the apple of his eye. Paris wanted to ask her if she was sure of what she was doing, but Alice had suggested she not do that. The girl said she was certain she didn't want the baby. She talked about her boyfriend then. She said it had been a very acrimonious break-up, and they didn't want to see each other again, for the moment.

"What if you get back together?" Paris asked quietly. "Do you think you would want the baby back?" Legally, they wouldn't have a leg to stand on, Alice had said, once the papers were signed, but Paris was worried about it anyway. What if they harassed her, or tried to overturn the adoption in court? They were all normal fears for her to have. It was all unfamiliar to her.

"No, I wouldn't. I don't want a baby. I want to go to school in Europe next year, and finish school. I can't do anything I want with a baby. And he wants to go to law school and doesn't want it either. I just can't take care of a baby, and my parents won't." She sounded as sensible as any nineteen-year-old girl, and sensible enough to know that she wasn't responsible enough to bring up a child. She was still one herself. She was the same age as Wim, and Paris couldn't imagine him with a baby for a long time to come. The birth mother's name was Jennifer, and they sat and talked for two hours. It was obvious that she liked Paris, and she said so when they left. And after that Paris went home and cooked dinner for Wim. They had an easy quiet evening, and she was dying to tell him about the baby, but she didn't want to tell him before she told Meg. She wanted to tell them together, it only seemed fair to both of them.

She spoke to Alice again on Monday, and she said it was looking good. The birth mother liked her a lot. And after she hung up, Paris was beaming when she came out of her office, and Bix looked upset.

"What's wrong?" She looked at him with a warm grin.

"You tell me," he said, and asked her to come into his office and sit down. "Paris, what the hell is going on?" She suddenly wondered if she'd screwed something up for a client, and was worried by the look on his face.

"With what?" He looked furious with her, but in truth he was scared.

"Either you're having an affair, or you're looking for a new job. And since you insist you won't date, I figure it's the latter. Every time I walk past your office, the door is closed, and you look like a Cheshire cat." He looked profoundly upset, and Paris felt badly to have caused him concern.

"I'm sorry, Bix," she said gently. "You're going to have to drag me out of here, if you ever want to get rid of me. I'm not going anywhere." She wanted to reassure him, but he only looked more confused.

"Then what the hell is it?" he asked, running a hand through his hair. And she smiled, just as he had said, like the proverbial Cheshire cat.

"It's something very wonderful. I think so anyway," she said proudly. "I'm going to adopt a baby, Bix." He just sat there and stared at her for endless minutes and then shook his head in disbelief.

"Oh my God. You're not." It was all he could think of to say.

"I am. At least I hope I am. I met the birth mother yesterday. I've been pursuing this for the past couple of weeks, but I've been planning to for months. I wanted to get Meg married first." It certainly explained the closed door.

"When did you decide that?"

"About six months ago. After Jean-Pierre. I don't want to do that again. And I don't want to be alone. Bix, when you think about it, it makes a lot of sense."

"Not to me. Do your kids know?"

"Not yet. I'm going to tell them when Meg gets home."

"When is this baby due, if you get this one?"

"December first."

"Shit. There goes Christmas. When were you going to tell me?" He looked even more upset at the prospect. His office was going to be in an uproar without her.

"When I know for sure. This may not be the one, but I hope it is. She's a lovely, wholesome girl, and she looks just like Meg, and me. But even if this comes through, I'm not going to leave you in the lurch over Christmas. I'd like maternity leave for a month or so, but I can take it in January, when things settle down. I'll let you know when I do, and we'll work it out." He was still staring at her in disbelief, and Paris looked frighteningly calm. She was absolutely sure she was doing the right thing, and it showed. She hadn't had a qualm or a hesitation since she'd met Alice Harper.

"Paris, are you sure? This sounds like a crazy thing to do."

"Believe me, it isn't. It's the first thing I've done in two and a half years that makes sense, except for coming to work for you. And I can do both. I didn't with Meg or Wim, but other women work." And she was mature enough now to handle a job and a baby. She wasn't worried about that either. She had thought it all out. "So," she asked, smiling at him across his desk, "are you going to congratulate me?" She was beaming, as he shook his head.

"No, I'm going to have you committed. I think it's time to call Sydney again, for another blind date. If I had thought that ending it with Jean-Pierre would lead to this, I would have either forced you to marry him, or shot him when he first came near you. I think this is a crazy thing to do. You need a husband, Paris, not a baby." And in part that was true. Or at best, she could have had both. But not the way things were.

"The baby is enough. I don't need a husband, Bix. I had one. It was great. But that's over."

"And you're just going to give up on men for the rest of your life? That's crazy." He looked genuinely upset for her. It was such a terrible waste.

"If it's meant to be, it'll happen someday, maybe when I fall off a ladder and break my arm," she said cryptically, and he looked confused.

"What does breaking your arm have to do with it?"

"That's how my lawyer met her husband. She broke her arm, he broke his toe, and they met in an emergency room."

"How cute," Bix said, still looking upset. She had given him a lot to digest. She came around the desk to give him a hug, and reassure him everything would be all right, and a few minutes later, Paris went back to her desk. Bix took a bottle of Valium out of his desk, started to open it, shook his head, muttered to himself, and put it back without taking one after all. At least he knew now, he reassured himself, that she wasn't going to quit. But adopting a baby sounded almost as bad to him.

Chapter 30

It was another week before Alice called, and Meg was nearly home by then. But it wasn't good news. Jennifer, the birth mother, had chosen one of the couples instead, and Paris was surprised by how disappointed she was. It felt like the ultimate rejection.

"It works that way sometimes," Alice said quietly. She knew how Paris felt. "When it's right, it will fall into place. You'll see. I have another option for you. I know you want a newborn, but I just want to run this by you. It never hurts to ask. We have a four-year-old in a Russian orphanage, alcoholic mother, unknown father, no HIV. She's been in the orphanage since she was two. There are two other siblings, and the Russians usually keep them together, but the couple who took them didn't want the little girl. She was scheduled to be adopted by an American family in Phoenix, and they backed out yesterday. The father has been diagnosed with a brain tumor, and they don't want to take on an adoption. So she's up for grabs. I have a picture of her I can e-mail to you. She looks very cute, but I know this wasn't what you had in mind." Paris thought about it for a second and was about to say no, and then wondered if this was fate, sending her this child.

"Can I think about it?" Paris asked cautiously.

"I'll send you the e-mail." And when she did, Paris thought she had never seen a sweeter face. She sat and stared at it as Bix came into her office and looked too.

"Who's that?"

"A four-year-old in a Russian orphanage. She's available for adoption. The birth mother I saw doesn't want me."

"Oh my God," Bix said, and turned away from the photograph. "Tell me this isn't happening. Paris, I'll marry you myself if you stop this nonsense." He was horrified by her adoption project, and said so whenever he got the chance.

"It's not nonsense," she said, looking at him. She was so calm it frightened him. He had never seen her so determined. "And I don't want to get married. Except for you, I might make an exception. What about Steven? Should we adopt him?"

Bix stared at her, it was a nightmare happening, as far as he was concerned. "I need a Valium."

"Do you want me to call your doctor?"

"Are you kidding?" He laughed. "I have about four hundred of them in my office. Would you like one?"

"No, thanks, I'm fine." And two hours later she called Alice and told her she had decided against the Russian orphan. She felt more comfortable about a newborn.

"I thought so. I just thought I'd ask. I think I have a lead on another birth mother for you, by the way. I'll know more in a few days. I'll call you."

And that weekend Meg and Richard came back from their honeymoon and called her. She invited them to come up and visit. She wanted Wim to be there with them, but they said they were busy. And Bix and Paris had Halloween to contend with.

It was early November when they finally made it up. They decided to have early Thanksgiving with her, since they were flying east to spend it with Peter. And shortly after they arrived, Richard mentioned to her that Andrew said he had called her. Paris looked faintly embarrassed.

"I know. I'm sorry. That was rude of me. I never called him." But she really didn't want to.

"I think he was afraid he had offended you. He's a hell of a nice guy," Richard staunchly defended him.

"If he calls again, I'll talk to him. I promise."

"I'll tell him."

And after that they sat down to dinner, and had a traditional Thanksgiving meal. But there was nothing traditional about the look on their faces when Paris told them she wanted to adopt a baby. Both her children looked like they were going into shock.

"You what?" Meg stared at her, for the first time not willing to support her. "Mom, that's crazy. You're too old to have a baby."

"That's possible," Paris conceded, "although I'm not entirely sure of that either. But that's not what I have in mind. I want to adopt one. And I'm certainly not too old to take care of a baby. Women older than I am are having them by in vitro fertilization." She defended her position, but so far hadn't convinced them.

"They have husbands." Meg was almost shouting, and she was looking to Richard to be her ally. So far he had said nothing. And Wim looked horrified. His whole family was going crazy. His parents had divorced, his father had married a girl almost half his age, now they had a six-month-old baby, he had two stepbrothers, and now his mom wanted to adopt a baby. Neither he nor Meg was enthused by the project, and they made no bones about it.

"Single women adopt babies, and so do single men," Paris said calmly.

"Let them," Meg said childishly. "I think it's stupid for you to adopt a baby. Why would you want to do that?"

"Because I'm lonely," Paris answered quietly, and both of her children stared at her. "You two are grown up, and have your own lives. I don't. Except for my job. You were my life. And I'm not your responsibility. I have to make my own life worthwhile. I want to have a baby, to love and take care of, and keep me company, until it grows up too. It doesn't mean I don't love both of you, of course I do. But I don't want to be alone either." There was a deafening silence, and Richard looked at her with great compassion, as though they were the only two adults in the room, and he got it. He put an arm around his wife and tried to explain it to her.

"Your mom has a right to do anything she thinks is right to make her life better. It's not easy being alone. This is hard for her. And it would be a wonderful thing to do for a baby."

"Why can't you just get married?" Meg asked plaintively.

"Because I can't, or I haven't," Paris answered, "and I'm not going to sit here and wait for the Messiah to come and improve my lot in life. That's pathetic. I need to take responsibility for my own life," Paris said, and Richard admired her for it.

"What if I have a baby? You won't even care about it, if you have your own," Meg asked, sounding pathetic, and Paris smiled at her. In her own way, Meg was still a baby herself. And so was Wim. Alice had been right. This wasn't as easy as she had thought.

"Of course, I'll care about your baby, sweetheart. And I'll care about both of you, and all the children you have. But I need to do something to make my own life better, and this is what seems right to me."

"It sounds pretty dumb to me," Wim contributed. "Babies make a big mess." He was seeing that with the half-sister Peter and Rachel had given him. Their baby seemed to scream all the time, and as far as Wim was concerned, every time he tried to play with her, she threw up, and Rachel got worried. It didn't sound like a terrific idea to him.

"Let's see what happens. I'll tell you both what I'm doing, and if a baby comes up. I just lost an opportunity recently, two actually. I turned one down, and the other one turned me down. This probably won't happen for quite a while," she reassured them.

"How long?" Meg asked, as though she'd just been told she had to face a firing squad.

"Maybe a year, more or less." All Meg could hope was that her mother would change her mind in the meantime.

And before they left on Sunday afternoon, Richard took a minute to talk to Paris alone. "Don't worry about Meg, Paris. She'll adjust. So will Wim. This is your life, and you have to do what's right for you. I admire what you're doing. It takes a lot of guts to take on a commitment like that at our age." He was, after all, only a year older than she was, and had a different perspective than her daughter, even though they were married.

"You'd better not say that." She smiled at him, grateful for his vote of confidence in her. "What if Meg has a baby?" She was hoping they would at some point, and from all they'd said, they intended to have children one day.

"That's different," he said to his mother-in-law. "I'm a lot more cowardly than you. I don't think I could adopt one. That doesn't worry you?" he asked her openly, and she shook her head, feeling great affection for him. He was not only her son-in-law, he was becoming her friend.

"It doesn't worry me at all."

Wim and Meg and Richard left on Sunday at the same time. It had been a turbulent weekend for all of them, but Paris was confident they'd calm down. And she knew Richard would help with Meg. And maybe even with Wim. He had promised to talk to him in a few days. God only knew what Peter would think of her plan when he heard of it. She wasn't counting on him to calm their children. He had his own life and problems, and his own baby they were somewhat hesitant about, because they still weren't sold on Rachel. And she had an unfailing knack for irritating them. She was a very strong woman, and she had broken up their parents' marriage, so she started out with two strikes against her in their eyes, if not three.

And as Richard and Meg drove away, he made a mental note to himself to say something to Andrew again. He still thought

Andrew should call Paris, even if they only became friends. They seemed so much alike to him. And this time, if for no other reason than out of respect for her son-in-law, she had promised to take the call, if he did. There was no harm in it. She wasn't going to date him, but as Bix said, it was always good to have another friend.

Chapter 31

The following week Andrew Warren called Paris again. He said he had come to town to work on a screenplay with one of his clients, who was having trouble modifying it, and he wondered if Paris had time for lunch. She remembered her conversation with Richard and her promise to him, so she agreed to see him that week when he got in. It was a courtesy lunch, if nothing else. He was, after all, her son-in-law's partner and friend, and she didn't want to seem rude, although she was frighteningly busy in the office. Christmas was coming. She almost canceled at the last minute when a new client came in to meet with Bix, and he threatened to throw Paris out of the office physically if she didn't go to lunch. He liked Andrew Warren a lot, and was convinced Paris would too, if she gave him a chance, even as a friend.

They met in a deli on Sacramento Street, which wasn't elegant, but it was quick, and she was embarrassed to tell him that she had very little time. But he seemed good-natured about it.

"I'm just happy to get out of my client's apartment. He's been staring at a blank sheet of paper for four weeks, and he says he's not coming out till he writes something. I feel like a psychiatric attendant. I may have to write it for him." He laughed, finishing his coffee.

"Can you write it?" Paris looked impressed.

"Not really, but I will if it will get him going. I was actually thinking about a stun gun, just to jolt him a bit."

"There's an idea." She laughed, and told him about the Christmas parties they were doing, when he asked her. He was fascinated by their business.

"I don't know how you do it. When I invite friends over, we order Chinese food, and eat it out of the cartons."

"Call Bixby Mason," she teased. "We'll take care of it for you."

"I'll bet you would. If Meg's wedding is any indication of what you two do, I'd say you throw a terrific party." He smiled at her appreciatively.

"We try to," she said blandly, thinking she had fulfilled her promise and didn't have to meet with him again.

He said he had to get back to his screenwriter then, and she had to get back to the office. It had been a pleasant interlude. He was very much like Richard, and she could see why they were partners. They were both easygoing, intelligent, unpretentious, and very good at their business. They both did a lot of hand-holding for their talent, which showed they had a nurturing nature. Paris couldn't think of a better husband for her daughter. Or maybe a friend for her in Andrew one day.

And as soon as Paris got back to the office, the secretary told her she had a call from Alice Harper.

"I have an interesting birth mother for you," Alice said, as Paris listened. She had just completed her home study and was ready to go, whenever it happened. "She's a little older than our run of the mill. And she's married. She's twenty-nine years old, and has four kids. She lives in the East Bay, and her husband is a lab tech. They're very tight on money. And apparently, he's been having an affair with their neighbor. He's leaving her, or in fact he's already left. And she didn't want this baby to begin with. I gather he's been pretty abusive to her. No drugs, no alcohol, she's very religious, and she wants this baby to have a good life. She knows it won't if she keeps it. She can't afford the ones she has, in fact, her sister is going to take her little girl who's three, and the birth mother is going to take the three boys, who are eleven and nine, and seven, and she wants to go east to get a job and live with her mother." It sounded like a tragedy to Paris. Fragmented lives and endless heartbreak. It had happened to her. She couldn't even imagine what it would have been like if she had had to break up her family, farm out her children, and give one up for adoption.

"What happens if she gets on her feet? Will she want this baby?"

"She says he raped her. She told him she wanted a divorce a year ago, and he didn't believe her. He sounds fairly abusive. So he raped her, and she got pregnant. But then he got involved with the neighbor. She filed the divorce yesterday. Now she wants to place the baby, and start life with a clean slate somewhere else. I'm not sure I blame her," Alice said. She had heard thirty years of these stories, and many of them were tragic. "What I like about her is that she's older, sensible. She knows what she's doing. She knows what it is to take care of a child, and she also knows what she can and can't handle. She's got more on her plate than she can cope with, and she knows it. You'd be a godsend for her." And maybe she for Paris.

"When's the baby due?" Paris asked, making notes on a scratchpad.

"There's the rub. In two weeks. It's a baby girl, by the way. She had a sonogram last month, and the baby is healthy." Paris had confided to Alice early on that she would prefer a little girl, it would be easier for her as she got older, particularly with no male role model for a little boy to rely on. But she was willing to take either sex.

"Two weeks?" Paris looked startled. "Next week is Thanksgiving."

"I know. Her due date is December fifth. Do you want to meet her?"

"I . . . sure . . ." She had told her kids it could take a year. But Paris felt that if this was right, she would know it. And she already had a good feeling about it.

Alice called her back half an hour later. She had made an appointment with the birth mother, for Paris, at a coffee shop in San Leandro, the next evening at seven. It was the most exciting dinner date Paris had had in months. Possibly in years.

And the next night she was hurrying out of the office when Bix saw her.

"I'd say you had a hot date, but unfortunately, I know better." He was extremely discouraged about Paris's current position on dating, although he knew she'd had lunch with Andrew Warren. She had told Bix pointedly that he'd make a great friend, and that was all either of them wanted. They were on the same page about that.

"I do have a hot date. I'm meeting a birth mother in San Leandro." Paris looked anxious and excited and hopeful all at once.

"You hang out in the nicest places," Bix teased.

With traffic, it took her an hour and a half to get there, but she had allowed enough time, and walked into the coffee shop minutes before the birth mother. She was a tired-looking blonde who looked as though she was ready to drop with exhaustion. But she was pretty, and gentle and bright when Paris talked to her. She'd had a year of community college, and wanted to go to nursing school one day. But for now, she was going to have to do whatever she could to support her children. Her husband sounded like a real bastard. And all this woman wanted to do was get on a plane after she had the baby, and go east to get away. She said her sister would send her little girl to her when she thought she could handle it. But she was frantic about trying to support her kids now, and she knew that they would all drown, if she had a fifth one. Her husband had recently lost his job, and he couldn't pay support. And every penny he had, he was spending on the other woman. Paris wanted to put her in the car and drive away with her, with the rest of her children. But she knew she couldn't. That wasn't what she was there for. They were there to talk about the baby that was due in two weeks.

Paris talked about her own family, and Meg and Wim, her house, her life, her job. But just as Alice had predicted, the birth mother wanted to know very little about her. All she wanted to know was that Paris was willing to take the baby. It was she who wanted Paris to approve of her, not the reverse, and get her out of the mess she was in, so she could get on her feet as quickly as possible, and help her other children. Giving someone the baby she was carrying was going to allow this girl to survive and take care of her other kids. She didn't care that Paris was single, or that she was older. She felt total confidence in her the minute she saw her. And from the moment Paris laid eyes on her, she knew this was the baby for her. They were halfway through the meal Paris had ordered for her, which neither of them barely touched, when Paris took the woman's hands in her own and held them, and as they looked at each other, there were tears rolling down their cheeks. They both knew at the same moment what had happened. The deal was done. The birth mother's name was Amy, and all she had to do now was have the baby, and give it to Paris. Paris and her attorney would take care of the rest.

"Thank you," Amy whispered, still clinging tightly to Paris's hands. And they sat there, talking and planning, and exchanging photographs until nine o'clock. There were no notable medical problems in Amy's family, one of her children had hay fever, and there was no history of mental illness. No alcoholism, no drugs. And all she wanted from Paris were photographs once a year. She did not plan to see the baby again. Both she and her husband were willing to sign off, and the baby would become the ward of the adoption agency then. And within four months, the baby would be legally hers. Once they signed off, and it was registered in Sacramento, neither she nor the father could change their minds. But Amy assured her there was no way they ever would. She was far more concerned that Paris would back out, and Paris assured her there was no question of it. She had made her decision, and stepped up to the plate. Now all Paris had to do was wait. And tell her kids.

And as she drove back to the city that night, she felt exactly the way she had the first time the doctor had told her she was pregnant. There was always that queasy little fear in the back of your mind that something could go wrong, but what you felt most of all was excitement and exultation. She had come running into the house to tell Peter victoriously, "I'm pregnant!" And she felt exactly that way now. She had given Amy all her phone numbers and told her to call the minute she went into labor. And they both had to call Alice Harper in the morning to tell her they had agreed, and it was a match.

The attorney called Paris at home while she was dressing for work, and Paris held her breath. What if Amy had changed her mind? She might have on the way home. Or maybe her husband had decided to stay with her after all.

"She wants you," Alice said simply. "How about you?"

"I love her," Paris said, with tears in her eyes again. They had even both noticed that they had the same color eyes and similar hands. As though God had made them sisters at one time, and separated them, and now brought them back together in the nick of time. Paris had two weeks to buy everything she needed. And she told Alice she would write a check that morning for everything Amy needed. The delivery was covered by Amy's medical plan. All she needed was some child care for her other kids while she was in the hospital, and Paris had volunteered to pay plane fare for Amy and her boys to go back east, after the birth. It seemed like the least she could do.

"I'll send the check over this morning," Paris said nervously.

"Don't worry. She's not going anywhere. She needs you," Alice said wisely.

"I need her too," Paris said. More than she had ever realized. But she knew it now. She called Meg and Wim before she left the house, and told them both.

Wim answered with a monotone "Whatever." And then said that whatever made her happy would be fine with him. And he sounded as though he meant it. Paris cried when she thanked him. His support was the greatest gift he had ever given her.

"Are you sure, sweetheart?"

"Yeah, Mom," he said, smiling at his end. "I still think it's a dumb thing to do. But if you want it, it'll be okay." Paris cried with relief and gratitude as she listened.

"I love you," she said fervently, touched to the core.

"Me too."

And the conversation with Meg went better than she had hoped it would too. She had had a long talk with her husband, and she could see her mother's point. If she really wasn't going to remarry, it was going to be a lonely life for her. And if this was what she wanted, Meg said she would support her. The only thing that worried her was that she thought that if her mother did want to start dating again, no man her age would want to get stuck with a baby. But Richard pointed out that he was her mother's age, and he wanted a baby with Meg. In fact, they'd been working on it. So in the end, she got Meg's blessing too. "This is pretty exciting, Mom," Meg conceded before they hung up.

"Yes, sweetheart, it is." And then she ran to the office to tell Bix.

"I'm having a baby!" she shouted as she came through the door, and then she saw that the accountant was with him. Fortunately there were no clients afoot.

"Congratulations!" the accountant said, looking stunned, but not as stunned as Bix. He looked up and stared at her and said a single word.

"When?" They had twenty-two Christmas parties on the books.

"In two weeks." She beamed, and Bix looked like he was going to faint. "Don't worry. I won't take off till January. I'll bring the baby to the office. I'll find a sitter. I'll take care of it. You can babysit for me," she said, and he groaned.

"Should I give you a baby shower?" he asked, looking panicked.

"Not till it's here, but thank you. We can play after Christmas." He was rummaging in his desk frantically as she said it. "What are you looking for?"

"My Valium. I may have to OD. What's the due date, or whatever you call it?"

"That's what you call it." She grinned. "December fifth."

"Oh my God, that's the night of the Addison wedding."

"I'll be there. With the baby, if I have to." She was going to find a sitter quickly, and already had a call in to a pediatrician. She was going to hire a baby nurse, to help get her through Christmas. And in January she was going to take care of her herself. Now all she had to do was think of a name. But that was the last thing on her mind, as she made hasty notes about what she'd need, and Bix followed her into her office.

"Are you sure you want to do this, Paris? A baby is forever," he said ominously.

"Yes, I know," Paris said, looking at him. "That's the only thing that is."

Chapter 32

Andrew Warren called Paris again the Monday before Thanksgiving. He said he had to come to town to see his client again that weekend. And while he waited around for him to write something, he wondered if she wanted to have dinner. She was spending Thanksgiving with Steven and Bix, and her kids were going to be in New York with Peter. Over the weekend she was going to buy things she needed for the baby, and beyond that she had nothing to do.

"That would be nice. Do you want to come here for dinner?" She didn't mind cooking for him. She had nothing else to do, and it might be easier for him, while he waited for his beleaguered screenwriter to hatch a script. They were within hours of the deadline, and the studio was making ugly legal sounds, so he wanted to stick around and breathe down the writer's neck.

"Is this what you always do, or is it above and beyond the call?" she asked after he said he'd like to come to dinner.

"Way beyond, but he's a nice kid, and I think he's in over his head. If I can help, I might as well. It's a quiet weekend for me." He said he was spending the holiday with friends, since both of his girls were in Europe, and he hadn't had time to fly over and see them for Thanksgiving this year. He asked how she was spending it, since he knew that Meg and Richard were going to New York to see Peter, and she told him she was going to spend it with Bix.

"It's always fun being with them," she said, and they agreed that he would come to her place for dinner on Friday night, strictly casual, sweaters and jeans.

But as it turned out, Thanksgiving with Steven and Bix was a lot less fun than she'd expected it to be. Steven cooked a perfect bird, and Bix's table was exquisite. But there were no other guests this year, except her, and Steven looked like he had a bad case of flu. He ate very little and went to lie down immediately after dinner. And while she helped Bix clear away the dishes and put them in the dishwasher, she saw tears roll down his cheeks.

"What's happening?" she asked as she put her arms around him, and he nearly collapsed against her. And before he even told her, she knew. It was Steven. He had AIDS. "Oh my God, no . . . it can't be . . ." But it was. She knew he had been HIV positive for many years. And they had both known it could happen one day.

"Paris, if something happens to him, I can't live through it. I just couldn't live without him anymore," Bix said as she hugged him, and he cried.

"Hopefully, you won't have to," she said, trying to be optimistic for him, but they both knew that sometimes life was cruel. "You just have to do the best you can, and do everything you can for him." And she knew Bix would.

"He started taking protease and nucleoside reverse transcriptase inhibitors last week, and it's making him feel really sick. Eventually, they said it would make him feel better. But right now he feels like shit." He had looked pretty rocky at the dinner table, but Paris also knew that he was still going to work. He had been on call earlier that day.

"Can you get him to take some time off?"

"I doubt it," Bix said, drying his eyes and loading the dishwasher again.

"I'll cover all the parties I can for you. Just tell me what you need."

"How are you going to do that?" he asked, looking discouraged. He couldn't even imagine a life without Steven at his side, but they had always known the risk was real.

"I found an adorable baby-sitter yesterday." It seemed funny even to her to have to worry about baby-sitters, and schedules and formula and diapers. But she didn't mind the responsibility or inconvenience of it. She could hardly wait. She was going shopping for everything she needed the next day. Amy's due date was eight days away. She was having the baby at Alta Bates Medical Center in Berkeley, and all Paris had to do when the call came was race over the bridge. She had promised to be at the delivery with her. And hopefully, the baby wouldn't come as fast as Jane's, so Paris could at least get there in time to see the baby born. Amy had asked Paris to be at the delivery with her. And if the baby was healthy, eight hours after the delivery, Paris could take the baby home. The one thing she didn't have for the baby yet was a name.

But she turned her attention back to Bix before she left that night. They went in to check on Steven, but he was sleeping, and Paris noticed that he seemed to have lost weight recently, and looked very thin, and in the past month or two, he seemed to have aged. Bix could see it too. They both knew he could have years left, if he was lucky. But battling AIDS and living on medications was not going to be easy for either of them.

She thought about them as she lay in bed that night, praying that Steven would get better, and live for a very long time. She knew how much they loved each other, and how unusual a relationship like theirs was. She didn't want anything bad to happen to them. Life was always so challenging, and so full of wicked, unexpected turns in the road. She had discovered that herself two and a half years before.

She fell into a fitful sleep and dreamed about the baby. She dreamed that she was having it and Amy was standing next to her, holding her hand, and as soon as the baby came, someone took it away, and in the dream Paris was screaming. And as she woke up with a start, she realized that that was what she was going to do to Amy. Amy was going to work so hard to have the baby, and then Paris was going to take the baby away. Her heart went out to her as she lay in bed and thought about it. Things seemed to be so hard for everyone. Bix, Steven, Amy . . . and in the midst of it there was innocence, and hope, and love. The baby seemed to personify all the good things in life, all the joy that came with a new life. And it was interesting that even in the midst of sorrow, there was always some small ray of light. And hope to make it all worthwhile.

The next morning Paris rushed out, as she had intended to, to buy everything she needed. She went to a fancy little baby store to buy a bassinet and a changing table, some adorable furniture, with pink bows and butterflies painted on it. And she bought little dresses and hats and booties and sweaters, and a layette fit for a princess. And then she went to three more stores to buy all the practical things. Her station wagon was so full, she could hardly see to drive it, and she got back just in time to unload the car, and put all of it in the guest room upstairs. She was going to put the baby in the bassinet in her own room. But she was going to put everything she needed in the guest room next to hers. She was planning to spend the rest of the weekend organizing it. But there was no hurry. She had all weekend to do it, and at five o'clock she started dinner for Andrew Warren. He had promised to come by at six. Or a little later, if his screenwriter was finally producing something.

She put a roast and some baked potatoes in the oven, and made a big salad. She had bought some crab on the way home, and she thought they could have cracked crab to start, and she put a bottle of white wine in the fridge.

He arrived promptly at six o'clock, and looked pleased to see her. She looked comfortable and relaxed in jeans, and loafers, and a pale blue turtleneck sweater. She didn't make any fuss for him. She didn't consider him a date, but a friend, and he seemed to feel the same. He was wearing an old leather jacket, a gray sweatshirt, and jeans as well.

"How's it going?" she asked him with a warm smile, and he laughed and rolled his eyes.

"God save me from writers with writer's block. When I left, he was on the phone to his shrink. And he had to go to the hospital for an anxiety attack last night. I may have to kill him before we're through." But he was remarkably patient. And he was more than willing to baby-sit him through it. The screenplay he was writing was for a major movie, with two very major stars, who were represented by her son-in-law. It was a family affair.

They sat in her living room while he ate peanuts and drank wine, and she put some music on.

"What did you do today?" Andrew asked comfortably. He liked her house, it was bright and cheerful, and on a sunny day it was awash with sunlight.

"I did some shopping," she said, not volunteering what she'd bought. She hadn't told anyone about the adoption, except her kids and Bix so far. And for the moment, she wanted to keep it that way. She didn't want a lot of comments from people she barely knew. And as much as she liked Andrew, they didn't know each other very well. Although he seemed to be very fond of Meg, and said a number of very nice things about her, which touched Paris's heart. He thought she and Richard were going to be a great match. And Paris agreed with him.

They had dinner around seven-thirty, and he loved the dinner she had prepared. He said that crab was his favorite, and the roast came out just right.

"I'm a little out of practice," she apologized. "I don't cook very often anymore. I'm either working, or I'm too tired to even think of food when I get home."

"It sounds like you and Bix work very hard."

"We do, but I love it. And so does he. Next month is going to be crazy for us, the holidays always are. Starting Monday we're going to be working almost every night." And it was going to be even more complicated for her once the baby came. She was almost hoping it would be late. It would make it a lot easier for her. And Bix had already agreed to let her take off the month of January. But she knew that babies came when they wanted to, witness Jane's, which she'd almost had to deliver herself. At least she wouldn't have to do that this time.

"Do you ever think about just taking some time off for a while?" Andrew asked her casually, and she smiled to herself, thinking of what she had planned.

"Not for very long. I'm actually planning to take some time off after the holidays, but no more than a month. That's a long time for me."

"I'd love to take a year off one of these days, and take an apartment in Paris or London, and just roam around Europe for a while. Maybe take a villa in Tuscany, or even Provence. It sounds like heaven to me. I keep telling Richard I'm going to do it, and he threatens to have a nervous breakdown every time I suggest it. His actors drive him crazy enough. I don't think he wants my writers on his neck too." The agency was a huge success, so it wasn't surprising that they had a vast number of difficult personalities to deal with. It was the nature of their work, just as parties and hostesses and brides and their mothers and hysterical caterers were the nature of what she did with Bix. It was obvious that they both enjoyed their work.

They talked about their children then, and inevitably their marriages to a minor extent. Although he was sorry that his marriage didn't work out, he didn't seem to have an ax to grind about his ex-wife, which was something of a relief. Paris was so tired of all the people who hated their ex-spouses, the energy they put into it ended up being draining for everyone else. And although she would always be sad about Peter, she wished him well. Whether she had wanted it that way or not, they had both moved on. It had seemed to take her forever, but she was there at last.

She had just poured him a cup of coffee, since he said he was going to be up most of the night after he went back to his writer, when her cell phone rang. It was sitting in the charger in the kitchen where they were eating, so she leaned over and picked it up. She was fairly certain it would be Meg. But it was an unfamiliar female voice, and in an instant she knew who it was. It was Amy, and she didn't sound like herself.

"Are you okay? Did something happen?" Paris asked, sounding motherly and concerned.

"I'm in the hospital," Amy said, sounding uncomfortable.

"Already? How did that happen?"

"I don't know. I had a lot of things to do with my boys. And my sister came today to pick up my little girl." Paris couldn't help wondering if she'd been upset, anyone would have been. She knew the sister lived in Oregon, and had been planning to come down and pick up the child. It was a loss to Amy, no matter how helpful it was. And maybe she was just ready to have the baby, now that she knew she had a home. The psyche did strange things to the body sometimes.

"What did the doctor say?"

"He says I'm in labor. I'm four centimeters dilated, and the contractions are about fifteen minutes apart. I think you still have time."

"Wow. Where are you? What room?" Paris grabbed a pen and paper and jotted it down, and Amy was having a contraction when she hung up. And suddenly Paris realized what was happening. The baby was coming. In a few hours, no matter how long it took, she'd be a mom again. And as it occurred to her, she looked at Andrew Warren, who'd been watching her and listening with a degree of concern. "I'm having a baby!" she said, right out of the blue, as though he knew what she was talking about, but he didn't.

"*Now?*" He looked shocked. He couldn't fathom what she meant.

"Yes . . . no . . . I mean, we're in labor. . . ." She was so excited she was incoherent, and he looked utterly confused.

"Who was that?"

"The birth mother. Her name is Amy." And then she realized she had to slow down, at least long enough to tell him why she had to leave. She wanted to get to the hospital right away. "I'm adopting a baby," she said, and smiled at him, and he was struck by how beautiful she was, but it seemed an inappropriate time to say anything about it to her, or maybe even notice it. She was a lovely-looking woman, and he liked her too.

"You are? What an amazing thing to do." He looked pleased for her as he sat back in his chair with a warm smile. "Good for you."

"Thank you. It's a week early. It's a girl. Thank God, I bought everything I needed today." She was definitely jangled but in a wonderful, joyous way. "I have to go to the hospital," she explained to him, as he smiled at her. There was something very touching about the whole scene. She looked like an excited little kid on Christmas Eve, knowing that Santa was coming any minute.

"Where? What hospital?" he asked, with a look of concern.

"Alta Bates in Berkeley," she said, looking around for her handbag, and stuffed the piece of paper with the room number into it.

"Are you driving?" he questioned her.

"Yes, I am."

"No, you're not." She was too distracted to be safe. "Let me drive you, Paris. We can take your car, and I'll take a cab home. I don't think you should be driving in the condition you're in. Besides, you're having a baby. You shouldn't be driving yourself," he teased, and she was touched.

"Are you sure?" She had to admit she didn't feel up to driving herself, and she was grateful to him.

"Perfectly. I'd much rather help you deliver a baby than my crazy client deliver a script. This is a lot more fun." He was excited for her, and pleased to be part of it. They left the house a few minutes later, and she chatted animatedly about the decision and how she had come to it. "That's kind of a radical position you've taken about dating, isn't it?" She had told him about that too.

"Believe me, after the blind dates I've had, you'd come to the same conclusion." She told him about the sculptor from Santa Fe Sydney had introduced her to, and Andrew roared as they crossed the Bay Bridge.

"I don't date a lot either," he said sensibly. "Or I haven't for a while. It gets so tedious exchanging all that pointless information about what you do and don't do, like and don't like, where you've been and where you haven't. And then you discover she's a dominatrix who feeds rats to her pet snake, and you can't help wondering what the hell you're doing there. Maybe you have a point. Maybe I should adopt a baby too." He smiled.

"You can come visit mine," she said proudly, and he looked over at her tenderly.

"Can I see the baby tomorrow after she's born and you bring her home? I'd really love to see her. I feel like I'm part of the official welcoming committee now."

"You are," Paris said, as they entered Berkeley. And a few minutes later he stopped at the hospital, and told her he'd park the car.

"Good luck," he said. She had remembered to put the baby seat in the car to bring the baby home in, and he told her to call him on his cell phone if she wanted him to come back in a cab and drive her. He handed her a card with the number. And she leaned over to kiss his cheek and thanked him.

"Thank you, Andrew. You've been terrific. You're the first real person I've told. Thank you for not telling me I'm crazy." It had been a reality check for her, particularly as she had a great deal of respect for him.

"You are crazy," he smiled at her, "good crazy. This is very good crazy. More people should do wonderful things like this. I hope you'll both be very happy, you and the baby."

"I feel so sorry for the birth mother," Paris said softly, and Andrew shook his head. He couldn't imagine giving up a baby and how awful that would be. Knowing how he loved his own children, it seemed like the ultimate agony to him, and to Paris. They felt deeply for her.

"So do I," Andrew said. "I hope everything goes smoothly." And as Paris got out of the car, he looked back up at her. "Call me when the baby gets here. I'll be dying to hear from you. I want to know who she looks like."

"Me, of course," Paris said, smiling happily, and waved as she walked into the hospital, and he drove into the parking lot in her car, smiling to himself. Richard had been right about his mother-in-law. She was a terrific woman.

Chapter 33

When Paris walked into the hospital, they directed her to the labor and delivery floor. She took the elevator, and two minutes later she was walking into Amy's room. By then she was already in heavy labor, and it was moving quickly. This was her fifth baby, and her other four had been fast deliveries. But she said this one hurt more. Maybe because she knew she was giving it up forever.

"How's it going?" Paris asked sympathetically as she arrived.

"Okay," Amy said, trying to be a good sport, but she groaned out loud when the next contraction hit her. They had an external monitor on her and the baby's heartbeat was fine, but the part of the monitor that showed the force of the contractions was nearly off the charts. The graphs on the paper tape looked like a major earthquake.

"Wow! Those are big ones," Paris said as the nurse showed her how to read it. She changed into hospital pajamas then, so she'd be ready for the delivery room, and took Amy's hand in hers. There was no one else with her. Her husband had been at the neighbor's when she left for the hospital in a taxi, and she had dropped off the boys at a friend's. It was a lonely way to have a baby. But at least Paris was there. And she had had the presence of mind to bring the papers she needed to have the baby released to her. And the hospital had been notified by Alice Harper about the adoption. Everything was in order. All they needed now was the baby.

Amy was doing her best to have it. And her body was cooperating nicely. The nurse said she was dilated to ten, an hour after Paris got there. From their point of view, it was going fine, but poor Amy was writhing in agony as she lay there, and she was determined to do it without medication. Paris didn't argue with her, although she herself had had an epidural and much preferred it to natural childbirth. But Amy insisted it was better for the baby. Maybe she felt it was her final gift to her.

They seemed to stay in the same place for a while. The doctor came in to check her, which hurt Amy more, and this time she screamed, and a few minutes later they rolled her down to the delivery room, and she started pushing. Paris was holding both her hands and trying to help her breathe, and after a while a nurse suggested that Paris get behind her and hold her in an upright position. It was uncomfortable for Paris, but it seemed to help Amy as she kept pushing, but the baby was going nowhere. They continued pushing, with no visible results for more than two hours, and Amy was screaming all the time now. Paris wished there were something more useful she could do for her, but she kept talking to her, and encouraging her, and all of a sudden Amy gave a hideous howl, and the doctor said the baby was finally coming.

"Come on, Amy . . . come on . . . that's it . . . push again . . ." Everyone was shouting at her, and Amy couldn't stop crying. Paris wondered if her own deliveries had been as awful. It didn't seem like it, but she couldn't remember. They had seemed easier than this one. And then finally, finally, they could see the top of the baby's head, as Amy worked harder than she ever had, and with three horrible screams, the baby finally slid out. Amy was sobbing in Paris's arms, and the baby girl's wail filled the room, as Paris saw her and began crying. The doctor cut the cord, and gently handing her over Amy, she handed her to Paris, as Paris leaned down to show her. "Look how beautiful she is," Paris whispered to Amy. "You did such a good job," she said, as Amy closed her eyes, and they finally gave her a shot, which made her woozy. The baby weighed eight pounds fourteen ounces. She was a big one, though Jane's had been bigger, but this had seemed harder and longer. It was four o'clock in the morning when they left the delivery room, and went back to the room that had been assigned to Amy. It was at the far end of the hall from the nursery. The hospital staff knew that this was an adoption, and Amy would be relinquishing her baby, and they tried to be sensitive about it.

They took the baby to the nursery to clean her up, give her eyedrops, and check her Apgar scores, as Paris sat in the room with Amy while she slept off the medication. And while she was still asleep, they brought back the baby. She was looking around, alert, with a little cotton cap on, wrapped in a pink blanket, and the nurse silently held her out to her new mother, and Paris took her, and held her close to her, as their eyes met.

"Hello, little one . . ." The baby had round pink cheeks, and big eyes that were baby color, and had yet to reveal what they would be, and a fuzz of white duck hair on the top of her head. She looked like a little doll in Paris's arms, and as Paris held her, she drifted off to sleep, as though she knew she had come home to her mother at last.

"What's her name?" the nurse whispered.

"Hope," Paris said, as she looked down at her. The word had just come to her as she saw her. She had been considering several others, but Hope seemed to suit her perfectly.

"I like that." The nurse smiled, as Paris sat looking down in wonder at the new life that was hers now. And she realized as she did that if Peter hadn't left her, this moment would never have happened. She had found it finally. The gift. The blessing that she hadn't been able to find in the agony for two and a half years. She knew it was there somewhere, but she had never found it, and now she had. The mystery of blessings tucked away in tragedies and disasters. This was the blessing. The hope she had longed for. It had come now in the form of this sleeping baby.

They sat that way for hours, as Amy slept off the drug, and Paris held the baby, and finally they both woke up. They gave Paris a little bottle with glucose in it to feed the baby, and they gave Amy a shot so she wouldn't lactate. They sat together all morning, quietly talking. The pediatrician had checked Hope out and said she could leave at six o'clock that evening, if Paris wanted. Amy was staying till the following morning, and Paris hated to leave her. She called Alice Harper at home to say that the baby had come, and she was delighted for her. Alice said that she should leave whenever the hospital said the baby could be discharged.

"What about Amy?" Paris asked, feeling anxious. She was calling from her cell phone in the hallway, and had left the baby in the nursery to do it.

"It's all right, Paris. They'll take care of her at the hospital. She knows what she's doing. She wants to do this. Don't make it harder for her." Paris understood then. They each had their role, their separate destinies to follow. It seemed so lonely to her. She called Bix then and told him too, and in spite of all his grumbling, he was happy for her. And then, feeling a little silly because she didn't know him very well, she called Andrew Warren on his cell phone. But he had driven her to the hospital and asked her to call him. She told him Hope had arrived and how much she weighed and how beautiful she was, as she described her to him. She didn't even realize she was crying as she did.

"I love her name," he said softly.

"So do I," Paris said. "It suits her." And it was what she had become to her mother, a symbol of hope for the future. The past was healed now. The gift had been delivered at last.

"I left your car keys at the information desk," he explained. "When are you going home?"

"They said we could leave at six o'clock tonight." She still sounded a little awestruck, and hadn't slept yet. She was too excited.

"Would you let me drive you?"

"Are you sure it wouldn't be a nuisance?" Bix hadn't offered, and she hadn't expected him to. Steven was still under the weather, and he wouldn't have anyway. Bix hated hospitals, and wasn't wildly fond of babies. This was her deal. And she did have her car there. She hadn't expected Andrew to renew his offer to drive her home.

"It would be an honor," he said solemnly. "I'll be there at five-thirty, in case they let you leave early."

"Thank you." It was a night that had solidified their friendship, and was an important moment for her, and her new daughter. He congratulated her again, and after that she called Meg and Wim on their cell phones. And they were surprised that the baby had come early. She was laughing and talking to them, and after she hung up, she went back to get the baby in the nursery, and was startled to discover that they had taken her to Amy. She was awake and had asked for her, which worried Paris. What if she changed her mind now? Paris already loved this baby. But Amy was still legally her mother.

And when she walked back into the room, Amy was holding her, looking into the baby's eyes and talking to her, as though she'd been saying something very important to her. And she had been, she'd been saying good-bye.

She looked up when she saw Paris, and without hesitating, she held the baby out to her, as Paris held her breath. "I was watching your baby for you," she said softly, acknowledging in one sentence all she was giving to her. Paris's eyes filled with tears as she took Hope from her. And a little while later the social worker came in with papers for Amy to sign.

Paris slept most of the afternoon, as the baby did. And at five o'clock they told her Hope could go home. Paris went to the nursery to dress her in the outfit she'd brought. It was just a nightgown and a blanket and an undershirt and a little cap. She hadn't had time to put something pretty together as she had done so long ago for Meg. But all that mattered now was that they were going home together.

When the baby was dressed, Paris walked back into Amy's room with Hope wrapped in the blanket in her arms. She wanted to give her one last look at her, and she was surprised by how calm Amy was, and she was sure that the drugs had worn off.

"Do you want to hold her?" Paris offered, but Amy shook her head. She looked sad, but she was very quiet. She just looked long and hard at the baby and then at Paris.

"Thank you," she said, which was what Paris wanted to say to her.

"Thank you . . . God bless you . . . please take care of yourself." She had promised to send her address so Paris would know where to send the photographs next year. It was so incredible to be walking away with this woman's child. But now she was hers. That was the most amazing part of it . . . this incredible baby was hers. "I love you," Paris said, and briefly touched her hand. Amy nodded, and said not a word, and as the door closed slowly behind her, Paris heard her say, "Good-bye."

There were tears streaming down Paris's cheeks, as a nurse escorted her downstairs. She felt like a kidnapper, spiriting this tiny bundle away. But everyone was smiling at her, and wishing her well, and Andrew was waiting for her downstairs in the lobby.

"Let me see her," he whispered, and found himself looking into two big bright eyes as Hope stared intently at him, as though wondering who he was.

"Isn't she gorgeous?" Paris grinned at him, and he nodded. He had the car waiting for them. And as he helped Paris put Hope in the baby seat and strap her in, she realized that he had been touched by the miracle too. They had come there together eighteen hours before, a man and a woman who barely knew each other, and had set out on an adventure together. And now they were friends, and there was a brand-new little person driving back across the bridge with them.

"It's amazing, isn't it?" Paris looked at him in wonder, and he nodded, bereft of words. There was nothing he could say to her to tell her what the moment meant to him. And every few minutes, on the drive home, Paris turned around and stared at Hope, with love and gratitude and disbelief. All she could think of now was how lucky she was. Hope was the long-awaited gift.

Chapter 34

Paris wanted to sit up all night and hold the baby, but she finally broke down and put her in her bassinet, and went to bed herself. She got up every few hours to check her, and kept waking up with a start, wondering if she had dreamed it, but she hadn't. Andrew had left around eleven, after helping her set things up for the baby. He helped her get the bassinet ready and even put the sheet on it for her while she held Hope.

"You're good at this," she teased him.

"I had a lot of practice. And I always enjoyed it." And it was obvious he was enjoying it now. He promised to come by the next day before he left for Los Angeles. The writer had finally finished the script. And Andrew was going back to the hotel to bed.

Bix and Steven came by on Sunday morning and saw her, and Bix brought a camera and took a million pictures. He had never seen Paris look better, and he had to admit, the baby was cute. Steven raved about her chin and her nose, which were perfectly formed. And by then, Paris had her in a tiny pink dress and a receiving blanket to keep her warm.

And at four o'clock Andrew came by again.

"I feel like I've been so fortunate to be part of a very special weekend," he said, looking very moved.

"Thank you for driving us back and forth," Paris said gratefully to him. "And for sharing this with us."

"I feel like the stork." They both laughed. He only stayed a few minutes, kissed the baby on the top of her downy head, and left. He promised to call Paris soon, and this time she didn't mind. He had become a friend overnight. Not a boyfriend or a lover or a suitor, or even a candidate for any of the above. Just a friend, which she valued far more.

And the next morning he sent her a huge bouquet of flowers, with a card that said, "In celebration of Hope! Love, Andrew." And Bixby sent one of his giant teddy bears made of pink roses. He had told her to take two days off, but she had to be back at work on Wednesday, and she had the baby nurse she'd be using that month all lined up.

And by Wednesday morning, when she went back to work, Paris was in full control. She knew the baby's schedule, which formula she liked, which position she slept in best. And everything in the guest room had been set up for Miss Hope, whose bassinet sat next to her mother's bed at night. All was well in their little world. And at every party they worked together that week, and there were many, Bix told their clients, "Isn't Paris amazing? She had a baby last Friday night!" And then they looked at her in awe, and she explained. By Friday, she had a mountain of gifts on her desk. The world was welcoming Hope.

She had to work straight through until Sunday, and on Sunday morning Andrew called. He had had a ridiculous week too, he said. And he reminded her that Hope was nine days old.

"I wanted to call her on Saturday to wish her a happy birthday, but I didn't have time. Another one of my writers went nuts and walked off a set. It took a while to smooth it out." He asked what she'd been doing, and she told him, and he said he thought he'd be coming up the following week and said he'd let her know.

And after that Meg called to ask about the baby. She, Richard, and Wim were spending Christmas with her, and they were planning to meet Hope then. It was less than three weeks away, and Paris could hardly wait for them to see her. Whatever their hesitations had been, they seemed excited about her now, if only to please their mother. And she was sure that when they saw her, it would be love at first sight. Who could possibly resist?

It was an insanely busy month for her. Between her work and the baby, she felt as though she were in a relay race, and despite the baby nurse, Paris was up with the baby every night, and wanted to be. But she was ready to drop by Christmas.

Andrew came up to see a client two days before, and she was half asleep on the couch, with Hope in her arms, when he arrived.

"You look beat," he said, as he handed her a box, which she unwrapped with glee. It was an outfit and a blanket for the baby with a matching doll.

"You're spoiling us. And yes, I am beat." She could hardly wait till January to get some rest. Jane had agreed to come back for a month to take Paris's place. She was pregnant again. And Bix was complaining that he was surrounded by women having babies. His life was complicated right now too. Steven hadn't been well since Thanksgiving.

And every day Paris was tempted to call Amy, to see how she was, but Alice had told her not to. Out of respect, if nothing else, Paris had to let go. So she did. And just enjoyed Hope as the gift she was. All of the paperwork was in order. Amy had signed everything without a murmur.

Andrew told Paris he was leaving for London, and both his daughters were going to celebrate Christmas with him there. And after that they were going skiing in Gstaad. It sounded very racy to Paris, and was. He said he would be back right after the New Year.

"I'd love to come up and see you when I get back. I'm sure Hope will be twice the size by then," although his return was only two weeks away. But there was something about the way he said it that filled Paris with concern. She didn't know what to say.

"I'd like to see you, Andrew," she said softly. But she wanted to see him as a friend, nothing more, and she wasn't sure that was what he had in mind. He clarified it for her.

"I know you have some very strong reservations about dating, and I can't say I blame you, or disagree with you. But if I promise to be extremely well behaved and not bring photographs of any phallic sculpture I may have made, and I don't arrive drunk, or order beans for dinner . . . do you suppose I could take you out for dinner sometime, and consider it a date?" He was being very careful with her, and she couldn't help but laugh.

"Am I as impossible as all that?" she asked as she laughed.

"Not impossible," he said fairly, "just cautious, and with good reason. I'd say you've had a tougher time than most. I don't blame you for being gun-shy, and if I do anything to upset you, I want to know."

"Like what? Spoil my daughter, send me flowers, drive me to and from the hospital when she's born? I'd say that's pretty offensive, wouldn't you?" They exchanged a long smile. "I just don't want to spoil our friendship. You're becoming too important to me. I don't want to blow that with something stupid that won't matter to us in two months." But he was hoping it would, and in truth so was she. He had to leave to catch his plane then, and he wanted to make sure they were on the same page.

"Are we on for a date when I get back? Officially, I mean?"

She smiled at him. "Officially, I'd say yes."

He didn't want to sneak up on her, or take advantage of her, or surprise her, or frighten her. He wanted to be her friend, but he also wanted to be more than that. He had enormous admiration for her, all she had survived, and all she'd done. "I'll call you from Europe," he promised. "Take care of Hope!" he shouted to her as he hurried down the stairs, having just kissed her on the cheek. And she waved as he drove away, wondering what she had just done, and if she'd regret it. She hoped not. She had sworn to herself she would never date again, and now she was sticking her nose out again. But it had been eight months. Maybe that was long enough to clear the air. And there was something very different about

Andrew Warren. More than anyone she had met since Peter, he was a man she could not only love, as a friend, but respect. The others had been fun, or good company, or sexy, or pathetic, but none had been worthy of respect. Andrew was.

He called her from the airport, from L.A., and from London when he got to Europe the next day. And by then her family had arrived.

Meg was excited to hold the baby. And Wim was grinning, as Paris hovered over them telling them to be careful of the baby, while Richard took pictures. And they all said she was the most beautiful baby they'd ever seen, which Paris knew anyway. Hope was almost smiling by then, and nearly four weeks old.

And as she set her gently down in the bassinet, Meg turned to her mother with a womanly smile that Paris had never seen before. "She'll be good practice for me," Meg said, smiling at her mother, then at Richard, and then back at Paris again.

"How's that?" Paris asked, feeling a little dim, but she was very tired.

"We're having a baby, Mom," Meg said as her mother threw her arms around her with tears in her eyes.

"How exciting! Congratulations, both of you! When?"

"It's due on the Fourth of July."

"How patriotic!" Paris laughed and kissed her son-in-law and congratulated him again, as Wim groaned and threw himself on the couch, while Meg held Hope again.

"What is this? An epidemic?" Wim asked the room in general. "Everyone's having babies."

"Well, you'd better not have one too," Paris warned, and they all laughed. And that night, when Paris came back in the living room after dinner, Wim was holding the baby, and Meg was next to him sound asleep on the couch. All her children were together. It was the perfect Christmas. Particularly now that they had Hope.

Chapter 35

The month that Paris took off in January turned out to be the best thing she'd ever done. She had time to spend with the baby, read books, go for walks with the baby in the stroller, visit Bix at the office and sympathize over his workload, and even see friends. She loved being a lady of leisure, but she was looking forward to going back to work again too. But not yet.

And Andrew Warren took two weeks off, and came to visit her in San Francisco. They drove to the Napa Valley, had lunch in Sonoma, strolled along Crissy Field with the baby. It was almost like being married again. And he took her out for several very fancy dinners that he claimed were their "official" dates.

"In that case, what's the rest of it?" she inquired. They had an easy relationship that seemed to be equal parts friendship and romance, and they both liked it that way.

"The rest of the time we're just friends," he explained. "It's only a date if I take you to a restaurant. How's that?"

"Excellent. Just the way I want it." And she really missed him when he left. He was wonderful with the baby, and they had a good time together. When he went back to work, he came up on weekends from L.A., and stayed in the mother-in-law apartment, once with Wim, since there were two bedrooms. Paris hadn't slept with him, and wasn't ready to yet. They had only been "dating" for about a month, although they'd seen a lot of each other when he came up for two weeks. They were together every day.

But on Valentine's Day their chastity came to an end. He took her out for a lovely dinner. She was back at work by then, and didn't even get home that day till eight-thirty. And at ten o'clock he spirited her away for a lovely meal. They came home at midnight, and he gave her a beautiful diamond bangle. She gave him a silly watch with a red alligator band, and he put it on. They sat and talked for hours, and finally they drifted into her bedroom and that which she had avoided and feared for so long became the easiest thing in the world. They made love like two people who had known each other forever and not strangers, she never had to ask him if it was "exclusive," it wasn't acrobatic or disappointing, exotic or terrifying. It was as though it had always been, which was the best way. And after they fell alseep in each other's arms, the baby woke them. Paris went to get her bottle ready, and Andrew gave it to her, and they went back to sleep with the baby between them and slept until the next day. Paris felt as though she'd come home. After nearly three years of loneliness and sorrow, she had found the man she had thought she would never find. She had stopped looking for him, and had long since ceased to believe that he existed. She had found the needle in the haystack after all. And so had Andrew. He had never been happier in his life.

It was a golden spring for them. They alternated weekends between San Francisco and L.A., and whenever he could get away from his office, he brought a stack of scripts up and stayed with her and Hope. Her children loved him, and when his daughters came to visit in June, they liked Paris as well. All the pieces of the puzzle fit, better even than they had with Peter. That was the odd part. It was almost as though she couldn't remember being married to him now. She felt as though she had always been with Andrew.

And when Meg's baby was due, she took two weeks off. Bix said he could manage without her, and much to everyone's relief, Steven was feeling much better. He was doing well.

Paris and Hope were staying with Andrew when Meg went into labor, right on her due date, and Andrew baby-sat for Hope while Paris went to the hospital with Richard and Meg. It was a long arduous labor, but Meg was very good about it. And Richard was wonderful with her. Paris sat in the labor room with them, and wasn't intending to be at the birth, but at the last minute Meg wanted her there, and Richard didn't mind. Paris didn't want to intrude, and as their son pushed his way into the world, Paris was watching her daughter and her husband and cried at how happy they were, and how beautiful their baby was. They named him Brandon. Brandon Bolen. He was a beautiful healthy boy, and as Paris held him in the delivery room, after they did, Meg looked up at her mother with a tired smile.

"I love you, Mom . . . thank you for being my mom." It was the best gift in the world. And she cried when she told Andrew about it. And when she lay in bed next to him that night, she sighed. There was something about having babies around. She was forty-nine years old, but she loved her babies, of all sizes and ages, as much as she had twenty-five years before.

"You know, I was thinking," she said to Andrew with a yawn, as she cuddled up next to him in the dark. "Maybe it's not such a great thing for Hope to be an only child. Maybe I should adopt another one." There was a long silent pause, as Andrew looked down at her with a smile.

"Is that what you've been thinking? She's not going to be an only child. She'll have her nephew to play with, they're only eight months apart."

"That's true," she said, nodding. She hadn't thought of that. Although they didn't live in the same town, so they wouldn't see each other every day. It wasn't the same as growing up in the same house with a sibling.

"Maybe we should really shake everyone up and have one of

our own." He had thought of it several times, but there were other things he wanted to do with her as well. And she didn't seem to object to his suggestion. It would take effort, but was not impossible these days, thanks to modern science and a little help from their friends at UCLA. But he didn't want to discuss that with her yet. "I have another idea. What do you say we get married, and go to Europe for a year?" He had wanted to do that for a long time, and now he wanted to do it with her.

"And leave Bix?" She sounded shocked, as she looked at him in the dark.

"Well, yes, for a year. You can always go back to work when we get back if you really want to. We could take him to Europe with us of course," he teased.

"He'd like that." And then she sat up and looked at him. "Did you just ask me to marry you?" She looked surprised but not shocked. She hadn't really expected him to ask, things were so comfortable as they were.

"Yes, I did," he said quietly. "How does that sound to you?" She answered him with a long heartfelt kiss. "Is that a yes?" She nodded. "Could you say it, please? I want to make sure I don't make any incorrect assumptions."

"Yes," she said with a big grin. "I will marry you. Will that mean we're exclusive?" She had told him that story too. She had told him all of them over the past seven months. She had no secrets from him.

"Yes, I think that would mean that we're exclusive. That would be a yes. So what do you think? Europe for a year?" She nodded. She liked that idea too. She'd help Bix train someone to take her place while she was gone, assuming they moved back to San Francisco, which she didn't know for sure. Once they got to Europe, who knew? Andrew was fifty-nine years old, and he kept threatening to retire early so they could roam around the world, and the idea appealed to her a great deal, and they didn't have to worry about Hope going to school yet.

"Shall we tell the children?" She beamed at him.

"I should think so. I don't think we should keep it a secret from them." He laughed and put his arms around her, and pulled her down next to him again in bed. "I love you, Paris . . . you'll never know how I love you. . . ." He had never loved anyone as much before, and it had grown on them slowly, in all the right ways, for both of them. They lay in bed talking about it. They were going to have a small wedding. She thought Bix should do it for them. And they agreed that they only wanted their children and a few friends there. And then they were going to leave for Europe, rent a place in Paris or London . . . a country house somewhere . . . maybe charter a yacht and spend a summer on it . . . it was all so perfect. But it would have been just as perfect if they never went anywhere. All she wanted was to be with him.

They told Richard and Meg the next day, and called Wim on his cell phone in the East, he was visiting Peter. And everyone was thrilled. And then she called Bix, and he was gracious enough to be thrilled for her too. "I told you you'd find the needle in the haystack. Now weren't all those blind dates worth it?"

"No," she laughed at him. "I didn't meet Andrew on a blind date. I met him at my daughter's wedding."

"Well, I knew it was something like that. Besides, the blind dates were good practice."

"For what?"

"Being charming to horrible clients, and running our business when you come back."

"Are you retiring?" She sounded shocked. She wondered just how sick Steven was.

"Not yet. But after you take a year off, so will I. Steven and I want to travel around the world. Maybe we'll close for a year. We'll figure it out. One thing I do know," he said, sounding happy for her, "the best is yet to come."

"Yes, it is," she said softly, and when she hung up, she told Andrew what he'd said.

"He's right." They had agreed to get married in August, and wanted to leave by September. She and Andrew went back to San Francisco the following week, to start making plans for their trip. He already had three apartments lined up in Paris, and a house in London. There was no limit to what they could do. And when she walked into the house in San Francisco, there was a box waiting for them, with a sprig of lily of the valley on top. And when she opened it, there was a beautiful oval antique silver box nestled in it, with engraving on the surface of the lid. She had to look at it carefully to read it because it was in a lacy old script.

"What does it say?" Andrew asked her, admiring it. Bix had such incredible taste.

"It says"—she held it carefully to the light and smiled at Andrew—"'The best is yet to come.'"

"So it is," he said, and kissed her. The past had brought infinite blessings and lessons, and had been what was meant to be at the time. It had given birth to the present, in all its beauty. And what would come next was unseen and unknown. But she was more than willing to believe that the best was in fact yet to come.